After Pentecost

Books by Richard Bankowsky

AFTER PENTECOST

A GLASS ROSE

After Pentecost

(AN EPISTLE TO THE ROMANS)

Richard Bankowsky

Random House — New York

For my father and his grandson, Jack, who together have instructed me in the mysterious and unfathomable meaning of Fatherhood

Man is an immigrant in Time yearning
constantly back to the eternal

PUBLISHER'S NOTE

The chapter titles and numbers
correspond to
the Gospel according to St. John

Chapter

After Pentecost

Chapters I & XVI

AUGSBURG CATHEDRAL, CHRISTMAS
MORNING, 1946

Because in the beginning, some-
body or something somewhere said BE THERE! Not BE GOOD or
BE BAD or BE-anything-else-but-here in Augsburg on Christmas
Eve. Said it not eighteen years ago when you were born (or
thirty-five when she was), but way back there along with BE
LIGHT and BE GONE when the whole round goddamned world
was.

Unless, maybe Johnny's right after all and "goddamned"
hasn't anything to do with it. Like the Ol' Man said back there
in the Orderly Room last July when you handed him the cablegrams, sitting there like that with his feet on the desk and blowing the cigar smoke, saying, "All of which goes to prove the

figure in the carpet's fornicating. Something you should have learned a long time ago, soldier. Because you should have had a pretty good idea long before last Christmas, long before you lost your own, that what they've been telling you the world is just a bowl of, doesn't grow on trees—not outside their convent gardens anyway. Not in Germany anyway. Not after a war."

Because in Augsburg back in '45 nothing grew on trees, neither money nor smokes nor food nor fuel either (so that before the winter was over there weren't even any trees left much less anything growing on them), nor immigration papers to America either where even wedding rings grow on trees, and like the Ol' Man said, "All she had to do to get one was shake the tree pretty much the way she shook the bed to get those immigration papers." Which may have been right. Which probably was right. Which may even have had something to do with explaining the second cable too. Only then you were *sure* there was a lot more to it than that. There had to be. Otherwise, he'd have been right about all of it. Not only about her, but all of it. And if he was, then they never should have handed out those sentences, there never even should have been a trial. And not just because it was Christmas Eve either. Because if he was right, there shouldn't even have been a Christmas Eve, or a Christmas after it—not even the first one—not then or now or ever. Because if he was right, it was all just one big fat waste of time back there in '45—all of it; the big soft flakes falling straight down under the streetlamps and against the courthouse windows, the room hushed and the singing from the cathedral across the square drifting under the doors and through the glass, and the gavel going, and the Colonel's voice rattling in the PA system, and the wailing, and the tearing of hair, and the wringing hands . . . all of it.

It must have been the singing that got you—*Stille Nacht, Heilige Nacht*—because through the whole damn sickening trial you'd been wishing they'd hang every last one of them and yet when it came time for the Colonel to read the sentences and the hush fell over the room and suddenly the singing was there, you somehow couldn't help wishing they had at least put it off until Wednesday instead of reconvening like that at 21:30 hours Christmas Eve just so they could tidy it all up before the holiday like the Colonel said, his voice rattling over the PA system, and you standing there at parade rest, your hands sweating in the white gloves around the billy, standing there like that in the dock with the accused but looking out of the side of your eye under the helmet liner and out the window and across the square to where the huge Christmas tree glowed blue on the steps of the cathedral, because you just didn't feel much like watching their faces when the Colonel handed them their Christmas presents, figuring he'd probably finish off with something nice and cheery like "Splendid work, gentlemen. I want to congratulate you all and wish you a Merry Christmas." Only, he let you down. Because after seeing the way some of them accepted their presents—especially the woman, wailing and tearing her hair and hanging on your arms like that when it came time to herd them back to the guardhouse (as though *you*, an MP corporal, could do anything about anything)—not even the Colonel felt much like a Merry Christmas.

And it was a cinch *you* didn't. You thought at first maybe you were even sorry tomorrow was a holiday (because there's nothing like work to keep your mind off things), not so much because of the sentences, since maybe they were only getting what was coming to them, including the doc (though they could have at least waited till Wednesday to tell them); not so much that, as all the business that came before, all the stuff you never in a million years would have believed if you hadn't actually heard them not only admit to it but even try to justify it, some of them. Anyway, you finally decided maybe there was something to be said for Christmas after all; for one thing there'd be no reveille come morning, and since the last thing you felt like doing was taking the trial to bed with you, and even though it was only a half hour or so short of midnight before you got out of your arm band and the braid and the white gloves and helmet liner and turned the forty-five back in at the arms room, you picked up your off-duty pass from the CQ and for no reason at all except maybe it was all written down before you were even capable of walking, you figured you'd walk across the square and hear midnight Mass in the cathedral, and then try to sleep away as much of the rest of Christmas morning as possible. And with the snow falling straight down like that and the streets all white under the lamps and the singing drifting out of the open portals, it didn't even have to be Germany any more but any place all white on Christmas Eve, like the Holy Rosary Church back home in Prescott for instance. And after the stuff at the trial, church didn't seem like such a bad idea at all.

Anyway, whatever the reason, you were there; standing there just inside the open portal, shaking the snow off your cap and folding it under your belt, the cathedral so crowded you couldn't really see very much more than the crucifix on the point of the altar and the tips of the candlesticks, the paint-and-plaster manger not even there unless you stood on tiptoe, the organ booming and the choir in the loft above your head just finishing a Latin carol and starting in on a French one, a bunch of troops from the French Zone across the river joining in, their voices rising along the high Gothic arches. All of it was pretty damn nice and kind of reassuring, and you were glad you'd thought of it, because the cathedral had it all over the compound chapel for making you feel like home again for Christmas, and the choir was really something to listen to (when you could hear it over the congregation; because it wasn't only the French troops after a while, but all the Frenchmen from the DP Center too, and then the Czechs and the Dutchmen and the Russians, and even some GI's helping along with the Italian carol) singing all the nations of Europe just the way they do back home on Christmas Eve. All of it was pretty damn nice, and you were feeling pretty homesick and you were waiting for them to start in on an English carol so you could join in yourself even though you never were much of a singer. And they had just finished the Italian one while you were thinking about it, and the organ boomed, and you had already gone through the first couple lines singing along with them before you realized they weren't singing in English at all, that they were singing "Today in Bethlehem," an old Polish carol they sing every year back home in Prescott, and you were singing right along with them, singing about a Virgin pure giving birth to a Son, and about great Kings adoring, and Angels singing, and cattle kneeling, and the amazing thing about it all was you were singing along with them in Polish just like back home again, and pretty damn good Polish at that.

At least she said it was pretty good, standing there like that in the snow after Mass, you looking, not down, but across at her because she was every bit of five foot ten in heels, and in the glow of the tree trying to figure out just how old she could be, trying to remember what she'd looked like back in the cathedral where the light was better—the pretty unpainted face framed in the shawl looking back at you over her shoulder around the ratty fur collar, her lips going with singing, smiling briefly that kind of sad faraway smile as though she had recognized you from some place, but only briefly, only for a second; you looking at the back of her in the shawl and the long winter coat, staring at her all through the rest of the Mass, thinking, "She's a looker all right. And I guess I'm just about as homesick as I'm ever liable to get. And I've got Christmas pay in my pocket. And I hope to Christ she doesn't pick on *me*, because if she does I'm just liable . . ." And so of course she did, because she really *had* recognized you, knew you were one of the American MP's she had seen ushering them in and out of the courthouse the past week, and you were young and you were made to order because you could speak Polish; looking across at you in the tree's blue glow, the snow falling straight down, her hair wisping blond over her forehead below the shawl and her lips moving like that for a while without even any voice behind them at first, saying finally, "I do not wish you to think . . . It is just that I . . . I have seen you at the courthouse . . ." saying it in that precise beautiful Polish; and you standing there looking across at her thinking exactly what she was trying to tell you she wished you wouldn't, thinking, "Even the beautiful ones. Even the Polish ones, goddamn it," as though beauty or national origin should impose a kind of immunity to want and need and corruption; looking at the shabby shawl tight around her head and criss-crossed under her folded arms, and the ratty fur collar turned up now on the threadbare long coat, thinking, "With Christmas pay in my pocket, I could sure play one hell of a Santa Claus."

But you were wrong (you were wrong about everything that morning), or at least you weren't completely right. She was looking for a Christmas present all right, but it wasn't the kind *you* thought—the eyes bright under the lashes and the lips even trembling a little, saying, "If you would just tell me. If you would only tell me what they are going to do to him. There will not be a newspaper till Wednesday, and if you could just tell me . . ." And you didn't even have to ask "Who?"—which one of the seven (or rather six, since one was a woman), which one was hers. You knew right off, without even having to think about it, that it couldn't be anyone else but the doctor, that Dr. Max Saulmann was the only one of the six that a beautiful young woman (no, not so young, because even then, even in the kind blue glow of the tree—though you were never much for guessing a woman's age, never found it necessary to, before—you could tell she was no kid), or anybody for that matter except maybe a mother, could possibly care anything about; though judging by what you heard at the trial you weren't sure that even *he* was worth spilling any tears over. But that's exactly what she was doing, right out there on the cathedral steps in the cool blue glow of the tree—the crowd pouring out of the portals and moving down the steps across the square to the rathskellers or hailing the horsecabs or the taxis or walking back to the compound or to their "shacks" or to one of the thousand cramped cots at the DP Center, walking through the fresh snow, most of them probably thanking God that after the freezing weather of the past few weeks He had, at least for Christmas, thought to give them a gift of weather warm enough for snow.

And it was a lovely snow (she said so), warm, clean, and kind of insulating almost. And you sat there in the booth watching it fall straight down under the streetlamps above in the rathskeller window, listening to the carols squeezing out of the accordion across the dance floor and drifting in the cigarette smoke over the heads of the dancers and over the GI's caroling around the long table beside the Christmas tree; sitting there with a quart of beer and two steins on the table in front of you waiting for her return from the *Mädchenzimmer*, wondering whether maybe you should have told her right off that they'd already sentenced him and, subject to review-board approval, he was already good as hanged by the neck until dead, instead of having taken her arm like that, saying in your best Polish, "Do not cry, Pani. They have not yet finished with the trial. It will not be until Monday before the sentences are passed." But what else could you do? Because, Jesus, that would have been one hell of a Christmas present to just hand her like that right out there on the cathedral steps, and you didn't need any special powers of perception to see the reprieve in her face when you lied to her, as though just allowing her to *hope* for another day was a damn fine present in itself. And one, two, three, just like that, you figured you knew pretty much what the story was, how she had managed to survive the war, and maybe if, like the Ol' Man said, you had been sensible enough to slap her across the mouth and ask her how she'd like it if you were to call some of her DP Polack friends and ask them why she, a Pole, was so interested in a condemned war criminal, none of it would have happened. But you weren't, and you didn't, and not only because you were new to it all, had only been over here a couple of weeks then, a late-comer who really didn't give a damn about any of it except the GI Bill. Maybe it was just because you kind of appreciated that thin blond hair wisping on her forehead beneath the shawl and didn't like to think how she'd look without it—her head shaved bald as a nun's. Or maybe it was just because it was Christmas after all, and you were feeling charitable, and anyway the war was over now, and if she felt about the doc the way it looked to you she did, in a couple of days when she'd get the news of his sentence they wouldn't be able to hurt her very much even if they pulled out those thin blond wisps of hair by the handful. Or maybe it was just that you were five thousand miles from home and she could talk Polish. Or maybe (which is most likely) it was just curiosity. Maybe you just wanted to be able to sit down with her and ask her if she had any idea . . . to sit there across from her and tell her, to repeat the accusations, the admissions, the whole filthy miserable business, to ask her to explain not only herself, but him too. Because he wasn't like the rest at the trial and you'd been thinking about his final words all through Mass (when you weren't thinking about her). Maybe you just couldn't believe she could possibly have any idea what it was all about. Maybe you just wanted to hear her say, "Oh God, I did not know! I never dreamed!" even though, even if she *had* said it, you wouldn't have believed her probably, because you had at least been overseas long enough to know that was what they all said, that was what the entire German nation said (not that you blamed them very much). Maybe you just wanted to hear her say it anyway, so you could start talking yourself into believing her. Because maybe even then, even standing there on the steps, saying, "Perhaps Pani would like to go and have something to drink and talk a little. It is Christmas after all, and I am sure they do not have a tree at the DP Center"; maybe even then, like the snow falling straight down under the lamps, you were already falling.

After all you were just a kid, not even eighteen yet, wouldn't be for another month and a half almost. And maybe you didn't know then she was old enough to be your mother—how could you? She certainly didn't look it, walking across the dance floor like that, the coat and shawl over her arm now, the accordion ceasing, the dancers paused waiting for the next number to begin, and surprisingly enough not one of them even thinking to whistle, not even the ones around the long table, not until after the music had already started up again and she was standing there before you, looking down at you; and you just sitting there as though she weren't really waiting for *you* to get up and help her with her chair, as though she hadn't been walking across the floor toward *you*, as though you weren't even in the picture, weren't there in the rathskeller at all but in some movie house or something, watching it all going on up there on the screen and expecting some guy, in tails and striped pants maybe, to stand up out of the bottom of it and bow and . . . You didn't even remember to stand up and help her with her chair, looking up at her looking down at you, smiling, only the lips a little reddened now; knowing all along that she was beautiful, unable to believe that just a shabby shawl and a threadbare coat with a ratty fur collar could possibly have hidden what you saw standing there before you. And it wasn't the dress, even though it was in better condition than the coat and shawl, because it really wasn't exactly what you'd call Paris France. It was just the way it fit, or rather didn't fit—because actually it had a little bit of a look of one of those before-Sanforizing ads. And maybe you should have known (no matter how young her face looked, especially before the lipstick, although even with her lips slightly reddened there was still something awfully young about it—not her eyes, just her face) that a woman couldn't possibly have developed that much in anything less than at least thirty years nor kept it looking that way much after thirty-five. But you were only seventeen then, and you didn't know anything then. And now it's a whole year later and you're eighteen and ten whole months, and you're so goddamned enlightened now you don't even need the Ol' Man to tell you that you were already "taken" even before she sat herself down—that you were banking on it.

It was just one of those things. Only, this time it wasn't just all light and shadow up on some screen. She was real, and she was sitting there across the table from you, and you couldn't believe it was actually happening to you, that you were anywhere in the picture at all, looking at her sitting there across from you blowing cigarette smoke like kisses, the smoke haloing the pale blond hair, shaping the air around her words, her voice soft as smoke saying no she did not mind the noise, she liked it that way and wasn't the snow lovely under the lamps and how nice it was to have snow for Christmas especially for the children at the Center when they would wake in the morning, though actually she had not really expected it and now her shoes were ruined but of course that did not really matter did it and though her feet were a little wet they would soon grow warm again; you imagining them—the two small un-stockinged feet warming themselves against each other, the ruined heels lying empty beside them under the table—already thinking, "I'll buy her a new pair. I've got Christmas pay in my pocket. I'll buy her some stockings too—silk ones too. Maybe a new dress even"; watching her sipping the beer, watching her smoking, your cigarette touching her lips, the smoke drifting and blowing on the air and you breathing it like a kiss; smoking yourself, actually trying to work it over to her without downright blowing it in her face, watching it wisp across the table and into her when she breathed, like playing some kind of bashful game of Dutch inhale. You were just that far gone, that far gone already and she hadn't even told you her name. She was just Pani this, and Pani that, and as far as she knew, you were nobody at all, just some young kid corporal. And when you asked her and she told you, it was like you had never heard the name before. And when you told her yours and she said it, it was like you had never heard "Roman" before either; watching the eyes over the rim of the glass, trying to read them, thinking, "She must know what she's doing to me," thinking, "She's right, all she has to do is snap her fingers." Only, you were wrong again. She wasn't thinking what you thought she was thinking at all. That faraway dreamy look in her eyes wasn't just put on to take you in, to take you in the way you were getting yourself set to be taken, saying to yourself, "I don't give a damn. I don't give a damn what happens as long as it does. I don't care if she's got somebody out there waiting to roll me. I don't care if I have to spend the rest of my tour on sick call. Just so long as it happens, just so long as it happens." That faraway dreamy look in her eyes wasn't put on at all, it was absolutely as real and white and innocent as the snowfall outside the window. Only trouble was, it not only didn't mean what you thought it meant, it had nothing to do with *you* at all, and when she spoke, it was like when all of a sudden the film snaps and the screen goes white and they throw up the house lights and you realize where you are and that it was somebody else up there in the picture with her all the while.

For a second you just felt like handing it to her right then and there, thinking, "Of course, the Christmas present. I forgot all about it. What a sap. Why do you think she's here with you in the first place—a two-bit snot-nosed corporal? She doesn't have to run around in those rags. With all she's got she could have generals—and maybe did once, German ones. Only these days she prefers doctors, and these days the kind of doctors she prefers they hang by the neck like an ornament on a Christmas tree." You felt like handing it to her all tied up in a nice green package with a big red ribbon around it, all tied up in the same box with the new shoes maybe and the silk stockings and the Sanforized dress you were planning to buy her—the stockings all filled up like Christmas with bones. But of course you didn't do it. But only because (though you didn't know it then) you were saving it for later so it would really come as a surprise, sort of like it had one of those Do Not Open Till Xmas stickers on it or something, and even though Christmas was already supposed to be over two hours old according to the rathskeller clock, there was still at least four hours to go according to your wristwatch which naturally was keeping Eastern Standard Time —for purely practical reasons of course, since it eliminated the terrific mathematical computations involved in determining what time it was at home whenever you happened to feel like wondering, "What are they doing back home right now?" which now that you've been overseas almost sixteen months really isn't very often any more, just about once every fifteen minutes. Like that night last July after you got the cable for instance; lying there in your sack looking at the radium dial glowing on your wrist, thinking, "Nine thirty-five yesterday evening. That would mean all of them are still sitting around the coffins praying the rosary, wondering why it happened, why you had to send her home, why you had to meet her in the first place, why you didn't just go straight back to the barracks after the trial and hit the sack and get some sleep, like you were trying to get then. Only, it didn't really matter then because you would sleep on the plane if you needed to and tomorrow at that time you'd be sitting there around the coffins with them, thinking about how it was already tomorrow over here, wishing it were seven months ago over here, wishing it were Christmas morning again and you had just handed her the present right

then and there in the rathskeller and headed back to the compound to your sack, or even better, wishing it were Christmas
Eve again, before you had even thought about going to midnight Mass; not nine thirty-five tomorrow evening in Prescott,
but nine thirty-five Christmas Eve in Augsburg even before the
trial was over, even before the sentences were read; standing
there in the dock with them, standing at parade rest, your hands
already sweating in the white gloves around the billy—looking
down at them under the brim of the helmet liner, thinking,
"They're as nervous and hopeful as a bunch of kids waiting for
Santa Claus."

All except the doc. Because Dr. Max Saulmann was the
oldest kid in the gang and had quit believing in Santa Claus
long ago. And anyway he knew that even if there did happen
to be one, the most a big bad boy like himself could expect in his
Christmas stocking was maybe enough coal and wood to start
his own little fire under him in hell. And maybe that was just
what he wanted, like, "All I want for Christmas is to believe
in it." Only, it was pretty hard to tell just *what* he wanted;
because it really didn't look like he knew, himself. Except
that it was pretty easy to see it wasn't anything like what the
others were hoping for. He wasn't anything like the others,
even sitting a little off from the rest in the dock, not speaking
to any of them, sitting there like that throughout the entire
trial, the entire six days, sitting there in the big winter coat,
his hat in his hand and his hands folded on his crossed knees, a
tall graying man with nothing at all in his face (not even bore-
dom), not even when it came time to defend himself, answering
the prosecution's questions in that calm unhurried voice which
had even less in it than the face, answering the questions just
as simply and frankly as though the prosecution were asking
him what he prescribed for the common cold or a nosebleed;
the strong deep voice droning in the PA system when it came

time for him to make his final statement; sitting there looking into the microphone or maybe past it at his hands flat atop the, table beside his hat, saying in that same grave becalmed voice, "I have nothing to say. As I have already stated I ordered the medications because I would have been executed if I had not.

"I am a doctor, and as a doctor I have always believed that the most important thing was to keep the patient alive—life was always the most important consideration no matter how it *had* been lived or had to *be* lived—in pain, in darkness, in a basket even. (Or as in my case, in shame and disgust and cowardice and abomination.) So you see I was always opposed to the government order theoretically. But what happened was that the doctor became his own patient, as it were, and the only way he could keep the patient alive was to prescribe compliance with the government order, even though it meant sacrificing in the case of others the very principle which justified the prescription in the first place. For it was the law and I knew that if I did not do it someone else would. And so I told myself, what is the sense of it, to get oneself killed, when alive as a doctor I would at least be able to help the others who were not labeled incurable. However, since the occupation my philosophy has changed. You see, I know I shall never be permitted to practice again under any circumstances even if the Commission were to free me—and certainly not in confinement. And furthermore, in the past several months I have come to consider that perhaps life is not the most important consideration after all, and that perhaps there really *is* something to this euthanasia business, that in certain cases perhaps death *can* be as good and beautiful as the term indicates, for you see, gentlemen—unless there is a hell—you will be doing me a service to hang me by the neck until dead; and who knows, perhaps even a bigger service if there is one."

That was all she came to hear. That was the reason she was there with you; sitting there, her eyes not looking *at* you but through you or past you somewhere, her hands flat on the table, the ashtray between them, the cigarette burning on its lip, almost as though she were acting it out as you told it, almost as though the hands flat on the table were his, and the nothing at all in her face the same "nothing" that was in his; sitting there listening to you tell it, the long pale hair wisping loosely over her forehead, the dim cellar light kind to the faint thin lines of age starting in her neck, and with her eyes closed and with most of her below the table (and if you didn't look at the dress pulling so tight across the anything but childish breasts) looking like a fifteen-year-old almost, because there was just something in her face that had nothing at all to do with the rest of her or her eyes either; sitting there across from you like that listening to you tell it, not only the part she came to hear, but all the rest of it too.

You told it because you got some kind of bastard pleasure out of it, like some ten-year-old in a soldier suit telling the cutest little girl on the block that when her little boy friend down the street wasn't playing doctor with her in the garbage shed he was cutting up sparrows under the fire escape; telling her how he admitted that many of the Poles and Russians sent to the institution as incurables were probably not incurable at all, that actually it was not very likely that a child of two or three and certainly not a baby hardly dry out of its mother's womb would have incurable tuberculosis; admitted that he did not even bother to examine them, that he did not even have the equipment necessary to do so, not even an x-ray machine since Bodemar was a mental hospital and not a tuberculosis sanitarium; there was even a letter he had written to the Overseer of Work in München which proved beyond a doubt that he was aware of the false diagnoses which appeared on the papers accompanying many of the laborers, a letter in which he outright asked that only tubercular patients be referred to him which were so advanced in their diseases that a cure seemed hopeless and death imminent and that the fresh cases should be sent to a sanitarium or back to their homes; admitted that after the first batch of laborers appeared at Bodemar he never even saw the patients referred to him until after they had already been sent to the cellar morgue, at which time it was necessary that he pronounce them dead prior to their cremation; admitted that in all cases he had falsified the cause of death—entering the cause as tuberculosis or heart ailment—just as he had previously done with German national mentally ill and deficient so as not needlessly to alarm the civilian population; told her all of it, watching her—her eyes closed through it all, her hands flat on the table—interrupting yourself once in a while to ask, "Shall I go on, Pani?" and she not even opening her eyes, as though she didn't even hear you, wasn't even there, not even nodding her head or shaking it or anything, just sitting there like that; and you going right on telling all of it, and through all of it expecting her to answer (knowing it would be a lie, but expecting it anyway)—when you came to the end and would finally ask, "But you knew this, didn't you, Pani?"—expecting her to answer (hoping she would answer), to shake her head at last, saying, "No! No! Good God no! I never knew he was cutting up sparrows."

But you were wrong again. She didn't say anything at all. She just sat there like a dead woman. She didn't bother to answer you one way or the other because none of that concerned her, she had not even heard it. All the while you were talking, all she was thinking about was how he had not only not bothered to defend himself but had actually asked for the rope, saying finally as though snapped awake by the absence of your voice, saying not to you really, not to anyone but herself, her eyes still closed, saying, "He wants to die. Now that I am no longer in danger, he wants to die. He wants to die because he knows that even if they send him to prison for life, I will wait for him." And it didn't do any good to ask, "Why? Why for Chrissake?" It was as though she didn't hear that either, as though you weren't in the picture at all; yelling finally—her eyes snapping awake—yelling, "Why for Chrissake?" yelling it so loud the barman came over, wiping his hands in his apron, saying, "Yes, yes! You should be a little patient, Corporal. For a bottle of beer you think I should kill myself maybe?" And you, "Make it Schnaps this time." And him, "Ah, ja, zwei Schnaps." And you, "Make it a bottle." And him, promoting you right there on the spot, "Ah, ja, Sergeant, mach schnell, sehr gut, Sergeant." And he was back even before she'd finished saying it—you paying him, hoping she'd notice all the cash you had in your wallet, because oh how you wanted to be taken, how you were dying to be taken.

But she didn't notice a thing. You weren't even there, you were just a voice. You might as well have been the doc sitting there, because you weren't in the picture at all. One thing was certain though, you were sure as hell going to be sooner or later if *you* had anything to say about it. And as you poured the glasses full, you watched her eyes, open but apparently unseeing, looking past you some place, no tears in them though, just nothing at all in them, her lips even curving a little as if to smile, saying, "It is such a long story," saying it as though she were already moving back into some depthless and spaceless past, as though she were really leaving you now, as though only her body remained sitting there. And you downed the whole glass straight and didn't even choke on it, didn't even feel it go down hardly, thinking, "This is going to be a cinch. And if I don't pass out of the picture completely, I'm going to damn sure drink myself into it, goddamn it"; saying, "All right, I bet it is. But I got all night. I got all damn night"; remembering that she didn't understand very much English, saying (in Polish this time), "He is not gone yet, Pani. And even if they should decide for the worst, that does not mean that you . . ." she, smiling like that, smiling that sad faraway smile, still looking somewhere beyond you, or rather before you, before you were

even born, before you were even around to imagine there
would come a day soon, even before you reached your eighteenth
birthday, when the only thing you'd want for Christmas was
to become part of a sordid and murky picture framed in the
faraway eyes of a woman not only twice your age, not only old
enough to be your mother, but one who supposedly wasn't even
alive; because when you said it, when you said, "Even if they
were to decide for the worst, even if he is as good as dead right
now, it does not mean *you* are," all she said was, "Oh, but I
am. I really am, don't you see. I was the first one he ever killed.
If there had been a death certificate for him to falsify, it would
have said, Magda Marya Nowina, died of appendicitis Christmas morning, 1926."

And maybe she was right. Anyway, it was like making love
to a corpse, like making love in a coffin, like it wasn't just a
dark horsecab you were riding in but one of those old-time
horse-drawn hearses; and with your head hanging out the window befouling the streets you felt all you had to do was look
back to see the long line of mourners trudging along behind,
their black umbrellas open against the snow gleaming under
the streetlamps—the horse's hoofs silent as death on the snow-
covered streets. You were sick, completely and thoroughly sick;
but not only from the booze, though you had gone through
an entire bottle between you back there in the cellar, she sitting
there as though she were not even aware she was drinking, just
lifting the glass to her lips and drinking like that, not tossing
it off like most people do a straight shot, but drinking it down
as though it were wine or something, not even letting you mix
them with soda like you were mixing your own (because after
that first one you just couldn't stomach the horrible stuff
straight), sitting there sipping it straight like that, smoking
your cigarettes; and you listening to her telling it, all of it, three
or four hours of it, because it was almost six o'clock in the
morning by the house clock when you left (not even midnight

on your wristwatch), all the stuff about Bodemar and the war
and all; but not only that, going way back before you were even
born, all of it, all the sordid fouled-up business about the priest
and all, and all of it was Max this and Max that, so that instead
of *you* drinking yourself into the picture, *she* was drinking you
completely out of it, going further and further away with every
sentence, with every drink, until the bottle was finally gone and
you asked her if she wanted another, and when she nodded like
that, her neck kind of rubbery and the long pale hair falling
loosely over her forehead, you figured she'd had it (not to mention five-star Corporal of the Army Roman Novak, RA 666
something or other, who had trouble remembering his own
damn serial number), helping her into her coat and shawl, the
cab horse snorting and stamping under the lamp, the snow
still falling straight down, the cab dark and warm and private
inside, the cabby just a voice up top somewhere, "Geh, geh!"
and the single slap of the reins.

You had no idea you were going to exchange Christmas
presents. You simply figured you'd drive around a little and talk
some more until the cabby felt you'd got your ten dollars'
worth, since you guessed maybe she no more wanted to hurry
back to her cot in the DP Center than you were dying to get
back to your bunk in the barracks. You never even thought of
anything like a hotel. You just weren't sighted in on that scene
at all. That may have been the most popular picture playing
in the European theater that Christmas morning but it just
wasn't showing on the screen you were watching, even though
you'd paid better than smoker prices for admission. And even if
maybe you did let it pass through your mind once or twice during
the evening, even with a half bottle of booze in you, you still
weren't *that* courageous, though no doubt about it you must have
been feeling pretty big and strong, saying, "Don't worry, Pani.
Don't worry about anything, because I'll take care of you. Don't

worry about a thing, because I'm here now and you just don't have to worry about A thing." With all the booze in you you weren't just a seventeen-year-old kid any more, you weren't just corporal, you were old enough to be her old man and a five-star general to boot, and she was just a little fifteen-year-old kid in your arms (admittedly a little big for her age), and you were going to take care of her from here on in, and there just wasn't anything she had to worry about any more. You didn't even try to kiss her, you didn't even think about it, thinking only about how you'd scrounge up a room for her near the Army compound first thing in the morning and get her out of that miserable DP Center, how with no sweat at all she could live pretty comfortably on a corporal's salary because you knew plenty guys who kept shacks on corporal's pay, and anyway you'd have time-in-grade for sergeant in another six months and there was no doubt in your mind the Ol' Man would pass over guys with twice as much time-in-grade as you because *you* were his boy, the finest jeep jockey in the European theater, and the sharpest soldier in that whole damn Army of conquering heroes and liberators, even though you were born too late, even though you wouldn't have touched the Army with a ten-foot pole if it weren't for the GI Bill. And she must have thought you were pretty damn funny talking the way you were, because she just leaned over and kissed you like that, smiling, saying, "You are a very nice boy. Now you will take me to the Center, yes? because I have drunk too much. And Monday you will come and tell me what the sentence is, yes?"

And just like that everything fell away from you, after all that talking you still weren't in the picture, thinking, "What the hell's the use. And after all the dough I spent. If all she wants is a messenger boy, goddamn it . . ." And it must have been the booze, it must have been. It wasn't *you* that was a cinch, not you who never even touched a woman before, except in dreams maybe, dreams you were even too shy to re-

member when you woke up in the morning, the whiskey talking,
saying, "Well, if I'm such a damn nice kid and I'm going to
run a messenger service between the courthouse and the DP
Center, what's in it for me, how 'bout an employee Christmas
bonus or something"; and she didn't even need to understand
what the whiskey was *saying* (it was American whiskey and
didn't talk Polish), because it was talking with your hands too
and so the point came across, and she just stiffened, saying,
"Please no. You are a nice boy, and you will come and tell me
Monday . . ." And that was exactly what you wanted her to
say, because you weren't even sure you'd know what to do if
she hadn't, that's what *you* wanted, but the whiskey had other
ideas, still talking, not only using your hands now, but even
getting you to translate into Polish, saying, "What for? Why
wait till Monday? I can tell you right now. The trial is all over,
Pani"; just like that, handing it to her right there in the horsecab, not even waiting to wrap it up in some Christmas ribbon
along with the new shoes and the silk stockings and the Sanforized dress, just handing it to her right then and there, not
because you were sore she had stopped you, holding your hands
like that and patting them like a nice little boy, because that
was what you wanted really, what you really wanted, that was
the picture *you'd* paid to see, the only one you *wanted* to see
really, except that you wanted it to be *you* up there with her,
and not him, *you* up there framed in her eyes. And so you said
it, saying it as though it were *your* voice rattling in the PA system and not the Colonel's, as though it were *your* vote had decided the issue, saying, "It's all over. They read the sentences
this evening. They're going to hang him, goddamn it." And she
just smiled that sad faraway smile, and it was like exchanging
gifts, under a gallows instead of a Christmas tree, she opening
her present and finding the bones there and just smiling like
that, that sad faraway smile like a disappointed kid finding
coal and wood in her stocking, sitting there like that watching

you open yours, watching you undoing the ribbons and fingering the wrappings like a timid seven-year-old expecting to find not just a spinning top inside but the whole round whirling world. And there in the back of the horsecab, dark as the inside of a hearse, the sound of the horse's hoofs silent as death on the snow-covered streets, that was exactly what you found. It wasn't a toy at all. It was the whole round spinning world whirling like a top, and playing with it only made you sick to the stomach, your head hanging out of the cab window befouling the snow.

"And so you came in here not even a week after you met her crying to me about wanting to marry her, and when I told you I'd do everything short of outright breaking regulations to stop you, you thought I was a bastard, right?"

"Yes, sir."

"And now seven months have gone by, and you've got two cablegrams in your hand to prove I was right, and you still think so."

"Yes, sir."

"You know what your trouble is, Novak? You're just looking for somebody to blame so you won't have to blame yourself. Because it was *you* sent her home to your old man and nobody else. All right, so it wasn't your old man you sent her to. Don't interrupt. You know what you are, Novak? You're one of these smart-ass kids who draws all kinds of fine distinctions about everything, the kind that's always interrupting people to tell them they're wrong about some petty little thing or other just to confuse the bigger issues, the ones that really count, like it wasn't your old man you sent her home to but your uncle who really isn't your uncle but just a friend of the family, a cousin or something, things like that, that make no never mind at all. A hell of a lot of difference it makes, doesn't it, since they all live in the same building? That's just it, you're always making fine distinctions about everything and everybody, and when it comes to something as basic and obvious as the difference between a decent woman and a tramp . . . I don't suppose you ever even gave a thought to how she managed to get those immigration papers so fast."

"I know how she got them."

"Like hell you do. Suppose I were to tell you I happen to know for a fact she paid for them on her back, in the bed *you* bought her, in the shack *you* paid the rent on every month? You wouldn't believe it, would you? After all that's happened, you still won't admit what she is. You got a picture in your head, even a good kick in the teeth like those cablegrams won't change. Well, you'd better shape up, soldier. Maybe that picture you're carrying around in your head is fine and noble and the way things ought to be, but they aren't, goddamn it, they just aren't. A kid with brains like you has got to learn sooner or later, otherwise there's going to be trouble. There already is, just because you couldn't tell the difference between a woman in love and a bitch in heat. Believe me, I'm not just making this up to prove a point, I happen to know for a fact how she got those papers. I checked it all out."

"That's pretty fast checking, sir, since you weren't even supposed to know I'd sent her home till I walked in here twenty minutes ago."

"All right, sit down, Roman," leaning back in the chair and lighting a cigar again—the smoke hanging low under the lamp above the desk—saying, "I don't know why I bother with you anyway. I don't know why I take any special interest at all. You haven't shown any respect for anything military and certainly not for these bars on my shoulder for almost seven months now. Now you come in here and show me a couple of cablegrams which only go to prove what I been telling you all along, and you practically order me to send you home Granite Mountain Special. When even if you had Red Cross

verification of the tragedy, which you don't, you know as well as
I do the Army doesn't send men home for funerals, not from
overseas. Sickness and imminent death all right, but not funerals, no matter how close the relationship, no matter how
many the hell coffins there are. You don't understand what the
word 'regulations' means any more, do you? So I don't know
what the hell I'm even giving you my time for."

"*I do.*"

"Now what's that supposed to mean? I'm telling you, Novak,
I'm taking all this down in the back of my head somewhere,
even though I don't want to. I know you're under a strain, and
I'm letting things ride. But there's only so much I'm going to
stand for. I know you think I got something against you. But
you're wrong. Anything I did to stop you from marrying her,
I did for your own good. I went out of my way, God knows.
And not because I'm one of these CO's who just because the
men call him the Ol' Man thinks he's got to be a father to
them. You know me, you know I don't run around wiping
anybody's nose. I wouldn't care if the whole damn company
went out tomorrow and married half the whores in Augsburg.
It was just that I took an interest in you. You used to be a
sharp soldier. I liked the way you handled a jeep. I liked the
way you used to listen on those trips to Dachau like you at least
had some idea what I was talking about. I still remember the
time I asked you how come you didn't tomcat it around like
all the rest and you said because it isn't right, that's all, just
like that. In fifteen years of service I can honestly say I've never
heard it put quite that way before. And so what do you do?
. . . a two-bit doxy twice your age . . ."

"If I were your age, it would be different, right, sir?"

"Shut up and listen. I don't know what you're driving at. I
don't know what you think you got up your sleeve. But whatever it is, remember you're just looking for somebody to blame
besides yourself . . . or her. Now don't interrupt. Before you

say something you're going to be sorry for, think it over. All right, I admit, I don't really know how she got those papers. Like you said, I didn't even know you'd sent her home till you came in here tonight. I made that up. All right. The point is you got to stop kidding yourself. You know damn well you never really wanted to marry her, and so you can't blame me for that. And even if I had let you marry her, you would have taken her home with you eventually and something just as bad would have happened. Anyway, you were relieved as hell when I told you I wouldn't process the papers. You could have gone over my head if you'd wanted to. You could have gone to see the IG or the Chaplain at least, but you didn't, did you? And don't tell me it was because she wouldn't have you. Not that she was crazy about you or anything, you're right about that. But you know as well as I do she'd have married a Private-1 in the colored platoon if she thought that was the only way she could get to the States. And you were happy as hell I turned you down. Only trouble was, when she saw she couldn't get you to marry her she worked on you till you got your Uncle whatever the hell his name is to sponsor her, and once she got that, getting the papers was a cinch with a little help from the right party. And don't tell any of the men in the barracks you had to talk her into going, because you'll be laughed right out of the theater. You see, Novak, I know exactly how it happened and I know why you did it too. You're one of these religious kids— and it doesn't matter what church you go to or how often, or if you even go to church at all even on Christmas—you're just one of these kids that thinks once you put it to a woman you got to marry her, or at least take care of her as though you owed her your whole damn life. And whether she happens to be your Virgin Mary or a two-bit tramp like Magda doesn't make a bit of difference, does it? I'm right, you know it. And that's why you came in here talking marriage, and that's why you sent her home. Because a kid like you just can't go on shacking even with a beauty like her and not start hating himself for it. And you couldn't just break it off, could you? You couldn't just leave her out in the cold, because you knew she wouldn't be out there very long. And even though you knew you couldn't go on with her without marrying her, you couldn't stand to think that if *you* didn't somebody else would, and that was why you sent her home, right? Listen, you may be able to fool yourself, Roman. But I know your kind. You're just a pushover for any beautiful bitch with a sad face and a sad enough story to go along with it. I *know* your kind."

"I guess you ought to, sir."

"What does that mean?"

"Nothing, except you ought to. Because after all, you've had about forty-five years to figure my kind out. Because you haven't only been talking about *me* the past few minutes, sir. Only difference is, we don't read the cablegrams the same way and so one of us has got to be wrong about what they prove, not only about her, but about that figure in the carpet we used to talk about on those jeep trips to Dachau. And so maybe you can't get me an emergency leave, but you're going to get me home somehow so I can get there in time to see that funeral and find out which one of us is right"—the cablegrams folded in your hand, one three days old dated July 20, 1946, reading, "ROMAN DARLING YOUR UNCLE GROSZEK AND I WERE MARRIED THIS MORNING LOVE MAGDA, and the other dated two days later, unsigned, reading, CONGRATULATIONS YOUR OLDMAN AND MINE KILLED THEMSELVES FIGHTING OVER HER—"Because, you see, you don't have a choice, sir. Because, you see, I really *do* know how she got those papers, sir."

Chapters II & XVII

MORNING

On the morning Roman got the first cable and two days before he got the second, the man he called his Uncle Groszek sat with his shoes off in an armchair in a hotel room in Atlantic City, New Jersey, listening to the sea booming against the beach below his window. He had been dreaming again, a dream in which he found himself kneeling under the kitchen sink in the tenement back in Prescott staring down into a hole in the floor into which somehow he was sure a penny had rolled. He had not had the dream more than a dozen times in the entire eighteen years since his first wife had died; however, in the past six months, ever since Magda arrived, he had had it at least once every night, and tonight (or rather this morning, the first morning of their honeymoon) several times.

And so following the cigar smoke rising round as a wedding ring against the shadowed ceiling he wonders what it all means, thinking, "There are only just so many things can happen to a man—and no more. It is the same thing over and over, like getting out of bed in the morning and lying down again at night except that you are one day older and maybe if you are lucky one day wiser too." For he has been to Atlantic City before, and in the darkness with only the moon in the open window and the fan on the dresser useless against the July night, it might even be the same room again for all the difference, and with Magda's breathing slow and steady from the bed it might even be his first wife lying there under the single sheet, her hair fanned blond against the pillow, her third finger left hand ringed with the identical piece of gold. Because when he thought about it, it was all just unlikely enough to make a man wonder whether perhaps it really wasn't so impossible to cross the same stream twice after all.

The stream, as Groszek sees it, had its source in a public urinal in First Ward Park the Saturday night of the Democratic fund-raising picnic back in 1927. Those were the days before he had thought to try his hand at politics, long before he ever dreamed he would one day find himself not only the Democratic leader of Prescott's First Ward but a duly elected representative of the people, sporting the title of City Councilman, and who as a candidate for the Mayor's chair come the November elections handed around favors with the same ease and flourish he handed out twenty-five-cent cigars. Those were the days when he was just another broken-English-speaking immigrant without a job, depending on the commissions he earned booking numbers to keep him in liquor and nickel cigars. But even in those days he was ambitious, planning and betting on marrying the

young and wealthy Pani Martha Sadovi long before her husband
had counted his final dollar, joking her about it in her candy
store every afternoon when he stopped by to collect the number
slips and pick up his daily supply of cigars, winking, saying, "I
wonder what it would be like, Pani, to wake up some morning
on a mattress full of money with nothing else to worry about
all day but making love to a clever young woman and running
a candy store and a tenement and collecting rents from fifteen
families every month."

Groszek knew of course that there wasn't a bachelor over
thirty in the entire First Ward who hadn't had his eye on the
mourning widow ever since the day of the funeral, that as soon
as a decent period of mourning had passed and she took off her
black clothes she'd be swamped with proposals; but the only
man he considered a really serious rival for the widow's hand
was Pan Jan Novak (or Janush, as the widow affectionately
called him). For though Novak had a lame left leg and limped
like a cripple, and though he was only thirty years old and so
really much too young for a thirty-year-old widow matured much
beyond her years after more than fifteen winters of marriage to
a man old enough to be her grandfather (Groszek himself was
thirty-six); nevertheless Groszek was not one to overlook the
fact that from a woman's point of view Jan Novak was after all
a rather tall good-looking fellow, what with his neat black mustache and all, and it was clear to everyone every time he opened
his mouth that he must really have been educated at the University at Lublin as he claimed, and he was after all a sober and
serious fellow who never set foot in the taverns, never touched
a drink, spending all his time in his room behind the candy store
studying the English language, which though he had only been
in the country less than four months he had already learned well
enough to teach others to read, holding a nightly class for recent
arrivals from the old country in a rented hall in the Polish People's Home (rented with money loaned him by the widow's dead

husband) and charging twenty-five cents per person per lesson, not to mention his already having been promised a job teaching in the new public grammar school across the river in Anderson come September. Despite all this, and despite the rumors which had linked Novak and the widow before her husband's death, right up until that morning two weeks ago when the widow's niece arrived from the old country, Groszek had been more or less confident that his own pressing and impulsive play on the very afternoon of her husband's funeral and his subsequent nightly visits to her bed, had forced the young and inexperienced Novak completely out of the game. In the past two weeks, however, two weeks during which every afternoon in her candy store the widow had whispered, "No, not tonight, Groszek. How can we with a child sleeping in the next room?" he had begun to wonder. Perhaps after getting a good look at his hand in those first few weeks after the funeral, the widow had decided the cards he held were not really higher than Novak's after all, that any stakes she had allowed him to pocket so far were simply due to Novak's inexperienced and fumbling play, that perhaps in the past two weeks . . .

He bit off the end of a new cigar and spat. He had already lost the day's commissions at the dice cages (it did not really matter, for it was already close to midnight and he had had more than enough to drink, and besides tomorrow was another day and surely the widow would stand him gas money and a handful of cigars even though she no longer proffered her bed), and so he parked himself on a bench near the dance pavilion, took off his shoes because as usual his corns were killing him, and prepared to watch the dancers for a while. From where he sat he could see—past the pavilion lights and above the trees bordering the park—the widow's tenement silhouetted against the sky, only a few lights glowing in the windows since at that hour the tenants who were not at the picnic were probably in bed. And that was exactly what worried him, because though he knew the widow

had never been one for community gatherings of any kind when
her husband was alive, and was not likely to change her ways
very much now that he was dead just because he, Groszek, had
happened to ask her in the candy store that afternoon to meet
him at the picnic tonight so they could talk over the impossible
situation of the past two weeks (especially since she was supposed to be in mourning and not dancing around at the picnic
with him); nevertheless, he could not help wondering whether
perhaps what with most of the tenants at the picnic and her
niece out of the house for the evening (he could see her dancing
with a girl friend under the pavilion lights) the widow was in
bed that very moment entertaining Novak just the way she had
entertained him, wondering whether perhaps she had been
doing so every night for the past two weeks just as (rumor had
it) she had done for more than three months before her husband
had died, ever since in fact that first week this Novak fellow had
arrived from the old country and taken up lodgings in the room
behind the candy store directly across the hall from the widow's
apartment.

There was no moon, and the sky was dark over the trees behind the tenement, and there were heat rumblings in the distance. The pavilion, however, was brightly lighted, and the band
was playing a polka, some of the musicians standing, singing of
sunshine and haystacks and the farmer's barefooted bowlegged
daughter who had never ridden a horse. He lubricated his cigar
and sat back watching the long straight legs and the bare feet of
the widow's niece flashing under the naked pavilion lights and
whirling skirt. She had taken off her shoes and he could tell by
the way she whirled around with her girl friend, throwing her
head back and laughing like that, that the number must have
been requested especially for her; he could tell from the way the
singing musicians stood with their instruments under their arms
clapping time and stamping their feet every time she stamped
hers, tossing her head and flinging her long blond hair. He knew

the girl she was dancing with, he knew her reputation and he knew she was at least seventeen or eighteen years old and no longer a child in either years or stature, and so he marveled to see how insignificant she looked next to the widow's niece, thinking, "At least from a distance nobody would ever take her for only fifteen." He shook his head, confident that it would not be long before the widow had trouble on her hands, remembering how he could not take his eyes off her in the rear-view mirror that morning coming home from the Hoboken pier, sitting there at the wheel of the big second-hand Packard the widow had bought for him (it was supposed to be a secret between them, just as the nightly visits to her bed were supposed to be a secret not only from her niece but from the entire neighborhood), sitting there watching the blond and rosy fifteen-year-old beauty taller than her aunt in the back seat smiling up at him in the rear-view mirror, thinking, "She is only a child and innocent, Groszek, but it will not be long before she discovers she is neither, and it would be something to be the one between the sheets with her when she does"—driving right through a red light, the police whistle blowing, thinking, "That is what comes of looking like that at fifteen-year-old children, Groszek —trouble."

And though trouble was the last thing he was looking for, sitting there in the shadows under the trees chewing on his unlit cigar and wiping the sweat out of the inside of his Panama with his noserag, it was like looking into the rear-view mirror all over again, sitting there watching the way the boys leaning against the pavilion railing hung on her every step, the musicians snapping their heads up from their music stands every once in a while, their eyes darting around the dance floor as though looking for their places on a music sheet or something, as though she were not only *dancing* to the music but was the *music* itself; watching her disappear into a crowd of boys on the far side of the bandstand when the set was finished; shaking his head again,

thinking, "She is trouble all right. Only two weeks in the neighborhood and she not only picks out the wildest one in the tenement for a girl friend but makes her look like the quietest compared to herself." He did not like it. After all, she was the
widow's niece and if things finally worked out the way he had
planned, she would one day be *his* niece too. Besides, he did
not like to think of such beauty wasted on some pimply neighborhood hoodlum. Somehow, he had always felt that innocence
and beauty should be like twin sisters dancing together, though
he knew that like sisters they very seldom chose each other as
partners. It was a shame perhaps but that was the way things
were, and there was nothing anybody could do about it. He had
slipped his feet back into his shoes and was just thinking about
going back and offering to spin the dice cages for a while, fanning himself with his hat and sucking on his cigar (it was his
last one and he was putting off lighting it as long as possible),
when he heard them.

They came running down the path through the trees, passing
right beside his bench and under the lamp and disappearing into
the ladies' side of the urinal. And though he could not help feeling uneasy about it, he told himself he owed it to the widow to
investigate, and anyway he had to go himself and it was not as
though he were really sneaking around, because he did snap the
light on and all; standing there listening to the voice rattling
away behind the wall, "This is the last time, Eva, the first and
the last. Maybe you look like eighteen but you sure don't act it.
I told you, didn't I? Just three little swallows, like me. Oh God,
I should have known. First you won't even talk to me, and all
of a sudden tonight . . . Well, just remember you asked for it.
Because don't think they're going to be satisfied with just a good-
night kiss or something, not after finishing half their bottle for
them"—the water flushing behind the wall, and then again, and
once more, the voice almost whispering now—"All right, shhh,
I hear them in there. You feel better now? I'll wait for you out-

side. Just wash up a little. You'll be all right, you'll see. In the car with the windows open and all . . ." And when he stepped out, he saw her throw the cigarette into the weeds behind her, saying, "Oh, Pan Groszek . . . I thought you were . . . Eva doesn't feel good. Something she ate at the stand, I think."

There was nothing else to do of course. He had decided that back in the urinal. Not only was it his duty to keep her away from her hoodlum boy friends in her condition, but bringing her home like that gave him a perfect excuse to visit the widow, thinking, "We could shake the bed to pieces tonight and Eva will sleep right through it." And so when he knocked at the widow's door and no one answered and he had to use the key he found knotted in the corner of Eva's handkerchief to let himself in, he could not keep himself from thinking, "By golly, I have been right all along. She is probably across the hall in his bed right now"; wondering, "How would it be if I just walked across the hall and pounded on the door?" thinking, "Yes, and how would I like a punch in the nose?" He did not even bother to snap on the lights. He just lifted her and carried her into her bedroom (she would not walk any further than the horsehair sofa) and sat her down on the edge of the bed—the streetlights bright on the sheets through the bedroom curtains—saying, "Now take off your clothes like a good girl and go to sleep." He found he was whispering, thinking, "They will be surprised all right. Or maybe it would be better just to sit in the dark and wait for her." He wanted to do both and neither, hoping the widow would come in before he had a chance to make up his mind either way, come in with a shawl on her head and maybe one of those baby doll prizes or something from the picnic saying she was out looking for Eva; Eva just sitting there on the edge of the bed, falling back across it again every time he let go of her shoulder, and he still whispering, saying, "Now be a good girl, Eva. You know you cannot sleep with your clothes on, besides they are dirty from being sick"; beginning to undo her bodice for her, saying, "If you take off your clothes like a good girl, your aunt will not even have to know"; thinking, "What are you doing, Groszek? What will she think if she comes in and finds you undressing her like this? All you would have to do is accuse her and like a woman she will start screaming about what are you doing to my niece."

So he just left her there sitting on the bed struggling with her clothes and went out into the parlor, leaving the bedroom door open, and just sat down on the sofa in the dark telling himself that he was out of breath from carrying Eva around, and besides, his corns hurt and so he would rest for a minute and then do what had to be done. He unlaced his shoes and aired his toes and finally lit his cigar, thinking how stupid he would feel waking Novak up after midnight, because suppose the widow really *had* only gone out to look for her niece, what would he say? "I just knocked to see if you were sleeping alone?"

The more he thought about it, the more he thought that maybe he should not have been so hasty back in the park, because where did it get him thinking only of his duty to the widow and her niece? recalling how Eva's girl friend Lottie had sidled up to him like that right in front of her boy friends, saying, "Why don't you take me home too? We could put her in the back seat and drive around in your car for a while and then her aunt won't have to know and she won't be able to tell my father and I didn't want to go out with these schoolboys anyway." And though he knew that would have only meant trouble, now after the way things had turned out he was not so sure it would not have been worth it. Because what was the good of being such a saint and thinking only of others? Where did it get him? Everybody was enjoying themselves except him—the widow and Novak, Eva's girl friend Lottie and her schoolboys. And anyway what was the good of it when tomorrow night Eva would probably just go out and do the same thing all over again and it would just be a question of time before one of those

pimply-faced hoodlums . . . He sat there wondering what it
might have been like if he had not been so decent—the car
parked somewhere in the Anderson hills, and the headlights off
and only the moon shining in through the windows, all alone
with the two of them—thinking, "But there *is* no moon tonight,
Groszek. It is going to rain." And he had just got finished telling
himself he was daydreaming like a schoolboy—watching the
wind blowing in the curtains over the parlor windows—when he
heard her calling him from the bedroom.

The light from the bedroom window curved naked over her
back, and the shift, pulled over her head, hung down between
her knees like an inverted umbrella. She was struggling and
whimpering, and when he moved to help her, reaching under
the shift where her chin should be and undoing the ribbon, her
hair spilled into his lap on top of it. She just sat there with her
head between her knees whimpering, and when he touched
her shoulder she just plopped back across the bed, the streetlight
bright through the lace curtains shadowing over her like a net.
It was as though he could feel it spreading over him too, the
damp wind blowing in the curtains, swinging the bedroom door
shut almost soundlessly, the room almost identical with the one
he knew on the other side of the wall, just reversed as in a
mirror, the door and the bed and the bureau on the right side
instead of the left, the window and the chair on the left instead
of the right, the chair almost identical with the one in the other
room on the edge of which he would always place his cigar—
the ash hanging over the floor—right after hanging his hat over
the bed post while slipping out of his already unlaced shoes and
just before taking off his coat and hunching out of his suspenders; the net spreading over him just as palpably as the lips
going against his palm, or the darkness and dissolution, or later
the defeat and disgust when he lifted his hand and found that
it was not "no" she had been whispering against his palm, that

Novak was not only in *his* bed across the hall with the widow, but in this bed too with her niece, her eyes still closed beneath him, her lips still going, breathing it over and over, the name drifting away into sleep, the room grown suddenly so quiet he heard the first light spatter of rain like a runaway horse galloping in the alley.

The rest was remorse.

Remorse and madness—but the quiet kind. Quiet for a year at least, at least until the morning of the attempted murder and suicide and the fall from the tenement roof—not the seven long murderous stories to the alley pavement below, but only five short humiliating feet into a top-floor fire escape in which only three small geranium pots were broken and one leg (Groszek's) —a fall following hard on an incident for which that first night Eva whispered Novak's name against his palm was just a kind of innocent dress rehearsal. Because somehow he had managed to keep his head that night, to climb out the window through the rain-soaked curtains and down the fire escape into the puddled alley, even though he had already heard the widow closing the windows out in the parlor before he had even had time to hunch back into his suspenders. He had even pulled the window shut behind him, remembering the widow's voice through the door, asking, "Is your window closed, Eva? It is raining." And back in his room behind the corner tavern he had even managed to drink himself to sleep. But the next morning, there she was, standing there before his bed, the folded umbrella dripping around her feet, her hair long and matted on her shoulders under the babushka and her eyes all ringed and swollen. And when she reached under her sleeve for the handkerchief, he saw —sitting there under the sheet in just his underdrawers—the candy store and the tenement and a mattress full of money floating away from him on her tears, thinking, "It is true what everybody says about you, Groszek, you are no damn good."

Only, she did not cry, she simply untied the handkerchief and handed him her dowry, which he unfolded into three one-hundred-dollar bills.

But for Groszek somehow that was even worse than a dowry of tears. At least that is the way he sees it now, believing that he had felt something then that he had never felt before, something he had never even guessed he was capable of feeling, handing the money back to her, saying, "Tell her it is no good. Tell her I will not do it, not for three hundred or for three hundred thousand"—because where else could she have gotten the money but from her aunt? Why else would she come to him like this when he knew as well as she did that it was Novak she cared for?—saying, "Do not be a fool, Eva. Do not let her frighten you. You do not have to marry me just because I have lain with you, because I have forced you . . . The world is not like that, it is not like she tells you at all. You are innocent and you believe her, and you think she gave you the money because she is only thinking of you. But do not believe it, it is crazy to think you have to marry me. She just tells you that to get you off her hands, and me too, so she and Novak . . ." And when she finally started to cry, unable to speak at all, he just told her to wait outside for him till he finished dressing, and when she was gone he threw on his clothes and went out the back door peeping out behind the back-yard fence to make sure she was waiting for him in the hall and not outside on the corner where she could see the car—the corner hardly visible through the huge rain. He did not know what he was going to do, where he was going to go, knowing only that he had to get away, thinking, "Maybe they have been right about you for a long time, Groszek. But not this time"; running for the car, splashing in the puddles, thinking, "And it has nothing to do with her aunt either, nothing at all. The three hundred was not even necessary, it is nothing but an insult. Because what she does not know is that you want her. Because until this morning, even *you* did

not know it. Until she came like that with that miserable three
hundred dollars, you never dreamed you could want anything so
much—more than all the candy stores and tenements and
widows in Prescott"; jumping into the car, the gears grinding,
thinking, "Because they are all wrong about you, Groszek. They
will say you are no damn good and that is why you ran away.
But they will be wrong. This time they will be wrong. Because
no matter how much you want her, you will not allow her to
throw herself away on a good-for-nothing like you just because
she is frightened. Because the world does not have to be that
way. The world just does not have to be that way, Groszek"; the
windshield wipers jumping and the car already pulling away
from the gutter when he looked up and saw her staring down at
him in the rear-view mirror.

That was nineteen years ago and now watching the cigar
smoke rise round as a wedding ring against the ceiling, wondering what the next week will be like with Magda—in the bars
and on the beaches and in bed—he knows it will be just as different from that week back in 1927 as the weather is. Because
even though it is Atlantic City all over again, even though the
season is the same, the month even; the weather is different,
the movement in the veins. Now, only the weather is hot, for the
blood has cooled. Then, only the weather was cool, the last cool
rain of the season before the August drought set in. It had
rained that entire week. And when they got back to Prescott
with the souvenirs—the satin pillows with "God Bless Our
Home" on them, and the Kewpie dolls, and the penny-arcade
photographs, and the three-pound tin "Treasure Chest" of salt-
water taffy, not to mention the piece of paper from Maryland
saying they were married—it was still raining, the rain booming
on her umbrella as he helped her out of the car in front of the
tenement, and rushing fearfully in the gutters toward the sewer.
There was nowhere else to take her but back to the tenement;

he could not very well take her to live with him in the room behind the corner tavern. And though they might very well have
gone to a hotel, Eva for some reason would not hear of it. She
would stay with her aunt until somebody moved out of the tenement and they could take the rooms, she said. If he wished, she
was sure her aunt would allow him to stay there also; but if he
would rather sleep in his room behind the corner tavern, it made
no difference to her. And though he knew *she* was looking forward to it, he did not like the idea of spending the night without her, much less the weeks or even months it might be before
a vacancy appeared. Still, he could not bring himself to go back
there and face the widow—not at least until he was completely
drunk.

And so at the corner tavern he just sat there quietly drinking
at the bar listening to old Nowicki the fiddler scraping away
amid the sandwich trays—the balls clicking on the pool table,
the pregnant old bitch dozing under it whining on the high
notes, her snout coming right up off her paws but her eyes
closed through all of it as in a dream. He spent a great deal of
time just watching the way Nowicki played and ate sandwiches
at the same time, holding a sandwich in his bow hand and taking a bite out of it every time it paused near his chin between
bars. For while he was still sober, Groszek paid very little attention to the joking and laughing going on behind him around the
pool table, but after three or four hours of drinking, somebody
said it just loud enough for him to hear, saying, "I agree with
you, my friend. He is not only a cradle stealer, he is a fool. Because maybe the widow's mattress is second-hand and no longer
so soft as her niece's but at least it has money under it"; and he
stood up, wheeled over to the table, grabbed a pool stick out of
the hands of one of the players and, steadying himself against
the table, shouted, "I will break the head of any man who even
so much as mentions her *name* in a saloon." He heard his voice
rattle in the overhead fan, but when all they did was laugh, he

slammed the stick across the table top and was disappointed to find that despite all the noise it had made it had not even broken. The fiddle ceased, however, and the old bitch came clattering out from under the table like a puppy, her huge belly rolling and her paws clacking and skidding on the linoleum, and somebody yelled, "Well, at least you have frightened the old lady, Groszek. Now goddamn, sit down before you fall down." And as he stood there with the pool stick in his hands thinking what it might cost him to act like a man for the first time in his life and maybe break a few heads, the door opened and everything stopped for a minute and there was Novak, standing there in the doorway like a drowned man, the rain dripping off his mustache and the peak of his cap (his pipe still smoking, however, turned upside down), the friendly old bitch sidling up to him, licking his hand and snuffling the rain puddle forming around his feet.

"It is the schoolteacher," somebody yelled, "come to sell English lessons for drinks"; Novak standing there tipping his hat, his mustache curving, saying, "No, gentlemen, not tonight. I have only come to take my *nephew* home to his wife." At first nobody understood, least of all Groszek. He was still in the dark long after Nowicki had begun scraping away on "Here Comes the Bride"; Novak saying, "This morning, Groszek, in the courthouse." And when it finally dawned on him—"The widow and Novak? Of course they are laughing! That makes him my uncle now"—he tried to laugh too, but it was no good, thinking, "So I was right all along. They have been playing around together all the while, and now . . ." And for a second he felt as though perhaps none of this were really happening to him at all, that he was only dreaming it, feeling the lips again and the name against his palm, and when he looked down and saw her—the old bitch sitting there at his feet, big-bellied, her tail sweeping the floor and her snout nuzzling against his palm—he understood—watching his foot go, thinking, "She sounds just like a woman when she screams"—for less than eight months later Roman was born.

There was talk of course. There were even those who, remembering his morning visits to the tenement, named *him* the father. Even he wondered about it, for the idea appealed to him. And at first, especially when Pani Novak named the child after him, he thought, "Why not?" However, as time passed and the talking died away, he began to think it unlikely that Pani Novak would be so forward and shameless as to name the child after him if he really *was* the father, unless of course that was precisely why she did it, since everyone would think it so unlikely. And after all, it was not so unusual to name a child after its godfather—though of course it was not a common thing either. And even though Novak acted as though he had no doubt whatsoever that the child was his, he must have known about those morning visits, and he must have known the widow was pregnant when he married her, otherwise why the rush, when she still had many months of mourning before her. Groszek knew that Novak was not a stupid man, and though he felt sure that he was not the kind of man who would knowingly marry a woman with another man's baby in her belly no matter how much money and property she had, still he could not help feeling that there must always be some question in Novak's mind and perhaps even in his wife's. After all, the only thing the business of the three hundred dollars proved was that the widow preferred Novak for a husband rather than himself. To Groszek it remained clearly a case of the widow's discovering her pregnancy and choosing Novak for the father though she could never really be sure she had made the right choice; and as luck would have it Groszek had just managed to arrange things so that she could send her niece after him the next morning with a bribe of three hundred dollars to take him off her hands, frightening the poor child with all kinds of stories about pregnancy and unmarried mothers. He believed this because there was no other way he could explain away the money or Eva's refusal to tell him how she had come by it. He believed it, because it seemed to confirm his suspicions about the widow's relations with Novak and gave him the comfort of feeling that he was not alone to blame for Eva's misery, that he was as much victim as she.

The only trouble was, Eva apparently did not see it that way. For though she seemed to despise her aunt, and as Groszek saw it, insisted on taking rooms in her aunt's tenement simply so she could silently torment her with her presence as a reminder of her betrayal of her own kin, Eva seemed to hold *him* equally guilty. For though he brought home every penny he made booking numbers and had stopped gambling completely except for the fifty cents he played on a number every day, there was no living with her. He told himself that she was just a child and could not be expected to understand what life was, could not be expected to know that people had to live with their mistakes and make the best of them, and he hoped that in time things would turn out for the best, that in time she would come to understand him. And so he was very patient with her when he would try to make love to her in the dark and she would lie there as though she were not even in the same bed with him. He knew that he could never expect her to care for him the way he had learned to care for her, but he hoped that perhaps when the baby came things would be different. He would tell himself, "Groszek, it is only natural. She is a child and she does not understand. She is blaming you for her discomfort, for making her go through all these months all blown up like that carrying a baby around in her belly in the heat of summer." He kept telling himself that right up until the day she gave birth, the day he found out that he had been wrong about all of it—even the three hundred dollars.

It happened in the fall.

They were sitting on the roof—Groszek smoking his cigar and Novak his long pipe—watching the park below turning green as the sky began to brighten over the factories in the east. Pani Nowicki the midwife had told them to go sit on the roof, that she would call when it was time, that it would be over even before Groszek finished his cigar and he should not worry because Eva was young and it would be an easy birth. He had seen Novak's wife Martha when Roman was born, clawing the pillows and biting her lips till they bled; and he had seen his Eva lying there in bed in her white cotton nightgown with the pink ribbon at the neck, saying, "No no. It does not hurt at all any more. Do as Pani says. Go smoke your cigar." So sitting there on the empty apple box—Eva's wash still on the clothesline, the sheets hanging straight down, the thin smoke from the factories rising straight up against the sky—watching the cigar drawing closer and closer to his fingers with every puff as though he were watching a clock; he told himself that he was not really worried. Nevertheless, he supposed he was glad to have somebody to talk to, to take his mind off things, even if it had to be Novak— Novak who thought it was something to "hit the numbers" on the very day before his wife was to give birth, saying, "It is *something*, my friend"; and he, "What is so unusual? It was the winning that brought it on. It was not supposed to happen for another week at least"; and Novak, "Well, it is *something*, nevertheless"; and he, "All right, so it is something," the cigar and pipe smoke glowing in the light over the open skylight, the voices of the women in the kitchen below, rattling against the glass, Novak's voice there again asking him whether he had perhaps dreamed the number; and he, puffing on his cigar, saying no, he had not dreamed it, "It was from a license plate."

"Well then, it is a shame you had to sell such a lucky car."

"Yes, it is a shame I did not marry a tenement and a candy

store so I could afford to keep it," looking away at the cigar smoke haloing out over the skylight, saying, "Besides, it was not the car. It was a junk wagon. But I do not see why it should interest you"; Novak smiling, saying he had only asked because he had thought perhaps an expectant father might like to talk a little to keep his mind off things, saying, "If you would like, however, I will be happy to go and smoke my pipe downstairs and leave you alone, my friend."

So he told him about it. He spat in the gravel and told Novak how he had been playing fifty cents a day on the same number for almost a year now, ever since the day he and Eva had married; telling how on that morning of the drive to Maryland, watching Eva in the rear-view mirror—the rain so heavy on the windshield that the wipers were practically useless—just as the car rose over the slope of the Market Street Bridge leading out of Prescott and he had let up on the gas pedal—the wiper jumping—there was this horse and wagon looming up in the wiper fan, the brakes screeching and the car swerving and climbing the gutter and coming to a halt less than a foot away from the railing and a ten-foot drop into twenty feet of river below; telling how when he opened the side window and yelled, the horse just plodded away, the old junk dealer all wrapped up in the canvas under the big umbrella not even hearing, the headlights glistening on the license plate nailed to the wagon tailboard and on the number 666.

He did not tell him any of the rest of it however—why he had made it a point to play exactly fifty cents a day with the pay-off at 600 to 1 and no commission subtracted since he played it on his own book, or why he was so sure it was a winning number, sure enough to play it for almost a year. Because in the glow of the skylight he thought he could read Novak's smile and he knew Novak was not the kind of man who would believe in signs, and to tell him about Eva's weeping and her crazy talk about wishing they had gone through the railing and how they had cheated the old man, had cheated Death, and now he would have to go back down to hell with an empty wagon, would only turn the smile into that superior educated grin Groszek had learned to regard as ridicule of everything he stood for and believed in, a grin that always made him think of the judge sitting in his court in Hackensack like God Almighty back when he had first come over from the old country, God Almighty grinning down at him, saying, "Don't you know, young man, that in this country we have laws. And two of them have to do specifically with bootlegging and booking numbers." Why, he would probably still be in jail today if it weren't for the lawyers from the syndicate he booked for, because it was useless to try to talk common sense to a judge, to try to tell him that he had always thought the police were the law and so how could it be against the law to book numbers when he booked more numbers in the Prescott Police Station than anywhere else. And as for bootlegging, what kind of law was it that said a man could not take a drink when he felt like it? What kind of law was it that said a poor factory worker could not risk a few pennies on the chance of winning himself a small fortune? Why, he would never forget the day old Nowicki the fiddler "hit" for a hundred and fifty dollars on a number from a fortune slip, he was like a new man. He bought presents for the whole family. His wife, whom Groszek could see down below in the kitchen and who had been calling her husband a drunkard for over twenty years, saying, "You are not a man, husband, you are a whiskey bottle, it would be better that you should die and leave us alone," completely forgot he was a drunkard and behaved like a bride again. His children treated him like a king. For a whole week his family worshipped him. Of course in the end he threw most of it away buying bootleg whiskey for his friends in the taverns. But who could blame him? It was not every day a weaver in a factory could throw money around like a king. Why, he could work the rest of his life and *never* again have so much money in his pocket at

one time. And all for a few pennies that he never missed anyway, all because some horses were running somewhere, horses
that he had never even seen, that did not even know how much
luck their running had brought him. "Why, you might as well
tell the *horses* it is wrong for them to run because Nowicki is going to play a number. It would make as much sense as trying to
tell Nowicki he is wrong to play it."

"Nowicki?"

"Never mind. I was just thinking out loud."

The cigar had already burned down to his fingers, and when
he looked down through the open skylight into the kitchen
there was no one there, neither Pani Nowicki, nor her daughter
Lottie, nor Novak's wife Martha nor any of the other women.
He started, saying, "They are all in the bedroom. Maybe I should
go down and . . ." and though Novak interrupted, saying,
"What for? They will only send you out again. There is nothing
a husband can do," he went down anyway, meeting Novak's
wife Martha on the stair, her voice all high and rattling in the
passageway, and her face wetting his shirt front. He held her,
steadying himself against the banister, saying, "What is it?
Pani? What?" thinking, "She does not need to tell me. I know
already. What a shame. And after all those months of carrying
it around like that," thinking, "Well, all right. So it is a pity.
Maybe it would have been different between us with a baby";
helping her back down the stairs, her face in her hands, Pani
Nowicki there at the door in her midwife's smock, crossing herself, whispering, "Hurry, hurry. I have already sent Lottie for the
priest"; Eva lying there like a child, the ribbon pink on the
nightgown beneath her chin, a string of rosary beads folded in
her hands across her breast, her eyes closed and her lips moving
silently in prayer, the glow from the kitchen light spreading
about the bed, and the first light of morning beginning to show
through the curtains. He thought for a second it was beginning
to rain, but it was only a sparrow fluttering against the screen;

standing there, laying his hand softly on hers, whispering, "Do not worry, Eva. It is all right. There will be others"; and she, not even opening her eyes, just lifting his hand to her mouth—the rosary beads rattling—and her lips kissing his palm, and her voice oh ever so faint amid the quarreling of the sparrows on the window sill, whispering what he thought surely (surely!) must be his name.

On the clothesline, Eva's sheets flapped in the morning breeze, and the smoke slanted out of the smokestacks in the east. Below, the park was green under the sun and the roofs of the neighborhood shone. He looked across them, leaning over the wall, and hooked on the bottle, thinking, "They do not even know she is gone. They will get up for work soon and nothing will even be different for them." He could see the sparrows picking around the garbage cans in the alley seven stories below. He smiled, thinking how they would scatter and fly up when his body flew down at them, how perhaps he might even catch some of them under him when he hit the pavement. It frightened him to think of it, so he went and sat down on the apple crate and watched the wash flapping on the clothesline, smoking, thinking, "There is still plenty to live for. There is the baby for one." But he knew he cared nothing for it—a red face bundled in a blanket—he had not even wanted to look at it when they showed it to him. He had been so sure it was the baby Martha had been weeping over, and it had not really come clear to him that Eva was gone until after the priest had already repeated the prayers and was daubing her forehead with the oil and cotton. It was all so mixed up that he did not even think it strange that right in the middle of the praying Martha should find it necessary to lean over to him and whisper, "It is to be the baby's name, Groszek. She told me he is to be named after her grandfather." He just stood there against the wall, his hands folded, his lips moving silently in prayer; thinking, "Well, it would have been nicer to name him after his

father than after *her* grandfather"; thinking about it so hard
that he had even forgotten to thank the priest; Martha taking
the bottle down from over the sink and handing it to him,
saying, "Go sit on the roof, Groszek. I will take care of the
priest and everything"—her eyes wet, her hands wringing her
handkerchief, the knuckles gone white—telling her husband to
go downstairs and see to Roman, to give him some sugar in a
handkerchief, that she would be down to feed him as soon as
she could.

And so sitting there on the roof, he told himself he would
have to find a better excuse than the baby; thinking, "Well,
she is probably on her way up there right now. So if you ever
hope to see her again, you would be a fool to jump. Because
just as sure as you are sitting here, you would not stop when
your body hit the pavement; you would continue straight on
down and only the birds would fly up." And he began thinking
of the past year; how she used to turn away from him; how
he had never really been himself since the day he had married
her; how he could never stand to be away from her even long
enough to book his numbers; how when he was with her, he
was almost content just to look at her, because she would never
allow him to touch her with the baby in her belly; and how she
hated to have him stare at her, saying, "Will you please go out
somewhere, Groszek. Go to the saloon. Go any place. Here, take
some money, and just go," digging into her money box in the
bottom bureau drawer (he gave her every penny he made except
for the fifty cents he played on the number every day and the few
nickels she allowed him for cigars), throwing the money on the
table, saying, "I am uncomfortable enough without you looking
at me all day. Go out and get drunk. Do anything. Just leave me
alone for a few hours at least," or going up to the roof, saying,
"I am going to get some air"; and he, "Well, maybe I will go
up too and smoke a cigar. I will help you up the stairs at least.
You must be careful, you know"; and she, "Oh please, for God's

sake, Groszek, just leave me alone. Leave me alone or I swear I will not be responsible"; and he, putting on his hat and going out, walking in the park looking up at the windows through the trees, or seeing her standing way up there big-bellied against the chimney—her hair blowing—thinking, "Well, she is only a child. You too would be crabby, Groszek, if you had to walk around all day in this heat with your belly blown up like that."

And on the last day, just last evening, coming home like that with the winnings and the bottle of wine to celebrate, emptying his pockets on the kitchen table beside the number books— exactly three hundred dollars when you subtracted the day's commissions, three hundred dollars in small bills and change, a 600-to-1 pay-off on a fifty-cent play—puffing on his cigar like a chimney, saying, "Well, here it is, Eva, here it is, my little Mamusha, three hundred to do with just as you wish, to pay back your aunt . . . anything"—Eva sitting there in the kitchen chair, the money piled up in front of her on the table, sitting there weeping into the hem of her apron; he opened the bottle of wine, thinking, "At last I have made her happy. From now on everything will be different." But when he tried to explain it to her, to explain why now it would surely be different, all he could do was tell her how he had been playing the number secretly for an entire year since the day they had almost crashed through the railing of the Market Street Bridge. When he tried to tell her *why* he had done it, *what* he had thought it would *mean* or *should* mean to *her*, to *both* of them, he found that he did not even know himself, except that he knew it was absolutely necessary to give her back in one lump sum the three hundred dollars she had paid him to marry her so that she could give it back to her aunt.

But why this was so absolutely necessary he was not sure or at least could not explain; and when he found out that her aunt had not really given her the money in the first place—standing there pouring the wine listening to her weeping into the apron, saying, "That day I came to you, she was not even out of bed yet when I left the house"—at first he was disappointed; it was as though the whole thing were a waste. But when she told him how she *had* come by the money, that it was passage money her aunt had sent to the family in Poland to bring them all over to America, passage money which she was supposed to have returned to her aunt, but which instead she had kept for herself telling her aunt that the money had been kept by the family back in Poland, kept it for herself so that she could be independent of her aunt in case she found she did not like her, and would be free to go back to Poland if she found she did not like the United States, when she told him all that, he decided that was just as good a reason for her to hate her aunt as the reason he had invented for her. And when she began talking faster and faster, saying, "I have been praying that you would not come home, that you would be run over by a car or something. Oh God, I wish we had gone off the bridge that first day," he kept trying to get her to drink, saying, "Do not think about it. Do not blame yourself. It is all over now. Done, finished." And when she threw out her arm and swept the table clean—the money, the number books, the glasses, the wine bottle, everything spilling all over the floor—crying, "Please, please, Groszek, leave me alone, just leave me alone," he got down on his knees on the floor and began scooping the bills into his pockets, reaching under the stove and the icebox and crawling under the sink after the rolling coins as though after an answer, saying, "Please, Eva. Please! You will make yourself sick again"; looking up at her standing there at the door holding it open with one hand, the other clutching her belly, saying, whispering, "Go, Groszek. Please go."

So he went; there was nothing else he could do. But he did not go far. He just sat down on the landing and tried to figure it out, counting the money as though somehow that was where the answer lay, surprised to find that he was only one penny short. It did not seem possible. With all the money scattered all over the floor like that, rolling under everything, it just did not seem possible. So he sat there and counted it again, pleading with her through the door to let him back in, thinking, "Well, this is not exactly the way other wives act when their husbands bring home their winnings. This is not the way I had planned it at all. But it is something anyway, at least maybe now I am beginning to understand her better"; realizing he must have made a mistake somewhere, because the second time through he found he was short almost fifteen dollars and change; starting in all over again, and this time the door opening right in the middle of the counting, and he turning to embrace the knees, thinking, "Ah, she is sorry. She has thought it over. Maybe it did not happen as I had planned it, but it has worked nevertheless because now that she has got it all out of her system . . ." But as he reached for her, she just moved back, standing there in the doorway holding her belly under the apron, her eyes rolling back in her head, whispering, "Go get her. Go get Pani Nowicki. Hurry, they are coming so fast now I cannot stand it."

And now it was all over. Sitting there alone on the roof—the morning breeze blowing in the sheets, the birds quarreling away down in the alley and the voices rattling in the kitchen below the open skylight—he thought of it all over again; thinking, "Well now, just what was it, Groszek? Try to remember one day that was not a fight, one minute of peace. What did she ever give you for the wonderful feeling you had for her? What kind of feeling was it to make you lose your dignity every time you went close to her? What was so wonderful about being chased out of the house every day?" He could not answer himself; thinking, "That is just it. It is just something, and if it could be explained it would not be the same thing any more." Still, he could not explain either the strange feeling of peace that had suddenly come over him. Perhaps it was simply the whiskey

beginning to do its work at last, because suddenly he felt no
remorse at her passing. He would miss her of course, and he
knew that despite everything he would not have traded the
past year for anything in the world, not even for a candy store
and a tenement. But somehow he was relieved that it was over.
He would never have wished it so, but now that it was . . . well
. . . He was just beginning to feel guilty about it when all of
a sudden he realized what they were saying, realized that they
were saying something he must have known all along; that all
the business of his making such a fuss over the three hundred
dollars was just an excuse to cover up what he must have known
was the real reason for their unhappiness all along but would
just not allow himself to admit it; their voices drifting up
through the open skylight, Pani Nowicki saying, "Calling for
him like that all through all of it, like she never had a husband.
Who does Martha think she is fooling with that talk of its being
a name for the baby. It is her husband's name, too. And never
mind, nobody has to tell *me* whose baby it is."

It was as though the sparrows had suddenly flown up out of
the alley and were rattling around his head, their dark wings
flapping in the sheets on the clothesline. He put the bottle to
his lips and when he brought it down again it was empty; feeling the lips against his palm again; knowing that he must have
known it all along, known not only that Martha had been lying
about the name, but that the reason her niece had hated her
so much had nothing to do with the three hundred dollars at
all, that she had hated her only because she was Pani Novak and
she (Eva) wasn't; knowing that he must have known it that
first night she had whispered Novak's name against his palm
and that he had spent the entire year trying to talk himself out
of believing it; the empty bottle shattering on the pavement
below, the sparrows scattering, flying up as he felt the arms
tighten around him and heard the voice, "No, Groszek. Do not
be a fool. Are you crazy?" And so he thought about it, amazed

to find how clear his head felt after nearly a full bottle of whiskey. The only thing was, that everything had slowed down a bit, everything seemed to be taking a very long time to happen; thinking, "Crazy? It is he who is crazy if he thinks I would ever jump. Even the thought of it almost makes me go in my pants"; not even struggling at first, allowing himself to be pulled away from the wall. And then all of a sudden, like a light going on somewhere, he thought of it; and he began to struggle, to struggle as though he really *were* trying to jump, shouting, "Let me go. I want to jump." And he watched his hands tightening on the throat, and the head and shoulders hanging over the wall, noticing that the sparrows were back again picking around the garbage cans amid the shattered fragments of whiskey bottle seven stories below; listening to his own voice as from a long way off, still shouting, "Let me jump. I cannot live without her"; smiling to himself, thinking, "What a joke—cannot live without her. Why, if she were alive now, I would kill her"; thinking also, "Well, good-bye, Novak. It is a shame a smart man like you has to go like this and leave a candy store and a tenement, not to mention two fine sons." Then it hit him—why not? At least it would give Novak something to think about on his way down to the pavement. And so though he did not really believe it himself, he said it anyway, saying it just as they went over the wall, smiling not two inches from Novak's face, saying, "But I have a son too, Novak. And his name is Roman." And with his hands clutched around his throat and their faces practically kissing, just before the fire escape began coming lazily up to meet them, he could feel the words starting in the throat beneath his palm, whispering, "You have *two* sons, Groszek. Two!"

Chapters III & XIII

NOON

Roman's mother believes he was conceived on the afternoon of her first husband's funeral. She believes it happened on the horsehair sofa amid the beaded lampshades and the palm-draped crucifix and the scent of Old Sadovi still lingering like candle smoke or the fallen petals of funeral bouquets left scattered on the rug. The coffin was gone and the funeral over, and of the six pallbearers she had invited back to her parlor for wine, only Groszek and Novak had remained; and as she had knelt beside Groszek's chair brushing the cigar ash off the rug into her palm—her widow's crepe whishing and the veil laid back on her new black hat—Groszek had joked her, saying, "The wine must be going to my head to make me so careless. Perhaps you should not allow me any more, Pani. Because once you get Groszek drunk, you know, you will no longer be safe in the same room with him, even on the afternoon of your husband's funeral."

She did not really mind his joking her; she had expected it. "I believe you, Pan Groszek," she said, smiling, sitting down on the sofa beside Novak. "You are not known in the neighborhood for your good manners. Besides, why should you think any differently from the rest?" her crepe tightening across her meager breasts as she removed the hatpin and lifted the hat off her head, her chestnut hair bunned severely in the tortoise-shell combs. "You see, I know what they are thinking," she said. "And you are no different, Pan. To be truthful, it is something to have you sitting here like this, to hear it right out to my face for a change, to have all they are thinking about me sitting right here in my own parlor—in my husband's chair even. However, I have a headache. So if you will excuse me, gentlemen, I will thank you again for everything and wish you good day."

But she did not rise, and neither did Groszek. And when Novak did, saying, "Yes, perhaps we should go. It has not been easy for you, Pani," she took his hand, saying, "Sit down. What does it matter? Yes, a woman should be tired and her eyes all red with watering her husband's grave. Only, I am not tired. I do not even have a headache really. And you saw I did not leave a single tear in the cemetery. My handkerchief is as dry as the day I ironed it"; removing the handkerchief from her sleeve, saying, "Besides, you have not even touched your wine. Do you want to disappoint them? Pani Nowicki and her daughter are lying with their ears to the linoleum upstairs, and they will be on the landing later to watch you leave, and if you do not at least stumble a little . . . And what about Pan Groszek here? We should give him something more to talk about in the taverns tonight than just joking the widow Sadovi on the afternoon of her husband's funeral"; Groszek, smiling at her speechmaking, leaning over and refilling her glass, saying, "You wrong me, Pani. There is not a man in the neighborhood who respects your feelings for your dead husband more than Groszek does."

She knew he did not mean what he said. She felt she could see through every word as through a window. And sitting there in her parlor with the cigar smoke hanging low under the ceiling, sitting as in a strange room, for her husband had never allowed anyone to smoke in his parlor—the flower petals still scattered on the rug—she felt, after the long and public funeral and the exhausting struggle with held-back tears, a kind of resignation and numbness in no way associated with relief at her husband's passing away (she knew that), but which nevertheless she could not help feeling guilty about; thinking, "Perhaps they are right after all. He is dead, and I feel nothing. I could not cry now even if I tried. Perhaps I really *have* been fooling myself all along"; accusing herself of something she knew she was not even guilty of, telling Groszek, a man she knew was scheming to compromise her out of everything her dead husband had left her (including her grief), telling him everything, deliberately accusing herself into his arms, saying, "Who knows? Perhaps you are right. How can I know? Perhaps I have been fooling myself all along. I was only a girl. I was not even sixteen years old when the letter came."

The letter. The cramped shaky minute miserly hand on the meager sheet of cheap paper, the page completely covered with writing—both sides—not an inch wasted and not a word wasted either. The letter from America, from Pan Isaac Abraham Sadovi, listing his assets: his prudence, his practicality, his sobriety; his candy store, his investments, his tenement. And, of course, his requirements: a clean, modest Polish girl (not a Jewess, because a Jewess always expects too much from a husband), a clean, modest Polish girl fresh from the old country—innocent, old-fashioned and unspoiled; a girl neither homely nor beautiful—simply plain; neither fat nor skinny—simply sound; a girl young and innocent, but clever with figures and capable of quickly learning the English language—yet not so clever as to hold too high an opinion of herself. In short, a girl modest and unspoiled and old-fashioned, who would respect the word of her husband and be grateful for his beneficence and support.

The letter was addressed to the Austrian Passage Director in Lublin, Poland, and forwarded by hand to Pan Ludz, tenant farmer on the Austrian's Polish estate, Pan Ludz, who just happened to have a pair of fifteen-year-old daughters—one a blond and rosy beauty, the queen of the countryside who even with a community baby in her belly could easily have married any of a dozen rural Romeos had her Tata the means to offer at least a cow or a horse for dowry; and the other a thin, pallid brunette who could certainly not be called homely but was not exactly pretty either (was in fact rather plain), but who was always very clever in her classes in the rural school and was very good at numbers and could speak the Austrian language almost as well as the schoolmaster and so should certainly be able to learn English quickly enough, and who as it happened did not have a single suitor though surely no one would ever think to call her homely, not even the Herr Passage Director in Lublin, who in determining the suitability of the bride-to-be looked down at the frightened Martusha and turned to her Mama, stroking his side whiskers, saying, "I do not know, Pani. She is rather skinny, you know, and pale, and . . . well, how shall I say it? Plain, eh?"

Yes, skinny and pale and plain, and oh so very thankful that this man with the side whiskers whom she did not even think of as simply the mediator, the go-between, seeing him as the actual ogre to whom she pictured herself betrothed; thankful that he had thought her plain, too plain—for the first time in her life happy to be just that, she who for as long as she could remember had always envied the plump and rosy beauty of her sister

Marya, dreamed of being pursued like her by all the overalled Romeos of the countryside, and now for the first time in her life actually thankful not only that she was plain, but *too* plain; crying, standing there with her hand hard in her Mama's, weeping into her shawl out of a joy and relief which unfortunately the Herr Passage Director must have interpreted as disappointment, relenting, saying, "But perhaps in a case like this . . . One cannot afford to be *too* particular in such matters. You say she is clever in the school, eh? Well then . . ." pinching her cheek, winking, saying, "Yes, my little goose, cheer up. In a few years you will be a rich widow. Sadovi cannot last forever. I shall make the arrangements. The amount agreed upon payable upon delivery of the article—subject to approval of course. Well, after all, Sadovi is a practical man. Yes, my little goose, you should be quite suitable; Sadovi is after all a practical man."

And there were many more tears after that. And not only Martusha's either—old Pan Ludz weeping into his bottle, crying the misfortune which had forced him to submit to his wife, to actually allow his daughter to be sold not only to a man even older than himself, a man old enough to be her grandfather, but to a Jew; weeping, cursing his wife's heartlessness and greed, cursing the day he had married her, this woman who had brought him so low as to allow his own flesh and blood to be no better than sold; for the first time since she had been born finding time out from his drinking friends and his bottle to kiss his "little Martusha," his "little angel" sold by his grasping wife "to the very devil." And his wife, crying too, insisting it was all for the best, that Martha would be a rich woman in a few years, that the old Jew could not last forever, that nothing could be as bad as living on a run-down worthless farm that was not even their own, with an equally worthless drunken pig of a Tata and a helpless disgusted Mama, doomed to be an old maid for the rest of her life because none of the stupid boys of the district had eyes for anything but the useless and temporary beauty of her sister, who cared nothing for soul or brain or goodness; and no matter how it was breaking her heart to have her little angel leave her, it was for the best. It had to be, if only because her husband was so violently opposed to it. For that reason alone, it could be nothing but for the best. "Yes, for the best."

She did not tell how much her husband had paid for her. She was ashamed to admit the mere three hundred dollars. But she told them all the rest of it—not really crying, just blowing her nose in her handkerchief from time to time. It was as though once she had begun talking, Groszek and Novak were not even there. It was almost as though she were talking to herself, watching Groszek lean forward filling her glass, but neither he nor Novak saying anything, almost as though she were dreaming and they did not wish to wake her—Groszek smoking his cigar and Novak sitting there with his forehead in his hand like a priest in a confessional. She told them how she carried on all the way over on the steamship. How she could think of nothing but her Tata crying into his bottle and calling her his little angel sold to the devil; and her Mama weeping too and telling her over and over again that it was "only for the best," and probably believing it too, but still unable to stop crying; and her beautiful blown-up sister Marya kissing her and whispering, "You do not fool me, sister. You are not doing me such a big favor going to America to become a rich woman. You know you are happy to go, and if I were not so fat it would have been me instead of you. But I will get there some day anyhow. Somehow. You just wait and see." And so who could blame her for thinking to throw herself over the rail on the boat? Only, somehow she could not, she said. Because somehow she felt that perhaps her Mama was right, that it would all turn out for the best. Yes, for the best, because though she had been married to a skeleton for over fifteen years, there she was only thirty years old and already a rich widow without even any children to hang on her skirts, and the choice of almost any bachelor in the neighborhood—two of whom were already sitting with her in her parlor almost before they had had time to take her husband's coffin out of it, and lay it decently in the ground.

Novak she had only known a little over two months. He had only been in the country that long. But in those two months, even though after fifteen years of marriage to a man old enough to be her grandfather she looked upon Novak as little more than a boy, the neighborhood came to look upon him as her lover whom she met nightly in his room behind the candy store across the hall from the room in which her husband lay dying. Groszek, on the other hand, she had known for years, ever since she had first come over from the old country. She knew him as a clown and a gambler, seeing him every day in the candy store when he would come around a few minutes after noon to collect the number slips and pick up his daily supply of cigars. She would make it a point never even to smile at him when sometimes he would touch her hand over the cigars and joke her about how lonely it must be at night married to a man as old as Sadovi. She would make it a point never to smile, but sometimes when the store was empty she would allow her hand to rest between his palms for a little (oh ever so little) longer than was necessary. So she was not surprised when as soon as the news got out that Sadovi had counted his last dollar, Groszek appeared at her door offering to help carry her husband to his grave. And in the cemetery that morning, all dressed up in her new black crepe and widow's hat and veil, feeling for the first time in her life like a *woman*, she thought she could almost feel her husband's eyes again (just as she had always felt them in the walls of the candy store whenever Groszek would stop by, as though he could watch her even from his bed), could feel them staring up through the lid of the coffin watching the ropes sliding out of the pallbearers' gloves, cursing not only Groszek for lowering him into his grave and planning to rob him of all he could not take with him, including his wife, but *her* too, for wanting it to happen.

She knew of course that Groszek would make the worst possible kind of husband. She knew he was as bad for her as the wine she was drinking, sitting there on the horsehair sofa feeling his eyes in her, knew that he was in a sense like wine himself, a wine distilled from the vine her Tata had planted in her garden that day fifteen years ago when he sat crying into his bottle over his little angel sold to the devil, her Tata, whom she had never really learned to love until that day she thought she despised him most, that moment when she taught herself to hate everything he stood for, to despise every Polish man she had ever known, looking upon them all as shiftless irresponsible drunkards who would never grow up, who dreamed impossible dreams and blamed everybody—their wives, their children, the very world—everybody but themselves when those dreams did not come true, drowning themselves in the bottom of a whiskey bottle instead of going out like her Sadovi and starting a business and making some money instead of sweating all their lives for pennies in a factory; admiring no man but Sadovi, loving him in a way, loving everything in him she could never touch, that could never touch her, loving the fifteen years of a next to nunlike existence, comparing every man she ever met to him, despising, perhaps even pitying, them in his shadow, everyone except Novak, that is; because Novak was somehow not like the rest; he was not Sadovi by any means, but he was Sadovi's one and only friend, and was more like *him* than he was like any of the rest, and was not at all like Groszek, who was everything she had taught herself to despise.

And so in the cemetery that morning amid the chanting of the priest and the singing and the tossing of the carnations and the handfuls of earth, she simply could not take her eyes off Groszek; watching him through her veil, his head bowed but his eyes following her, making her feel in the new hat and dress not at all like the faded shawl-wrapped Martha she had always thought herself, but somehow for the first time in her life like a woman, the very woman the neighborhood had painted in its rumors; knowing that at that very moment he was wondering whether the rumors were true, wondering just what the surest, smartest way into her pocketbook would be, and (assuming the rumors *were* true) figuring the surest, smartest way would be through her bed. And that was exactly how she wanted him to think; knowing that like the rest of the neighborhood he no doubt believed she was not at all grieved over her husband's death, believed she had been hoping and praying for his death for almost fifteen years, believed only a fool would ever consider remaining faithful to a bedridden and sour and complaining old skeleton who just out of spite persisted in living on from day to day and year after year as her youth flitted hopelessly away from her, believed she must surely feel she had been cheated out of fifteen of the best years of her life. She wanted him to believe that. She wanted him and everyone else to believe it, because none of it was true—none of it; wanted everyone to believe it because perhaps that way she might possibly even get herself to believe it, because that was the only way she could possibly justify what she knew she wanted to happen, what she knew she was going to make happen, whether she could ever get herself to believe she was justified or not.

She had made it a point not to allow herself to weep at the wake or in the cemetery. And the only time she could not control herself and the tears welled up in her eyes behind the veil, was when she thought how the only reason her husband, who had never had a friend in the neighborhood besides Novak, had so many people at his grave was because of the scandal; not only the scandal involving her and Novak, but the scandal of a Jew being buried in St. Michael's Cemetery. It made her weep to think how when the end had grown near he had finally agreed to turn to the Church, to even allow her to bring in a priest to marry them all over again in the eyes of God, even though when he had found out she had bought a plot for him and that turning to the Church meant he would have to be buried in St. Michael's alongside some of his very own tenants, he had absolutely refused to die, hanging on for days and days after that, cursing her and calling for the priest to come back and turn him back into a Jew again so he could be decently burned instead of rotting away under the same ground as his neighbors. But in the end his strength had failed and he had gone like all good Catholics with the balls of cotton and the oil and the priest singing him six feet under St. Michael's Cemetery. "What is a little self-respect in the face of eternity," he had said in the last hour. "Besides, a promise is a promise, my wife." And standing there beside his grave looking down at the cheap wooden casket under the meager flower blanket, she wished she had not agreed to spend as little as possible on the funeral, though she had no qualms whatsoever about the shameful reception she had planned, a reception for the pallbearers alone; for like her husband she had no use for any of her neighbors or her tenants, and she knew why they were there, just as she knew why it had been so easy to get six men to carry his coffin—it was no accident that they were all middle-aged bachelors like Groszek. For like her husband, she knew she did not have a friend in the neighborhood besides Novak, who in the last two months had become fast friends not only with her husband but with her too. And she knew that everyone said she was just like her husband, like a Jew herself—and she was proud of it—knew that the salesmen who had to deal with her in the store and her tenants and those in the neighborhood whose notes she held, swore that she was even *more* tight-fisted than her husband (even Groszek used to accuse her of masquerading as a Christian when she would not trust him even for a nickel cigar—"But I admire you for it," he said). For she had learned plenty from her husband, learned that one way to save money was not to make any friends you would have to spend it on. And as long as she had Sadovi, she did not need friends. And now that he was gone, she felt she still did not need friends. She was not even sure she needed a husband. She was not sure what she needed. However, she knew she needed something.

And now, almost nineteen years later, sitting here in her kitchen thinking about it, she believes she knows what it was she needed that day, knows at least that it was not just passion and abandonment and release and the headlong spiraling fall from grace as she had thought then; believes it was not only she and Groszek and Novak sitting there that afternoon, sitting there on the horsehair sofa in the tight airless parlor amid the cigar smoke and the forgotten flower petals scattered on the rug, she with her hands folded in her lap—her knuckles gone white with wringing the handkerchief as though trying to wring tears out of it, the two slim but not exactly pretty fingers (even at thirty already laundry- and dish-worn) slipping the tarnished wedding band up and back over her knuckle—thinking, "Do not be a fool, Martha. What will you trade it for, the paper band off his cigar?"—her hat in her lap, the long chestnut hair bunned high atop her head already beginning to fall in wisps over her forehead, the wine glass on the table staring up at her emptily, but only for a second as Groszek leaned long over the coffee table and drained the bottle into it. She knows it was not only three of them sitting there when she reached out her hand —ringless now, the ring round between the two slim fingers— reached to stop him, touching the back of his hand curved around the wine bottle, shaking her head but still talking as he placed his other hand over hers just as he had sometimes done in the candy store over the cigars, her hand caught between his, riding the bottle in its slant over the wine glass, the port bleeding out of the bottle warmed by that trinity of hands which was already Roman, Roman staring out of her eyes at the man who would become his father and out of his eyes at her, Roman standing there with her as she stood with her back to the door removing the combs from her hair listening to himself out in the hall—the wine glass winking in the dim afternoon light, the ring lying there beside it beside the ashtray, the cigar burning on the lip—listening to Groszek's voice out there saying, "Goodbye, young fellow. I will return the suit to the tuxedo store to-morrow," and Novak's door closing and finally the glass and iron front door slamming, echoing in the hall. And when she heard the parlor door open again as she knew it would, she did not even turn, standing there holding the wine glass, her eyes closed and her hair falling long to her waist; did not turn until she heard the voice whispering, "Excuse me, Pani, but I have left my cigar." And when she did turn, the glass tipped in her hand and the wine ran dark down the front of her funeral crepe. And it was Roman who had tilted the glass, Roman swimming on the wine whirling around so sweetly in her brain, hurling him-self around inside of her, inside of both of them as she watched his hands wiping the handkerchief across the lace jabot, Roman rushing down the passage and through the door and into her womb, rushing headlong to meet himself, to complete himself, absolutely dying to be born.

At least that is what she believes. She believes Roman was just as much to blame then as he is now—"if anybody is ever really to blame for anything," she thinks. Because, for a mo-ment she seems fully to see, sees Roman loving his rib not only on the horsehair sofa amid forgotten flower petals dying on the rug, but long before that amid remembered flowers and a gar-den lost; knowing without even needing to put it into words that Roman was more than just a judgment on them; he *was* them, was them long before he ever was, long before *they* were, long before he found himself with only eight more months to go to his birth day, staring out of her eyes at the cold cigar stub and the burn in the bedroom chair. And it seems to her now, some kind of purposeful miscarriage of divine justice which had allowed Roman to be born without a harelip he could point to and say, "See, Mama, here's that little worm of a cigar burn in that chair"; a harelip or a stunted leg or anything that might have kept him out of the Army and out of Europe and that woman. Because for Martha, Roman's sending Magda to them was just divine judgment delayed. For her, Magda was just Eva all over again.

Not that they looked alike, really. She could not really convince herself that they did, though that was actually the only way she could begin to explain to herself her husband's strange behavior during the past six months, explain his refusing to sponsor Magda even though he knew that was the only way they could possibly be sure of keeping her away from Roman, forcing her therefore to go secretly to Groszek and practically openly admit to him that Roman was his son (something she had vowed she would never do, even though she knew her husband had confessed it to him that morning of the fall from the roof), not actually admitting it, but not denying it either (at least not convincingly); Groszek assuring her that he had known it all along, saying, "Because why should I believe he was telling the truth about Johnny and lying about Roman, as you have always tried to make me believe, Pani? Either he was lying or telling the truth, not half and half as you say. How stupid do you think Groszek is? Either they are both mine or they are both his; make up your mind. Either he was lying or telling the truth—now which is it?" saying, "Pah, you do not have to say it. He has said it for you. Because why else would he refuse to sponsor her? Because what does he care what happens to Roman any more than he cares what happens to Johnny. They are nothing to him. There is probably nothing he would like better than to see my son get mixed up with a tramp. Of *course* I will sponsor her! You have done right to come to me, Martha." She herself, however, was not so sure. For she had felt just from the way her husband had crossed himself that morning the photograph arrived (something she had never seen him do before in the almost twenty years she had known him, for if her husband was anything he was surely not a religious man), felt that she was not the only one for whom the woman in the photograph was just Eva all over again even though the resemblance between the blurred brown image and her memory of Eva was even less than slight. They were both blond and beautiful, and to Martha, who had never been either and had always secretly yearned to be both, they were the kind of women created solely to make fools of men and to break the hearts of the plain good women like herself who were married to them.

For Martha this was an axiom, something she had learned way back even before she had learned to count on her fingers, an axiom her twin sister Marya had taught her long ago. And so she knew when she first laid eyes on the photograph, just as she thinks she must have known that day she first saw Eva, that there would surely be trouble. Because for Martha, Eva and the woman in the photograph were not only the same *kind* of woman, they were the *same* woman. They were Marya, her twin sister Marya, in whose belly Eva was still only a scandal that day Sadovi's letter arrived in the old country, Marya, the plump and rosy beauty who had half a dozen rural Romeos proposing to her the very next day after her Tata named the three-hundred-dollar dowry, but who never married any of them, who died instead in the summer after her sister Martha had left for America, died in the bloom of her plump and rosy and galloping-consumptive beauty, died with the still unhatched Eva in her belly, though for Martha, standing there along the pier fence with Groszek, calling, "Eva, Eva, over here!" it was only the name that had died. For Martha, the blond and rosy beauty in the

white full-skirted cotton, the girl running down the gangway of
the broken-down steamer with the cardboard suitcases in her
hands that morning back in July, 1927, her long hair blowing
blond beneath the flowered babushka, for her she was as much
Marya as though the boat had sailed not only across the ocean
but across the years too, returned from whatever distant shore
Marya had journeyed to fifteen years before. And when they embraced, she almost expected to hear her say, "See, Sister, I told
you I would get to America. I told you I would get to America
somehow."

And so she must have known right then and there on the pier
(just as she knew the minute she saw the photograph) that it
would not be long (not even two weeks) before she would find
herself sitting in her kitchen (just as she is sitting now—only
then, Roman had almost eight months to go to his birth day and
now has put eighteen birthdays behind him), sitting there
watching the rain weeping down the windows, wishing she
could just faint away again as she had done the morning she
found the burn in the bedroom chair, wishing she could have
just fainted away once and for all then, because it would have
been so much easier, so much more merciful if she could
have just turned away from all of it leaving her body lying there
empty on the bedroom floor like a pile of old clothes to be
gathered up and boxed and buried away in the cellar—or perhaps even better, burned. For then there would have been no
sitting there like that imitating the rain, thinking, "Martha, you
do not deserve this. What have you done to deserve this? After
all those years of being good. Just one little mistake, Martha?"
remembering all those nights of having a skeleton crawl into bed
with her and turn off the lights—the bed smelling of nothing so
much as the grave; and the other nights too, those last few years
in which her husband was confined to his bed, lying there alone
at night glad that he could no longer come to her, that at last

she could love him without having to submit to his making love to her, but hoping he would call, would need her, would allow her to make love to him the only way she knew how, the only way she felt she was made to make love—wiping the fever out of his eyes, and tending the bedpan, bathing the smelly bedsores on the shrunken withered back, the bones sticking up like wings. For that was the only way she could possibly ever have loved him; thinking, "Because maybe that is the only way you *can* love, Martha, the only way you were made to love, ought to love. Not like with Groszek; that is not for you. That is for the others, not for you—for Marya, for her daughter." For during those fifteen not unhappy, not even vaguely unhappy years of marriage, Old Sadovi had been much more father than husband to her, kind, generous (even with his reputation for greed, to her generous—and could well afford to be since she would no sooner spend money on herself than he would on anyone *but* her), tender, asking nothing of her but hard work, good sense and unquestioning respect for her husband, all of which she considered nothing less than his due, not even requiring fidelity (anyway not after he could no longer come to her at night), never even mentioning it to her, never needing to, since not requiring it was perhaps the very thing that guaranteed it.

Indeed, near the end he had even encouraged her to justify the rumors about Novak and herself, saying, "You will need a man when I am gone, and I have brought this fellow from the old country to take my place. I will make a bargain with you, my child. You have wished me to marry you over again in the Church. I will do it, if you promise . . . I have talked with him about it. He says he will never marry. He does not know that he needs you. But I know it. So you will have to begin immediately; it will not be easy to convince him, but a woman has ways. I will turn to the Church if you promise it, I will do anything you ask if only you will promise me you will marry Novak and not this good-for-nothing Groszek." She could not imagine how he had learned of her feeling for Groszek when even she was not sure just what it was she felt, unless he really *could* see through walls as she sometimes felt when she met Groszek in the store. Because of course she did not believe his jokes about how the movements of the rats in the walls during the long nights he lay awake unable to sleep told him of the most secret goings-on in the tenement, saying, "The rats are always in the walls listening, and they hear the most secret and sinful things, and when you lie in bed for five years like me and sleep all day and stare at the ceiling all night you begin to hear with them. Wherever there is filth there are rats." It was from her husband that she had first learned about the rumors going around the neighborhood about her and Novak. He had told her that he knew they were not true of course, that they were just talk, though he wished they weren't. And so she had promised to marry Novak if her husband would turn to the Church for her, and she had tried even before he had died, as he had insisted she should, only to find that Novak would never look at her as anything but a friend, and even now almost twenty years later she cannot bear to think of that night her husband had actually sent her to Novak's room to . . .

But as it turned out, she had been able to keep her promise after all, not only despite, but because of, that sweet and spiraling fall from grace—sweet for a time at least, a month of secret delirious and sinful nightly entanglements, of pleasure (unsuspected, never even dreamed of) found, and after Eva had arrived, lost, lost and missed, desperately missed, almost two long weeks of missing, of rising pale at night from remembered love, walking the floor, or sitting at the kitchen table watching dawn rose the window shades and blow damp in the starched white curtains, the sparrows already quarreling in the alley; thinking, "You do not deserve this, Martha. You have been good so long. You do not deserve to be torn like this, to desire like this. You have made a promise, Martha"; counting her rosary, trying to pray herself to sleep, trying to find the strength to break off with him; thinking, "How can you allow yourself to miss him so, when you know he is only interested in your money and property and not you? It was bad enough when you were dizzy with wine, but to allow him to come like this for almost a month. Oh God, you *know* why he is interested in you, Martha!" She knew, and she was grateful for it, thankful that though she had nothing else, none of the things her sister Marya had had, she *did* have the one thing she felt a man was always interested in— money and property; thinking, "Yes, you are lucky, Martha. Because how else could a man be interested in just plain you?" thinking also, "But he is no good for you, Martha, no good. And, Martha, you have made a promise."

And that was the way it went for those entire two weeks, praying she might break off with him, and at the same time wanting him; wishing she had never sent the letter to the old country, the letter telling of her husband's imminent death, the money order enclosed sufficient to buy steamship passage for five, but only Eva arriving, explaining that Pan Ludz would not leave his old drinking friends and Pani Ludz could not leave *him* no matter how much she would have liked to, and that her brothers were at the border with the cavalry and that Pani Ludz had decided to keep the unused passage money since Martha was now a rich widow and would surely not miss it; wishing this at night, and yet thankful every afternoon that Eva *had* come so that she had no other choice but to forbid him to visit her at night, hoping that in time she would be able to break off with him completely. For no matter how much she might need him at night, she knew she could never allow him to come to her with Eva sleeping right behind the wall in the next room; telling herself every night for two weeks that the next day in the store she would tell him to come despite everything, knowing all along that in the cold light of day, handing him his cigars and the number slips she would say as usual, "No, Groszek, not tonight. Yes, I know it cannot go on like this. But please, not tonight, not yet"; seeing him for only those few minutes each day, hoping she would be strong enough to hold out, wishing she had not been such a fool in those first weeks, during which she had abandoned herself so completely to her passion that she had even allowed him to talk her into buying him a car. Because, even if she *did* find herself strong enough to give him up completely, how would she ever be able to show her face again; for surely he would boast in the taverns not only how he had visited her bed all those weeks, but how she had even given him a car to try to bribe him into marrying her, and how he had thrown her over anyway? And she felt too, that even if he were gentleman enough not to boast in the taverns, surely someone must have seen him leaving or entering the tenement on at least one of those mornings, and everyone knew that Groszek did not have the kind of money required to buy a car even if it was only second-hand. It was no good trying to convince herself that any-one actually believed the story he had made up about hitting the numbers and putting a down payment on the car and looking for a job so he could pay it off.

Actually, it was the business of looking for a job that had convinced her she ought to buy him the car. He had told her that it would look better if he had some kind of steady job be-fore he married her, that then it would not look so much as though he were just marrying her for her money, as some in the neighborhood seemed to think. Of course, he would quit work just as soon as they married so he could devote full time to run-ning the store and the tenement, but nevertheless in the mean-time it would look better if he had a job; as a matter of fact it just so happened there was an advertisement in the news-paper for a vacuum-cleaner salesman, however it was for a man who owned his own car. She should have known that he only wanted the car for show, and so he wouldn't have to walk from butcher shop to candy store to saloon on his number route, especially since he had such terrible corns. Because as it turned out he never did find a job, coming in every day as usual to collect the number slips, saying, "There is a job in the paper in Newark, and one in Paterson, but it takes money to buy gas and oil to go riding all over the state following the advertisements"; handing her a dollar for ten nickel cigars for which she would give him back five dollars change. And the next day it would be the same story all over again because, as he would say, "Good jobs with a little dignity are hard to find—jobs with a little dignity to suit a man who owns his own car and all." She could just imagine him walking up to an employer and handing him a cigar and pointing to the big Packard outside in the parking lot, acting not only like a man who did not need a job but like one who should be employing the employer; wishing she had not been such a fool, that she would be able to give him up despite the scandal she was sure would follow, not knowing what to do, where to turn, and so, relieved in a way when she discovered that perhaps there was no need to question, that perhaps there was only one thing to do, that perhaps there was not even a question of waiting for the mourning period to decently pass.

It was on a Wednesday in the second week when she first thought of it. On Thursday she began to worry about it a little. On Friday she tried desperately to remember when she had last had it. And on Saturday, the night of the Democratic picnic in the park, she was convinced that she had certainly missed it, though of course it did not necessarily mean anything more than a bad case of nerves. It was about nine o'clock that evening that Eva came running into the kitchen weeping, locking herself in her room even before Martha could ask her what was wrong; Martha standing there talking through the door, asking, "What is it, Eva? Are you hurt? Is there something . . ." getting no answer but "Leave me alone. Go away. I have my head in the pillow so I cannot even hear you. Just leave me alone, please." And so she just smiled and sat down at the kitchen table, thinking, "She is just like her Mama. Every little thing that happens to her is such a big heartbreaking thing. It is probably nothing more than a broken fingernail and she acts as though it were the end of the world. She will be over it in five minutes." And it looked as though she was right because not more than five minutes later Eva walked out of the bedroom with her kerchief tied over her hair, and her eyes a little red but no longer crying, saying she was going to the picnic, Martha shouting after her to be back before eleven because they had to get up for Mass tomorrow; thinking, "She is Marya all over again," wishing she had the courage to go to the picnic herself, Groszek having asked her in the store that afternoon to meet him near the dance pavilion so they could talk things over. But she had never gone to any community functions when her husband was alive, and she did not intend to start now that she was in mourning, and anyway that kind of thing was not for her, after fifteen years she had probably forgotten how to dance anyway; thinking, "It would be something though just to go and watch them. If Eva is like her Mama it would be beautiful just to watch her"; thinking about it until it was almost midnight, and finally throwing on her shawl and climbing the seven flights to the roof to see whether the picnic was still in progress, Novak there leaning against the chimney, smoking and looking down over the wall, the colored lights glowing through the trees in the park below and the polka music drifting up on the damp air, the basket full of clean clothes she had sent Eva to gather off the lines earlier that evening still there beside the chimney and the rain on its way—standing there shaking her head under her shawl, saying, "She can never do anything right, nothing"; and he, "Oh, good evening, Pani"; and she, "Well, they are still dancing I see"; and he, "Yes, at least until the rain begins. Listen to the thunder"; and she, as out of a clear blue sky, because she just had to tell somebody, "Janush, I am going to have his child."

There was nothing for a while, just the music drifting up from the park below, blowing on the damp breeze. And she watched him leaning there silently against the chimney, puffing on the long pipe Sadovi had left him, the bowl glowing; and in the darkness she almost felt it was Sadovi again, smelling the familiar tobacco smoke, knowing Novak would understand just as she knew Sadovi would understand if he could have heard her—and perhaps he could; Novak not even bothering to ask, "Why tell *me*, Martha? What do I have to do with it?" saying simply, "Have you told him?" and she, "I am still not sure"; and he, "Tell him immediately. Take him to a priest, and tell him so you can be married as soon as possible"; she, surprised to hear Janush talk of priests, since everybody knew he was as much opposed to priests and Church as her dead husband had always been, even as a convert, saying, "I suppose there is no longer any choice. I know he is no good for me, that he is only after my money and property. And these last two weeks I have even thought to give him up. But now there is no more choice, and shameful as it may sound to you, Janush, I think maybe I am even glad of it," saying, "But it might just be nerves after all, and there is the mourning period. How would it look?" and he, "You care for him; marry him. The mourning period is nothing. Why must you think the only reason he wants you is for your money? Why do people always suspect the worst of a man? Perhaps Groszek is the man he is only because people have come to expect nothing better of him. Perhaps he has got so used to it that now he expects nothing better of himself. He knows you believe like all the rest that he is only interested in your money. He even believes it himself, perhaps. He is the kind who will have a good feeling like caring for you and will say to himself that he is not worthy of such a feeling, and so will find another reason for chasing after you, one more like what people have made him believe of himself, like wanting only your money. You know, Pani, people think that I am only a friend to you for your money, that I am waiting for the mourning period to end and then I will ask for your hand because I want your money. They cannot believe I can admire you and care for you like a friend just for yourself. Even your niece has accused me of it tonight."

Martha was grateful to him. She was grateful for the things he had said about Groszek. She did not believe that he actually meant all he said; she believed he had said it just to give her peace. But she was grateful nevertheless because his words *had* given her peace. It was almost as though the dark roof were some kind of huge confessional, and she would have liked to talk more, but the rain began and so they walked together down the seven flights to the bottom hall and at his door she stopped for a minute and looked up at him and said thank you and took his hand and just for a second even thought to kiss it, but of course she didn't. She had completely forgotten about Eva, and when she got to her own door—choosing the key from the ring on her belt—and found it partly open, she remembered Eva at the same moment she remembered the rain, running into the dark parlor and slamming the windows, thinking, "I want him so much, I even imagine I can smell his cigar smoke"; trying Eva's bedroom door, saying, "Are you asleep already, Eva? Why do you lock the door? Why are you so stubborn? Did you have a nice time at the picnic?" And when there was no answer, she listened with her ear to the door, hearing the sobbing, saying, "Do not cry, Eva. Tomorrow is another day. Is your window closed, Eva?" And when she heard the window slam behind the door she just smiled, saying, "All right, good night then. We will talk tomorrow. Do not cry, and get some sleep. We will go to a late Mass." And she took down her hair, and went to bed and knew she would sleep very well, what with the rain outside the window and feeling so unburdened after having talked to

Novak, glad that she had told him all, because it was almost as though she had told it to her husband in a way, almost as though it were Sadovi who had said, "Marry him, Martha. Marry him right away."

And just before sleep, she lay there thinking, "She is only a child, but she feels as much as you, Martha," remembering what Novak had said about Eva's accusing him of wanting to marry her for her money, thinking, "So that was why she was crying. She thinks he will not pay any attention to her because of me. She too has heard the rumors. But it will all turn out all right. Because I have not only noticed the way she looks at him, but the way he cannot take his eyes off her either ever since she arrived. He is just shy, and no young man likes to think of marriage, but she is so beautiful, and in time, who knows?" So she told herself everything would be fine. She liked the idea of Novak and Eva, of herself and Groszek, wishing he were there with her so she could tell him how she felt, what she felt must be going on in her belly and how happy she was about all of it, how really there was nothing like what a man and woman could feel for each other, could make out of each other—like the baby in her belly—looking over at the chair beside her bed almost expecting to see his cigar there on the edge of it where he would always place it just before crawling into bed with her—almost smelling the smoke. She did not care any longer what the neighbors would think about her marrying so soon after her husband's death, or what they would think if she had a baby in only eight months. She would have a husband she cared for as she never knew she could care before, and not only that but his child. And so what did she care about talk? it would pass in time. Because in time everything always turns out all right if you just look at things calmly. She was a practical woman. She was not a schoolgirl like her niece, who made such a big thing out of every little thing, like everything was the end of the world. She was a practical woman who could make the best of anything if she just used her head, she told herself—and her heart too of course, as Janush had said, but not just her heart, not like a schoolgirl. They could be married in a week. All they would have to do is go to the priest and tell him about the baby and he would put aside the three weeks for announcing the banns. She felt she had never been so happy before, praying, "Oh please, God. Please make it a baby," feeling that if her prayer was answered, she would at last be getting everything she had ever really hoped for out of life.

Perhaps Groszek was not exactly the kind of man who would make the best husband, she was not fooling herself about that. But she did not care any more. She would have his baby, and when he saw how much she cared for him and how she had given him a son (it *had* to be a son), he would do anything she wished. And even if he beat her every night and drank like a pig and made her do all the work in the store and the tenement, it would be no different from the way all the rest in the tenement treated their wives and what mattered was that he would be hers. And he was such a fine-looking man, with his cigars and all, like a politician or something; and it would be so nice to be able to smell the cigar smoke in her rooms in the curtains and on the sofa, everywhere; she would not be like the rest of the women who made their husbands go up on the roof to smoke. With his cigars and all, and the way he dressed, people who did not know him never even suspected that he did not even have a steady job. And when they were married and he owned a tenement and a candy store he would not only *look* like an important man, he would *be* one. She only hoped people would eventually come to understand him, the way she did—the way Janush had said. But people always looked at the wrong side of things, always expecting the worst as though the worst had to be the truth and the best always a lie, like suspecting Groszek of only wanting her for her money, always looking for something bad to happen, like the fortune teller who came around with the parrot

—good fortunes a nickel, but bad fortunes a dime, because people would always rather know the bad side of life. "Like even if there is no baby in there now, and after you are married it really *is* just a case of early birth, they will begin to count on their fingers anyway. Because even if a thing is right, people will make it wrong if they can. So what is the use, Martha? What is the use?"

The next morning, when she awoke, it was still raining, and for the first time in over fifteen years she felt she could sleep until noon. But there was Mass to go to, and so she got up, put up her hair, made the wood fire in the stove against the damp, cooked breakfast and then called to Eva. When Eva did not answer, she went to the door and knocked, and when there was still no answer she turned the knob and, finding the door open, looked in on the empty unmade bed. She had not seen Eva in the hall or the toilet when she had gone to put up her hair, and since it was raining she knew she could not have gone to the roof, so she assumed Eva had gone to an early Mass without her. But stooping to make the bed she saw it on the floor beside the chair. She could not believe it. "It is only a dream," she thought. "I will wake up soon and find myself back in bed because it is getting so frightening now that I will not be able to stand it much longer and wake myself up. And it will be morning, but with no rain behind the shades, only the sun, and I will get up and come in here and wake her for church and we will meet him on the steps and I will tell him about this crazy dream I am having and he will laugh like he does. And when I tell him, whispering, that we may have to get married sooner than we had planned, he will puff on his cigar and stare shamelessly at my belly right in front of all the ladies. Because it is only a bad dream, and so wake up, Martha, and tomorrow will be real. Because it just has to be, Martha, it just has to be!" Kneeling there hearing the milk wagon out in the street, the damp hoofs ticking away in the kitchen clock like the incubus, the blind nocturnal mare; kneeling there beside the bed, her finger going up and back in the wormlike burn in the edge of the chair, saying to herself, "No, Martha, it is no dream. Why should it be? Because what else can a woman like you expect out of life," seeing it as from a long way off, seeing it lying there on the floor swimming in her eyes—the chewed slimy stump of cold cigar.

Chapters IV & XIII

AFTERNOON

Magda had awakened at noon to the smell of her husband's cigar. Even before she had time to rub the dream out of her eyes, to find that she was not really a fifteen-year-old back in her old-country bed in Porgorze, that it was not Max standing over her and what she smelled was not the stench of burning flesh after all, Groszek's voice was there rattling over her in the electric fan, saying, "So you cannot be without him for even one night, eh? You have to dream of him even on your honeymoon."

She had thought at first he meant Max. But after a while, sitting there in bed with the sheet hugged tight to her chin as if to proclaim not only her innocence but her modesty too, she suddenly realized he was talking not about Max but about (as far as she knew then) a man she had never even met until just last night, and even then had not been properly introduced to, so that not until the early hours of this morning, just before falling off to sleep in the hotel bed while Groszek sat smoking fully clothed in the armchair beside the window, had she even begun to guess who the stranger might be. And so when her husband woke her like that, standing there over her bed with his suitcase in his hand and his cigar smoking like an incinerator under his Panama, his voice rattling, saying, "Groszek is not so much the fool the two of you think he is. How long did you think it would take me anyway? How long did you think I could go on telling myself he was not really there at all, that it was all just that crazy dream of the hole under the sink, the need for sleep driving me out of my head. That I just imagined him standing there in the Erie station all those nights, that the business with the flowers, the thing in the park last night . . . Good God, woman! How long did you think it would take Groszek?" she could not believe it.

She hardly even had time to protest, much less to question, getting a chance to say little more than, "Are you crazy, Groszek?" before the door slammed and he was gone, leaving her there to finish rubbing the sleep out of her eyes and to roll lazily out of bed and holding her aching head cross over to the window in her bare feet and look down the seven stories to the boardwalk below just as he stepped out from under the canopy —his suitcase bouncing against his leg and his glasses glinting under the sun—looking back and up over his shoulder, just as she knew he would, to make sure she'd see which one of the boardwalk bars he disappeared into so that later (after she had finished bathing and breakfasting and washing and setting her hair and had given him plenty of time to drown in the bottom of a whiskey bottle the schoolboy suspicion she was sure he had probably already recognized as foolishness even before the elevator had reached the lobby) she could go down and meet him there before dinner and tell him that she did not blame him at all for acting the way he did because after all what could a man expect from a woman who would give herself to an eighteen-year-old boy; and he would grumble for a while and shake his head and finally apologize, saying, "Sometimes I just do not understand myself. Because, surely, if Groszek is anything, he is not a jealous man."

For that was not the first time she had seen Groszek behave like a schoolboy. Just three weeks ago, on the evening of the very afternoon he had proposed to her—driving her home from her job at the City Hall, saying, "There is no hurry. Take your time. Think it over"—on that very same evening he had pressed her for an answer. He would not even allow her to explain—the two of them sitting there in the tight cheerless hotel room, he in the soft chair by the window, his shoes off, his cigar smoking, and she on the edge of the bed with her hat in her lap, saying, "I can never tell you how grateful I am to have you ask me, Groszek. But truly, I cannot allow you . . ." He just stood up out of his chair like that before the window, and fingering the draperies, said in that winking, grinning way of his, "It could not be that there is someone else, eh, Pani? It could not be that, could it?" She just smiled at first, thinking he was joking, saying simply, "Groszek, you know better than that"; but when he turned from the window, flicking his cigar ashes into his palm, saying, "I know better? What do I know, Pani? I know you are not chained to the bed here all day, *that* I know. I know as a welfare worker you are supposed to go all over the Ward helping people. But how do I know *where* you go, *who* you see? How do I know who waits outside every night to come up here when I am gone? How do I know who else sits in this chair and takes off his shoes, who is maybe already lying here in that bed every night laughing into the pillow slips listening to me asking you for a good-night kiss at the door like a bashful schoolboy. How do I know, eh? Tell me that, Pani. How do I know?" she did not know what to think.

At first she even smiled a little to think he could be so jealous. She had not thought he could care for her so much. Until then, she had not even really taken the marriage proposal very seriously. Because though he had made it a point to see her every single evening ever since she had arrived in Prescott, he had never once talked to her in any kind of serious way. It had been she who had *offered* the good-night kisses; he had never needed to ask. And so she smiled now to see him so jealous, saying, "Why, Groszek, you are jealous. How nice that you should be so jealous." But he did not smile back, he just glared at her, saying, "What is so funny? Is it so funny for Groszek to ask a woman to marry him? Maybe if *he* asked you, eh?" and she, "Who, Groszek? I do not understand you"; and he, pulling the draperies aside, "*Him.* Down there! Down there in the station! There with the pipe in his mouth. You do not see him, eh?" she looking down, but seeing only a crowd of shoppers and movie-goers waiting in the station bus stop out of the rain. There was no one there she recognized. She could not even see their faces, just the tops of their hats in the neon glare. And there were *several* men smoking pipes. And then the bus was there splashing in the gutter puddles and then it was gone and there was only the station empty behind the rain.

It did not matter, however. Because it was all just foolishness anyway. She told him so, told him that nobody had ever been to visit her at night, and if he did not believe her why didn't he ask the people at the desk downstairs. And when he asked her what for, saying, "They are no better than you. For a penny they would lie to the Pope. So why should I believe them? Why should I believe anybody?" she told him, saying, "You have asked me to marry you, Groszek. Why would you ask to marry a woman you are sure has been running around behind your back? Running around even after all you have done for her these three months, and without asking anything in return, a woman who would let you spend your money on her and buy her dinner every evening and get her such a nice job and drive her up and back to work every day and take her to meet all your political friends in the taverns and introduce her like she was really worth something after all even when you know she is the kind of woman who would give herself to an eighteen-year-old boy, a woman who would let you do all this for her and then run after another man when you turn your back. Why would you want to marry a woman you think this of, Groszek? Tell me that, Groszek. Tell me that and you will not need to ask me. Because, Groszek, I do not ask you to believe *anybody*, only yourself."

He simply shook his head after that, shook his head and sat down in the chair, blowing into his palm, saying, "You will forgive me, Pani, I am afraid I have dirtied your rug," having flicked not only the *ash* of his cigar into the cup of his palm but the coal too—the chewed cigar lying dead on the floor beside the drape. And when she asked to look at it and thought to call down to the drugstore for some ointment, he just put his hand on hers over the receiver, saying, "It is nothing, just clumsiness. Already it is better just from touching you." And when she kissed it, kneeling there at his knees, and when she began to remove his shoes, and he just sat there shaking his head, saying, "I do not know. Sometimes I think I do not understand myself at all," she tried to tell him. Sitting there like that at his feet, her head on his knee, she tried to tell him all of it, everything, but he would not listen. He would not even allow her to tell him about Roman, much less about the Captain and Max and all the rest of it. Because as he had said before, if he was *anything*, surely he was not a *jealous* man, and he just sat there and removed the cellophane from a fresh cigar, saying, "If I wanted a saint to marry, Pani, I would not have asked you. Save your

confession for the priests. Groszek likes you the way you are.
What you had to do to become what you are does not matter. I
am glad for all of it, because how could any of it be bad if you
have come from it. I am *happy* you took up with Roman. Yes,
happy. Because how else would I have ever found you?" taking
the paper band off the new cigar and slipping it over the little
finger of her left hand, saying, "You see, you will not be getting
any prize if you say yes. I have not even thought to buy you a
ring," saying, "So now make up your mind, goddamn. Are you
going to marry Groszck or no? Make up your mind because in
five minutes Groszek has a Council meeting to go to."

And so nothing is ever *all* bad, she thinks, never, not even a
thirty-five-year-old woman taking up with a boy young enough
to be her own, not even all that had had to happen in the past
twenty years (had begun happening even before that boy was
born) just so that she might be there in Augsburg in the winter
of 1945, so that she might sit there in the bed he had bought for
her or at the window in the tight cheerless room he had rented
for her, to sit there (just as she is sitting now drying her hair at
a hotel window in Atlantic City looking down not at ruined
walls and burning rubble heaps in an alleyway, but across the
boardwalk and the beach to the ocean where the children roll
in the surf like fishes) to sit there in Augsburg thinking about
what else she might tell him when he returned after duty hours
with the bag of groceries and the cigarettes and would make dinner and sit across the table from her listening to her telling it
over and over again, saying, "You know what you're doing, Mag?
You're trying to blame yourself for everything gone wrong in the
whole goddamn world. It just can't be done," the clothes he had
washed the night before still hanging on the line strung across
the room, the flatiron heating on the gas range, the moon
through the skylight bright on the table during the meal before
the lamp was lit to iron by. And after he had finished the iron-

ing and the lamp was snuffed out again, lying there in the bed
beside him she would continue telling it, all of it, over twenty
years of it, going way back before he was even born, telling it
even after she knew he had already fallen asleep—his breathing
regular beside her, his boyish shoulders bony above the blanket
—lying there beside him whispering herself to sleep, and snapping suddenly awake and shaking him gently, saying, "I have
just remembered something"; and he, not even opening his eyes
for more than a look up at the skylight to see that it was still
the moon up there and not the cold winter dawn, mumbling,
"Now what?" and she, telling it to him and knowing even before
she would finish the sentence that it was not anything she had
not already told him, that it was not the answer after all, that
it was only the answer in the dream, for only in the dream did it
remain the one thing she had not told him, the one hole in the
story which once closed would scab over and heal like a wound,
telling it to him; and he, "You didn't wake me up just to tell me
that, did you?" and then, "Okay, I'm sorry. I don't mind. Now
try to get back to sleep, will you"; lying there beside him—his
breathing gone shallow again—and looking up at the stars above
the skylight, thinking, "You have to turn all the lights out down
here before you can see them. But they are always there just the
same," just as it seems to her now that the pounding on the
door that night in late February, just a few days after she and
Roman had celebrated his eighteenth birthday over a bottle of
real French wine, had been there all the time, all during those
two months she had lived with Roman, and that she had just
never stopped confessing long enough to hear it.

Because the moment after she opened the door, the moment
the words "Roman" and "jeep accident" and "hospital" came
clear to her amid the stream of English words the Captain
poured over her like water from some profane baptismal font,
it seemed to her that her eyes were opened for the first time
since Christmas. And sitting there across the table from him in

the cold, not even remembering to throw her coat on over her nightgown, not even thinking to light the lamp, the moon through the skylight curling in the cigar smoke rising between his fingers, she did not even have to be told that it was all her fault, that Roman had been (as the Captain put it) "walking around like a sleepwalker since Christmas," that instead of his mind being on the road, it was "somewhere in the gutter" with *her*. She did not need to be told because she knew all that herself, wondering how she could possibly have been such a fool the past two months; the Captain saying, "I knew there'd be trouble. I could see it coming that first morning he walked into my office talking marriage"; saying it, and she not understanding at first, thinking perhaps it was simply a matter of her not understanding English very well, especially when it was spoken as fast as the Captain spoke it. Because that was the first time she had ever heard anything about Roman's wanting to marry her. Roman had never even mentioned it to her, much less his having gone in to see his commanding officer about processing the necessary papers. And when she asked the Captain to repeat it for her slowly, and he did, she just closed her eyes and sat there unspeaking, her hands folded quietly in her lap, letting him go on and on about how he was there to see to it that she got out of town before Roman was released from the hospital, that it would do her no good to "blubber and bawl" because he "damn well knew her kind"; she knowing that it would do her no good to tell him that she had had no idea it had come to that, that she had never dreamed Roman had ever thought of her as anything more than what the Captain had just finished saying she was, knowing that he would not believe her anyway. And besides, perhaps it would not be the complete and absolute truth, after all. Because even in her most profound retreat from the world she must have known that at least part of her reason for telling Roman her story, telling him all of it the way she had, was simply to help him think of her as the Captain thought of her; the Captain sitting there under the skylight amid the cigar smoke, saying, "What the hell kind of a tramp are you anyway, taking up with a kid like that? You're old enough to be his old lady, goddamnit. What the hell kind of a tramp are you anyway?" and she, nodding her head finally, her eyes still closed, saying, "Yes, I will go away. I will go somewhere. If only you would allow me to see him, to see that he is all right. Yes, I will go away, somewhere."

And so for the first time in almost two months, she left the room; sitting there beside the hospital cot trying to smile back at him, his legs hoisted up in the casts, his voice high, breathless almost, saying, "I got good news for us, Mag. The letter came in the morning mail before we left for München. I guess I just couldn't wait to get back and tell you"; telling her how it had happened, how with the Captain asleep beside him and with nobody to remind him about speeding . . . "The Ol' Man was thrown free when we went through the railing and if it wasn't for him diving after me and pulling me out they'd be dragging the bottom for me now, because there wasn't much chance of my swimming very far with both of them broken like this"; lying there and trying to tell everything at once and translate the letter from America at the same time, the letter she did not even understand at first because he had never mentioned that he had even written home about her, much less that he had asked his family to sponsor her immigration; explaining it to her, saying, "My uncle'll be sponsoring you instead of my folks because he's got connections in the courthouse. He'll see to it things really move on his end. So now all *we* got to do is get you a visa, which may not be so easy considering the kind of company you kept during the war"; and she, "I am leaving Augsburg tomorrow"; and he, "Don't *be* like that, Mag. You don't have to worry. Maybe I can't keep you any more the way I have been. Maybe you'll have to go back to the DP Center for a while. Because somebody's got to sign a statement of charges for that drowned jeep and I know damn well you wouldn't have any use for me if I let the Captain do it like he wants to. Especially after he pulled me out like that and all. So it's going to have to come out of my salary, and I don't know how we're going to manage, but we will somehow. You got to trust me, Mag. Because if you think I'm going to let you go back home to Poland with the Russians there. If you think I'm going to let you . . ."

That night as she packed the single cardboard suitcase, she wept; not only because she had to leave, but because of the reasons Roman had invented for her leaving, the reasons which she had to allow him to go on believing, since she had promised Captain Johnson she would not tell Roman that it was he who was responsible—that being the condition on which he had allowed her to visit Roman in the first place. And she would have left the following morning if the Captain had not appeared at her door, his arms loaded with groceries and his breath reeking of whiskey, saying, "There's no hurry, there's plenty of time," dumping the clothes back out of her suitcase onto the bed, saying, "He won't be out for weeks, months maybe. So what's the hurry. Don't think I'm getting soft either, because you're still going to scram long before he's up and humpin', but there's no hurry"; the two of them sitting there across the table from each other, she with her coat wrapped tight over her night-gown this time, watching the smoke from his cigar curling up under the skylight, the lamp unlit and the space heater gone cold because the daily quart of Diesel Roman brought in the jeep's spare gas can had run out, the moonlight bright on the white helmet liner lying in the middle of the table and glinting in the freshly opened whiskey bottle. She talked about Roman, as though she knew if she could just keep Roman between them, what she knew even then was going to happen, would not happen, as though as long as she talked about Roman the Captain would stay there on his side of the table like drawing a ring around herself as a little girl through which the devil could not pass; thanking him for risking his own life to save Roman's, and telling him that she understood perhaps how *he* felt about Roman and that he should try to understand how *she* felt, saying, "I do not expect you to believe me, Captain. I know what you think of me, and of course you are right in a way." And she tried to tell him how it had been between her and Roman, not because she expected him to believe her and certainly not because she had any hopes of his allowing her to stay on in Augsburg (she was more anxious to leave before she did any more harm, than even the Captain was to have her leave), but simply because she knew that once she stopped talking it would begin happening. And she was right, because she was not a child any more and the circle went up in a puff of smoke and when she heard the door go and opened her eyes again, looking across the barren waste of her unclothed body and between the bed posts to the empty table and the moonlit smoke hanging low above it under the skylight, she had actually had to *tell* herself that of course he had used the door, and that the smoke hanging low under the skylight was only the ghost of his last cigar.

And though the very next morning she left the room with her suitcase to take a cot back at the DP Center again until such time as she could get permission to leave the city, that was not the last she saw of the Captain. At the DP Center they told her that her request for transfer to Frankfurt could not be processed until her papers were returned from the Military Police Detachment and that in the meantime she might work as a waitress at the Compound Civilian and Officer Mess in the Farben Building, a job which at first she could not understand how she had come by, since there were many in the Center who had priority over her and were working at much less desirable jobs. It was not until her third day on the job that she first noticed him at one of the tables opposite the ones she served. He pretended not to see her, just as she pretended not to see him, but she could feel his eyes on her all the time, knowing that she had been feeling them since the very first meal she had served. She did not understand. It did not make sense. Almost four weeks passed, four weeks in which she never left the DP Center except to travel to and from her work at the Farben Building (she did not even visit Roman at the hospital, feeling it would be better for him to think she had already left the city), four weeks during which all they could tell her at the DP Center was that they could not process her request for transfer until her papers were returned from the Military Police Detachment and that no other information concerning her case was available to them at that time, four weeks during which she felt his eyes in her every breakfast, lunch and dinner.

Then on the very evening she had vowed she would approach him and ask him straight out what it all meant, she could not find him anywhere in the dining room. She had not imagined it would be like that, thinking all during those four weeks during every breakfast, lunch and dinner that she would give anything to be able to walk out of the kitchen to take her first order and not find him there. She had not imagined that the very first time he failed to appear she would actually resort to giving herself excuses as to why he would be late, looking over the heads as she served, staring into the far corners of the great room, so that she was admonished twice by the supervisor and ended up almost spilling a tray over a group of colonels; and later walking back to the Center that night in the rain, thinking, "How did he know? How did he know I would ask him tonight?" remembering the puff of cigar smoke hanging low under the skylight and how for a minute she had allowed her imagination to run away with her just like a child, but only for a minute; wondering, "Could it be? Could it be that he cares for me?" She did not even turn when she heard the jeep following in the gutter behind her, heard it over the click of her heels on the pavement and the rain booming on her umbrella; she did not even have to look back to know that it was an MP jeep, the very one in fact that she had so often seen from her window during those two months after Christmas parked empty in the alley below as Roman worked over the range making her lunch. And when she got to the square, and she heard the motor die behind her, and he was there under the umbrella with her, saying, "Where you going anyway? The DP Center's back that way," all she said was, "Back to the room," not even nodding, not even needing to, when he asked, "What room? You mean the kid's shack?" And when he told her there was somebody else living there now and what the hell did she have in mind anyway, and she simply said, "Of course. I was not thinking. Where then?" he just grabbed the umbrella and took her by the arm and hustled her up the cathedral steps out of the rain, saying, "I don't know what you got in mind. I'm not even going to ask. I don't know what you're thinking and I don't want to know. All I come to do is say good-bye and to tell you not to go round thinking I did it for *you*." And before she was even completely aware of what he was talking about, he had kissed her and was gone, leaving her kneeling there before the votive candles racked like a heart beneath the paint-and-plaster statue of the Mater Dolorosa, wondering about the ocean, and the waves and the words, "You leave on the *Bismarck* Sunday morning. I'm nuts I know. I could be booted out of the service for messing with those papers. But I didn't do it for you. I want you to know that. Or for Roman either. It's just that I got a wife and kids back home, and I know damn well if there isn't an ocean between us, inside of a week, Roman wouldn't be the only damn fool chasing all over half of Europe looking for you."

From the hotel window she can see the ocean between them —the children rolling in the surf like fishes, crawling up on the beach as though washed up from somewhere long past the horizon, as though that really were the end of the world out there after all and you could just swim right back the way you came, right out into the sky like birds swim in air. Groszek had been there to meet her at the Hoboken pier. She recognized him immediately as she came through the immigration line; Groszek standing there in his homburg hat and black velvet-collared coat and white scarf and gray gloves, puffing on a cigar and looking as though he had just stepped out of the Easter Parade, which she found out during the drive to Prescott had actually been the case, for just before driving to Hoboken to meet her he had had his picture taken on the steps of the Holy Rosary Church presenting a basket of Easter eggs to a seven-year-old to signal the start of the annual First Ward Easter Egg Rolling Contest in the park; Groszek standing there before the shiny black limousine big as a hearse holding the back door open for her, his big face grinning down at her from the rear-view mirror as he drove, the limousine hurtling crazily down the highway, so that she was certain he would run into something, the cigar going in his mouth as he talked, and after they had finally careened over the bridge into Prescott, waving to the traffic policemen in the corner huts, even pointing out the window, his voice rattling, saying, "And that is the YMCA and that is the courthouse, and that is the Holy Rosary Church and there is the park," driving her all over town, through all four wards, talking so much and so fast that she did not even dare to interrupt to tell him that his driving was frightening her, though he must have noticed how pale she was (she could see her face in the rear-view mirror as she was getting out of the car) when they pulled up in front of the hotel, saying, "So, I frightened you, eh? You would never think I have been driving over twenty years and have only had one accident in my whole life, eh?"

But it was not really the driving that had frightened her so much as the prospect of having to meet Roman's people. She had gladly sat through the tour of Prescott, since it had meant at least an hour's delay, not knowing then that Groszek had had no intention of taking her anywhere near the Novak tenement; helping her out of the limousine, saying, "You will stay here in the hotel. It will be better. After all, Roman is her son . . . You understand." Of course she understood. She was completely aware that the only reason they had consented to sponsor her in the first place was simply to get her away from Roman, and she had never for a minute expected them to greet her with open arms, as Roman had been innocent enough to think they would; Roman saying, that evening she had gone to him and told him that she was leaving for America in the morning and that it was the Captain who was responsible for getting her the papers even though she had promised the Captain she would not even mention his name (to her woman's way of thinking it was not even really a promise broken, just so long as Roman kept his promise not ever to let on to the Captain that he knew), Roman saying, "Okay, I promise. I know how you feel. And I know why you're willing to go too. Even aside from the fact that he'd be in a hell of a lot of trouble if you didn't. That's why I never mentioned I tried to process those marriage forms; I knew you'd take off if I did. But you don't have to worry, Mag. Not about me anyway. Because I know it can't ever be between us. Not that I wouldn't marry you tomorrow if you'd have me, because I don't have any wife and kids to worry about. But I know it can't be, and still . . ." saying finally, lying there practically helpless with his legs still up in traction, saying, "I just want to be able to do *something*, Mag. Because that's the way it's going to be from here on in for you, you wait and see. Because there just isn't going to be anybody gets to know you isn't going to want to do *something* for you, and no strings attached either. Just like with me there are no strings. That's the way it's going to be in the States too, with my people too, you'll see. Once they get to know you, Mag. Once they really get to know you."

But of course she knew better than that. Because no matter

what Roman had said, or even the Captain for that matter, who she was perfectly aware knew better (she had seen him that afternoon; they had walked for a while, a short while, along the canal, and on the way to the hospital in the cab she had promised again that she would not tell Roman about them, and he had told her not to worry, that they were all sure to love her in America), she had not even expected to be met at the pier. And she was grateful for the hotel and for not having to meet the Novaks; Groszek moving about in the single tight room like an entire inspection team, opening and slamming empty bureau drawers, saying, "Pah, this is a pigsty, but how did Groszek know you would be such a Pani? That little photograph with only your head . . . If I had known, I would have rented a *house* for you"; laughing and handing the bellboy a bill, and standing there against the door, saying, "To tell the truth, I will tell you . . . you are better off. Because let me tell you. If you ever meet them some time, do not mind them. They are just naturally sour people, as tight as a fist about every penny, especially Martha. That is why she never smiles, she is afraid somebody will think she is friendly and ask her for charity. I tell you this so you will know. You are better off here, believe me. In the tenement after a week, you would not be able to stomach them. I have lived there over eighteen years and I do not know how I have put up with them so long. But I have a son, you know, and anyway there are six flights between us and I am seldom home except to sleep. I am so busy, you know . . . Roman has told you, eh? In November, I am running for Mayor"; laughing, saying, "So you see, do not think I am being so friendly only because you are such a Pani. Because when you get to know Groszek you will see that a politician never does anything for nothing. There is always a string attached somewhere. You see, it is a politician's *job* to be nice to people. Who knows, some day you may become a citizen and I will need your vote," lubricating his cigar, saying, "Besides, I am your sponsor, no? It is the law that I must take care of you, eh? To see that you do not become a liability on the community, as the contract says."

It must have been her nerves, the excitement, the anticipated meeting with the Novaks, because when he sat down in the single soft chair by the window, flicking his cigar ashes absently on the rug, saying, "And the first string attached is that you allow me to telephone the bellboy to bring us up something to drink. Though I will warn you now, if you get Groszek drunk you will not be safe in the same room with him even though you *are* such a Pani," she just stood there looking at herself in the mirror, her hat in her hand, her hair wisping out of the bun falling pale over her forehead, her face all red and contorted and homely with crying, standing there, listening to herself trying to talk amid the sobbing, saying nothing that made any kind of sense, just letting herself go completely, hardly even recognizing her own voice, saying, "But this is America. Roman said it would be different, the Captain said it would be different," falling back on the bed, sitting there sobbing into a tent of hair, hearing the door go, and looking up to see only the cigar there smoking in the ashtray beside the telephone next to the empty soft chair.

She missed him terribly that first afternoon. It was understandable. After all, she did not know another soul and under the circumstances the two or three hours they had spent together since her arrival at the pier was enough to make her feel they were old friends. And now almost three months later and more than a hundred miles away, looking down across the boardwalk toward the Fisherman's Bar and Grill sardined between the salt-water taffy stand and the souvenir-photo parlor, she dries her hair and tells herself that she is surely not the first woman this has happened to, that indeed in the old country it is almost a custom that the groom should get drunk and act jealous of every man who dances with his bride. Though of

course in her case it had not quite happened that way. Because
actually, though Groszek had got himself very drunk indeed, he
did not appear to be in the least jealous of any of the many men
she had danced with last evening. Instead, he had rather forced
partners on her, even at times when she thought surely she could
not possibly dance another step—the Mayor, his Council, the
entire Democratic party it sometimes seemed to her—forced
partners on her even after she pleaded sore feet and an absolutely
unbelievable headache. He would just hand her another drink,
saying, "Here, if your feet hurt take off your shoes. You have
not had enough to drink, that is all. Now dance with my friend
Dr. Paulus here and show him a good time. I am counting on
him to deliver the Third Ward to me in November. That is
where all the rich Jews live. Like the doctor here; is that not
right, my friend?" slapping the doctor on the back, and winking, and raising his glass as he danced a little circle around them
stamping his feet in the polka, just as drunk as she had ever
seen him before, and having an absolutely wonderful time,
laughing and pointing at them with his cigar, as the doctor
whirled her around the floor—her white veil wheeling. And it
was not until later, not until she and Groszek ran arm in arm
together down the path from the dance pavilion to the parking
lot, her shoes in her hand and her feet tender against the gravel,
the voice of the best man booming over the PA system in some
meaningless speech designed to occupy the guests so that the
bridal couple might make their getaway before anyone noticed
they were leaving; not till they practically *ran* into him standing
there in the dark amid the trees beside the public rest rooms,
not until she actually recognized him in the moonlight diffusing
through the trees, the whiskey whirling around in her head as
though she were still dancing, saying, "I remember you. You
are the man with the flowers. Why did you not ask me to dance
with *him*, Groszek? I do not even know what ward I am to get
him to deliver"; extending her hand and giggling into her hand-

kerchief at her drunkenness, saying, "You should not be afraid
to shake my hand. Groszek will not charge you many votes . . ."
Groszek pulling her away rudely by the arm and her laughter
turning finally to tears when she felt herself still dancing, still
whirling around and around in the back seat as the car careened
up and over the Market Street Bridge, her belly coming up into
her mouth just as she got the window rolled down, befouling the
Anderson streets, begging him to slow down, but the car only
jolting ahead, the motor roaring, and his voice there from the
front seat, rattling, "What are you afraid of? Have I not told
you I have only had one accident in my whole life. Besides, your
funeral will give him an excuse to bring you flowers again."

Even in her stupor, she understood him. But she did not have
the strength to answer. Besides, she did not know herself quite
what to think of it. It was just last evening, or rather Friday
evening. They were having dinner in the second-story Chinese
restaurant just across the street from her hotel, when she happened to look up from her plate and saw through the large
window beside her and across the telephone wires a man standing in the hall window just outside the door of her second-story
hotel room, a man with a huge bouquet of flowers in his arms.
She had smiled to Groszek across the table, saying, "Thank you,
Groszek. You are very thoughtful"; but all he did was look up
from his tea, his mouth full of fortune cookie, saying, "What
for? For a plate of cooked grass and noodles?" she smiling, saying, "For the flowers, foolish"; and he, "What flowers?" and
she, pointing, smiling as he stood up over the table and leaned
around the drapery, his napkin tucked behind his collar slop-
ping in her teacup, "Not in the street, Groszek. Across, in the
window there." Only, it was too late by then, and the hotel
window was empty; Groszek saying, "Well, I am sorry I did not
think of it. But I have enough to think of with the wedding
tomorrow. I am afraid those were not for you. You are not the
only one who lives on the second floor, you know. But I will

have some sent to your room. I will telephone right now. What kind do you like?" and she, "The same kind. Costmarys, or what do you call them here, chrysanthemums?"

But she did not begin to put one and one together until much later, not until long after they had arrived in Atlantic City and she lay there in the hotel bed trying to fall back into the sleep she had begun in the back seat of the limousine, where sprawled in her soiled wedding gown—the veil crumpled on the floor beside her—she had thought, "I will be glad to get out of it when we reach the motel. It is only a mile or two and so I should not fall asleep." As it turned out, however, Groszek had not bothered to stop at the motel he had reserved for them on the highway outside Prescott, but instead had driven all the way to Atlantic City, over a hundred miles, in less than four hours; the man at the hotel desk telling them they were almost a day early but they were lucky because though the room they had reserved would be occupied until tomorrow afternoon, they might have the wedding suite for the night; Groszek just standing there before the window in the fifty-dollar-a-day suite, puffing on his cigar and fingering the satin draperies, not even answering her questions, her "What is wrong, Groszek? What is bothering you? Did I behave badly? Was I so terribly drunk? Why will you not talk to me, Groszek?" still not speaking to her long after she had got undressed and showered and into bed, just sitting there in the soft chair silhouetted before the window amid the sound of the surf and the rattle of the electric fan atop the dresser, the smell of his cigar drifting across the dark room to her. So she just lay there alone in the big double bed trying to sleep, thinking, "It has something to do with the man with the flowers of course. But who is he? Why was he hiding like that in the trees, and why the flowers?" when all of a sudden, for no reason at all (except perhaps that he and his wife were the only ones who had not at least replied to the wedding invitation, the only one of Groszek's acquaintances she had never been introduced to, the only man in America besides Groszek who could possibly have had the remotest reason for bringing her flowers), all of it just fell together, like one and one—"He is Roman's father." She said it to herself at first, though out loud; and Groszek just sat there in the moonlight, still chewing on his cigar, still not speaking. And so she asked him right out, whispering it almost, saying, "Tell me, Groszek, and I will be quiet. The man with the bouquet . . . is he Roman's father?" And when he finally answered her, speaking out of the darkness amid the electric fan's rattle and the sound of surf booming against the shore, it struck her as no less strange than did the rest of the dark hours of that morning in which she would awake out of her dream and see him still sitting there, the cigar smoke still wisping up thin against the open window, would wake out of her dream wondering what it could all mean, thinking perhaps he had not really heard her correctly, lying there repeating the question over to herself, "The man with the bouquet . . . is he Roman's father?" and then his answer, cryptic as cigar smoke in a recurring dream, "Only God and Martha know. And as for Johnny? Only God."

Chapters V & XV

EVENING

Not until just five days ago during one of their usual arguments over her daily baths had Marya ever imagined it possible. Her mother had told her to go out and find herself a husband to pay her water bills, and Marya instead of simply ignoring her as usual had screamed, "I don't have to look for a husband. Johnny's going to marry me," to which her mother, almost as though she were not aware she was thinking aloud, said simply, "Yes, why not? It would be nothing more than what everybody has come to expect from this family —a brother and a sister marrying."

It had always been completely out of the question, not so much because if it happened to be true it might cast some odor of scandal upon the family, for it had not been until just recently that it had even occurred to her that if it *were* true after all, it would mean that one or the other of her parents could not possibly be the sober and righteous paragon she had always taken for granted all parents must by definition be—a woman like the widow Nowicki being the exception that proved the rule, her defection as a parent accounted for by her widowhood, just as her Uncle Groszek's widowerhood not only accounted for but excused his. It had always been out of the question simply because, as she so often told the widow Nowicki and her daughter Lottie to their faces whenever they happened to tease her about it, they were liars and were just jealous like her mother said—her mother having many times warned her as a child not to linger on the second-floor landing on her way to her Uncle Groszek's rooms or to the roof, saying, "They have nothing better to do with themselves than to smoke and to drink and to go around to the taverns and the dance halls and to tease children. So you should not mind them, daughter. They are liars, and they are only jealous of us, just as the bad are always jealous of the good"—they were liars and they were jealous and so anything they might offer as truth, simply by virtue of *their* having offered it, was double-your-money-back guaranteed to be false.

But now, kneeling in the bathtub washing the ring around the receding water line and watching the dirty water swirl down the drain, she wonders how it could possibly have come to this, how things could possibly have got themselves so all mixed up that when she finally got up the courage last Wednesday to stop Johnny on the stairs and tell him about it, tell him that it was true after all, that they really *were* brother and sister, that her own mother had actually admitted it to her, Johnny had just sat down right on the stairs and outright wept into his hands—Johnny, whose entire childhood had been, just as hers and Roman's had too, shaped and cast and colored by the unfortu-

nate and unforgivable circumstance of his having allowed himself to be born a *mere* cousin to them, rather than a brother, who
in those days before her Uncle Groszek's luck had changed lived
with them like part of the family, even sleeping in the same bed
with them, crosswise—Johnny at the head and she at the foot
and Roman in the middle between them—sleeping together
like that right up until that year when everything began to
change the way it did, everything, the whole world in fact; because in that year 1939, just fourteen weeks after her First Holy
Communion, on the very first day of the month of the feasts
of the nativity, the holy name and the seven dolors of the
Blessed Virgin Mary, the earthly realm of the Queen of Peace
(who as Marya had learned from the nuns at Polish School was
in addition to being the Mother of God and her very own name-
sake, also the Queen of Poland) was invaded by the Prince of
this world.

After that, it seemed to Marya that all everybody in the neighborhood ever did was listen to the radio and run out three or
four times a day to buy a paper from one of the newsboys yelling *Extra* in the streets. Even her Uncle Groszek, who during
those noontimes when he came home from his number route
to count his money and number slips had never listened to anything but the horse-racing news when he bothered to listen to
the radio at all, suddenly on that first day of September—coming home as usual to meet her on the stairs and hand her the
moneybags and the number books and lift her in his arms to
carry her up the six flights to his rooms, his breath wheezing the
usual combination of whiskey and tobacco which she could
never quite bring herself to overlook since it always somehow
seemed to ally him with the widow Nowicki, whose breath was
no more pleasant and whose daughter Lottie would almost
every day just happen to pass them on the second-floor landing
on her way to the hall bathroom with her towel and toothbrush,
still all sleepy-eyed and fuzzy in her bathrobe but not without

her lips all painted up and smiling, and to whom her uncle always tipped his hat and said good morning even though it was always already past noon; tipping his hat and smiling as usual on that first day of September, carrying her, Marya, up the remaining five flights to his kitchen, but instead of the usual business of his lighting a fresh cigar and slipping the paper band off it and over her finger like a ring before sitting down across the table from her to count the pennies and dimes and nickels and quarters and half-dollars into piles and fit them into the green and pink and blue and yellow paper sleeves; five pennies of which he would give to her for helping him, because as he had so often said she was almost as fast as he was—which was something because really she knew of no one except perhaps her mother who could count coins as fast as her Uncle Groszek, who still never made a mistake even though he would finish almost half a bottle of whiskey every afternoon while he was doing it—three pennies going into the penny bank she had made for herself by cutting a slit in an empty cigar box and taping the cover shut and which she kept in various hiding places in the bedroom downstairs in order to keep Johnny from finding it and shaking the pennies out; the remaining two pennies going most often to the old Greek who came around almost every evening during the warm months with his box of fortune cards and his parrot and his truck with the merry-go-round on the back and the sign "2¢ a ride 2¢," which ride not until that spring after her First Holy Communion, when everything began to change the way it did, did Marya begin to feel herself too grown-up really to enjoy, just as she had begun to feel that she no longer really enjoyed helping her uncle count his number money, not the way she used to anyway, though of course she had no choice but to pretend that she was as pleased to help him as ever because it just so happened that was when he needed her help most of all, because on that first day of September, he did not even bother to count out so much as a single

pile of pennies himself, leaving it all to her—he just turned on
the radio over the icebox and sat there across from her fingering
the dials as she counted, his eyes all watery "from the bottle"
she thought. And in the weeks that followed, up until that day
late in September when the whole neighborhood seemed to her
to have gone completely crazy, the women running weeping into
the streets and crying on their way to the church, "Warszawa
has fallen, Warszawa is gone," her uncle not only listened to the
radio all during the noon hours but far into the nights too so
that some of the tenants even complained to her mother and
father that with the windows open against the September heat
nobody in the tenement could sleep. But by the end of September it was all over, and he never bothered with the radio after
that; though it was not until late in December, during the
Christmas holiday from school, that she found out why.

He came home that day long before noon, and without any
moneybags or number slips, and he was so drunk that she did
not even allow him to carry her upstairs, handing him instead
the bundle of clean laundry that had been waiting for him in
the hall. And sitting there on the edge of the bed beside her as
she separated the sheets from the rest of the laundry because
he had opened the bottom bureau drawer where the sheets belonged, he did not even bother to answer her questions, just
shaking his head and smiling that terrible drunken smile; and
instead of taking the sheets she handed to him and laying them
in the drawer, he simply laid them back down on the bed beside
him and removed several others from the drawer, out from
under which he reached the green tin box that once before,
when she had come across it while putting his laundry away for
him, he had told her only had "some old papers and things in
it," and which though it looked to her very much like a little
treasure chest, what with the shiny brass corners and the handle
and the miniature hasp and lock, she never dreamed would,

when he opened it on the kitchen table with the aid of one of her hairpins, overflow with all those crumpled-up one- and five- and ten-dollar bills.

It was not the most money she had ever seen in her life, for she had many times seen her mother and father counting piles of bills out of the safe behind the candy store, especially on the days they collected the rents; and even her Uncle Groszek had once or twice brought home as much and more in his moneybags when one of his customers happened to "hit." But there *was* after all quite a bit there to be all in one little box, enough any- way "to bring a whole *family* over from the old country," as her uncle had put it, "somewhere right around three hundred dollars anyway," though he could not say exactly. But even if it were only a hundred or fifty or fifteen or even one, it would still have been the most money she had ever seen go up in smoke before; her uncle standing there fumbling in his vest pockets with his thumbs and coming up with the folded envelope and tossing it across the table to her, saying, "Read it out loud. I wish to hear it one more time"; she sitting there unfolding the unstamped and unpostmarked small envelope addressed in a flourishing hand to Pan Roman Pawel Groszek, Prescott, New Jersey, U.S.A., hardly getting the letter out of the envelope to read the date and the salutation (not even noticing that he had removed the box from the table) when out of the side of her eye she saw, just as though hell itself had somehow worked its way up through the plumbing—the bright hot flames leaping up out of the kitchen sink.

It was unforgivable she thought; and she wept when he stopped her from running to the sink to turn on the faucet, sweeping her up into his arms to watch the flames finally die in the box and the wisps of black burning ash rise drunkenly up along the kitchen wall toward the skylight. It seemed to her that not only he, but she too had done something dreadful, as though they together had committed some unpardonable sin.

And later after it was all over and her uncle had gone, and she had taken the somewhat charred box and the picture and the ring and the rosary back downstairs with her and her mother made her take it back up again and then gave her a spanking and made her kneel on rice in the bedroom corner facing the wall (a punishment which till then had been reserved exclusively for the boys), she did not question the justice of it all, even though she had not even told her mother about the money, did not tell her anything in fact except that her Uncle Groszek had said that she might keep the box and the ring and the rosary and the picture too and so it was not as though she had stolen anything, which was not exactly the complete truth anyway and which suspicion it seemed to her must be the logical explanation of her mother's wrath. She did not tell her about the burning, or how after it was all over her uncle had put her down and gone over and run water from the faucet over the ashes, scratching his head, saying, "Pah, I forgot about the change," the coins there on top of the pile after he had poured the water out of the box into the sink and emptied it out over the table, not even scorched, nor the wedding band either, nor the string of white rosary beads, nor the large water-soaked paper-framed photograph of a young man and woman leaning against a railing with a painted moonlit sea behind them and beneath the gilded inscription, "Souvenir of Atlantic City."

Nor did she tell her mother about the letter. She had completely forgotten about it until after her uncle had already gone, rushing off the way he did after palming the pile of coins into his overcoat pockets even before she could finish asking whether he meant the ring and the rosary and the photograph too when she asked him if she could have the box for a penny bank since it looked like he was through with it, and with the hasp and lock and all Johnny would have a harder time of it even if he did find out it could be opened with a hairpin, and her uncle had just nodded, saying, "Yes, yes! Of course. Take it, take it," and was gone with his overcoat pockets bulging, leaving her there still kneeling on the kitchen chair examining the ring and the rosary and the photograph. Because it was not until then, till she was alone and had time to wonder what it all meant, that she even remembered the letter, finding it lying there under the kitchen sink next to the garbage pail where it had fallen when her uncle had swept her up into his arms; the first and last pages of the folded sheet smeared and blurred from the water that had splashed on the floor when he had doused the ashes, so blurred and smeared that she could not read any of it; the inside pages, however, hardly smeared at all, the fine Polish script—even finer than the nuns' at school—almost as easy to read as her Polish catechism; beginning right in the middle of a sentence, reading "and so I am grateful that I do not have to tell you of it face to face but can write it like this (which is difficult enough) without even knowing if this letter will ever get out of the country, or my friends either who have promised to take it with them tomorrow (may God help them). But if this letter does find you, I hope it finds you well. She talked of you often, how she had never seen you, how she was not even born yet when you left for America in 1910. She had talked about how you were going to send for her some day ever since she first came to us from Krakow thirteen years ago to teach the little ones in the school. If only you could have somehow got together the passage money; but of course she told us too how very poor you are yourself and that it is not in America as everybody thinks it is over here, everybody is not really a millionaire. She was even ashamed to ask it of you, she said, except that she felt that once she could get to America she could take a job and help support the children and be a mother to them. The little ones would have loved her as did all the little ones here in the school. And it would have been so good for her, because after all she was not the kind of girl who would have anything to do with men, such a devout plain girl, like a nun almost, and except for the children in the school, well, she was sometimes lonely. Of all who were taken last night, you would think God would have spared her. If only she had not been home in her bed but out running around with men like some of the others on a Saturday night, some of the others who were made for the kind of thing that will happen to your poor sister, and who were spared because they were not at home when the German trucks came shining their lights on the doors. There were three trucks, almost all the girls and younger women of the neighborhood. There is hardly a girl left over fifteen or under thirty. And how she wept when they took her, and how she swore on her brother's name that she would kill herself, and on the name of every one of your seven motherless children . . ."

And so in that year 1939 everything changed in the world. Not only in the big world, but in Marya's world too. For one thing, she never counted coins again under the skylight in her uncle's kitchen, for after that Christmas season her uncle had little to do with pennies and nickels and dimes any more. As he said himself his luck had changed, and so had his job, and his habits too. And she rarely ever got to see him any more, for since he had given up his number route and had become Councilman he was a very busy man and only came home sometimes to sleep at night long after she was already in bed. But it was not as though she minded very much, she told herself. After all, she was getting a little too grown-up to be carried up the six flights at noon to count coins for pennies, or to report to him like to a judge and jury how her mother had put her to bed almost all of yesterday afternoon simply because she had maybe broken a dish while she was drying or perhaps fallen down and skinned her knees on the pavement jumping rope or had maybe just forgotten herself and bitten off all her fingernails again; too old to have him take her on his lap and stroke her hair, saying, "My nervous little bird, if you were mine I would let you bite your fingernails all you want, and when you skinned your knees, I would go outside and put the sidewalk to bed for the afternoon," or like one time when he was a little drunker even than usual actually taking a stack of dusty and spidery old dishes out of the closet over the sink and telling her to smash as many as she liked right there on the kitchen floor, actually smashing one to show her he wasn't fooling, "because what are dishes anyway, even if you have somebody to use them"; she simply shaking her head telling him that it was silly to smash good dishes unless of course they happened to slip when you were drying them and you couldn't help it, because after all she wasn't a baby any more, she understood that much.

In fact sometimes she was sure she understood a lot more than a lot of people a lot older than herself, like her Uncle Groszek for example and the business with the dishes. Although really that wasn't half so bad as her father and mother the time the stray dog got into the garbage shed and had her puppies there—her own mother taking the poor blind-eyed little things and putting them into an empty potato bag when the old mama dog finally got hungry enough to leave her babies for awhile and go looking for food, her own mother actually giving Johnny a quarter to throw them off the bridge into the river because it was the only decent thing to do, she said, since nobody wanted the homely little mongrels. And that would have been the end of them too if she hadn't gone crying to her father, who finally allowed her to keep one and telephoned some people who came with a truck to take away the others, allowed her to keep the white one which she used to cuddle and wrap in a blanket and sing "Lullaby and Good Night" to, and feed candy because he liked it as much as she did, so that he got worms and one morning she found him in the shed all bloated and stiff as a plaster doll, and she thought she would never get over it; marveling at how stupid her father could be to try to console her by telling her he would get her another puppy, that she would get over it just the way she got over the time the nest of baby sparrows was blown off the fire escape in the storm (as though a bird and a puppy were the same thing, as though you could cuddle a bird in a blanket and sing it lullabies, or feed it candy so it should die); not knowing how to tell him that it was no good, that it just wouldn't do, screaming, "Why didn't you let Johnny drown them? Why didn't you let him? Why didn't you?" weeping in her Uncle Groszek's arms that noon, his voice there almost as though it were her own, saying, "A new puppy? Is he crazy? Does he not know there will never be another puppy like your little Tuffush again? Sometimes I wonder who is more stupid, little one, your Mama or your Tata."

But that was all behind, and she did not miss any of it. After all she was not a baby any more. She was at least grown-up enough during that Christmas season of 1939 to realize that the change that had come over her uncle was something to be grateful for rather than to regret. Because after those terrible days of wondering what had happened to him, those three days before Christmas following the day he burned the money and left the tenement with his overcoat pockets bulging with coins— three days during which at least twice a day a big car would pull up in front of the candy store and one of the men in the tight black coats and derbys and gray gloves (her mother said they were gangsters) would come into the store and ask her father if her uncle had come home yet—he returned just before midnight on Christmas Eve all dressed up ("like a professional pallbearer," her mother had said) in a black homburg hat and chesterfield coat and white silk scarf and undertaker gray gloves, his face all smooth and smiling as though he had spent half the day in a barber's chair, and a big cigar going in his mouth and his arms full of all kinds of Christmas presents for everybody, including a bottle of perfume for Lottie upstairs and as he said, "Flowers for Lottie's Mama the widow—Four Roses, the kind that comes in a bottle," saying over and over that he was a new man, and had no hard feelings for anybody, even shaking her father's hand and kissing her mother on the forehead, and telling how his luck had finally changed, how he felt it in his bones, how he had walked out of the tenement three days ago a bum with his last seventy-one dollars and some sixty-odd cents in his overcoat pockets ready to throw it all away on drink, when who should he bump into on the second-floor landing but Lottie, Lottie who took a five-dollar bill out of her bathrobe pocket and asked him if he would please play it on a horse for her on his way past the pool parlor because she had a "hot tip" on the noon race in Florida and would not be able to get dressed and get down to the corner on time to place the bet herself, and he in his drunkenness just pushing her aside and calling her a tramp and a great many other insulting things he said he could not repeat in front of children, and for no reason at all he said except that he was half crazy with drink; saying, "Perhaps Marya has told you how by accident I even burned a few dollars I have been saving"—she sitting there under the tree amid her presents chewing on her fingernails, shaking her head and feeling somehow that he had betrayed her by telling of it—smiling, saying, "No? Well, it was just a foolish accident anyway, a few dollars, nothing worth mentioning"; not mentioning the letter either, looking at her as though now that he was sober he could not quite remember whether he had showed her the letter or not, saying, "A drunk is not responsible"; saying, "But anyway, by the time I came to the pool parlor on my way to the tavern, maybe I was already beginning to get a little sober, because I went upstairs and I not only put five dollars of my own money on Lottie's horse for her, but all the rest I had in my pockets too, for myself. And you know what? They have been looking for me for three days now to give me my winnings. Thirty to one, can you imagine it?—Groszek, who has had no luck at all, not even at cards, for over ten years now. And where was Groszek all the while? Drunk as a pig in a wino shack by the railroad tracks, not even knowing how all of a sudden his luck had changed."

But it was not only her uncle's *luck* that had changed, but her uncle and a great many other things too. For that was the spring Johnny was caught playing "doctor" in the alley garbage shed with her brother Roman's twelve-year-old girl friend, Petronila, and after that Marya began to sleep all alone in the big double bed, biting her fingernails under the sheets because she was always so afraid of the dark, Roman sleeping for a time on the horsehair sofa in the parlor until he finally outgrew it and moved onto the cot in the storeroom behind the candy store and Johnny, now that his father's luck had changed, moving upstairs onto the cot in his father's kitchen. She had the entire bedroom to herself now, and the bureau too and the mirror above it in which one day she suddenly discovered that despite what her uncle thought, she was not really very pretty at all, that in fact she was rather plain—even when she smiled only a little so her teeth wouldn't show. And by the time she was twelve and going to St. Mary's High School, having skipped the eighth grade completely, she had come to think of herself as not merely plain but downright homely, having refused to wear braces on her teeth, not only because they made her unbearably nervous but because she was afraid that once her teeth were straightened she would no longer have any excuse to give herself, knowing that even then she would still be plain (or rather homely, as she saw it), even if her teeth were as straight and white and beautiful as Lottie's upstairs.

Though Marya had, ever since she could remember, looked upon the widow and her daughter as tramps, by the time she got to high school she could not help admitting that Lottie was really the prettiest woman she had ever seen outside the movies even with the bags under her eyes and her skin all flaky with too much powder. She was a bigger tramp than ever during the war

—a regular "Victory Girl" Johnny called her—but her looks were exactly what Marya pictured her own might be if it weren't for her teeth. She had long chestnut hair just like Lottie's, and though her mother would never allow her to wear it hanging loose like that down over one eye as Lottie did, but up in combs and a bun, just before going to bed at night she would stand there before the bureau mirror with her hair down over one eye, unsmiling and with an eyebrow lifted like Lottie's whenever she talked to anyone (especially a man), and with her thin breast-less body hidden under the big baggy cotton nightdress and below the bureau top, and only her head and shoulders visible in the mirror and a skirt or blouse or something thrown over the lampshade to dim and color the light, she could almost imagine that the reflection in the mirror was not only beautiful as Lottie but sometimes actually Lottie herself, the thin bony shoulders under the cotton nightdress suddenly blossoming full and naked under one of those filmy nightgowns Lottie would sometimes hang out on the roof clothesline amid all the other pretty underclothes; Lottie, who on those sunny summer after-noons would lie up there on the roof in her sunglasses and bath-ing suit with the oil all over her, and the portable radio blaring and the movie and confession magazines scattered all over the blanket, and the pink-tipped cigarette butts all over the gravel; Lottie, who worked nights as a waitress in the Owl's Tavern, and who in the fall of forty-five just after the war ended began suddenly putting on weight, and who the following March, just five months ago (to the scandal of the entire neighborhood, in-cluding Marya's mother whom Marya had overheard saying to her father, "Do not speak to me of the law. Her whole life is against the law. Any decent woman would have run to a doctor and had an operation the minute she found she could not get anyone to marry her") had herself a baby boy.

Marya not only thought Lottie's son was the prettiest baby she had ever seen, but somehow Lottie herself lying there pale-lipped in a white cotton nightdress, makeupless with the baby there beside her, and even with the cigarette between her fingers, seemed to her more beautiful than ever, cleansed somehow, no longer a tramp, no matter what she had done. For though Marya could not even begin to imagine what really went on in the back seats of parked cars, having no more than blurred and fleeting visions of two monstrously entangled beasts bare-bottomed like a couple of obscene baboons tearing and devouring away at each other with crooked teeth of lust, nevertheless she knew without even needing to think it, and certainly without ever trying to put it into words, that *one* time, no matter when it was, or where or with whom, no matter how perverse or abandoned or sinful; that *one* time, that *one* moment, the moment when that beautiful little boy ran headlong down the corridors of time to meet himself, to be born, it was *holy*; and it seemed to her that the real sin lay not in any of the other things, not in the lust, or the teeth tearing or anything else, but that amid all of it, the moment of holiness was not even recognized; that that baby was being born, that a new life was issuing from the hand of God, was being handed right down there to her in the back seat of that car or in the motel bed or wherever, was being breathed into her belly and she did not even know it, did not feel at all different for having two souls inside her now instead of one, was not aware (how could she be?) that perhaps at the very moment when she felt herself spiraling down into the lowest depths of herself, suddenly, somewhere inside her, in the blackest depths of her bowels, was born the purest whitest human innocence possible; did not feel the slightest bit different than she had felt all the other times when it was all just devouring and dying and endings and no beginning; because there was no heavenly glow, the back seat of the car did not suddenly become refulgent, except perhaps in the beam of the highway patrolman's torch; the night was not suddenly resonant of angelic choirs heralding the newborn, there was only dance music on the car radio; it felt just like all the other times, no better no worse, just as exhausting, just as final; and so how could she have known? Because as far as Marya was concerned, after seeing Lottie lying there beside her baby, there was no question in her mind that even Lottie if she had known at the time what was happening to her, what miracle was taking place inside her very own belly, if the back seat *had* glowed, if the choirs *had* sung, if the angel *had* appeared there at the window instead of the patrolman, appeared saying, "Behold, thou shalt conceive in thy womb and bring forth a son"; even if he had had to go on and say, "He shall be insignificant and shall be called a bastard among men, and he shall have no inheritance, and shall be subject to all, and meet with a bad end"; even so she might have looked up there into her lover's eyes, not only bright amid the heavenly glow, but radiant with lust, and would have beheld there, as in a mirror reflected back on her, not only a shameless and insatiable tramp, but a "Handmaid of the Lord."

But perhaps it was only the feeling that she herself had failed her which caused Marya to change her attitude toward Lottie. Because, that day last March on her way down from the roof after hanging out her mother's wash, when she heard the screaming through the door on the second-floor landing and rushed into the rooms with the clothes basket still in her arms to find there the widow Nowicki passed out at the kitchen table with a whiskey bottle still clutched in her hand, and beyond her through the open bedroom door Lottie with her legs spread wider on the bed than ever in the back seat of any car grunting and sweating and screaming in the throes of birth, she could not bring herself to do anything more than freeze—Lottie screaming, "Help me for God's sake! Don't just stand there, help me!"—and only after what seemed like hours finally break away from herself and run down the stairs weeping so hysterically that she could not get her mother to understand anything more than that whatever it was that had horrified her so was somewhere upstairs. And it was not until several days later, after it was all over—her mother and father having helped Lottie deliver her baby—that she even got up enough courage to climb the stairs and beg Lottie to forgive her for failing her; seeing her with the baby beside her, and thinking how terrible it was for God to make a woman go through so much to get her to help Him create life, no matter how much of a sinner she had been, and that the pain and suffering Lottie had gone through helping Him do what He had to do, ought to satisfy Him, that she had paid for her past, *whatever* it might have been, and that if He was not satisfied that was too bad for Him, because it certainly satisfied Marya, especially since Lottie did not even complain, saying, when Marya went to her and told her that she was sorry she had had to suffer so much and she couldn't help her, saying, "It wasn't bad at all, honey," and taking her hand and smiling between the pale lips with the cigarette smoke coming out of her nose, "I didn't have hardly any labor at all. You should have seen your old lady when *you* were born. Thanks anyway though, you're a sweet kid. Here, you want to hold him awhile?" And Marya did. And she held him quite a bit after that, every day in fact during those two months, helping Lottie bathe and feed and change him and make up his crib in the open bureau drawer, cuddling him in a blanket and singing him to sleep like a little seven-year-old again playing house; playing house for over two months until that hot almost breathless Saturday afternoon early in May, cuddling the baby up there on the roof amid the weekend wash hanging limp on the clothesline, while Lottie in her bathing suit lay on the blanket amid the dance music on the portable radio, smoking and rubbing baby oil over herself, saying, "Thank God I got my figure back. Now all I need is a little color. Though from what I hear, it looks like I might have to change the color of my hair too if I'm ever going to get your Uncle Groszek back."

It was not until later that night, however, that she found out
what Lottie meant—that night just a little less than three
months ago, just a little after midnight after she had taken her
bath and watched the dirty water swirl down the drain, thinking
then, just as she thinks now, "Almost sixteen years old already,
and still nothing there at all, like a boy." Only, then it was just
a matter of wanting to be more beautiful, like Lottie with her
breasts full under her sweater, so that maybe, if for no other
reason, maybe at least one or two of the boys at the Saturday
night dance would want to dance with her. She was oh so very
tired of arguing with her mother every week and having to tell
her over and over again that no she was not going to the dance
to find a husband, that she did not like dancing in the first place
and that she did not want the kind of husband she would have
to go out and chase, that when the time came he would come
and find her, and besides she had homework to do and wanted
to get to bed early and go to six-o'clock Mass tomorrow morning. But now, just three months later, it is not that at all any
more, because tonight she *is* going to the dance and there will
be no argument with her mother; looking down at herself now
naked in the tub and remembering Lottie with her baby at her
breast for those first few days at least, thinking, "And with her
always so big and all and still nothing. And so what will I do
when he's all crying and hungry and all? And what if when I
tell him to hush, that his Mama is warming his bottle, he won't
even be able to hear me? What then? Or maybe he won't even
be *able* to cry, not when he's hungry or ever, just never"; telling
herself not to even think about it, because now it would never
be anyway. Because tonight it would be all over and done with
once and for good. Johnny would be there to meet her at the
dance, and they'd get into the car and drive across the tracks
into the Third Ward and up to the big house in the park and
it would be like having your tonsils out where you didn't even

have to go to the hospital, just the doctor all by himself and a nurse to hold the pan for you to spit the blood into. For tonsils, they didn't even have to put you to sleep like they did the time in the dentist's chair when she had every one of those first ones pulled out and he showed her the new penny and said it would be hers when she woke up if she was a good girl, and she breathed deep with the mask over her face and everything went away and away and only the penny was there in the sky big and round as the moon and the clouds swirled round it, round and round, and all of a sudden it wasn't a penny at all, just a hole in the water-swirled basin into which she was spitting her blood. Only, this time she knows it would not be quite that easy, that it would not be simply sitting there terrified in the dentist's chair or on the edge of the doctor's table without so much as even having to take off her clothes. And so she'd better find the newest pair of pants in the drawer and the newest slip too, even though even the newest are all so raggedy and yellow and holey with washing that it is going to be shameful for her to have to be seen in them, especially if there is a nurse too; thinking, "Because she always buys the cheapest she can find. Because 'New this, new that, every month. What do you think your father and I are, millionaires? So long as they are clean what does it matter? Nobody looks under your dress, do they?' "

And so tonight Marya *is* going to the dance, going because that Saturday night three months ago, that Saturday night early in May, she did *not* go, went to bed instead after she had argued with her mother over her bath as usual and had finished doing some of her homework, sweating there under the single sheet in the still, hot, almost breathless night, unable to sleep and so getting up, and in her long modest cotton nightdress and bare feet, tiptoeing past her mother's room and down the hall past the little room behind the candy store—the light still on behind the transom and her father probably still counting his books or reading the newspapers because as her mother was always saying, "Lately, he never sleeps any more"—and climbing up the seven flights to the roof, her bare feet smooth on the stairs and tender on the gravel just as the midnight mail plane droned low overhead like a bunch of stars blinking its lights for the landing at the New York airport; the skylight over her Uncle Groszek's kitchen lighting up and then darkening and then light again and dark again, and then again light and dark, and light and dark, and light and dark again even before she had time to cross the six or seven feet from the storm door to the skylight, standing there cool against the chimney and looking down into the kitchen lit only by the soft yellow light from her uncle's bedroom; hearing the voice which she did not even recognize at first—the light flashing on again and then off again three times in rapid succession—the voice saying, "That's SOS, a flier boy friend of mine taught it to me. Save Our Souls, somebody—anybody!"

It was like looking at three different stills made from the same movie film of Lottie in nothing but heels (one of them on the floor beside her chair) and the filmy white nightgown Marya had always admired so much on the clothesline, Lottie kneeling on a chair and leaning (it was not until the second still that Marya thought "drunkenly," and not till the third that she added "shamelessly"), leaning across the table toward Johnny, who sat there with a whiskey bottle in front of him drinking (the glass in his hand halfway between the table and his lips in the first still, at his lips in the second, and back down empty on the table in the third), drinking and smiling across at her as she leaned pulling on the light cord over the middle of the table, saying, "He's dead now. He asked me to marry him before he left, but he was only a kid"; and Johnny, "Why don't you leave it on?" and she, "Never mind."

"Well, then how can I see to fill your glass?"

"You seen too much already. Now be a good kid and go back to your college girl. What are you doing home anyway?"

"I live here, remember?"

"She sent you home. I do that too when I got somebody else waitin'. That's what I call a double date."

"I thought what you call a double date's takin' on two guys at once."

"Very funny."

"All right, so let's put on the lights."

"You're a scream, just like your old man. You even sound like him in the dark."

"Swell, put on the light."

"Sometimes I even forget you're not related. Anyway, how'd you like it if I took your old man to court?"

"I don't know. With half the neighborhood up on the witness stand swearing how they paid you for it . . . It'd be lively anyway."

"It'd be in all the papers too; and what about the election?"

"What about it?"

"You know damn well what about it. But don't worry, I'm not going to do it. I told him that. Because I want him to be Mayor as much as he does. I didn't even ask him to marry me, if you want to know. All I wanted was to be the one behind the veil in the limousine, that's all. I knew he was seeing that blond DP. I didn't even complain. I knew I couldn't do him any good so soon after the baby. But now that the doctor says its okay, I thought tonight . . ."

"What are you bawlin' about?"

"He wouldn't even come out to say hello. He gave them orders not to even let me in. Who does he think he is anyway? He's not Mayor *yet*. I got as much right in the Democratic Club dance as anybody. I'm a registered Democrat."

"Right now you're a drunken registered Democrat."

"I could see him dancing inside with that DP. They had to throw me out. And you know what Joey the Cop said? He said he had orders to lock me up even, if I didn't behave myself.

Well, it's not going to be that easy. Because I'm not leaving till I see him. I don't care if I have to sit here all morning. So be a sweet kid and blow, I didn't climb five flights of fire escape in these heels just to sit here and jaw with you."

"You were pretty damned surprised when that door opened and it was only me."

"*I* was surprised? You looked like your eyes were going to pop out of your head."

"It's not every night I come home and find a half-undressed dame guzzling my old man's booze. You really got it in that nightgown, no bull. So why don't you give me a break and lean over like that again and put the light on."

"Just remember your place, sonny. I'm not one of your little college girls, remember. I'm old enough to be your old lady. Just remember that."

"Okay, just so *you* remember you're not."

"Not what?"

"My old lady."

"Well, suppose I was? Suppose he decides to marry me after all?"

"Fat chance."

"You could do worse."

"Maybe so. But I'd sure as hell hate to be that poor little bastard downstairs in that bureau drawer."

"Listen, I wouldn't go round callin' names if I was you. Your old lady wasn't exactly a saint, you know. She didn't get married when she was fifteen for nothing. Because we used to double date together, and let me tell you, your old lady'd outdo me any time in the back seat of a car. Because maybe you were *born* in that bed in there, sonny, but you sure as hell weren't conceived in it . . . unless maybe it was one of those mornings that big shot you call your old man was out booking numbers and dreaming about what it would be like to be back in bed here with his bride, and all the while she was rollin' around in it under old man Novak gettin' herself completely and properly . . ."

Marya heard the slap almost before she saw Johnny stand up in the light from the bedroom and lean across the table; saw Lottie's head fling back and the chair go out from under her, sprawling her to the floor under the sink, Johnny almost instantly down on his knees beside her in the pool of light from the bedroom, muttering, "Are you okay? I'm sorry. Are you okay?" and holding her head in his lap. She just stood there against the chimney unbelieving, her hands to her mouth, biting her fingernails, unable to break away from herself, unable even to speak as she saw the arm reach around Johnny's neck and his head bending over her; breaking away finally as though out of the embrace itself, and running across the gravel, her bare feet not even tender any more, like floating, running across the roof and through the storm door and down the flight of stairs and through the hall and the door into the kitchen, the light no longer on in the bedroom, and the kitchen lit only by the hall light shining in behind her through the opened door, falling bright across the floor and bending around the bedroom door just enough for her to see Lottie rise from the edge of the bed which she could have no more than just sat down upon, throwing her nightgown on over her head, which she could have no more than just finished removing, and pushing past her and out the bedroom and through the kitchen into the hall slamming the kitchen door behind her, leaving her there to find Johnny in the dark, leaving her there sobbing aloud and choking and pounding against his lifted arms and scratching at his face with her nailless fingers until she heard it (heard it long before she felt it), heard the slap across her face and felt herself sinking down to her knees before him as he sat there, still sat there, on the edge of the bed, his breath full of whiskey and cigarettes; feeling his arms around her and his chin atop her head; feeling, as she lifted her face to his and threw her arms about him and hugged him to her, her lips in the darkness searching his face as for an answer, feeling all limp, all blown about in a hot wind like a nightgown on a clothesline as all of it began swirling away; feeling just as she would feel a few weeks later when she discovered what must be happening inside her, just as she feels now after almost three months, kneeling here in the bathtub watching the dirty bath water swirling down the drain.

Chapters VI & XIV

NIGHT

In the six months since the letter arrived Novak had never once considered that Magda might *not* recognize him. And so when they finally met last night at the wedding reception, he simply could not bring himself to believe that she might actually have supposed him merely a storekeeper, merely the man Roman called his father, supposed apparently that his appearance in the park was nothing more than curiosity, his hiding there amid the trees and his refusal even to shake her hand when they discovered him merely another example of bad manners like the business of his and Martha's failure to RSVP to the invitation or their neglecting to invite her to the tenement for even a single visit in the entire three months she had been in the country.

He simply could not bring himself to believe that after meeting him face to face like that, even amid the darkness of the trees with only the moon and the distant light of the dance pavilion to see by, that she could possibly fail to recognize him —the graying smoke-stained mustache, the glasses, and the limp, and the balding head and all the other marvelous disguises of time notwithstanding. To think that he might actually have been so completely forgotten, had never occurred to him. He never dreamed that her sudden and completely improbable entrance might have been arranged (he never for a moment considered it chance) simply and specifically to demonstrate that his prayer had finally been answered, that he had succeeded in actually *becoming* the man he had been pretending to be for almost twenty years now, that he really *was* only and simply the man others thought him to be, that that was all anyone *ever* was or could ever hope to be, that he might actually stand before her (before *her*) as before a mirror and confront not himself, but a stranger, the stranger he confronted whenever he looked at himself staring back out of other people's eyes.

It had been almost twenty years now since Novak had last looked into a pair of eyes and confronted himself. For here in America, only in the watery old eyes of Old Sadovi had the image ever even remotely coincided with the man. And Sadovi was dead, had been for almost twenty years now—ancient ailing Sadovi, who during that first interview in April, 1927, was still able to sit up against the pillows, his long pipe smoking in his mouth between the store teeth, his ancient thin voice rattling against the naked crucifixed walls under the lightbulb's glare, the watery old eyes unblinking as though already looking beyond the veil, the bald skull shining through the wizened thin old flesh, nodding, saying, "All of us wander the same road, my boy;

you and I and our relative the cobbler in Krakow. Because what
are we, eh? We are all descended from Abraham, true. But what
are we? Surely, we are not Jews; that is merely a mistake Christians make about us. I myself have never even seen the inside of
a synagogue, nor has my brother-in-law the cobbler, nor your
poor dead mother either—rest her soul"; grinning, saying, "But
do not fear; your secret is safe with Sadovi. Sadovi will take it
with him to the grave."

For Sadovi had been the only man in America who had
known him; Sadovi, his uncle, his mother's brother, who by the
time his youngest sister was born was already old enough to be
her father, and who when she died in childbirth just five months
after turning Christian in order to marry the father of her child,
was himself already a wealthy tenement owner and money
lender in America, who just thirty years later would agree not
only to sponsor the immigration to America of his poor dead
baby-sister's only son, but to do so under any and all circumstances, replying in the cramped clumsy Hebrew script to his
brother-in-law the cobbler in Krakow, "Every man should break
the law at least once in his lifetime, and I do not have very much
life time left. So buy him the necessary papers no matter what
the cost and put him on the first boat and the law go hang"; in
the meantime confiding to Martha *not* that he was sponsoring
his long-lost nephew outside the law, but simply some penniless
stranger named Jan Novak, a schoolteacher whom his brother-
in-law in the Krakow ghetto had asked him to take in not only
as a favor to himself, since the cobbler, he lied, owed Novak
money, but as a business venture too, since this schoolteacher
had promised in writing to pay back double the sum he had
been advanced for passage, plus room and board and the like
until he could stand on his own two feet; promised all this in a
note which in their last interview (just about two months after
the first) he called for, and in the presence of Martha, wadded
in his palsied hand and burned like an offering in the ashtray

on his night table, giving as an explanation—his watery old eyes winking—his wish as a Christian to perform at least one "good work" to accompany him on his journey, saying, "Besides, I would like you to be *completely* indebted to me, my boy. Perhaps then you will think again about helping Martha keep her promise to me"; grinning, his lips drawn thin against the store teeth, grown huge in the shrunken head, almost giggling as Martha reddened and hurried blushing from the room; his old voice rattling there against the closed door, saying, "Because what good does it do to be so stubborn, my son. According to your papers you are free to marry, and so who will ever know? And why should it bother *you*, when you have thrown it all up anyway? You are not even a believer any longer much less a Papist like myself"; laughing, as he leaned over the side of the bed and spat into the chamber pot.

"But no, I am serious," he said, wiping his mouth on his sleeve, "I had hoped when I sent her to your bed last night . . . Yes, do not look so surprised, it was I who sent her; so you must not think badly of Martha; it was part of her promise to me. And it was foolish for you to be so stubborn. You could spoil everything. And after all I have gone through, starting the rumors and everything. Maybe you think it is easy for a sick man who cannot even get up and walk about the town, who has to lie here and wait for somebody like Pani Nowicki to come down and make excuses about her rent, who has to depend on somebody like her to start the rumors for him"; saying, "All right, do not turn away. I know what you think. You think I am a foolish old man—in my second childhood, eh? Well, perhaps you are right," saying how not since he was seven, had he believed in anything but the dollar. But now? "Well, who knows? Maybe there is something to this second-childhood business after all. For you see, my boy, you have in some ways come to me like my childhood again. I know you are thirty, and think yourself a man, but to me at my age you are like a twelve-year-old," going on to tell how he had leaned hard on his nephew's words, and how in all their talks in the past two months, it had almost been like learning the alphabet or something all over again, like learning it from the beginning to the end, from A to Z and all that he had missed in between, saying, "I do not say it was your story alone which has turned me to the Church, even though your trying to confirm my skepticism may have had something to do with it after all—because as we Christians say, the ways of God are as strange as the ways *to* Him are many. Nor was it only Martha, though she has been at me for a long time now; and to be truthful, for many years I have been praying to *something*, something I did not even believe was there at the time (and I am still not sure I believe it, perhaps)."

Nevertheless, he had prayed to this something to give him whatever it was that was necessary to satisfy Martha, who had believed that for fifteen years she had been living in sin with him; that is, to satisfy her without having to completely lose his own self-respect and become a convert, his breath wheezing, saying, "What happened was, I had always hoped to have a son in my old age. I thought perhaps with a young girl like Martha . . . but well, it did not happen. So I made a bargain with whatever or whoever it was I was praying to. What could I lose, eh? Anyway, to make a long story short, look what happened; here you are. I made a bargain I thought surely I would never have to keep—because how could it happen, me an eighty-year-old man dead down there since seventy? I have always been a practical man. How could I have even dreamed there would be a miracle? Yes, I believe it. A miracle. I am still dead down here, and yet here you are. What else could it be?

"No. Do not turn away, my son. At least allow me to finish. You owe me that much. Because there is really more to it than you think. Because tell me, why did I want a son so bad in the first place? Not for any kind of sentimental reasons you might name. No, I wanted a son only so I could leave all that I have worked for all my life—the tenement, the candy store, all the unpaid notes and the money in the strong boxes . . . I wanted a son I could leave it to. Because what happens to me after I am gone, I do not care, but what I leave behind—all that I have worked for all these years denying myself . . . Pah, I do not care if I were already up there in that heaven Martha is always talking about . . . If I had to look down and see all that I have worked for all these years in the hands of some good-for-nothing drunkard like this Groszek fellow . . . If I had to look down and see it, I would walk over to that throne Martha says He sits on and call him every name I could think of, and not in Latin either, but in plain everyday Yiddish he could understand."

It was not that he wished to keep Martha from getting anything that was due her, he said. For he knew her, knew she was a good woman and a wise one and deserved every penny he would leave her. But he knew too that after fifteen years of marriage to an old corpse like himself, a man could easily make a fool of her. And he had known for some time that Groszek had had his eye on her and was just waiting for him to die and leave her everything. But if he had a son, he could leave everything to him in trust to his mother. That way it would be safe from the hands of adventurers like Groszek. But now Novak was there, and it was as though all that had happened to this nephew of his in the old country was simply and only an answer to his prayer. For now that Novak was there, there was no need for a son, no need to deprive Martha of anything, no need for trusts. For if Novak married her, then surely Groszek could not. And all of it would be Novak's and hers equally in marriage—Novak his sister's boy and Martha his wife who had kept his keys all these years and would go right on keeping them after he was gone—under her husband's supervision, of course. And that was why he had made her promise, why he had agreed to turn to the Church for her, why he had sent her to him last night, why he had started the rumors so that the whole neighborhood was expecting a wedding almost the minute they lowered his coffin into the ground.

He smiled, his too-big store teeth gleaming in his mouth and his breath wheezing like a race horse. "I have only one fear," he said. "Now that I have kept my part of the bargain, I hope He does not try to cheat me, and will see to it that you and Martha come together in this bed. For I will climb the stairs slowly, and I will keep one eye looking back over my shoulder, and if I see that business is not what it should be down here, I will crawl back out of that filthy Christian grave in St. Michael's and you will hear me in these walls at night, my son, you will hear me just like my friends the rats." And with his breath wheezing, and his eyes gone far away under the lightbulb, he spat once into his noserag and settled back against the pillows, saying, "Well, I will say good night now. Only, remember! Think about it. On your papers you are free, and she is a good woman. And in time, you will learn to care for her, just as I have. Think of the tenement, of the candy store. Be practical, my boy"—his pipe cold on the night table now, his hand already cold as the grave—"All right, tomorrow then. Only, one more thing before you say good night. Let me tell you of this Groszck fellow. I know him. And so I tell you beware. It is not that he is a bad man. It is only that he believes what other people say of him, and there is no more dangerous kind of fool. Let me warn you . . . But tomorrow. Tonight I am tired. Good night, my son." And sitting up like that with his hands folded quietly before him on the sheet and his breath already rattling away into sleep in the lipless skull, he closed his eyes, and on the bed table the too-big store-bought teeth grinned like a nightmare in the water glass.

And so when the next evening, just before he left for his night classes at the Polish Home, Martha appeared at his door,

saying simply, "I think he is gone, Janush. However, his eyes
. . ." and he followed her back to her husband's room and
pressed the lids closed over them, it was like dropping a curtain
over himself, over himself mirrored there, as though time might,
after all, actually be divided up in threes like acts. It was hardly
six weeks later however that Eva appeared, appeared as though
out of another world, a world separated from this one by oceans
of more than water. It was as though she had been sent by
Sadovi himself, sent because business was not at all what it
should be down here. For after his discovery in the very first
week after the funeral that Groszek was visiting her rooms at
night, Novak avoided meeting Martha just as much as she
seemed to avoid meeting him, feeling a kind of embarrassment
whenever it became necessary for them to exchange greetings
in the hall, and it was their drifting apart like that which was
responsible for his never having learned of Eva's expected arrival until the very evening before she appeared; appeared as
though out of Sadovi's dead eyes almost, as though out of the
very past over which that evening just six weeks earlier he had
drawn the ancient lids.

Martha had appeared at his door that evening before the boat
docked just as she had appeared the evening of her husband's
death, standing there rather grim and haggard and worn, wringing her hands and begging his pardon but she had no one else
to ask, and since he did not work mornings except on his studies,
which he could do in the store between customers, and if he
would not mind wearing the apron for just a few hours while
she went to the Hoboken pier to meet her niece; standing there
the following morning in the empty store preparing his lesson
for the evening class on the soda counter, hearing the car pull
up outside, and—between the potted plants and the flypaper
twists hanging from the light cords in the store-front windows
—seeing her standing there on the sidewalk as Groszek helped
her aunt out of the car, seeing the bright hair under the July

sky blond above the peasant cotton and beneath the flowered babushka, and feeling for a second (just as he had felt last night in the park when Magda offered him her hand) that it was not possible that she did not recognize him; though of course (unlike last night) he recognized almost immediately that it was all foolishness—extending his hand and looking across into the unfamiliar eyes—realizing that the resemblance really ended with the long blond hair and the age, except perhaps for the look that was already there in the eyes as she looked across at him—Martha saying, "Eva, this is Pan Novak, the one I told you of who will teach the English to you before the school opens again in the fall"—a look which he must have recognized immediately that first morning, even though he refused to admit it to himself until that evening on the roof two weeks later.

During the two weeks, he found himself five nights out of the seven standing there before his beginning class in English at the Polish Home as in a dream, as in another world, as though she had not only just arrived from the old country but had brought it with her; standing there before his class of factory workers and housewives—new citizens who wished to learn to read the morning newspapers or apply for better jobs, or those just fresh from the old country preparing to file their first papers —standing there, confusing the English with the old Latin lessons in the schoolroom back in Porgorze, saying, "*Nowy* in English is *novus* . . . Ah, you will excuse me, I mean to say, 'new,' of course," or perhaps, " 'Coin' in English is not horse, not *kon*, but like when you say . . ." and going on to give the Latin instead of the Polish, and then needing to correct himself, saying, "That is to say, *pieniadz* or *grosz* even, excuse me"; trying not to look down into the eyes responsible for his confusion, which he knew of course were staring up at him even when he had his back to the class writing on the portable blackboard, knowing that she did not even see what he was writing, much less hear what he was saying.

In those two weeks she seemed to learn nothing at all about English, sitting there in the front row, blushing the few scattered times he called on her to recite, *not*, he knew, only because she did not know what he had asked much less the answer, but simply because *he* was speaking to her; knowing (and so did all the others—some of the ladies joking her right out loud there in the class so that he too would be sure to hear, saying, "You should study harder, young one. Do you not know the schoolteacher likes clever women like your aunt?" and, "You will have plenty time to make eyes at him when he is your uncle counting your aunt's money"), knowing, on that evening of the picnic in the park, sitting there on the roof smoking Sadovi's long pipe, watching the evening settle down over the smokestacks in the east, and the roof door going, and she standing there amid the sheets blowing on the clothesline; knowing exactly what was going to happen, or at least should have known, because after all it had all happened before. Now it was only the day that was different, only the words, the reading now in some old newspapers she had brought up to the roof with her in the clothes basket, spreading them flat upon the gravel and picking the clothespins off the line, the dry sheets flapping in the wet breeze blowing up from the east, tangling round her and soiling on the gravel as she tried to fold them, despite the spread newspapers; he helping her finally, saying, "You are no better with your aunt's wash than you are with your English, are you, Eva?" but she, not speaking, kneeling there on the newspapers, smoothing the pile of folded sheets, still kneeling there after he had helped her to fold them all neatly into the basket, her finger moving under a random line of newsprint, the words meaningless on her lips as she tried to render the English sounds, he correcting her pronunciation in his own still heavily accented English, kneeling there beside her, reading with her, haltingly, the two of them down on their elbows like children over the Sunday funny papers, bottoms up, their faces side by side, and all of a sudden as out of a dream, her lips all trembling on his.

She of course could not have known why he had thrust her away like that—sprawling her into the gravel—her voice still there long after she was gone—"If I had money like my aunt. If I were smart like her . . ."—the taper twist of newspaper flaming over the bowl of the grown cold pipe and the ashes blowing. She could not have known, because nobody knew. Because as far as anybody but himself knew, he was Jan Novak, except of course for the cobbler in the Krakow ghetto who on that twenty-seventh day of December, 1926, had jokingly sprinkled some drinking water over his head out of a carafe beside the bed in which he lay—his leg hoisted up in a cast—burning with fever; the old cobbler giggling, saying, "I christen you Jan Novak. I hope you will like your new name. You were unconscious and I had to tell the doctor something," telling him to try to sleep, and not to worry, that he was safe, that they had burned his clothes, and the horse was hidden in the storeroom, and that tomorrow night they would take him out of the city, and after the holidays the merchants would be traveling again to the markets in Nowy Targ and there would be news of the mountain people then, and that everything would be all right, for he had already written about him to their relative Sadovi in America—Sadovi who when he died left everything to him, not only the pipe and the tobacco, not only the tenement and the candy store and the unpaid notes and the strong boxes hidden away all over the tenement in greater profusion even than Martha's rattraps, hidden under the beds and behind the chiffoniers, and in the trunks and under the floor boards in the closets—left him not only his wife, but his wife's faith and trust and respect for himself.

Because, it seemed to him that for Martha, he was not really

Jan Novak at all, he was Sadovi, was the dead old man resur-
rected, as though for her the old man would live forever, had
simply fallen into a fit or trance or something and had waked
up again fifty years younger. He was aware of course that up
until that evening on the roof she had always looked upon him
as little more than a boy (though she was only thirty years old
herself), but he was not really surprised when she came to him
that evening, not six hours after Eva, all tears, had slammed
the roof door behind her and left him standing there as in a
dream—six hours during which he had simply sat there on the
orange crate against the chimney puffing on his pipe, and after
the sun had set over the factories in the east, looking down at
the colored lights bright around the dance pavilion in the park
below, the waltzes and mazurkas and polkas drifting up on the
damp air—six hours during which (it seems to him now) he
must have actually been *waiting* for Martha to come to him,
come to him shaking her head under her shawl over the basket
still there full of clothes and the rain on its way, saying, "She
can never do anything right, nothing," the thunder there rolling in the distance like a signal; and all of a sudden, without any
preamble, calmly and almost unashamedly confessing it all to
him as though he alone could grant her forgiveness and absolution or whatever it was she was looking for, as though it were
he and not Sadovi she had made the promise to, the promise
which with Groszek's baby in her belly she was sure she would
have to break, probably not even knowing *why* she had come
to him; knowing only that she had to tell it to someone and
he was the only real friend she had in the neighborhood; probably not knowing the next night either when she stood there
pounding at his door and he rose from his newspaper and the
table above which the rats rattled around in the wall, and found
her sobbing there, weeping about the phone call from Atlantic
City, saying, "She called me. Yes, they are married, Janush.
Janush, they are married"; no doubt thinking, when he finally

quieted her down enough to make her understand he was asking
her to marry him, to marry him right away, that he was doing
it for *her*, or for her money perhaps, or maybe even for Sadovi,
for anyone or anything other than the real reason, never dreaming (because how could she?) that he was not doing it for her
or for himself or even for the unborn baby in her belly or for
anybody who ever was or ever would be born, standing there
like that before him—her hands going in her hair as in a tangle
of vipers—absolutely screaming for abortion.

But no matter what she thought, *why* she thought he had
done it, he knew that for her he had become not the *new* husband the judge had given her in the courthouse that summer day
in 1927 but the one as far as she seemed to be concerned she
had never lost. At least that was the way it looked, and that was
the way he was happy to have it—the bedroom wall separating
their separate beds, her aspect, even before her aprons began to
belly the way they did, much too maternal for even a kiss on
the cheek or the forehead, the belly always there between them
like dotage between hundred-year-old lovers. For in the first
ten or eleven months of marriage he came to feel as though they
had lived with each other for at least half a century or more, as
though all the heat and passion of young love had been left so
far behind them as to be forgotten, as though they had already
had all that, had gone through all that together in some other
life perhaps, all the dark smoke and the searing and crackling
of young love green in the fire gone now and not even flame
left, just the small warm glow of the coals; the baby in her belly,
simply and matter-of-factly a miracle in their old age, the miracle Sadovi had prayed for perhaps, which had somehow got
delayed in its passage between the worlds and had turned up
somewhat embarrassingly late; a miracle which Martha never
allowed him to touch in her belly, and which after a screaming
and lip-biting delivery following almost three days of unspeakable labor she would not even allow the midwife to handle,

doting over it for more than six solid months like a mad woman, never taking it out of the apartment except out onto the fire escape for air.

During those six months, she never even allowed him, her own husband, to see her bathe it or dress it, much less suckle it at her breast, her bedroom door almost always locked; six months during which he had to take care of the candy store and the tenement alone and make his own breakfast, lunch and dinner, and hers too, coaxing her to eat, getting her to do so only by reminding her that her breasts would dry up if she didn't; for she had no time for anything but her baby, no time even to talk to him very much more than to remind him three times a day to check and rebait the rattraps. And it was not until the evening after Eva's death, the evening after his fortunate fall off the roof—fortunate because it was only five feet into the fire escape rather than the seven stories to the alley pavement, and though Groszek had ended up with a broken leg he (having fallen on top of Groszek) had emerged unscratched —it was not until that evening, finding her sitting there in the rocking chair in their kitchen with her own baby rocking in the cradle at her feet and Eva's baby at her breast, not until then that she smiled up at him, her eyes full of tears, saying, "Janush, I have been sick. But I am all right again. I have been such a fool. All the time I thought you must hate him because he is not yours. But now I know. How could anyone hate a baby? What does it matter who his father is, who is his mother? I do not care, Janush, just as you do not, have not all these months right from the beginning. And I know you will allow me to care for him, Janush. I know you will allow me to care for him like my own. For I have milk for both of them, Janush, for your son and for mine. And it is pure, Janush. And it is white and unsoiled, even though my soul is black"; taking his hand and pressing it to her cheek and kissing his palm, the tears weeping down her naked breasts; and that night—the babies asleep,

Roman in his cradle and Johnny in an open bureau drawer—coming to him for the first time, climbing into his bed and whispering, "I do not ask you to care for me as you did for her, Janush, the way she cared for you. But she is gone now, Janush, and there is only you and me and the children, Janush. And now I know what it was I have been blaming you for all these months. It was that I did not wish to believe you could be such a saint and marry me even with another man's baby in my belly. Because I have always known you did not do it for the money, even though I tried to tell myself you did. But now I know, and I promise you, my husband, it will be different from now on. We will make a good life together, Janush. I promise it. Because oh, Janush, I am so thankful you are not a saint. I am so glad that you have lain with her, that you are no better than *me*, Janush."

Of course, he had denied it. But it had not mattered because he knew that as far as she was concerned it was completely understandable that he should—simply for convention's sake, if for nothing else. The fact that he had never so much as touched Eva except for the kiss on the roof, the fact that he had told the truth that morning when he and Groszek toppled into the fire escape, that Groszek really did have *two* sons . . . none of it really mattered, because as far as Martha was concerned he was guilty.

And for almost nineteen years now he has lived with it, nineteen years of a good life (just as Martha had promised); nineteen years in which he looked back upon the past before his marriage as something which had happened to him in another life, a life which in time he no longer even needed to remember to forget, saying to himself that day Marya was born in the fourth year of their marriage, "You owe it to all of them not to remember, to Martha, to the boys—to Marya, your only hope, your own blood and bone. Because you have

made your choice, made it the day you decided to marry her."
In time he even got to a point where he not only spoke *of* himself as Jan Novak, but *to* himself too, telling himself, "Jan, you
are only what Martha and the children think you are, and
nothing else. Anything else you might have been that they do
not know of, was never you. Because your vocation now is to be
a husband and a father they can respect and admire, and everything that could destroy the picture of you they carry around
in their heads must be forgotten"; even agreeing after the birth
of Marya, to remarry Martha in the Church, not actually turning to the Church himself as Sadovi had, but at least allowing
the priest to say the necessary words over them in the rectory
and promising to allow Martha to raise the children as Catholics
even though he himself would remain an unbeliever. And after
that Martha stopped her constant nagging, and after that it
was all peace and forgetfulness for almost fifteen years, except
for that one day eight years after Marya was born, the day of
her First Holy Communion.

Three years earlier, the day the boys had received for the
first time all dressed up in their velvet suits and starched col-
lars (both receiving in the same month because they had only
been born six months apart), he had been sick in bed with
what the doctor called a nervous fever brought on by too much
work and so could not have attended the Sunday ceremony
even if he had wanted to. But in 1939, four months before the
war broke out in Poland, kneeling there in church for the first
time in thirteen years, watching his little daughter in the white
bridal veil and sandals kneeling at the communion rail amid
all the other seven- and eight-year-olds under the watchful hands
of the nuns, watching her head tilt over the paten and the
priest placing the host on her tongue amid the *Corpus Dómini
nostri Jesu Christi* . . . suddenly he began to weep so uncon-
trollably that he had to get up and leave the church before the
end of the ceremony—Groszek saying later after a few drinks

at the communion celebration back at the tenement, "Well, of course I wept too to see such innocence and beauty at the communion rail. But then everybody knows I am a sentimentalist. But Novak. Who would ever have thought it?"—awakening that night out of a dream with the sweat in his mouth and "Remember me" on his lips, a dream of which he could remember nothing but its terror; Martha waking beside him and starting in all over again about his acting so foolish in church being a sign of God, insisting again that if Sadovi, who was a Jew, could turn to the Church, so could he.

He simply told her that she was mistaken, that it was nothing but nerves, and that he was going out on the stoop to smoke his pipe. But instead of going out on the stoop, he climbed the seven flights to the roof in his slippers, his nightshirt tucked into his trousers under the suspenders, the light there shining up through the skylight and Groszek as usual sprawled asleep on the kitchen table below with the whiskey bottle at his elbow; and he knelt down there beside the chimney as dawn began to brighten the sky over the smokestacks in the east, whispering, "I ask You once and for all to forget me. Now and forever. Believe it, I am lost to You. All that the thing in the church meant is that I still believe. That is all. So after ten years You have got me to admit that much. But think! What does it mean? It only means that believing, I still wish nothing to do with You"; whispering, "What is it You wish of me? Why should I be so precious to You. Of all You have allowed to slip away from You, why concern Yourself with me? Is it because You know even better than I, that it was all Your fault; that I did it all for love of *You*. Well, I will tell You, You are wasting Your time, and if You do not leave me alone, despite Martha and the children, there is always the river again and this time I will not allow You to save me."

And it looked as though his prayer was answered. For during the next seven years as the horse of war rode red across the

world, he awoke every morning out of a sleep sweeter than
death, and all things came to him and he was at peace. He
had his children about him, and he could have washed his
steps in butter if he had wanted to, but instead he put on
righteousness like a robe and like a Sadovi in a diadem rode
charity like a white horse across the neighborhood, lending
money without collateral and charging little or no interest,
attracting not only those in the neighborhood who were still
afraid of banks after the crash in '29, but even the banks'
regular customers, saying, "Give me your money and I will
double it for you in a year," offering as high as twenty-five and
thirty per cent annual interest on loans made to him, and invest-
ing the money even before he got it into his hands, so that
though the strong boxes scattered all over the apartment lay
empty, there was more money than ever to be had, just as when
Martha's rattraps lay empty there were always that many more
rats in the walls. He invested the money with a shrewdness
and sureness in those boom years that even Sadovi would have
envied him. Indeed, everybody envied him, the entire neighborhood envied him, so that when he walked out of his store into
the neighborhood on his daily evening walk around town, men
tipped their hats to him and women blessed him and all gave
their ear to him and waited and kept silent at his counsel and
went away comforted. And the years spun by like a gambler's
wheel on which he never lost. And his luck seemed to rub off
on others too; for even Groszek, who insisted the prosperity in
the neighborhood was due simply to all the overtime at the war
plants and nothing else, suddenly himself got lucky at horses
and no longer sat in his kitchen under the skylight hooking on
a bottle, having bought his way not only into the Democratic
leadership of Prescott's First Ward but into a chair on the
Mayor's Council, an office for which Novak himself had been
asked to run, but which he had turned down in favor of Groszek, saying he was not a politician but a businessman and was

content with that. Yes, content. He was content even when Roman came to him on his seventeenth birthday to sign the papers; content even though it looked as though his wife would never forgive him for sending her son to war, saying, "What do *you* care if he gets killed, he is not yours. Why should *you* care?" content even when four months later Roman was shipped overseas to Germany, and Martha refused to talk to him at all because he had not kept his promise to her and gone out to pay somebody off at the army camp to keep Roman in the country; he knowing that it was useless to tell her that he could not do it if only because Roman would never forgive either of them if he ever found out about it, and that it did not really make any difference anyway since it was 1945 by then and the war was already over in Europe anyway and there was little chance of his being killed; content until that morning in January, 1946, when the letter came; content because he had his consolation.

"How round the world runs, how circular the days," he thinks now, slipping down through the cool water, his eyes lifted to a light he still believes is nothing more than the glow of the streetlamps on the river's surface. "The years wheel the sky like pigeons above the rooftops. And the breath corrupts, and the days extinguish, and grave thou art my house, and darkness my bed, and corruption thou art my father, and worm my mother, daughter and bride; and still there is no hope, no hope at all. Because once it starts to tick away inside you, it is for always and ever and even after the clock runs down, you still *are* and always will be and there is nothing you can do about it, Novak, nothing. Because even at the bottom of the river, in the deepest pit of hell, you still are, even though He has forgotten you. Because even there *He* still remembers. Maybe He does not remember *you*, but at least He remembers what you *should* have been which is really *you* after all. And so even if *she* has forgotten, *He* has not; because it was *He* who sent her." The light is bright above the water now, and it is not simply the streetlamps along the bridge any more, he knows that; knows too that it is no good to struggle, because the more he struggles the more the water lifts him, the closer the light floats downward; wondering now, *why* he had done it, why he had chosen the river. Was it because in those six months he had never once thought of it as anything else but inevitable, the inevitable and necessary last and final act of self-assertion to guarantee his being permanently and eternally forgotten? "Or was it only euthanasia?" he thinks, only self-renunciation because he could not bear the pain of living forgotten after all—not even by her; even though that had been the very thing he had yearned for for almost twenty years.

For ever since that morning he had read the letter in which her photograph was enclosed—reading it and crossing himself, something he had not done in almost twenty years, so that Martha, who was in the store with him at the time and must have noticed the foreign stamps on the envelope when the postman handed it to him, seeing him pale and for the first time since she had known him cross himself, no doubt thinking something unspeakable had happened to her son, snatched the letter out of his hand even before he had time to hide it from her, to realize what he was doing standing there like that looking up at the fan-swirled ceiling, saying, "Behold, here I am"—ever since that day six months ago he had been planning it, planning to meet her, to hear her say, "Remember me"; six months of knowing that refusing to sponsor her was like throwing dust against the wind; six months of finding himself walking past the Main Avenue movie house every evening during his customary stroll, not only after he had found out from Martha that Groszek was keeping her in the hotel over the movie house, not only during those three months that he knew she was living there, but before she had even arrived in

Prescott, every night since the letter had come; finding himself every evening walking all the way across town to the Third Ward, walking past the movie house and looking up at the hotel windows almost as though he somehow knew she was going to stay there when she finally arrived, almost as though for him she were already there. For though that had been his usual route during his evening strolls ever since he had begun taking evening strolls that year he married Martha, it seems to him now that somehow he had always known in the back of his mind somewhere that she would some day appear at the window of that hotel, that he would meet her some evening, just bump into her unexpectedly some evening, would meet her and would say, "Remember me?" and then walk back across the street, and through the trestle under the tracks and down Lexington Avenue to the Main Avenue Bridge and into the river under it.

But he never saw her—except at her window several times. And once he even walked across the street into the hotel lobby, walked in and continued right around and out again in the revolving door when he saw Groszek standing there at the desk; and finally, the night before the wedding in the park, Thursday night, he had actually walked into the lobby flower shop and bought the bouquet of white chrysanthemums and walked up to the hotel clerk and asked for her room number, the clerk ringing at the switchboard, saying, "That's going to be some wedding. The presents for 3C been coming in all day. Maybe she's in the bath or something. If you want to sit down and wait, I'll ring again in a couple minutes"; leaving the clerk standing there at the switchboard, and walking up the three flights and through the hall, 3C big on the door with the telephone ringing behind it, the knock echoing in the tight hall; standing there and knocking amid the odor of chrysanthemums long after the phone had stopped ringing, long after the neon hands on the clock across the street above the second-floor

Chinese restaurant had traversed the hour. For only after the hands had come together at nine did he realize that looking out the hall window and across the telephone wires he had not only been looking at the clock entangled in the coils of a neon green and red dragon on the restaurant marquee, realized too that she was looking right back at him, that she was even smiling at him across the telephone wires—Groszek's head there popping around the curtain and leaning over the table looking down into the street. Then the window was gone, and the hall was there and the steps—the clerk at the desk saying, "You been up there all that time. If you'd waited a minute like I said, I could of told you . . ."—hurrying out of the lobby, not through the revolving door but down the one step into the movie lobby and through it out onto Main Avenue so they wouldn't be as likely to see him if they still happened to be looking down out of the restaurant window, though God knows he could not imagine what difference it would make now since he was absolutely sure she had recognized him; thinking, as he cut across the tracks and walked back down Monroe Street toward the tenement, "It will be a simple matter now. They will not even wait to finish their dinner. They will be waiting at the tenement with the police when I arrive."

But he was wrong. Only Martha was there waiting for him, looking at him like that, saying, "You must be crazy, Janush!" when she asked him what the flowers were for (he had carried them all the way home all big and blowy in his arms without even realizing it) and he had told her that they were for her. And maybe that was it. Maybe he really had gone out of his mind. The following day, all yesterday morning and throughout the afternoon, he just stood there behind the candy counter expecting the bell to tinkle over the jamb any minute and the door to open and his life to end. He could not even remember the orders from one minute to the next, asking his customers to repeat themselves three or four times before he could remember what they wanted long enough to get it for them, not even able to make change, to remember the prices of the things he had been selling for almost twenty years; the ladies asking him, "Are you sick, Pan?" telling him, "You look pale. You have not been looking yourself for months now. You have been working too hard. You had better begin taking care of yourself." It was as though he did not even hear them; thinking, "Could it be? Could it be she does not know me? It could not be"; turning the store over to Martha at six as usual, but instead of going in to sit at the table with Marya and eat dinner, taking his cap and leaving the tenement and walking as usual across town, just walking without any particular destination in mind, thinking, "How could she? Between two panes of glass, across a street, after twenty years?" suddenly coming upon himself standing there in the dark amid the trees looking across the lighted dance pavilion, watching her in her bridal gown whirling around the floor in her stocking feet, first with the doctor and then with the Mayor and then with the doctor again; Groszek standing there at the bar in his tails and striped trousers like a pallbearer, drinking toasts with his political friends and stamping his feet every once in a while in time to the music, and the best man climbing onto the bandstand and calling for all to gather round him and making some kind of meaningless speech, distracting him just long enough to lose sight of them in the crowd, so that she and Groszek were upon him and gone even before he had time to fully realize what had happened, to realize that she had actually not recognized him, that face to face she had actually not recognized him.

He was unable to sleep at night, as usual; lying there beside Martha in the familiar bed, thinking, "It is unbelievable. Nothing has changed. Everything is just as it was before. Nothing is different. She does not ever need to know. There is no need ever to meet her again. No reason why anyone has to know— neither Martha, nor the children, nor anyone"; getting out of bed this morning and opening up the store as usual, and without any sleep at all, feeling like a new man, not even needing to sleep on his feet the few seconds or minutes or whatever between serving one customer and the next. Even Martha commented when he turned the store over to her as usual at six, saying he must have slept very well indeed last night because he looked like a new man today, saying, "You know, my husband, this is the first time I have seen you smile in six months. I have been so worried. But now that it is all over . . . Tell me it is over, Janush. I do not have to know why—because they are married or what. I do not wish you to explain anything. Only tell me that everything is going to be all right again, that you are not going to let anyone make a fool of you. Tell me, husband, because I have been so afraid."

He knew she was afraid to tell him what it was she had been thinking all these months, but he was able to guess, saying, "There is nothing to worry about, Martha. I have been a fool. I cannot explain. And I am grateful to you for not asking. But now it is all right again. Everything is going to be all right." He even joked her a little, saying, "After almost twenty years of marriage, you have to expect a man to play the fool sometime"; and she, "Oh God, I do not blame you, Janush. She must be very beautiful. I could see just from the photograph. And I know that I am not . . ." he stopping her, kissing her eyes, feeling rather foolish after doing it, saying, "We are getting a little old to be so romantic"; and she, "Oh yes, Janush. Thank God we are getting old. Old together. And soon we will both of us be too old to ever play the fool again. Janush, I pray it. It is like all my life I have been waiting only to grow old, waiting for peace, Janush, where nothing can ever happen to me any more, where everything will be behind, where only the good is there to be remembered and even the bad does not seem so bad any more because at least it is finished and done with"; and he, "Yes, Martha. For it is all over and done with now, and the rest will be growing old together, and peace, Martha, only peace."

And he supposed he had actually believed it; kissing her forehead, saying, "I will be home early tonight. I will not walk long. Just down Monroe Street. I will be home long before Marya returns from the dance"; walking down Monroe Street, thinking, "Nothing has changed," wondering how he could possibly have been such a fool all those months, when common sense alone should have told him that after almost twenty years—with a mustache, and the balding head, and the limp and everything else Time had done for him . . . "How could she possibly have recognized me? How could I ever even have dreamed she would?" walking down Monroe Street and across the tracks to Main Avenue, finding himself looking up at the hotel windows over the movie house, smiling to himself this time, thinking, "I must have been crazy with lack of sleep. If she had been there the day with the flowers, she would have probably just said, 'Oh, thank you, Pan Novak. How good of you to come like this to show that you do not really think wrong of me after all,' and that would have been it. What else could I have expected? What could I have said? Remember me? Please remember me! I want you to remember me so that my whole life will come to an end. I want you to remember so that it will all come out after twenty years, so that it will break the hearts of my wife and children"; walking down Main Avenue and across Lexington and over the bridge out of the Third Ward and into Anderson, thinking, "I should not have come so far. I promised her I would be home early, and with Marya out of the house for the evening it will be nice just the two of us together. Because nothing has changed. I should never even have come out tonight at all, because suddenly I am so tired I can hardly stay awake on my feet"; hurrying down Anderson's Main Avenue and then up Anderson Avenue to the Market Street Bridge leading back into the

First Ward, having completed the circle; thinking, "She has forgotten me completely and nothing is different. She has forgotten me completely"; feeling as though he were walking with his eyes closed, as though he were already asleep, saying it over and over again, hearing his voice as from a great way off, saying, "She has forgotten me. Forgotten me completely," marveling how after six months of thinking so foolishly, today, all of a sudden, as tired as he was, he was thinking as clearly and sensibly as he had ever thought in his life; standing there at the railing looking down into the still water as though waiting for something to appear suddenly out from under the bridge, watching his leg rising over the rail, and just smiling to himself, thinking, "Yes, I must be only dreaming after all. Because there is no reason for it now, she has forgotten me, and nothing is different. And I have the children and Martha. And we will grow old together, and there will be peace. And that is all I need now. I am just so tired . . . I feel I could sleep forever," looking down into the dark water, the streetlights mirrored in the flat surface below the bridge, thinking, "I have been thinking about the river for so long now, that I am even dreaming of it. It must be; only a dream could be so unreasonable. Because what would be the reason to do it now when there is no need for it at all since nothing at all is different, nothing has changed? She has forgotten me and all I need is a little sleep, which is exactly what I am doing now, dreaming it all away once and for all and forever. Why, today has probably not even come yet, and where I really am right now is still back in bed last night only dreaming it is today"; the water, looking solid enough to walk on, beginning to rise now, coming up to claim him lazily as in a dream, a dream almost twenty years long out of which he would wake with "Remember me" on his lips, because forgotten, he could not even bear to dream.

Chapters VII & XIX

MORNING

When old Jozef Janosz's Zofia died, all the good women of Anderson who saw him sitting there beside the coffin—sitting there with his eyes open but not seeing and with his lips going but not speaking and with the rosary beads wrapped around his hands—all of them agreed that it would have been kinder if he too had died, for surely now there was nothing for him, nothing but to sit there in the great house and wait to die himself, in the great unpainted house which he had built with his own hands and which had been fifteen long years in the building.

In the old country, Janosz had been a carpenter, a very fine carpenter, and so it had not been possible, as it had been for the others who had been only farmers, for Janosz to go to work in a factory. And since here in Anderson there was never any work for a fine carpenter, and no one could expect Janosz to go to work for one of those pushing construction companies across the river in Prescott, where there would always be some stupid Irish or Italian foreman trying to tell him how he should drive a nail, telling *him*, Janosz, who had been the finest carpenter in the entire section of the old country, how to build a house; so rather than go to work in the factory, Janosz the carpenter became Janosz the junkman, for whom there was always plenty of work.

The good women of the town would see him early every morning sitting there in his wagon under the beach umbrella, the reins loose in his hands and his mouth going with tobacco, his already tired but steady horse clopping along toward the bridge to Prescott and the towns beyond, where Janosz would ring the old cowbells strung across the wagon bed and yell in his best English, "Reksy, papiry, junky." And at night, the wagon full of old automobile tires and all kinds of rags and papers and junk, they would see him slumped there under the umbrella, probably already asleep, the wagon rumbling back over the bridge into Anderson behind the still tired but steady horse, and the old cowbells quietly rattling complines under the lamps.

There was so much work for Janosz the junkman, in fact, that it was not very long before he had sent back to the old country for his family and his good wife, and it was then that he first began making the great boast in the taverns. He would say that when his family got to America he would make sure that none of his sons ever had to go to work in a factory, and that with them helping him in his junk business he would some day build his family a great house, a regular castle, and that this house would have twenty rooms and each of them would be twice as large as any two rooms in the usual house of the town, and that he would build it all himself, with the help of his sons of course, for surely no one could dispute that Janosz had been the finest carpenter in the entire section of the old country. He would only talk like this when he had had a little too much to drink of course, and then he would sing very loudly, and show them his money and laugh at them for having to break their backs in the factories to make somebody else rich, and brag like that about the great house with the twenty rooms. And so when his good wife and his family finally came to live with him together with the horse and the junk, all in the tin-and-tarpaper shack on the edge of town at the foot of the Anderson Hill, the good women of the town would yell at him from their windows as he rumbled by in his wagon. "Pan Janosz," they would yell, "when will you invite us of the town to see your fine new house?" and, "Tell us, Pan Janosz, how does your good wife keep such a fine big house clean, Janosz? Twenty rooms, Janosz." And the men would joke him at the taverns, and so he soon stopped going to them and kept to himself, and after a while the good women even stopped yelling at him from their windows.

His good wife would tell the women at the meat market that her husband was a good man but was stubborn as a cow, and his sons would tell the Sisters at the school that though their Tata could not come to Mass with his family on Sunday morning, because that was the only free time he had to sort the junk since the rest of the week was all work from before sunup till long after sundown, that he would always say the rosary with them every night before they went to bed. But what was the good of money if you had to sacrifice your immortal soul for it, the good women would tell his wife, and what was the good of money if you could not at least enjoy it a little, when you had to live in a tarpaper shack together with a horse and a pile of junk and you never went to the beer gardens or had any friends and your young boys never even went

out to the picture houses in Prescott across the river. But they
had all of them forgotten about the boast of the great house.
And so on that morning in 1910 when Janosz rumbled down
the side of the hill and through the town toward the bridge
with the wagon full of sawed-off sections of the trunks of trees,
the good women of the town, hanging out of their windows or
coming from the grocery stores with the hard rolls and the
pickles for their husbands' lunch pails before the whistles blew
in the factories across the river, just looked, because for the
first time in over a dozen years Janosz, instead of simply spitting tobacco juice into the street as he passed, actually rattled
his old cowbells at them and tipped his battered old cap.

They soon learned that he had bought an acre of land atop
the Anderson Hill, bought it the very week after his wife had
told him she was pregnant again. And it was many months
before he had even a small section of the land cleared, and all
the good women were sure he would be dead long before the
year ended, what with his working all day with his junk business
and half the night up on the hill. But at the end of the year
he was still very much alive, and when Zofia was born his
wife told how happy he was that she was a girl because he
already had three sons and that was enough, and how he
told her that since this was the first of their children to be
born in the new country, the great house he would build would
be especially for her, and that very night he went out and
started digging the cellar of his "castle for my Zofia."

Zofia was already seven years old when the Great War came
and it was clear to all by that time that Janosz had not just
been talking when he had boasted that his house would be a
castle. It had taken him four years just to dig his cellar, and the
good women understood how terrible it must have been every
single day of that entire four years for his wife to get up in
the morning and be drawn to the window to look out on that
little hole in the side of that great hill and not be able to notice

any change at all. For there was not much one spade could do to the side of a hill in a few hours of a night, and Janosz got very little help from his sons. Two of them had to go to work in the factory in order to support the family because Janosz now put away every penny he made in his junk business for his house, and the youngest one was still going to school and was truly a lazy boy. And so Janosz had to work alone, even in the wintertime before the snow came, picking away in the frozen ground; and when the snow finally would come covering the hill and lying deep in the hole that was to be the cellar of Janosz's house, his good wife would tell how difficult it was to live with him, and that it was a crazy man who would fight with his sons like that and call them worthless and lazy when really they worked very hard in the factories to support him and his family, a crazy man who would curse at them and then stomp out of the shack and trudge up the side of the hill with the kerosene lamp and just stand there in the snow spitting tobacco juice into a hole in the ground.

And when the war came and his sons left the factory and said good-bye to their younger brother and kissed their little sister and their good mother and then trudged up the side of the hill in the snow to say good-bye to their father and went away to France and never came home again, his wife told the good women that she thanked God, yes thanked Him for taking her sons from her if that was the only way He could get her husband to give up his foolish dream. Because when the news came that first Alex had been lost and then Thaddeus, Janosz just stopped working on the hill and never even went up there for almost a year. But on the Sunday night after little Zofia's First Holy Communion there was a light up on the hill again, the light of a small kerosene lamp moving in the dark clearing atop the moon-bright hill. And then the building began. And on Sundays, which Janosz would spend almost entirely up on the hill after the junk had been sorted, he would have the company of his little Zofia, who would come home from Mass with her good mother and take off her white communion veil and white shoes and put on her overalls and sneakers and after helping her Tata finish sorting the junk would walk with him up the side of the hill to work on their house. For as Janosz would say, he could not ever hope to get it done if it was not for his little Zofia's big help, and that if his son would do even half as much work as she did, instead of spending all his time at the dances in the Prescott Polish Home and in the car of that good-for-nothing Italian girl from Prescott, whose brothers would surely make him marry her, that it would be no time at all before the work would be finished and the house done.

But the brothers of the good-for-nothing Italian girl from Prescott did not make Janosz's son marry their sister; instead, he ran away with her one spring and then there was only Janosz and his good wife and his little Zofia and the horse and junk left in the tin-and-tarpaper shack at the foot of the Anderson Hill. And then it was not long until there were only the two of them and the horse and junk, for that winter they carried the coffin out of the shack and buried it in the frozen cemetery. Old Janosz cried of course when he threw the carnation into the hole, and he cried even harder when he knelt down in the snow to wipe the tears out of little Zofia's eyes. But that night there was a light on the hill as usual, and the next morning the good women of the town began yelling out of their windows again as he rumbled out of town in the wagon. "Pan Janosz," they yelled, "how is it you found time to go to the funeral of your poor dead wife? Surely, Janosz, you cannot afford to miss a whole day away from your house," and, "Who will live in your big house now, Janosz, when your Zofia takes a husband? Your horse, Janosz?" But he just spat some tobacco juice into the street and rode on by and at night there were the cowbells rattling complines in the streets as usual and later the small light on the hill.

And when the good women sent the pastor of the Holy Rosary Church to talk to him because they were worried about Zofia's having to sleep all alone in that shed half the night there on the very edge of town, he told the pastor that surely he could take care of his own, that his Zofia was happy and they needed nothing from anybody. "Father, I send my Zofia to your school, and she has never missed Mass a single day since her Mama died. So please be so good as to leave us alone, Father. My Zofia is healthy and she is happy. All you need to do is look at her and you can see. Zofia, are you not happy?" And so the Pastor came back and told them that Pan Janosz had been very polite and that he was bringing up his daughter as a good Catholic and that surely it was his privilege to be left alone if he wished it. After that the good women of the town washed their hands of old Jozef Janosz and his little daughter Zofia, and every morning from their windows in the town they would see Janosz's house growing up out of the side of the hill, mysteriously almost, almost as though it were not really being built by a man at all.

It was, just as Janosz had promised, a truly great house. It had twenty-one rooms, and sitting up there atop the hill under the sun it looked like nothing less than a castle. The entire first floor was built of stone, and it was larger than any of the great houses of the rich in Prescott's Third Ward or in the other towns Janosz visited with his junk wagon, and it had many more balconies, and its spires were like that of a cathedral. Indeed, it was the spires which brought the men up the side of the hill that Sunday. It was spring and the trees were still without leaves. Janosz and his Zofia were working on the skeleton of the tallest spire, each of them on separate ladders reaching up from the point of the main roof. She was helping him hold the young pine tree which by custom was nailed to the highest point on the house when the frame was completed, and which when finally taken down was a sign to all that the building was finally finished and only the painting remained. Janosz was tied to the spire with ropes, and hammering, and every once in a while spitting into the wind, and so he did not even hear them when they hollered up at him. Zofia came down however and talked to them for a few minutes. They told her that they had got together at Mass and decided to come and help him with the spires, because surely this was no kind of work for a man who was no longer as young as he used to be and whose ladders were surely not the best—not to mention a thirteen-year-old girl who could get dizzy climbing so high and fall. But she simply thanked them, and said that her Tata would refuse, that it was good of them but she and her Tata needed no help and they would be done soon anyway, and then went back into the house and climbed back out of the attic window onto the main roof and back up the ladder to the spire, her pale blond hair blowing long in the wind.

And then the real spring came and the trees were no longer without leaves, and then the summer was there, and then it was gone, and by the time the first snow came the roofs were all finished, and just in time too. For it was true, Janosz was no longer as young as he used to be and now he slept slumped over the reins in his wagon every morning and did not even seem to see the women hanging out of their windows or going to the store for their husbands' lunches, for the horse knew the way as well as he—down Maple Avenue, to Main and then to Anderson Avenue and over the Market Street Bridge into Prescott. And though he still had plenty of strength, more than most men half his age, it was still plain to all that there was pain in his bones when he lifted a barrel of scrap iron into the wagon, and the good women said among themselves when they saw that the roofs were finally completed, that if there had been one more shingle to place or one more nail to drive up there in the wind, surely Janosz could not have done it, for it was certain that a man of his age had long passed the days of climbing ladders. But the roofs were finished and all the work was being done on the inside of the house, and by the time spring came round again the day finally arrived when the young pine tree could be removed from the spire as a sign that, except for the painting, Janosz's castle was finished at last.

At that point in his story the old man paused and spat against the pot stove, the tobacco juice sizzling and skittering against the glowing iron. The old gaunt skeleton of a horse, still harnessed to the junk wagon, nosed about in the haymow, intermittently and quietly clattering the cowbells strung across the wagon bed full of old automobile tires and all kinds of rags and papers and junk, and the rain was loud on the tin-and-tarpaper roof. From the pallet beside the haymow, naked and warm under the horse blanket after the hot wine—the wet tin cups empty now, sizzling and skittering on the pot stove—Novak watched the old man in the kerosene glow of the lamp, wringing out his soaking-wet clothes over the catch-buckets scattered about under the roof, and hanging them in the rafters over the stove to dry; the old man all shaking and bent over with too much age and drink, who in his junk-buying trips across the river in Prescott and the towns beyond was perhaps no longer strong enough to lift a barrel of scrap iron into the wagon bed all alone, but was nonetheless capable of dragging a full-grown and unconscious man out of the Prescott River and lifting him unaided into that same wagon bed; puttering about now and telling his story, for what reason or to make what point Novak did not even bother to consider, lying there half dozing in the old man's pallet after the warm wine, listening, the story told in the good adequate peasant Polish, the old man's healthy tobacco-stained teeth gleaming in the ancient skull, his voice rattling away again amid the rafters, saying, "It snowed that Sunday, or rather the night before. A beautiful warm moist snow that whitened the branches of the trees below the hill and the roofs of the town beyond—the first Easter snow in thirty years. And we stood there on the main roof, me and my Zofia, reaching the ladder up to the high spire and watching the good women of the town in their coats and shawls and galoshes coming down Maple Avenue past my shack and toward the hill, together with their husbands and children and dogs even, so that it looked like not only the entire neighborhood but the entire town was coming to celebrate the completion of our house. For even though from the roofs we could not see what it was they were carrying, I knew they were coming with the Easter roasts and the wine and the home-made breads I had not tasted since my good wife died. And so I did not know what to think even after my Zofia told me how just before Mass that morning she had gone and told the Sister that today would be the day of the taking down of the young pine, and how after the Gospel, the pastor had put aside his written-down Easter sermon and talked instead all about how with the aid of grace and complete faith, men could still make miracles in this world, and how with much hard work and much faith, even the poorest of our people could some day hope to build a great castle in this country, even if the castle only existed in the cathedral of his immortal soul. And as my Zofia told me of it, the church bells in the steeple of the Holy Rosary Church rang out the consecration of the Host at the noon Mass across the bridge and the valley and up the side of the hill. And then my Zofia climbed up the ladder, her long hair blowing in the wind. And as I stood there on the main roof holding the ladder against the spire, I watched her remove the young pine and stand there on the rungs waving to the good women of the town and their husbands and their children and even their dogs who were coming across the fields from the shack and up the side of the hill. And I could see them waving back. And then the snow began to slide out from under me and I could hear the good women of the town scream against the side of the hill."

He did not even cry at the funeral, he said. And all the good women of the town said many kind things to him, but he did not hear; and after the casket was in the ground, he just walked with his eyes staring but not seeing and with his lips moving but not speaking and with the rosary beads wrapped around his hands. He walked straight out of the cemetery without even saying thank you to the good women who had been so kind. And as he walked back "home" down the slush-covered streets—the first April snow in thirty years—he agreed with the women that it would have been kinder if he too had died, for surely now there was nothing for him. "And I could not understand it, I could not understand any of it. Why would a good and merciful God allow such a thing. And I tried to explain it to myself. I told myself that perhaps I had been wrong from the very beginning, that surely it had always been as my wife had said, I was a stubborn and willful man and now God had punished me. But then it was not for me to try to explain the ways of God, I told myself finally, and I spat into the snow and just sat there on the stump looking up at my Zofia's castle and thought what a good joke it would be to turn the whole thing into a stable for my horse."

And as the old man spoke, Novak could almost see him sitting there as darkness fell, spitting and thinking how he had built himself a house to die in; his castle there amid the radiant clean snow, looming big as a cathedral under the moon; the lights of the town below one after the other slowly and steadily going out until finally the whole town was dark and asleep; then the sky turning red over the hill, the great flames rosing the snow and scorching the leafless trees, and the lights of the town below one after the other coming on again, and the shouting and the running about; the good women in their shawls and overcoats and galoshes hurrying down Maple Avenue together with their husbands and children and dogs even, so that it looked as if not only the entire neighborhood but the entire town was coming to warm their hands, all of them amazed to find only the horse and the wagon and the unsorted junk there in the shack at the foot of the hill, saying later among themselves as they stood there in the circle around Janosz's castle looking up at the great devouring flames, saying it looked as though they had not only lost Janosz's miracle, but old Jozef Janosz himself.

"But they were wrong," the old man said, "because the next morning my old wagon was there in the streets under their windows as always." And as he went on, Novak did not even need to listen to the rest of it, for he could see it all himself, could see the old man slumped there under the umbrella behind the already tired and now almost unmoving horse, the reins loose in his hands and his mouth going with the tobacco; just sitting there under the umbrella paying no attention at all to the nods of the good women of the town hanging out of their windows or going to the store for the hard rolls and the sour pickles for their husbands' lunch pails, probably not even hearing the good mornings, just sitting there and spitting the tobacco juice into the cool morning air, the wagon bed full of all kinds of charred and blackened timbers and sinks and faucets and bathtubs and pipes and doorknobs and chandeliers and probably even a spire or two above which the old cowbells rattled matins in the slush-covered Anderson streets.

How he had managed to stay awake as the old man told his sentimental story, Novak did not consider. But almost immediately the old man finished, his voice rattling amid the rafters, saying, "I have been telling myself all these years that it was simply a matter of cowardice; that any real man would have set himself afire along with the house. But now I see that it was not that, after all. Because, tell me, my foolish friend, where would you be now if Janosz had done twenty years ago what you had tried to do last night, eh? Janosz would not only have set himself on fire that night, but you too, eh, my son," Novak fell asleep.

And he dreamed. He dreamed he was standing there naked beside the haymow, the horse blanket fallen to his feet, holding his hands up like a surrendering criminal; except that his thumbs and forefingers were pressed together as in the offering of the victim and he could hear the tinkling of an acolyte's bell. But when he woke again, the acolyte's bell turned out to be nothing more than the rattling of the cowbells over the wagon bed, and the old horse was still grinding away at the same mouthful of straw. And so he just lay there on the pallet under the horse blanket pretending to sleep, watching in the window above him —just as regular as clockwork, even though the war was long over—the air-spotter's beam atop the Anderson Hill washing like a huge windshield wiper across the raining sky.

It was one of those dreams that do not even need to fool the dreamer, for the dreamer knows it is not the dreaming that matters so much as the dream. From the very beginning he kept telling himself he would wake up any minute. And not on any pallet in a junk dealer's shack either, but back in his own bed in the tenement with Martha by his side; thinking, "I am just snoring away on my back dreaming this, all of it, including the business in the river. Because what reason would I have to kill myself in the first place?" Besides, he had told the junk dealer (if indeed there had ever been a junk dealer) little more about himself than his name and how he had "accidentally" happened to fall off the bridge, certainly nothing to give the old man cause to slip out into the rain just as soon as he had fallen asleep and fetch not only the police, but the soldiers from the Signal Installation on the hill, and the priests too. It was all too absurd. How could anything so improbable as the gibbeting of three practically naked men to some Signal Installation telegraph poles up on the Anderson Hill be anything else but a dream; the three of them, himself, Groszek, and, *reductio ad absurdum*, a blond and perfectly beautiful picture postcard of a Christ, somewhat immature perhaps, somewhat softened and sentimentalized but nevertheless unmistakable, hanging there like criminals on Calvary above the overgrown ruins of some old burned-out stone house just outside the army compound, their arms roped back over the crossbars amid the glass insulators and telegraph wires, and the crowds literally swarming up the hillside out of Anderson and Prescott and the towns beyond, so that the sound of their coming rose out of the valley like a huge lament, frightening rabbits out of their hillside burrows and even the garter snakes out from under their rocks; at least until *ecce homo* himself finally hurled his voice down over the crowd, at which point even the leaves ceased to stir, even the birds, and the silence just seemed to hush down the hillside and out across the towns and cities of the valley and slip up the side of the Paterson mountains blue in the distance and off into the universe itself —the voice there cajoling as birdsong amid the arboreal green, promising, "I shall exterminate poverty.

"All that humbles you and makes you long-suffering, I shall exterminate.

"I shall exterminate injustice; no mercy shall be shown those guilty of crimes against you; them and their crimes shall I exterminate.

"I shall exterminate unhappy marriages.

"I shall exterminate war.

"I shall exterminate all hatred spoken against you, all persecution.

"I shall exterminate all discomfort, all disease, and all pain.

"I shall in the end exterminate all sorrow and the source of all human tears"—the voice there promising its promises as the whispering began to rise out of the crowd like a chapter right out of Scripture, "Take him down, he is a good man," and, "No, let him save himself. If he can do all he says he can do, why does he not come down?" And even the pastor was there among them like one of the Pharisees—though too old and feeble and racked with illness to go about tearing his robes—crying, "Blasphemy!" his cancerous unnatural voice hurling itself out over the crowd from his sedan chair in the wagon bed of old Jozef Janosz's junk wagon, crying out, "It is written, if anyone say to you, 'Behold, here is the Christ!' or, 'There He is!' do not believe it. For false Christs and false prophets will arise and will show great signs and wonders, so as to lead astray, if possible, even the elect"; Novak thinking, as his own lips moved on the words, "I have put the words into their mouths myself, every one of them, because they are all only part of my dream, and I am responsible for the *pro* as well as the *contra*"; the man calling down from his telegraph cross again, saying, "If anyone thirst, let him come to me and drink. If anyone hunger, let him come to me and eat"; and then suddenly as out of a clear blue sky Magda's voice there (for they were all there, Martha, Marya, Johnny and Magda too) calling up to him from the clearing below, asking, "Who are you? Who? Tell us once and for all, is it really You?" and as a great black cloud rose out of the burning garbage dumps in the valley below, he answered her, saying, "Woman, behold thy son"; and as the sun darkened and the curtain of the temple was torn down the middle, he cried out in a loud voice, "I am who am not!" and came unaided down from the cross.

And so now he is alone up here. For they have taken Groszek down, Groszek who just a few minutes ago still dressed in only his undershorts and socks climbed up a ladder to him and tried to convince him to join them, saying, "I do not believe all those campaign promises any more than you do, my friend. But anybody with any sense knows that it is stupid to try to go against public opinion. Use your head, Novak, get on the bandwagon, cast your vote with us. What can you lose? Even a janitor's job in the City Hall is better than rotting up here on a telegraph pole"; Groszek, who now, all dressed up in his wedding tails and striped trousers again like a professional pallbearer, his cigar smoking in his mouth and fanning himself with his Panama, leads by the halter down the winding hillside road the gaunt gray skeleton of a horse, old Jozef Janosz sitting useless on the wagon seat under the beach umbrella, the reins wrapped loose around the hands in his lap, and behind him, standing tall in the wagon bed on the left hand of the helplessly protesting pastor's chair, The People's Choice himself, all dressed up now in tails and gray gloves like a bridegroom or an undertaker, smiling through his beard and like the piper in the tale or Nero while the world burns, scraping away on Nowicki's old fiddle; the huge impossible crowds strung out behind the wagon snaking down the hillside to the fiddled strains of "Here Comes the Bride," and out into the streets of Anderson and under the Erie trestle to the sand pits and the city dumps where the huge fires blaze out over the garbage fill and over the flotsamed slick floating on the pond, so that the water itself seems ablaze and a stench like roasting flesh steams out over the cities and rises black over the hill, the horse and wagon like some neon dragon over a Chinese restaurant going red and green and black, hub-deep amid the flaming waste, the crowd following behind, ravening in the garbage heaps like Romans at a wedding feast, gorging and orgying, rolling swollen-bellied and belching amid the cast-off shawls and shoes and underclothes, amid the million broken whiskey bottles and the boxes empty of cigars, amid the million mucked-up condoms and syringes and diaphragms and toilet bowls and kitchen sinks and bureau drawers and broken-headed Kewpie dolls and carriages and rockless horses and worn-out automobile tires and license plates and all kinds of rags and papers and junk; men, women, children and beasts all wedded together in a tangle of arms and legs and claw and hoof, feeding and fornicating, vomiting and voiding, as the fiddler walks slowly out over the burning water and like some Grand Exterminator living up to an unconditional guarantee, stands there in the steaming center of the pond summoning them all festering and hemorrhaging like rats in a plague, summons them, in one total and ultimate act of euthanasia, into the bubbling, charitable soup of suicide.

Looking up into the darkness, Novak thinks at first that he is looking up into the face of Old Sadovi, grotesquely lighted grinning down at him from heaven or hell or wherever, his too-large store teeth gleaming in the withered old face like a skeleton out of a closet, saying, "How do you feel, my boy? The fever is over, eh?" But it is only the junkman he realizes, somewhat disappointed to find himself back on the pallet in the shack at the foot of the hill rather than in his own bed back in the tenement, the old junkman leaning over him with the kerosene lamp glowing under his chin, saying, "You will dress and have some breakfast, and then Janosz will drive you home in the wagon"; the wagon still there under the tin-and-tarpaper roof, still full of old automobile tires and all kinds of rags and papers and junk, the same wagon he had spied way off in the improbable distance of his dream floating toward him after the flotsamed water (in accord with all the laws of displacement) had flooded up out of the pit and out over the entire valley and the hill, flooding into his mouth as he tried to call out, covering him, so that it was not until long after he was sure he had already drowned that the light appeared shining above the surface of the waters and the hand reached down for him, old Jozef Janosz's hand, reaching down for him out of the floating junk wagon, the old gaunt horse unharnessed there in the wagon bed behind him, and the ailing pastor there too seated in his sedan chair like a sultan, a huge white rooster crowing away on his shoulder over the charred and blackened timbers and the sinks and faucets and bathtubs and pipes and doorknobs and chandeliers and even a spire or two, big as any cathedral's, the old cowbells rattling matins amid the sound of trumpets blowing about the far four corners of the silent world—which as it turned out of course was only the Signal Installation loudspeaker blowing reveille up on the Anderson Hill; the raining sky beginning to brighten now behind the window above the pallet, a lone rooster crowing away outside in some chicken yard somewhere, and the old man over by the haymow hitching up the horse, spitting into a catch-bucket under the leaking roof, saying, "Tell me, my son. Who is it you want so bad to remember you?"

Chapters VIII & XVIII

NOON

In a churchyard cemetery in a remote and forgotten region of the western Carpathians, Pani Marya Baranek remembers, knecling now just as she has knelt every Sunday for almost twenty years after hearing ten-o'clock Mass and just before starting home to finish preparing the Sunday dinner she had begun at the crack of dawn—the roast going into the oven just before she left for Mass—though it would not be eaten until two-thirty or three that afternoon, when the assistant pastor bicycled the half-mile down from the rectory to the Baranek cabin to join her husband and herself at table. She remembers all of it, kneeling here before a monument erected to the memory of her husband's only son, lost (along with her first husband) in the frozen Dunajec on Christmas Day, 1926.

Her husband, whom she had married a short year after the tragedy and who now sits in the wagon behind the single gaunt horse, smoking his long pipe and spitting into the gravel path waiting for her to finish her prayers, had told her all about his son; told her in fits of drunken and weeping rage all that she had not had time to learn from his son himself during his short year in Porgorze, but which during the eighteen or nineteen years she has had to think about it now she has come to feel she had always known, had known the first time she had ever set eyes on him that winter of 1925, known that he must truly have been destined for the priesthood from birth, that he most certainly must have been weaned on the lives of the saints, and that the first intelligible sound to issue from his lips other than the customary infant wailing must surely have been not "Mama" or "Tata" but *"Boze,"* not "go" or "ga" but "God." Indeed, in the years since the tragedy she had come to make little if any distinction between what her husband had told her in drunken ingeniousness and what she herself had learned directly from the lips of his son himself—not to mention what she and the other good women of the parish had *invented* to tell about him—so that she had come to look upon the story of the "first word" as having come to her not from the lips of the father but of the son, who, she was careful to have her lady friends understand, surely did not believe the story himself but nevertheless loved to pretend he did, cherishing as one might a birthright the memory of this tale his drunkard father used to publish about the taverns of Krakow when his son was still a boy, along with various other boasts about how his son would surely grow up to become a bishop some day if not indeed a cardinal or perhaps even (why not?) Pope.

Believing that she had first heard the story from the lips of the son allowed her to endow with some aura of sanctity a story which she felt was much too beautiful to dismiss completely

and so she refused to allow herself any more than a suspicion
that it might after all be only the ravings of a good-for-nothing
drunkard, invented simply to pander to her own teary-eyed senti-
mentality and thereby win his way into her dead husband's
homemade whiskey supply and consequently, as he henceforth
bewailed, into her bed. As he told it, she had veritably led him to
the altar dangling a whiskey bottle before him like a carrot on
a string, just as his first wife had led him to the altar dangling
not a whiskey bottle before him but her bed, the only difference
being that in the first instance the whiskey bottle had turned out
to be the consequence rather than the lure. For as he had told it
to Marya in the hour of their mutual bereavement, it was the
pleasures of his first wife's bed and the fruits of that pleasure
which had lured him from his true vocation and caused him to
seriously take up the business of becoming a drunkard instead.
Indeed, even she, who had had some twenty years' experience
with a drunkard (her first husband was as accomplished an im-
biber as he was a distiller), had to admit that Pan Baranek was
truly an inspired drinker, that he had been, as it were, truly
"called." He had grown as fond of the bottle, he assured her, as
he had once been fond of his wife's bed—or to put it more deli-
cately as he was wont to do in those early days, apologizing to
her, the bereaved widow, amid drunken flourish and bow—as
he had once been fond of his wife, his little sixteen-year-old
Jewess, which fondness had led him to ruin his life, had turned
him away from God and his vocation in His Church and left
him with nothing but the consolations of the whiskey bottle and
of course a son whose birth had been responsible for his
mother's death and who through no fault of his father's—who
was usually too drunk in the Krakow taverns to do very much
more than boast about him to his drinking friends, leaving the
business of his upbringing to his dead wife's relatives in the
Krakow ghetto—happened to finish grammar school at the age
of ten, graduate from the seminary at sixteen, and at the age of

twenty-two be ordained a priest of the Holy Roman Catholic Church.

It was at the celebration following his son's ordination, he told Marya, that in a fit of wet-eyed rapture and remorse he had first confessed his monstrous sin, confessing aloud before the entire assembly of friends and prelates, that before his son's birth he had actually prayed to God that both his wife and his son would fail to survive the delivery so that he might return to the seminary he had deserted and resume his abandoned studies. As he told it to Marya, it was actually the most glorious day of his entire life, standing right up there at the banquet table with all those big churchmen listening to him, telling them that God had seen fit to answer only half his prayer, and had committed him to drink away the rest of his life in the horror of it. Every drink he took, he said, was a toast to his damnation. Because on that day of all days when he should fall on his knees and thank God for allowing his criminal and dissolute existence to bear such glorious fruit, in all the joy and pride he took in his son's ordination, he still could not help wishing that his prayer of twenty-two years ago had been answered *completely*. He simply could not help himself, he told the company. For no matter how he tried, he simply could not help feeling it was his son who had ruined his life for him, for it was after all his son's growing there in his mother's belly which caused him to give up his studies at the seminary, give up his true vocation and to become nothing but a husband and a father, and not a husband for very long. He told how he had assured the august body that he had considered the possibility many times over that perhaps it was simply because he was doing so poorly at the seminary that he had become attached to his son's mother in the first place, that he had not really been "called." However, he would leave such complex matters for them to decide among themselves, since after all he was simply a humble drunkard and did not pretend to know the mind of God, as most assuredly his august listeners did. "Still, perhaps there is some kind of chance for a good-for-nothing like Baranek," he told them. "Who can say that it was not my drinking all these years, my corruption and dissolution which is responsible for turning my Piotrush to the Church. Who knows, perhaps some day my son will achieve a prominence in the hierarchy from which he will look down and order the rest of you to drag me into heaven despite myself. Perhaps for some of us there *is* no other way to heaven but through the neck of a whiskey bottle. But be that as it may, gentlemen, you have your vocation and I am left with mine. And wherever it is I finally receive my reward, I am sure I will meet a good many of you there. Shall we drink on it, gentlemen?"

At least that was the way he told it to her, and knowing him, Marya could accept it without a great deal of qualification just as she knew she could believe the rest of it—about the letter for instance, the letter in which his son, the fall following his ordination, told him that he was studying medicine at the university in Lublin preparing for missionary work in China, the letter to which he replied that a priest's career in the Church was as good as finished if he allowed himself to be buried away in some rice field on the other side of the world, and that it was his son's business to see to it that he somehow got himself transferred out of the university and into a parish in Lublin or Warsaw or Krakow, a parish in which he could make a name for himself and rise in the hierarchy of the Church. His son wrote back that he of course agreed with his father but surely his father must realize that his vows of obedience prevented his doing anything other than what he was then doing. However, in the spring of 1925, though he had been one of the most brilliant students at the university, his son wrote him that he had failed his qualifying examinations in oriental medicine and would be home for a visit prior to taking up his new assignment in Porgorze. He greeted his son warmly at the home of his relations in the Krakow ghetto and joked about how unhappy he was he had failed his examinations, but that surely it was a sign he was destined for something bigger than a rice-field parish in China. Of course, a little mountain village in the Carpathians was not exactly on the main road to Rome, but with industry and ambition the petty jealousy of his superiors could be overcome—for there was no doubt about it, envy among his superiors had caused his son's exile to the Carpathians. The Church after all was run by mere mortals and one had to expect "politics." However, with industry and ambition his son might cut a road to Rome even through the remote and desolate Carpathians. And that was how it came to pass, Marya learned, that in the late fall of 1925, in the season of Advent, Father Piotr Baranek came to be the assistant to the ailing pastor of the parish of the Holy Family in Porgorze.

She had not known any of this, of course, that day she first met the new assistant. The name Baranek then was as strange to her as it is now familiar. But the moment she saw him that day at the rectory door—taking his bags and half curtsying and dismissing the shepherd who had volunteered his time and his sleigh to drive the new Father the thirty miles up the mountain roads from the train station in Nowy Targ—she knew immediately that somehow he was not like the other assistants who had come and gone during her forty years in Porgorze, almost twenty years of which, ever since she was a child old enough to help her mother with rectory chores, had been spent in addition to marrying and bearing four children, two of which had died at birth, cooking and washing and cleaning at the rectory and tending to the church altar and the sacerdotal robes, since there were no resident nuns at Porgorze. It was nothing he had said or done particularly. He had simply smiled and thanked her for taking his bags and showing him up to the ailing pastor's room. It was just the way he looked, she supposed; later that evening around the supper table spooning the cabbage soup out of the pot into her husband's plate, saying to her daughter loud enough so that her husband might hear, since she never spoke directly to her husband any more or he to her unless they were arguing; saying, "It is just something about him. I do not know. Perhaps it was just the way he walked into the rectory like he was not only the assistant pastor, but the pastor himself. And yet he is so young, he almost looks like he does not even need to shave. I do not know how I can ever bring myself to confess to such a boy"; her husband laughing between the spoonfuls of soup, saying, "I do not know what your Mama is worried about. The only sins she needs to confess to him are the ones they commit together there in the rectory. The ones she commits with the pastor, she can confess to the pastor as usual"; and she, wiping her hands on her apron and hustling her daughter off to her bed in the loft, saying, "Husband, I know you do not respect me, but think of your daughter. What kind of talk is this in front of a fifteen-year-old?" and the argument beginning as usual until he would finally rise from the table and go slamming out of the cabin and out to his horse and his bottle in the barn, leaving her to weep into her apron as her daughter came back down from the loft and standing behind her chair removed the combs from her hair; sitting there at the table feeling her daughter's hands running the combs through her long chestnut hair flecked with the soft silvery traces of age; no longer weeping now because she had not really been seriously weeping in the first place, since she was quite used to her husband and his talk, and though she might not ever have actually gone so far as to admit it to herself she actually needed if not enjoyed his accusations, which were of course totally untrue, as she knew very well her husband realized, weeping for no other reason perhaps than sorrow at how absurd and utterly remote was the possibility of her ever even psychically justifying her husband's accusations.

Because God knew, if she was *anything* she was not that kind of woman. Everyone knew she was a good and faithful wife and mother and a devout woman of the church. She had never once in her entire life ever looked at a man the way her husband implied she did. Why, she had never even looked at her own husband that way, not even when they were first married, and it was only in the filthy mind of a drunkard that the thought that a woman could actually think such things, that a woman could actually enjoy such filth and look for it . . . only in the mind of a good-for-nothing drunkard could such a thought even come to be (why, if he had seen her kissing the feet of Christ Himself he would probably accuse her). Before they were married, while he was still courting her, he had never had such thoughts. He had never even tried to touch her. He had married her for her beautiful long hair, he had told her, and for her chastity. And only after they had been married for a while, only after he had begun to drink the plum brandy he distilled, did he begin to accuse her of such nonsense, going so far as to say, "I do not even think any of them are mine. Why should I? Four children in twenty years, and we have only been to bed together *three* times." Which of course was completely untrue, because from Marya's point of view it seemed he hardly let her alone for a minute those first few years of their marriage, and every night it was the same old thing, closing her eyes and pretending to be already asleep and waiting for his mustache against the back of her neck, until of course he eventually got to be so fond of his bottle he was usually already asleep even before he had time to remove his trousers and crawl into bed beside her, or would fall asleep by the fire, bottle in hand; and in the last fifteen years, ever since the birth of their daughter, he no longer even slept in the bed with her, sleeping out in the barn instead with the sheep and the cow and the horse, "out in the barn with the rest of the animals," Marya would say, "where he belongs."

Through the open kitchen window and across the yard beyond the plum orchard she could hear the horse whinnying and stamping in the barn as she told her daughter about the new assistant, feeling the comb smooth as sleep playing through her hair, trying to imagine that the flecks of silver in the strands she fingered were just an illusion of the kitchen light, for though she knew her hands were wash- and dish-worn and her legs were blue with veins and swollen thick about the ankles, nevertheless, there was still *something* in her face she told herself whenever she found time to steal a look into the single mirror over the bureau in her bedroom, whenever her hair was down and dark around it; *something* that was not there when she wore her hair bunned severely up in combs during the day, *something* she knew would not be there when it was no longer chestnut flecked with gray but the other way round; saying, "Yes, you will meet him tomorrow in the school and then you will see. How I wish our Jan would have gone on to the seminary. But he is like your Tata. Both of them, all they know is horses and the bottle. For what do they need the cavalry at the border? There is no war. At least if he would write sometime. He probably does not even wear his scapular any more"; realizing that she was digressing, saying, "He is very smart. I can tell it just to look at him. And he will teach you the Latin and the rest, and when you take the veil, my darling, you will not have to be a scullery maid. You will be a teaching Sister, and in time, who knows, maybe even a Mother Superior. Because I can tell it just to look at him. Because he is somehow different. He will change everything in Porgorze. I can tell it just to look at him."

It was as though she had mouthed a prophecy, for in the little mountain village of Porgorze, with the old pastor devoting so much of his time to nursing and cherishing what he called his "beloved cancer" and unable to do much more than hear confessions and serve his daily Mass, Father Piotr found himself called upon to minister not only to the minds and souls of his flock—hearing confessions, and serving Masses and teaching in the school—but since the nearest town was located almost thirty miles away over mountainous terrain accessible in winter only by sleigh, he had also to minister to the physical body of his parishioners—tending the colics, the snakebites and the thousand and one ailments of the mountain community, not to mention assisting the harassed midwife during particularly complicated births—the midwife being Marya herself. Furthermore, he organized a Third Order of St. Francis for the women of the parish of which Marya was president, a Living Rosary Society of which Marya was vice-president, a Rosary Confraternity of which Marya was financial secretary, a Sacred Heart Society of which she was recording secretary, and a St. Anne's Society of which she was treasurer. For the children of the parish, he organized a Children of Mary Sodality of which Marya's daughter was assistant to the moderator, an Ave Maria Choir in which Marya's daughter sang a sweet and angelic alto; and for the men of the parish, he organized a Holy Name Society of which Marya's husband was conspicuously not a member. On Sundays the new assistant's sermons hurled themselves about the eaves of the little village church and seemed actually to bring down the reproof of heaven upon the heads of those who distilled or drank or were less disposed to constant church activity than Marya and her like, those who were, as he put it, "the slaves of gluttony and sloth." And more than one drunkard confessed to his wife that the new Father had actually denied him absolution and forbidden him the Host unless he promised to give up drinking completely. Indeed, all the good women of the parish agreed with Marya that the young assistant pastor was truly a godsend to the flock.

The men it seemed had certain reservations, however, as did the women of the parish who might be considered something other than "good." Marya had known from the very beginning of course that Father Piotr was not exactly a popular confessor.

However, it was not until that afternoon late in the month of July almost eight months after he had taken up his office that she first realized how serious the situation had become, at least as far as Father Piotr himself was concerned. But that was not all she came to realize that afternoon. For ever since the old pastor had, several months before, taken to his bed permanently with his affliction, the number of parishioners who confessed and received communion daily and on Sundays had fallen off considerably. By the time July was there, the only man in the parish who continued to receive the sacraments regularly each week was the church organist, who was a bachelor and not a drinker and as far as most of the other men in the parish were concerned, not even a man. Indeed, the only members of the parish regularly seen at the altar rail on Sundays were the younger children of the parish and the older women, and of course Marya and her daughter. And on that particular Saturday afternoon in late July, the church was nearly empty as usual when Marya emerged from the confessional and recited her penance at the altar rail. And later, standing at the sink in the rectory kitchen mixing the flour and water in a pot, she heard him come in from the sacristy and climb the stairs to the pastor's room, and with the flue open in the fireplace could hear them through the common chimney connecting the kitchen fireplace and the fireplace in the room above; taking her batter and sitting in the July heat on the bench beside the fire, mixing and listening, the voice of the pastor, who was a little hard of hearing, descending loud and raucous down the flue.

"It is because you are so hard on them, my son. So the parish is famous all over the Carpathians for its drinking. What does it matter? It is not because they drink that they sin. It is because they sin that they drink. You cannot stop it by refusing them absolution. It just gives them more to drown in the bottle."

She could imagine the pastor sitting there in his bed against the pillows puffing his cigar and sipping his plum brandy every once in a while, the smoke circling his head like a halo, as he laughed.

"Do not worry, my boy. It will be all right again in time. In the end you will not lose a single one. But it takes time for them to get used to you, to your heavy hand. Just as it will take time for you to get used to their backsliding. And it will do you no good to protest, for I have already written to the bishop. No, no, never mind. I told you it will do no good. I am an old man; I am used to having my own way. Yes. Believe me, my son, some day you will smile at all this. Yes, there will come a time when you will lie here in this bed just as I am lying now, and God willing with as fortunate an affliction. (Yes, yes, I have seen to it and it will do you no good to protest.) And by that time, you too will perhaps have learned the consolations of a good cigar and a finger of brandy. You will lie here and blow a half-century of wisdom about the head of some young assistant, who if God has mercy on these humble people will perhaps show as much promise and zeal as you do, my boy. And just as you are doing now, he will beg you to reconsider, and you will say, 'But I am an old man, and I am used to having my way, and what is done is done.' You will tell him that you too once hoped to get a parish in Krakow or Lublin, that you too thought it was your destiny to some day serve Mass in the cathedral at Rome, but that an old priest puffing on a cigar and teetering on the very brink of eternity told you that Rome is where the heart is, and you were much too solemn in those days to even smile at an old man's foolish pun."

"Father, with your permission. I shall return when your mood is more serious."

"So, you see! Even the pastor is subject to your reproof. Forgive me. No, no. It does not matter. Do not apologize. I know you mean no disrespect. After all, you are right, you know. This is a serious matter. It is just that I myself have been through all of it myself and so . . . well, it is difficult not to at least smile. However, I know for you it is a serious matter. And so it is. So it is. Yes, how the old world grinds and grunts on its axis when we are young and devout, eh? How out of tune with the music we hear. Eh, yes, I know. In time, however, you find your ears become attuned to it, and what you heard as discord before, you find is harmony after all, and the sweet thin music of innocence in time becomes so rich and full and overwhelming, there is nothing else to do but smile. Believe an old sinner, there is no help for it. Ah, but I see you have no wish to indulge an old fool in his heresy. Yes, I know where such thinking can lead. We have been through all that many times before in these past eight months. And perhaps that is precisely why He chooses to take me now, before my senility leads me into the heretical maze. But have no fear, my son, I am too old for revolutions. Mine is the way of acceptance, of infinite resignation. And if I accept too much, if I am perhaps too resigned—well, there will always be those like yourself who lean off the other edge of the razor. The Church is catholic, there is room in it for all of us.

"Perhaps that is why He sent *you* to me, to them out there. Perhaps I have not really been enough for them—though I will go to Him convinced that I have not lost one of them, not a single one. It is my consolation here at least. Yet who knows, when I step into my cathedral up there (you see I am an incurable optimist), who knows, perhaps I will find a few of the back pews empty. It could be. And though I digress, the fact remains that in less than a year you have done more for the physical well-being of my parish than I have done in fifty. All right, perhaps I exaggerate a bit. But how much can one man be expected to do in the short time you have been with us? So what does it mean? Does it mean you should be sent to another parish, larger, more responsibilities, where your talents can be used? Perhaps. But I have taken it upon myself, and God will judge me if I am wrong. The empty confessional means nothing.

In time it will work itself out. Even without the crowded altar rail on Sunday it is still clear that He pours down His grace upon your parish. Yes, *your* parish. They *work* for you, my boy. The new school will be a monument to your zeal. I only pray I live long enough to see the ground broken. But that is another matter. Perhaps all they have needed all along was a sterner hand than mine. I had thought a new school was hopeless, but already it is almost reality. They may not tell you their sins, my boy, but they give you their money and their time. And in time they will change you, and the altar rail will be full again and there will be a new school too, eh?

"Yes, it will just be a question of time, of getting used to each other. Here on the mountain away from the world you will get to know every one of them like a son or a daughter, and you will come to think that the responsibility for their souls is yours alone. But I would caution you on this. You must not allow your children to overwhelm you. They will ask for more than any one man can possibly give. And you will in time find it so necessary to be needed, that you will revel in their need like a drunkard and come to think your power to give of yourself is unlimited. I see it already, my boy, and you have not even been here a year. And so I caution you not to allow yourself to be devoured by them. Remember that one day you will lie here like me and another will come to take your place, and you will warn him that one day he too shall pass away. Remember that you must not indulge yourself. That you cannot give all of yourself no matter how great their need, no matter how much you may long to. You must remember that each time they call on you, you must cheat a little, save a little of yourself for yourself, saying each time, 'All right, I grieve with you, I weep with you, I minister to you and cure you, but I cannot climb up on the Cross for you, not that.' Because you must remember, if Peter had not denied Him, not once but three times, there would not even be a Church today to which they can turn. Remember, that no matter what they will expect from you, no matter what you *think* they expect from you, you are not Christ. You are only a man after all, only Peter's brother at best. And you must not only deny Him three times before the cock crows, but three times three, and more. And the cock crows every single morning."

There was nothing for a while, and Marya's stirring began again, the wooden spoon knocking against the pot, the unleavened dough thickening, the young voice there in the fireplace softer than the pastor's so that she had to lean into it to hear, the sweat pouring down her face as she listened.

"You are not speaking of me, Father. As usual you speak only of yourself. You judge me in terms of your experience. But you forget I am not *you*. I am different. And you are not me, and you do not understand."

He must have been pacing about the room, for she could hear his footsteps overhead and then his voice would die away and then come back again so that she could hear only fragments of his conversation, and even the fragments were not always clear because his voice was naturally soft and only in the pulpit did it boom out across the church, hurling itself around the arches and up into the choir loft. What she did hear, however, she put together into something that made perfect sense in her own mind. She felt she knew exactly why he was so desperate to be sent out of the parish. And it was certainly not what he was trying to make it out to be for the pastor's benefit; saying, his voice clear and close again in the fire, "Suppose I were to tell you, Father, that I do not deserve to be a priest. That really I despise being a priest, or at least a parish priest. That I despise the parish. That I despise almost every single one of them out there. That it is not a question of getting a larger parish in a city. That I really have no ambition to rise in the hierarchy of the Church. That all I want is to be left alone with Him, to go out into the desert and be alone with Him, just He and I alone with no one."

"Well, what I would say is that if what you say is true, then if you went into the desert you would indeed be alone, because He would not be there. For you would simply be indulging yourself. The Desert Fathers went out of the world because they loved it too much, not because they despised it as you say you do. They were not indulging themselves but mortifying themselves. But for you, if what you say is true . . . and quite frankly I will tell you now, that I do not believe what you say, not because I believe you are lying to me, but because you simply misinterpret your intuitions . . . if what you say is true, then you are indeed blessed with your vocation; because you are given a chance to mortify yourself for Him and at the same time help His children perhaps more than most of us. For you have a talent, a capacity for doing good works much beyond that of the average young priest or even an old one like myself. But as I say, I do not really believe you long so desperately for the desert. It is after all the old story all over again. You wish a personal contact with Him, just you and He alone. But so do we all, my son. Even the biggest drunkard in the village. The drunkard no less than the saint, is mortifying himself, trying to find Him in the desert bottom of a whiskey bottle. It is the same old story. Though we all know better, or at least should know better, we cannot help feeling that it is the body of the world which comes between us and Him. And like some naïve Platonist we begin to think of the world itself as evil and we despise it, simply and only because we are so desperately in love with it. As though somehow this must mean we have less time to love Him, instead of seeing that every act of love is a sacrament, instead of living our everyday normal lives, even to the business of emptying the chamber pot, as a sacrament. Only then is the Epiphany possible. Only after we have come to accept His creation, the world in which He Himself walked and wondered, the body in which He Himself breathed and bled."

"*His* creation I can accept, Father. He created Eden and

Adam in it. But it was Adam created the world just as sure as Satan created hell. And it is the world I cannot accept."

After that, there was nothing for a while, and she could not tell whether it was because they had both fallen silent above, or whether perhaps Father Piotr was still talking but had moved away from the fireplace again, hearing his footsteps above her moving across the ceiling and then back again.

"Give yourself time, my boy." It was the pastor again. "It will work itself out." And then another long silence, and Father Piotr, "But, Father, I have been dreaming."

"Well, good. It makes the nights more interesting. Let me tell you, since the German has given me the sleeping powders I have not had a single dream I can remember in the morning. Believe me, it makes for a very dull night in retrospect. But I suppose there is no help for it. What can I do? It is either the sleeping powders or the drugs. He is a very impractical man, the German. He cannot understand when I tell him I am grateful for every little twinge of pain He will consent to send me."

"Father, I have been dreaming of the flesh."

"Ah, so that is your problem, eh? At last. Why did you not say so in the first place instead of wandering all over the map. So, the contact with the women of the parish is giving you bad dreams, eh? Well, what did I say, eh? Deep down inside, you are a sensualist after all. Pah, do not be a fool. Do not let it bother you. It is natural. This is not the seminary. You are a handsome boy—firm as Peter perhaps, but beautiful as the brother of James. It would be a shame if some of the hussies of the parish did not flirt with you a little. Come, you can tell an old sinner . . ."

"Father, you *must* write to the bishop again."

"No no no, my boy, that will not be necessary. Why, even the saints have bad dreams. In more naïve times they used to throw shoes at them. Now we know better, or think we do. Perhaps we should go back to throwing shoes at them to remind us that they are merely physical after all, merely something we ate. You are a man, my boy, not a eunuch. As I have told you as your confessor, it is scrupulosity, nothing more. You want perfection, my boy. You will not tolerate adulteration. You insist on sainthood or nothing and cannot accept the physical corruptible body of the world. But you will learn. Besides, you exaggerate. Well, enough of this. Suddenly I am very tired. We will talk more tomorrow. And do not worry about the confessional, in time it will work itself out."

When she finally sat back, she felt her face was scorched, and the perspiration poured down her neck and she could feel it running between her meager breasts under the housedress and apron. But it was not only the heat of the fire, it was also what she had heard. Because, could it be? Was it possible? She was not sure whether she was merely blushing to think of it, or whether her face really was scorched in the flames, looking at herself in the bottom of a pan, as she stood there at the sideboard molding the dough and shaping it into the wafer tins for the morning communion, thinking, "It could not be simply coincidence. Not even three days after the dinner." It was not as though he had not had dinner at her home many times before; he had dined with them at least once or twice every month on Sunday afternoons. But he had never dined with them in the evening before, and never when her husband was at table, for her husband never joined them for Sunday afternoon dinner. On this occasion, however, the fifteenth anniversary of her daughter's name day, her daughter had insisted that her Tata celebrate with them, and though the last thing in the world her husband would ever consider doing was sharing one of her dinners with a priest, there was nothing he would not do for their daughter, except perhaps give up his bottle or say a decent word to her mother, which of course was the case that evening, for though he came to the table washed and shaved for a change and not smelling of sheep and horses, there was nevertheless whiskey on his breath though he had promised his daughter on *that* one evening he would forget his bottle completely; sitting down at the table rather sheepishly at first because it was obvious that he had had even more than usual to drink, the three of them at the table, her husband, her daughter and the good Father; she bringing the lamb roast and placing it not before her husband, because as drunk as he was she was sure he would make a mess of the carving, but in front of Father Piotr, who always did the carving whenever she had him in on Sundays. And that was the beginning of it, her husband smiling under his mustache as the Father carved, saying not to her or to the Father, but to their daughter, saying very softly in a nice relaxed conversational tone, "So you see what it has come to, my angel?" writing absently with his fork upon the tablecloth. "In my own house I am only a guest. At my own table. Well, so it goes. Maybe she has married *me* instead of the Church as she had hoped, but nevertheless it is the Church she lies with in the rectory."

His voice did not change, and his mustache still curved in a grin, and when she dropped the gravy bowl and just stood there with her hands over her mouth as though it were she herself who had uttered the words, he simply continued to write absently on the tablecloth with his fork, and if Pani Babka's Jozef had not burst in at the front door at that very moment she could not think what she might have done; Pani Babka's Jozef begging her to hurry because his wife sounded as though she were about to breathe her last, standing there in the doorway with his cap in his hand bowing to the Father, saying, "I am sorry to interrupt your dinner, Father," and wishing her daughter a happy name day, the poor man pale as a ghost, after five children just as pale and frightened as if it were the first; the Father offering to go with her and help in the delivery, but she telling him that it surely would not be necessary, that Pani Babka was never any trouble at all, and besides the dinner would go to waste, and she would try to be back as soon as possible; throwing her shawl over her head and taking her carpetbag from her daughter and kissing her on the cheek and telling her not to forget to serve the plum brandy after the dessert; Pani Babka's Jozef bowing to the Father at least twenty times through all of it and shaking his head at her husband's offer of a quick swallow out in the barn just to keep up his courage, though of course if Father Piotr had not been there, it was doubtful whether he would have refused, his hands shaking on the reins as the weathered and run-down old wagon bounced along the mountain roads under the moon; she sitting there beside him, thinking, "He was very anxious to come and help me. He must have asked five times if I would like to have him come along, when everybody knows Pani Babka is healthy as a horse and gives birth like a hen laying eggs although she always screams enough to make her husband think she is in her death agony just to make him suffer a little too. Why was he so anxious to come with me?"

She had put it out of her head as soon as she arrived at Pani Babka's, and when she got home several hours later than she had expected, since Pani Babka had not really been ready for her when she arrived but had been putting up such a fuss for her husband's benefit that he had been unable to stand it any more and had rushed over before his wife was really ready; when she got home Father Piotr had already left of course and her daughter was asleep in the loft and she herself was so tired that she fell asleep even over the singing of her husband and Pani Babka's Jozef out in the barn. And what with the business of her husband's having gotten drunk enough that night to have beaten the horse blind with a hickory switch, and her daughter's not feeling well after having eaten too much of her name-day dinner, she had not had time to think about very much of anything, and so it was not until three days later on that Saturday when she overheard him and the pastor through the fireplace

that she began to put two and two together, congratulating herself on being wise enough to have recognized the situation for
what it was almost immediately and having insisted as she had
that he remain that evening and finish his dinner rather than
allow him to accompany her to Pani Babka's. Because, after all,
he was young and it had been up to her to use her discretion
and not to allow him an opportunity to betray himself and his
collar, to lose his head and perhaps say something to her in a
weak moment that would embarrass them both and make the
whole thing impossible. It was just fate perhaps, or more likely
the devil tempting the poor boy, the devil using her in his
scheme, she who would be the last one to ever allow anything
like that to happen. And it was just lucky, or perhaps it was the
grace of God, that she was sensible enough to realize it, had
recognized the schemer's hand in it that very evening of the
name-day dinner, sitting there like that before the fire in the
rocking chair with her hair down as her daughter combed it long
and smooth before putting it back up in the bun—the roast on
the spit, and the table set and everything all ready for the meal,
she and her daughter having already taken their baths and washed
and dried their hair—sitting there feeling the comb smooth as
sleep and the hair down all soft around her face, and not expecting him to appear for another hour yet, when suddenly there he
was standing there in the opened doorway, looking down at his
pocket watch, saying, "It seems I am early"; and she, "It does
not matter, we are happy to have you with us longer, if you
would not mind waiting while I finish putting up my hair"; and
he, "Perhaps my watch is wrong, what time is it?" and just then
the clock in the bedroom chiming five; and he, "Five, yes, that
is what I have. It was five you told me, Pani. I have it written
in my book"; and she, "Perhaps I made a mistake. But it does
not matter. Daughter, go call your Tata."

And so that must have been it, for she could not imagine how
she could ever have made such a mistake telling him five, when

they never ate before six, ever. But as though it were not enough he had to see her like that with her hair down and soft around her face, her husband had to go and say those terrible things right in front of him like that, and he *was* much much too anxious to accompany her to Pani Babka's, practically pleading with her right there in front of all of them, her husband, her daughter, Pani Babka's Jozef. She only hoped it had not been so obvious to the rest of them, though she was afraid it had been. Well, anyway, it was clear why he was so desperate about being sent to another parish, poor boy. But God willing, as the pastor had said, perhaps he would get over it. She would see to it that he did. She would stay out of his way as much as possible from here on. And there would be no more invitations for him to dine with them; after all, if he was young and incapable of controlling himself she at least would keep temptation out of his reach as much as possible. After that she did no more than nod to him around the rectory and say good day, and she lit candles for him every morning and prayed he would not succumb and that God would give him strength as He had given her, and she even made it a point to disguise her voice in the confessional though actually she never had anything to confess that ever really mattered one way or another, and she had infinite pity for the boy because obviously all of it had wrought a great change in him.

Although his sermons still brought the wrath of heaven itself down upon the slothful and the gluttonous and were indeed more frightening than ever before, slowly but surely Father Piotr's confessional became as popular as the old pastor's had ever been. It had all started that very Sunday after the name-day dinner. Pani Babka's Jozef, who had not received the sacraments ever since the old pastor had taken to his bed, had promised God he would go to confession and receive communion even if it meant he would have to promise to give up the bottle, if only

He would allow his wife, who had only been capable of giving him daughters in the past, five of them, if only God would this time present him with a son. That was what all the singing had been about in the barn that night after the dinner. And that Saturday afternoon, the very afternoon she had overheard Father Piotr and the pastor discussing the poor showing at the confessional, Pani Babka's Jozef told to the awe and amazement of the entire village—riding out in his wagon and stopping at all the cabins between the church and his own and taking the men aside from their shearing or running out into the meadows and up the slopes where they sat amid their flocks and waving a whiskey bottle over his head, shouting— the news of Father Piotr's reformation, telling how the good Father had absolved him of his sins without making him promise to give up drinking, without so much as even mentioning the bottle at all, without even lecturing him, having simply sat there behind the gauze curtain with his forehead in his hand mumbling the words of absolution. It had been as easy as that, and Pani Babka's Jozef did not know who to thank more, God or the good Father. He supposed ultimately he should thank them both, equally. And though he was the only man at the communion rail that Sunday, besides the organist of course, the following Saturday it seemed as though all the men in the village had been waiting for months with one foot in the wagon ready to whip their horses down to the confessional as soon as word was brought to them that the pastor was hearing confessions again or that another assistant had perhaps arrived in the parish, because the Saturday after Pani Babka's Jozef brought them the news they fell all over themselves trying to beat each other down to the confessional.

That Sunday the altar rail was filled at least ten times with kneeling open-mouthed parishioners devouring like starved men the Hosts Marya had prepared the preceding afternoon, more than a dozen tins of them, almost as many as she would ordinarily prepare only during the Lenten and Christmas seasons. And though everyone else in the parish marveled and wondered at this sudden change that had come over their priest, Marya did not. She did not dare think it right out, but the thought always lay somewhere close enough to the surface of her mind so that she would sometimes have to pause and smile sadly to herself thinking about the grace God was pouring down lovingly upon her little parish. For not only was everybody but her husband and a few other hidebound anticlerics receiving the sacrament regularly again just as they had done before the old pastor took to his bed, but they were also helping with the construction of the new school and just generally taking a greater interest in the church simply in order to help lighten as much as possible the immense burden which their return to the confessional and communion rail had imposed upon the young assistant, who was not only doing the work of two men since the pastor was confined to his bed and the bishop was for some reason taking his reverent time about sending the parish another assistant, but had started enough new projects on his own which alone would require more time than any ordinary man could possibly find within himself to give. How strange were the workings of God. How unbelievable that she, a useless old woman, should be responsible for such a miracle. Though, as the months passed and summer left and the fall arrived and went, she began to light candles for the bishop praying that he would see fit to delay no longer the sending of another assistant. For it was plain to all, by the time the Christmas season rolled around, that Father Piotr was not well, that he was "killing himself with service" as the pastor put it that Christmas Eve—Marya sitting there on the bench before the scorching fire, with the sound of her batter spoon knocking against the wooden bowl, listening to them, up in the pastor's room, their voices drifting down the flue and out of the fire, the pastor's voice rasping and unnatural from the cancer, sounding like something out of the grave.

"I have warned you again and again about giving too much of yourself. And it will not do to blame the bishop either. Because there is no question that you can do the work of two, even during the Christmas season; *you* could do it with ease, I know this, though it is not what I have been writing to the bishop. But you are not content with the work of two, you have to overreach yourself, you have to begin new projects, you have to do everything as though it meant the end of the world if you held back even that little bit of yourself you need for your own sustenance. Tell me, my son, what are you trying to do? Is this your way of spiting an old man? of seeing to it that you get your transfer out of the parish even if you have to kill yourself to do it? Be done with it. I submit. After the holidays I will write to the bishop again and ask that you be transferred."

"Father, I beg you . . ."

"No need to beg. No need to deny . . . I have said it."

"But, Father, you do not understand."

"What is there to understand? You are like a ghost. I can see in your eyes that you are burning with fever. How you are going to get through the midnight Mass, I dare not imagine, and as for the morning Masses tomorrow . . . My boy, why are you killing yourself?"

"Father, I am not. I am only doing what is necessary. You would do wrong to send me away now. You said yourself that I am blessed to be allowed to do this work."

"Pah! What else did I tell you? I told you I did not believe you in the first place—all this foolish talk about despising the parish, about not being fit for the priesthood. Hate could never accomplish all *you* have done. Love is what is killing you, my son, love."

"But not for them, Father."

"No, do not tell me again. I know, not for them, for Him. Only for Him. You know, I have heard you say it so many times since the summer that I am fed up with it. Who would believe it, after all these years, now on my deathbed, I am fed up with talk of loving Him. I am a humble priest, I do not understand all this talk of love and sacrifice, of making up to Him all that the others refuse Him, of despising them for refusing even to give up the things that are forbidden them much less sacrifice anything that is due them, as we do. You talk as though the sacrifice of the priesthood is superior even to that of the Cross. He sacrificed His Son for the world He loved, you say, but *you,* you sacrifice yours for the world you despise, because He loves them and you love Him, and . . . Pah, you tire me with your infernal metaphysics. What kind of maze is this? To compare priestly chastity and the sacrifice of reproducing yourself to the sacrifice of the Cross . . ."

"No, not that, Father. But if a man were willing to sacrifice his very soul, to sacrifice the reward of seeing Him he has loved beyond all reason just to be able to go on helping the people he would as soon see all burn in hell as they deserved were it not that *He* desired differently . . ."

"Enough! It is clear, you are having hallucinations. It is the fever."

"But, Father . . ."

"Enough, enough! You will not say another word, and you will do exactly as I say without any question. You need sleep. I have heard you in your room at night. You have been scourging yourself out of all proportion . . . You *know* that is indulgence. I have sent for the German. He will be here before morning. He will look at you and see if you are fit to serve the morning Masses. If not, there will be no morning Masses. In the meantime you will take some of my powders and get some sleep before the midnight Mass. You will send Marya to spread the word that as many as possible attend tonight, the children too. The others will have to do without. It is my error. I was wrong from the beginning. I have allowed this to get out of hand."

And when he came down and told her, she thought her heart

would surely break just to look at him, standing there like that with the package of sleeping powders in his hand looking like he was already asleep, his eyes burning with fever, just standing there watching her as she took her hat and coat and umbrella from behind the door, saying, "I will finish my baking later. Do not worry, I will see to it that they are all there tonight"; thinking how terrible it all was that it should be because of her that he was killing himself like that, burying himself in his work in order to help forget his sad and hopeless feeling for her; thinking it and blushing as she pushed out into the snow, her umbrella trembling against the wind, remembering again the part of the discussion about reproduction, wondering whether after the holidays it would not be better if she just gave up her church work and her duties at the rectory. And she probably *would have*, too, if God had not seen fit to solve the problem in His own way. It had seemed oh so very sad and pitiable when it happened, but that was only, she knows now, because as usual we never see the whole picture. Actually, the way she sees it now, almost twenty years later, kneeling here before the monument in the churchyard erected in his memory, it was simply another example of God's mercy, of His taking him unto Himself. Indeed, it was like killing two birds with one stone, she thinks. Because God took him unto Himself and sent her good-for-nothing animal of a husband to hell, both on the very same day in the very same hour and in the same buggy behind the same blind horse. Because such are the ways of God.

It happened sometime after midnight Mass around three o'clock Christmas morning. Almost the entire village had been at the Mass. It was the only time Marya had ever been to a midnight Mass and heard babies crying over the caroling. The altar rail was full to overflowing several times before she and her daughter got a place side by side at the rail; and just before she closed her eyes as she raised her face and opened her mouth to receive the Host, she could see his hands trembling as he reached into the ciborium; and as the Host melted on the roof of her mouth amid his words *"Corpus Dómini nostri Jesu Christi"* and she made the sign of the Cross and was about to vacate her place at the rail and go back to her pew, she heard behind her the huge voice of the congregation hurl itself up against the arches in one prolonged gasp, and looking up saw there behind the altar rail, the ciborium beside him lying on its side and the Hosts scattered around him, Father Piotr sprawled like a dead man upon the marble floor.

There was some delay of the Mass after that, but not much. Several men carried him to the rectory and brought back the pastor ensconced in a big wooden chair looking like nothing less than a shrunken corpse, his color horrible, and his fat man's robes at least a dozen sizes too large for him; the pastor, who leaned grotesquely out of his chair and one by one reverently picked the Hosts off the floor and placed them back in the ciborium, and then as the men carried him in his chair back up to the altar, took another ciborium out of the sepulcher and continued distributing the communion, repeating the *Corpus Dómini nostri Jesu Christi* in the rasping unnatural voice, moving up and back along the altar rail like a sultan in a sedan chair.

She did not even bother to go to the rectory after the Mass. She felt she had caused enough trouble. It seemed obvious to her what had happened. It was not mere coincidence that he should have collapsed right after giving *her* communion (or at least right after her daughter, who was right beside her at the rail). It would be better if from that day on she stayed away from the rectory completely, she told herself. She learned from the others that he had merely fainted and that it was surely nothing serious, since he had come to even before they had got him into his bed, and had argued with the pastor that he was capable of going back and finishing the Mass himself. So she

just got into the wagon beside her husband, who was a regular
Christmas and Easter churchgoer, and they drove back over the
rutted snow-covered roads as their daughter sat bundled in a
blanket behind them in the straw-covered wagon bed. She did
not think anything of it at first when upon arriving home they
found her asleep there sitting up—her father carrying her into
the house and up into the loft to her bed prior to adjourning to
the barn and his bottle. However, when she tried to get her to
undress, she marveled at how tired her daughter was, unable
even to keep her eyes open for more than a few seconds at a
time, sitting there like that on the edge of the bed trying to get
her clothes off but only succeeding in getting the shift pulled up
and over her head before she was fast asleep again, the shift
hanging down between her knees like an inverted umbrella and
the overhead lamp curving naked along her back; and when
Marya began to undress her daughter herself and knelt down before her and reached under her chin and undid the ribbon and
the long blond hair spilled out onto her lap atop the shift . . .
it was then that she noticed the corset for the first time, plopping her daughter back across the bed, one of her own old cor-
sets which had been packed away in a trunk since her wedding
day; realizing even before she got it off why her daughter had
been wearing it, and slapping her, and slapping her again, asking, "Who? Who?" and again and again, but none of it doing
any good, screaming; and her husband coming, but none of it
doing any good because there was nothing they could think to
do that would wake her.

By the time her husband got back in the wagon with Father
Piotr, Marya was in a state of hysteria, apologizing to him over
and over for having to call him out like that when she knew he
was not well, when he himself should have a doctor, weeping
hysterically as he administered the sacrament of extreme unction with the little balls of cotton and the oil, her husband yelling through all of it, "Do something for her. Do something, in-

stead of only praying her into a grave"; she taking strength after
the Father's calm and sad "There is nothing any of us can do
now. But do not worry. I have absolved her of her sins and she
goes to Him in a state of grace"; the rest of it happening so fast
that even after almost twenty years of thinking about it she still
cannot remember exactly how it had happened. She cannot even
remember how she had come to ask the questions, but she can
even now see him standing there so calm and serious, not at all
like the nervous shaking assistant who had collapsed at the altar
rail a few hours before, his voice unhurried, completely con-
trolled, telling how her daughter had stopped by the rectory that
afternoon after she herself had left, saying that her mother had
left her umbrella in the hall closet on the second floor, and how
she had gone up while the pastor was asleep and come down a
little later apparently empty-handed, saying that her mother
must have been mistaken; "She must have gone into his room
and taken some of the powders off the night table"; and she,
"But who? Who?" and he, "I cannot say, Pani"; and then her
husband, "Cannot say? Cannot say?" And then it was there all
of a sudden as out of nowhere, "Of course. Of course, he cannot
say, because it is *him*."

She could not believe her ears, her knees going right out from
under her as she stood there holding on to the kitchen table,
falling into a chair and just sitting there unable to move, listening to her husband's voice whirling about her, saying, "Of
course. That night. The night of the name-day dinner"; and
then the Father's voice there, just as calm as ever, saying, "Pani,
if you like I will stay till the end"; and her husband, "The end,
eh? Nothing you can do, eh? You had better do something,
priest. Because if she dies, you have killed her just as sure as if
you had given her the powders to drink. Because that is your
baby in her belly, priest!" She could not believe it. She could
not speak. She just sat there and waited, and as though in answer to her prayer his voice came to her as from a long way off,

saying, "It will do no good to accuse me, Pan. It is foolish to even think anyone would believe you. You will only throw suspicion on yourself. You do not have to be afraid of me, Pan, I am a priest; I can never repeat what your daughter has told me in the secret of the confessional."

It was her prayer answered, and she actually felt herself begin to smile through her tears, just begin to smile before she began screaming. And she was up out of the chair, and she was clawing at her husband's face, feeling the hand slam against her head only after she was already sprawled out on the floor, her head practically in the fireplace, scorching the side of her face. And she could hear herself screaming, "Animal, animal," through the hair which had come loose from her bun, her screams echoing up the chimney; and her husband just standing there over her, saying, "You believe it of me, my wife? You believe it of your husband, my wife?" And through her own tears she could see *his* starting in his unshaven face. "You believe it of me, my wife? You believe it of your husband, my wife?" And she could not bear to look at him, she felt she was going to throw up; hearing his voice yelling, "Priest, priest, it is you. It was you that evening of the name day." And she did not even have to wait for the Father's denial, because her daughter had told her the following morning that he had left right after the dinner. And lying there with her head practically in the fire, she recalled how the dinner dishes lay piled in the sink when she finally got home from Pani Babka's and how the next morning her daughter had complained that she did not feel well and did not even wish to get out of bed and told how she had heard the horse screaming last night; recalled how she had learned later that day that her husband had beaten the horse blind and that the horse had probably stood bleeding there in his stall all the while he and Pani Babka's Jozef drank and sang and celebrated the birth of Jozef's son. And thinking about it, all she could do was scream, watching her husband moving toward the Father, and the

Father backing toward the door and then the door open and her husband framed in it and the Father beyond climbing into the wagon under the moon and the reins slapping and her husband running and throwing himself into the back of the wagon just as she got to the door and watched them rolling together in the wagon bed, the blind horse galloping away into the white night, as behind her her daughter lay swollen-bellied and dying in her bed.

Chapters IX & XIII

When Magda finally awoke that Christmas morning back in 1926, her eyes tearing in the smoke, she wondered how it was possible that she could smell so distinctly the reek and stench of flame consuming her flesh and yet not feel any pain, none at all; realizing only later after she had time to look it all out, that the faces hovering over her belonged not to some fallen angels all hot and smoldering in hell, that she was not really in hell at all but back in her own bed in Porgorze; though after her mother and the German doctor told her what they had done to her (or rather *for* her, as they put it), and she discovered herself all flat and corsetless beneath the sheets again, she was not so sure, not so sure at all, even though her mother very nicely explained it all away as merely the burning of the Christmas roast.

She did not question, however. Nor did she ever reveal to them the terrible mistake they had made, never during those days in which she slowly recuperated under the watchful hand of the German, who drove the thirty miles by sled every day from Nowy Targ to see her, and of her mother, who little by little explained it all to her, telling how nobody could ever blame her for taking the sleeping powders if they knew the truth, but that luckily thanks to the German, whom surely they would never be able to repay for all he had done—compromising his principles and even breaking the law just to help them in their hour of shame—no one other than herself and the German need ever know the truth, especially since her husband had gone to his reward and was no doubt burning in hell that very moment just as sure as Father Piotr, who unfortunately had to be in the wagon with him behind the blind horse that Christmas morning when it careened through the bridge rail and fell the hundred and fifty feet into the frozen Dunajec, was at that very moment seated among the saints in heaven, while their lost bodies floated somewhere under the foot-thick ice toward the sea.

She allowed them to go right on believing they knew the truth, to believe that she actually had tried to take her own life, that she was inexpressibly grateful to them for ridding her of her "shame." What else was there to do? What was the use of throwing it up to their faces when after all they had only been trying to help her, to do what they thought necessary? She allowed them to believe it when actually it was no closer to the truth than the ridiculous story they had invented to tell the village, the same story they told Pan Baranek when he appeared that day in Porgorze for his son's mock funeral, all about how she had suffered a ruptured appendix on her way home from midnight Mass and how her father had gone to fetch Father

Piotr, who performed the operation but could not stop the hemorrhaging, and while driving back to the rectory with her father
to get word by telephone to the German in Nowy Targ, had
died in the accident on the bridge, the German having almost
miraculously appeared on the scene at dawn just in time to save
her life.

The German was the Herr Doktor Maximilian Saulmann,
whom in time Magda learned to call Max, and to whom she
could no more ever bring herself to tell the truth about that
Christmas morning in 1926, than she could ever say "yes" to; not
so much because she would never be able to give him children,
and certainly not because she believed in her mother's old-
country superstitions about people who lived on after receiving
extreme unction, superstitions which precluded, among other
things like walking barefoot, eating flesh and making a will, their
contracting of a holy marriage. It was simply that she could never
quite bring herself to put aside the feeling that after all that had
happened to her, the only bridal veil she should ever wear, the
only wedding ring she should ever allow to encircle her finger,
should be the black coarse veil of the postulant or the golden
wedding band of the nun. She felt that the only passion her lips
should ever again taste should be the eternal one pressed against
the bleeding feet of a crucifix; her only lover He whom she could
never quite bring herself around to saying "yes" to, could never
quite get herself to accept as a husband any more than she could
accept Max; because even though she sometimes did manage to
convince herself that He had proposed to her in her prayers
many times, that He really did care for her despite herself, she
nevertheless could never bring herself around to believing she
was worthy of Him any more than she was worthy of Max,
whose veil and ring she could never bring herself to accept
either, despite her having accepted his passion, a passion celebrated in the open carriage behind the dozing horse while sheep
grazed the slopes above the clouds and swans dipped their heads

in silken pools that first summer, or that fall and winter in the office in Nowy Targ after the long drive in the sleigh down the side of the mountain, or that spring after the drive down the dust roads, there in the small bright room over the cello-maker's shop, with the fire smoldering on the hearth and the music of the sorrowful instrument there in the garden below where the old cello-maker perched on the edge of the garden chair ("As though on the brink of eternity," Max had said) played Bach and Beethoven for his German friend and mazurkas "for the beautiful lady," at least, as he said, "Until I can play Mendelssohn for both of you."

But that was long ago, and now driving back to Prescott in the huge rain, her husband of one day hunched over the wheel as though driving under water, his cigar practically touching itself glowing back at him out of the windshield amid the ticking but useless wipers, and behind them in the back seat, sitting there with his head against the window, their only son, who less than an hour ago, precisely at noon, had appeared at their hotel door crying, "Marya's bleeding to death"; she wonders, not about Marya whom she has never even met, nor even about what it must feel like to die, but about the baby instead, about what it must feel like to die without ever even having been born; dreaming back in the silence amid the ticking of the useless wipers and the insulating roar of the rain and the stench of Groszek's cigar in the closed car, dreaming back to those ember days after the passion had smoldered, after the flight from the rooms above the cello-maker's in Nowy Targ, and the rooms above the blacksmith's in Krakow, and back up and over the mountains again to Prague, and finally after the occupation and the ethnic reorganizations to Bodemar on the Lech, and all along the way, around every turn but the last, the pure-white and pompous geese squawking amid the horse's hoofs like outraged and scandalized old women; Bodemar Castle high

up on the mountain side above the town, only the spires and
the chimneys showing above the trees whenever she looked out
of their cottage window to watch him white on his bicycle disappear down the road every morning during the warm months
and in the hospital car in the cold; wondering just when it was
she first recognized the odor and knew that the stench rising
out of the castle chimneys in the huge clouds of black smoke
and pressing down the mountain side in damp weather and
hovering over the valley; knew that it was no more the stench
of burning garbage, as Max had told her it was, than the stench
she had awakened to that Christmas morning almost fifteen
years before was merely the burning of her mother's Christmas
roast.

But she never questioned, never let on to him she knew,
just as she had never in all those years ever questioned how he
could possibly have buried anything that winter in the iron-
hard ground under three feet of snow, not even on that last
day, that twenty-fifth day of January in 1946, when he stood
there in his cell saying in his heavily accented but beautiful
Polish, "The trial has been a revelation to me, Magda, like the
scales falling from my eyes at last. I understand now their talk
of Apocalypse, of Final Judgment. It is as psychologically sound
as the principle upon which the criminal acts when he revisits
the scene of his crime. It is Adam returning to Eden and
coughing up the apple stuck in his throat since Genesis. Only,
what the innocent Americans do not know is that it is not
simply a matter of choking it out of the throat with a rope and
handing it back to the Gardener. That is like the camel thinking to squeeze through the eye of the needle simply by molting
his hump. But without his hump, what is the camel, eh? Maybe
a horse, eh? Or even better, a jackass. But surely not a camel
any longer. And what is Man without his apple? Yes, but what
the attic philosopher forgot to add when he talked about his
apple a day keeping the doctor away, is that they must not

under any circumstances be stolen apples, for then they will only stick in the throat."

And he went to the gallows like that without ever knowing, because the only person she ever told it to was one of those innocent Americans that had hanged him, the very most innocent American of them all; told it to him because Max was gone then, and Roman had not only accused, tried and sentenced him, but just happened to understand the language in which it had happened, the language in which she could tell how her mother and her new husband had erected in the churchyard the huge monument over the vacant grave of their lost son, and the not extravagant but certainly substantial headstone over her father's equally vacant grave in the hillside cemetery, which her mother visited every day just as she did the churchyard, for no other reason than to reinforce the story she had invented to tell the village and her new husband, since according to that story there was no reason in the world other than that her dead husband had been a drunkard and they had lived as strangers for the last fifteen years of their marriage, no good reason at all why she should not have cherished her dead husband's memory, Magda's father, the drunkard who had sat there that evening of the name-day dinner after her mother had left with Pani Babka's Jozef, sat there at the table with his daughter and their guest, still drawing with his fork on the tablecloth, saying, "Now that she is gone, priest, let me tell you in all seriousness that it is indeed an honor to have your highness share my humble table with me like this. For a humble shepherd like myself to have such an educated man at my table is indeed an honor. So if you will be so charitable and forgive the talk of a few minutes ago . . . for I do not really believe what I say; it is just to embarrass her of course . . . and I apologize for giving in to temptation in your exalted presence.

"No, no! Do not look away"; Father Piotr sitting there looking helplessly toward her but her father going right on, saying, "I mean what I say, as foolish as it sounds, as insincere . . . I mean it. Really, deep down I have the deepest respect for priests. You would not believe it, eh? But then, it does not matter what you believe. It is true nevertheless, and you are a fool if you think for one minute I mean anything I have said against my wife's purity. I feel it an insult to me that you should believe it. I know my wife is as pure as my little Magdalene, yes, as pure, as virginal even, though we have been married twenty years and have had four children. Can you understand that? No, of course you cannot. All you understand is that it is very dull in the confessional for you when she kneels there on the other side of the screen, eh? Not like some of the others, eh? No! Do not get up. Do not go. I beg you to sit and eat and listen to me, and when a man begs a priest for help, what kind of priest is it who refuses? Priest, do not laugh, but I am asking you to save my soul."

There was silence after that, and Father Piotr sat down again and the plates were passed and filled, and her father took a drink of the plum brandy, saying, "Besides, Pani will be angry if her roast goes to waste"; laughing, saying, "I would offer you a drink, priest, but I know your reputation. Yes, they tell me you are a hard confessor, not only about the drinking but about everything. They say that you ask all kinds of questions which to some would not seem necessary. Excuse me, but I have heard it said that it is almost like you enjoyed hearing sins. Of course, you must not think for a minute I myself would ever believe such stories . . . still, you hear things, like some of the younger women say you ask too much about everything, like where did he touch you, where you sit down, or where, and for how long? and all sorts of things like that which to some would seem unnecessary . . . Wait, allow me to finish. I myself know you are not the kind to turn the confessional into an in-and-out affair like the pastor, and I know it is not because you enjoy hearing such things. I know this, and I would like to know how it is possible. Is it not a temptation? How can you help it when you look at the women of the parish and you know all their secrets. It is not a big parish, and though the confessional is dark, there are still the voices. All I wish to say in mentioning these things which embarrass you and turn your face red is that I admire you for it. I admire all you priests, as I have already said. I admire how you can overcome such great temptation every single day."

It was at that point that she had decided to go out to the well and fill the bucket for the dishes, and though she tried to draw out the process as long as possible, even filling the bucket a few times and carrying it to the barn to water the flock and play awhile with the newborns, and then pausing in the orchard on her way back to the house to bite into an unripe plum and look at the moon; when she got back to the porch, she could hear them through the screen door, still talking, or rather her father still talking, saying, "Yes, it is easy for *you* to say that. Throw the bottle away and receive the Host every morning. But I am not a priest like you. I am a man, and I am not so old yet that I do not sometimes want to behave like a man, and since I am married to a woman like Pani and must remain so chaste like a priest, I would like you to tell me *how*, Father. How can it be done without the bottle at least? God strike me down if I do not believe, no matter what I say or have said, that not only you but the pastor also are as pure as the day you came out of your mother's belly. I swear on the Cross I believe it. But how? How does a man do it? Are there different kinds of men, are there men who do not need to be men? What is it? What is the secret? Why do you keep it only for yourselves? Why not tell the world, or if not the world, at least us, us whose wives . . . Pah! Let me tell you. You know why I married her? Not because she was beautiful . . . though she was as beautiful as you could imagine, like my Magdalene almost,

only with dark hair . . . not like now, not with the swollen
ankles and the cheeks hollow like milk saucers and her hair
always tied up so tight in the combs . . . No, it was not for
her beauty I married her. It was for her chastity."

On the porch in the darkness she could hear the sheep bleating away in the barn beyond the plum grove, the plum trees
glazed bright under the moon, her father's voice rattling on the
night air, saying, "Ah, I see you smile, priest. That is good. You
cannot believe it of a man like me, eh? She was like a nun, I
tell you. But that is no surprise to you, eh? She is a nun now,
only without a veil. She was so innocent, so holy-looking with
her eyes always turned away and the blush there in her cheek
whenever I looked toward her. I could not even bear to touch
her hand without feeling that I was molesting her. I could not
bear it, I wanted her so much. And not for the reason you might
think. True, I was not exactly a saint in my youth. I had plenty
of girls. But Marya was not just one more I wished to deflower,
not just the biggest challenge of all, as the village thought. No,
I wanted her just the way she was, the way I saw her, so modest,
so innocent that her cheek would burn under my eyes. The
others of the village would say, 'Ha, Jozef will have to marry
Marya if he wants her, she is not like the rest.' They said that
was the way it always was, the pure woman always gets the
good-for-nothing, because the good-for-nothing always marries
only the one he cannot have otherwise. But they were wrong,
at least the reason they gave was wrong. At least I went so far
as to promise her that if we married I would never touch her.
We both knew of course that it would not be possible. But we
said it to each other anyway. It was what we wanted, even
though we knew it was impossible, for the world was not made
that way. But I promised, and of course at the wedding they
got me drunk, and I took her that first night even before we
got home to our bed. I took her right there in the carriage, just
as though she were any of the others.

"Only, of course she was not like any of the others, not at all; and I pitied her those closed eyes, the hardness of her, but after that somehow I could not leave her alone. I hated myself every morning, but every night I just could not help myself. I do not know why. I did not enjoy it surely. I hated myself even as I was doing it. It would seem as though she would just stop breathing as soon as I got near the bed, like she would just die, all of her going away some place and only her body left there in the bed with me dead and cold as stone. She never spoke, never opened her eyes. Oh, how I pitied her. How I loved her, and hated myself. And she never blamed me. She never said a word to me about it. She was happy with her work at the rectory, and her midwifing, and then when our Jan came she had a very hard time but she did not even blame me then. She was grateful to me she said for giving her a son. She as much as told me she was grateful to me for being willing to sleep with her, as though she were some kind of monster or something. She thanked me for forcing myself on her.

"But I could not stand myself. And I took more and more to the bottle, because it helped a little. And then when my little Magdalene was born, Marya had such a terrible time she nearly died, and that was the last of it. Since then I have never touched her. Since then I have been as pure as a priest. So now you see why I believe in your purity, priest, when I myself, a good-for-nothing animal as she now calls me, have been chaste for fifteen years. But of course I have my bottle. But what do *you* have, priest? I will admit, at first the whiskey only made me want her more, and so you are right when you say the bottle can lead to sin and maybe you are right to forbid absolution to the drinker. With a little whiskey, it got to where I could take her without guilt. But in time it got so the whiskey was enough in itself—a few pulls on the bottle and I could lie back in the hay and just talk to my horse all evening. *Kon,* I say, horse, you are lucky to be a horse. And he looks back at me from the stall, with that long face and those sad eyes, and he flicks his ears a little as if to say, Are you crazy, old man, talking to a horse? But that does not bother me, I go right on telling him how lucky he is, how it is no wonder it is not in the nature of things that a horse should need to take a pull on the bottle once in a while. A little hay is all he needs and nothing bothers him, nobody ever blames him for anything, nothing is ever his fault. Like the time I was mending the shoe and he kicked me in the stomach so that I almost died . . . Nobody thought to blame the horse. It was my fault for being drunk and not careful and allowing myself to be kicked. And so it is clear why he does not need a bottle, eh? But how about me, priest? A day will come when he will break his leg and be as useless as me, and I will put a bullet in his head, and it will all be over for him. But what about me, priest? Will the day ever come when it will be all over for me, when I will be no more? What about me, priest? What about if I were to put a bullet in *my* head?"

So that was her father. That was the man she had never really known until that evening, the man she discovered as though by stealth, as though by eavesdropping on a confessional, standing there out on the porch through all of it as her father's voice drifted and blew through the screen door on the tobacco smoke. And after it was over, after the long pause in which she waited expecting to hear Father Piotr's voice boom out the answer as from the pulpit—but only the night sounds there, the crickets praying in the trees, and the single solemn call of some night bird out of the valley below and the sheep bleating in the fold—she heard her father's voice again, laughing now, saying, "Well then, I might as well go and talk to my horse, eh? Yes, I might as well go and talk to my horse," calling back through the screen door, as he pushed past her and staggered down the path through the orchard toward the barn, "And thank you for all the good advice, priest," laughing and swearing drunkenly across the orchard to his horse.

That was the first time in her life she had ever thought of her father as having any kind of past at all. She always thought of him and of her mother too, for that matter, as simply *her* parents with no identity whatsoever separate and apart from their relationship to her, as though they always were and always would be simply and only and ever her mother and her father, as though they had been born her parents, as though that day some fifteen years before, that day she herself was born, they too (and not only they, but her older brother Jan too) had been born, as though the entire family had issued from the hand of God in the same instant, complete and whole and permanent, just exactly as the four of them appeared in the brown and faded baptismal photograph framed on the bureau top in her mother's bedroom beside the palm-draped crucifix and the votive candles—her father a strikingly handsome and mustached young man with plastered-down hair, his felt sea-shell-banded mountaineer hat crooked in his arm, his chin tilted up stiffly above the sheepskin jacket and the embroidered white homespun trousers and leather moccasins, her mother seated there on the bench beside him, beautiful in the peasant cotton and the embroidered shawl, her five-year-old brother standing stiff as a general at her knee, and she herself bundled in a blanket in her mother's arms, the pastor standing plump in the background smiling in his cassock, a crucifix held against his chest and his two fingers raised in benediction, just as she in time came to imagine God Himself must have raised His two fingers when he uttered, "Let there be Life."

She learned early that the pastor was not actually God Himself, but simply one of His representatives here on earth. Nevertheless, whenever she thought of God, God the Father at least, of whom there were no pictures in her missal or statues in the church as there were of His Son (and everybody knew the Holy Ghost was a pigeon), she always thought of Him as pretty much resembling the pastor. Standing there in the photograph with the crucifix held to his breast (the very same crucifix that stood on her mother's bureau top, the outsized head of the German-made Corpus easily discernible in the large eight-by-ten photograph), he lent to it that air of sanctity which led her to remark the resemblance of the arrangement of the family in the photograph and the position of the altars in the village Church of the Holy Family—the main altar topped by the crucifix and flanked by two smaller altars, the right devoted to Joseph and the left to Mary. The appearance of her brother and herself in the holy scene, which at first seemed an intrusion, resolved itself when two days after Christmas on the eleventh or twelfth anniversary of her brother's name day, during an argument growing out of his having had to do on his own name day her chores as well as his own because her mother had dressed her up specially for the name-day company and did not wish her to get dirty, an argument in which she assured her brother she had not allowed her mother to dress her up simply to celebrate *his* stupid old name day at all, but rather the feast day of Jesus' brother, Saint John the Apostle.

She attributed her brother's laughter rather to his ignorance than to her own unsuspected confusion over the pastor's catechism lesson that morning before his class of seven- and eight-year-old pre-first communicants which, apropos of the feast day, included a brief description of the "disciple whom Jesus loved," and to whom He had referred when speaking to His mother from the Cross, saying, "Woman, behold thy son," and to whom He had spoken the beautiful "Behold thy mother!" She deplored at first the coincidence that her brother's name day happened to fall on the very same day as the feast of the saint, but marveled later, after her brother explained to her the meaning of "name day," that not only her brother, but she too had been named after a saint, a real honest-to-goodness saint that was written about in her missal, and who (as she understood her missal then) had personally written the Epistle to the Mass commemorating her feast day, had personally written, "I will rise and go about the city: in the streets and the broad ways I will seek Him whom my soul loves: . . . and I will not let Him go, till I bring Him into my mother's house, and into the chamber of her that bore me." And after that, in the light of her discovery (and as deliberately as any of those old masters who, as Max was to explain to her one afternoon in the Augsburg museum, painted their mistresses as madonnas), she came to think of her own and her brother's appearance in the baptismal photograph as no more incongruous than the appearance of their namesakes at the foot of the Cross on Calvary.

And so for her to have tried to imagine then at the age of seven and eight, and perhaps even nine and ten, that her parents had had a life prior to that enchanted in the photograph, that there could possibly have been a time when they existed as something other than *her* mother and *her* father, something other than the perfect saints all mothers and fathers must by definition be, regardless of some of them drinking a little too much; to have tried to imagine it then, would have been like trying to imagine Mary and Joseph as not only having had a life of their own prior to the Annunciation, but an unholy one at that.

However, by the time she was fifteen, the disenchantment had long been accepted. She had stopped thinking of her parents as saints just as she had long ago ceased thinking of the photograph as anything more than a rather old-fashioned brown and ugly family portrait, when she bothered to think of it at all, bothered even so much as to notice it while kneeling before her mother's bureau in prayer, since what seemed to her as a

child crawling up on a bedroom chair to explore the mystery
on the bureau top, or even at seven and eight standing on tiptoe with her nose over the edge of the bureau, what seemed to
her then something immense and wonderful, at nine and ten
and eleven grew smaller and less wonderful as she herself grew
taller, until at twelve and thirteen amid the aura of her own
image filling the bureau mirror, not only did she cease to notice
it, but at somewhere around thirteen or fourteen it was like her
childhood itself relegated to her mother's bottom drawer along
with the baptismal certificate, the communion veil, the con-
firmation candle and most of her childhood illusions.

She had learned not only that her father's drinking was
shameful and selfish, but that her mother's devotion to the
Church was not entirely selfless either, just as in the past she
had discovered, along with her discovery of the magic of her
mother's mirror, that her own devotion to the Church was not
quite as selfless as it had previously been, for her work at the
rectory helping her mother, and her work at the school doing
her own studying and helping the pastor with the lower classes,
and her singing in the choir and all the rest of it, had slowly
during the ages of twelve and thirteen and fourteen ceased to
engender the feeling of necessity, of satisfaction, of joy it had
engendered before, had become indeed joyless drudgery. What
had once been privilege, suddenly became penance, and though
she never ceased to perform her chores or to perform them with
at least an outward show of satisfaction, she would really have
preferred to sit alone doing nothing, perhaps watching the
swans dipping their necks lovingly into the pond or the sheep
grazing the slopes while the lambs cavorted; anything rather
than help in the rectory, because as much as she loved and
revered the old pastor she could not prevent herself from noting
that no matter how often she or her mother might wash his
cassock, he smelled bad; could not prevent herself from admitting to herself that aside from teaching the children in the

lower grades she no longer found any joy whatsoever in school and study.

Indeed, if it had not been for her mother's wish that she learn all the good pastor had the time and inclination to teach her prior to her entrance into the convent, so that she might be chosen to serve as a teaching Sister rather than as a convent scullery maid or laundress, she would have been content to forgo the studies completely and simply spend her time smiling at herself in her mother's mirror. She looked forward to her morning and evening prayers before the bureau crucifix as an excuse to kneel before it, telling herself that God was being kind to her, that of course all her good works during that time when she had still enjoyed performing them were not worth half so much in His eyes as they were now, now when though she really would much rather have been doing something else, she nevertheless continued to perform them, and with a good will, even going so far as to suggest to herself that God was allowing the devil to tempt His servant just as He had allowed him to tempt Job and for the very same reasons. However, at other times she told herself that even suggesting such a comparison was simply one more indication of her growing and uncontrollable vanity and her consequent fall from grace, a fall from which, as she came to think of it during that year prior to the fifteenth anniversary of her name day, only miraculously did she manage to recover.

As she saw it then, it had been the children who were for the most part responsible for her recovery. She so enjoyed teaching the lower grades that she suddenly, somewhere around Easter in that year 1926, resolved that the only way she would ever be able to persevere in her mother's ambition was to assure herself that once she had taken the veil she might look forward once more to teaching children. Scullery and laundry work which had grown so tedious for her at the rectory and at home certainly would not be any less tedious at the convent. And only through concentrated and constant study could she possibly hope—a peasant girl like herself—to display enough talent as a novice to guarantee selection as a candidate for the teaching sisterhood. It was, as she saw it, this rekindled interest in learning which slowly but certainly returned to her God's grace, since she once again found herself happy, pleased and gratified not only with her studies but with her chores too, just as almost miraculously (she thought then) her mother's mirror had grown tedious and unsatisfying, so that her appearances in it, which were even more frequent now than ever, became a penance rather than a joy, revealing as they would never fail to do, some slight blemish in her flesh which to her would appear nothing less than a canker mirroring imperfections within. And though she felt certain that grace had been revisited upon her for her *own* sake, as a reward for her determination to go on performing her good works even when she found no joy in them, she did not entirely discount the fact that the presence in the parish of the new assistant was a visible manifestation of the bestowal of God's grace upon the parish as a whole, a parish which like herself, she felt, considering the amount of drinking that went on, did not really merit it.

She certainly could not deny that the new assistant had helped at least to restore her interest in learning, allowing her as he did to select Latin texts from the rectory library which the old pastor would surely have considered much too advanced for her. She realized with the very first book the new assistant allowed her to choose as a text, that some part of her lack of interest in learning prior to his arrival was certainly due to the fact that she had been advancing in her studies at a rate more rapid than the old pastor was disposed to admit, and hence the material he gave her to read (books almost purely devotional which she had at first found beautiful and touching) only bored her. The new assistant supplied her texts which not only allowed her to study the language but also to obtain some knowledge of Latin literature and thought, as for example did the selections found in the text she happened to be studying that week of the name-day celebration, in which text, after she had re-entered the house with the water bucket and placed it under the sink—her father's drunken yelling to his horse across the plum orchard still out there beyond the screen door —in which text *somehow* she found herself reading aloud that night. And now almost twenty years later, just quite *how* she cannot even begin to imagine, though in all those years she must have gone over the incident in her mind only God would ever know how many times, all of it like some dream you try to remember and try, wondering just how much of it was really dream and how much of it you've invented in remembering it.

Only, it was not a dream. At least the changes she watched and felt taking place inside her those next five months were not a dream, unless (regardless of how she chose to think of that night) perhaps a nightmare might actually impregnate, could like the incubus summoned on the secret wings of adolescent desire and with plum brandy on his breath climb upon her atop the sheets of her mother's bed, a nightmare which she never revealed to anyone before that Christmas morning in a horse-cab in Augsburg, revealed to a boy voiding his stomach in the snow, a boy young enough to be her own, to whom she told it all, for no other reason perhaps than that now Max was gone and could no longer hear or care about what really happened that night. She chose the first person to come along; it didn't have to be Roman, it could have been anybody, she supposes now sitting here in the car amid the insulating roar of the rain, except that Roman quite coincidentally, she thinks, just happened to understand Polish so that she might tell it to him in the language in which it happened, telling how she put the water bucket back under the sink and instead of doing the dishes as she had planned (or had she?) . . . "Oh, I do not

know how it happened, whether I said we could study the lesson before Mama came back, or whether as he told me later
in the confessional it was he who suggested it. Perhaps it was
neither. Because it was the usual thing after dinner on Sundays.
Mama would clear some of the dishes before us, and I would
get the book down from the shelf and we would study as she
did the dishes"; telling it to him that way one day, and then
the next, or perhaps even waking him at night, telling him,
"No, I am sure now. It was I who suggested it. He wanted to
go back to the rectory"; telling how she cleared the table before
him, asking him to help her only with one page which she was
finding very difficult; and then right in the middle of the telling
changing the story again, saying, "No, it could not have been
that way. Because I did not even reach that place in the book
yet—I do not *think* I had reached that place in the book yet.
It was another selection I could not understand, the one from
the *Expositio* about Atonement and Original Sin"; and then
the next morning over the breakfast table under the skylight
and the cold Augsburg dawn, "But perhaps I did. Because
perhaps he told me what to read, but it was I who opened to
that page even if, as he said, it was only by accident"; telling
how she read the lines, saying one day that of course she understood what she was reading, saying she had read it all before
many times, that she herself had selected that particular chapter and paragraph, telling her teacher that she was having diffi-
culty translating it, and then the next day saying that it was he
who had done the selecting, that she had never read it before,
that she did not even understand really what she was reading,
that she was too busy thinking about her father, about all he
had revealed of his and her mother's past, remembering, as she
read the meaningless words, the long-forgotten family photograph in the bottom drawer of her mother's bureau—the pastor
with his hand raised in blessing like the hand of God Himself
out of which her entire family had just then issued complete

and permanent, his other hand clutching to his breast his son crucified on the Cross—kneeling there on the chair beside him translating the Latin words riding over his finger, translating just words, she said sometimes, just as sometimes she assured him she knew very well what she was reading, the two of them there alone without suspicion, their heads together over the book and under the lamp, their chairs side by side, she reading aloud haltingly, reading how those famous lovers were constrained in the ancient net, reading, "So under the pretext of discipline, we abandoned ourselves utterly to love, and those secret retreats which love demands, the study of our texts afforded us. And so our books lying open before us, more words of love rose to our lips than of literature, kisses were more frequent than speech. Oftener went our hands to each other's bosom than to the pages; love turned our eyes more frequently to itself than it directed them to the study of the texts," reading on until the book and he who wrote it like a panderer urged their eyes to meet and changed the color of their faces, till he— he who even then she knew would never be divided from her—all trembling kissed her mouth. And as the blood-blind horse wailed wild across the plum grove and round about the spinning world, she lifted up her face to his, lifted it as though it were already Christmas morning at the altar rail, lifted it and fed upon those chastened lips as on the soporific sop and drank deep the poisoned chalice wherein the winged serpent coiled— for that night they read no further.

Chapters X & XIII

EVENING

Martha knew that in the eyes of the Church it was sinful to buy a fortune, whether you believed in it or not, and it was not as though she were one of those women of the tenement who looked forward every evening to the coming of the old Greek and his parrot, like the widow Nowicki, for instance, who could never manage to pay her rent on time but who nevertheless always seemed to be able to scrape up enough change to buy herself a fortune every evening and to play the number on it at the corner tavern the next morning. It was the widow's having won a hundred and fifty dollars on a number just a few days before which was, in

part at least, responsible for Martha's buying herself a fortune
for the first time in her life.

Yesterday evening, after her husband had gone out for his
walk and Marya had gone out supposedly to the dance at the
Polish People's Home, Martha, having heard from one of the
ladies in the store that the widow had "hit" for over a hundred
and fifty dollars, climbed the flight of stairs to the widow's flat
and notified her amid the wailing of Lottie's baby somewhere
back in the bedroom that she had heard of her good fortune
and just happening to be on her way to the roof thought to
stop by and congratulate her; the widow, shaking her head,
saying, "Yes, Pani, I have been expecting you. I know, you
would like some company on the roof, eh?" excusing herself
and disappearing into the flat for a moment, and coming back
and handing her the roll of bills and the coins, saying, "It is all
there. Three months. Now when you sit on the roof and talk
to yourself, you will at least have an excuse. You can say you
were counting your money," the door slamming in her face, and
she climbing the remaining six flights still hearing the baby's
wailing through the door echoing through the hall, thinking
how stupid it was for her husband, baby or no baby, to allow
women like the widow and her daughter to stay on in their flat
owing three months' back rent, giving them charity like that
when even the widow's own sons ever since they had married
and moved away had given their mother and sister up as hopeless tramps. Why, if it were not for her taking it on herself to
go up there and collect, her husband would probably have
allowed the widow to put him off again so that she could throw
away *all* her winnings on drink and married men at the corner
tavern, instead of just the eighty-some dollars left her after
subtracting the sixty-six seventy-five which Martha counted out
of her apron pocket into her lap sitting there on the apple crate
against the chimney, the music of the Greek's merry-go-round
drifting up from the street below on the small breeze blowing

damp in Lottie's sheets and diapers still hanging on the clothesline.

Suddenly, the widow's rattling voice was there, yelling down
out of her front window no doubt, "Ho, *Grecya*, here is something for you. Catch. You should buy your polly a cracker for
bringing a poor old woman some luck"; Martha sitting there,
thinking, "Why not? What is ten cents? Of course it is foolishness; but what is ten cents? Besides, it will give them something
else to talk about instead of how I am always talking to myself."
And then again, it might even make them feel for once that she
was after all just a woman like themselves despite the fact that
she was also their landlady. For some reason, sitting there on
the roof last night listening to the merry-go-round grinding away
some meaningless tune, she had felt strangely lonely; "strangely"
because somehow it was not like anything she had ever felt before, nothing like what she had felt when Roman left her to
join the Army, or even what she had been feeling for almost six
months now ever since the letter had arrived with the picture in
it, or even whatever it was that had gripped her heart that morning back in 1927 when a slimy stump of cold cigar burned a
scar into her consciousness much deeper than in the edge
of any bedroom chair. It had been simple to account for her
loneliness then, she had lost something, her son, her husband,
the father of her unborn child; but last night, sitting there on
the roof hearing the organ grinding away below just as she had
sat there the night before, Friday night, hearing the music from
the dance pavilion in the park to which she could imagine him
dancing with his bride just as twenty years ago she had sat there
with the man who would be her husband listening to the music
drifting up from the pavilion, while below, the cigar already
smoldered on the bedroom chair—what was it she had lost?

Anyway, last night she had at least not wept over it, had instead gone down the seven flights and out into the street and
bought herself a fortune, "Because, after all what is ten cents,"

only to find that for ten cents she could not even buy one of
the yellow "good" fortunes, much less one of the green "bad"
ones, the ladies on the stoop laughing, saying, "What do you
think, Pani, only your store prices and your rents have gone
up?" the fortunes no longer a nickel and a dime, but fifteen
cents and a quarter; the old Greek grinning as she handed him
the coin, his teeth glistening in his shrunken skull above the
parrot on the stick pecking silken-headed at the *green* slips in
the twenty-five-cent drawer and coming up with a *yellow* one in
his bill; apologizing for the bird, saying, "There is a mistake.
I make a mistake. When I fill up the drawer, the good sometimes she gets mixed up with the bad. My eyes are not young
no more. My Klotho, she pick again, eh?" but the widow Nowicki screaming down from her second-floor window like a
drunken old witch, "Do not be a fool, Pani. He only wants your
quarter. He knows it is a sign. It would be bad luck for you to
pick again." And so she took the *yellow* slip, and not forgetting
to ask for her dime change, she went back into the tenement
and into her kitchen and before opening the fortune, counted
out the sixty-six dollars and change again—sixty-six dollars and
six dimes, which she counted over three times before remembering that the missing fifteen cents had of course gone to pay for
the fortune—for though she assured herself that she did not
really believe in such things, and had gone down more to give
the ladies something other to talk about than her habit of talking to herself, she found herself reluctant to open the fortune
and read it, knowing that once she looked at it she would find
it was nothing special after all regardless of what the widow had
said, that it would be just another one of those foolish things
nobody with any sense would ever put any faith in even without
the guidance of the Church to assure one not only of their
worthlessness but their sinfulness too, because after all, she was
not a superstitious drunken old witch like the widow Nowicki,
she was a practical woman; putting the money away, and sitting

down on the horsehair sofa, and taking the little yellow slip out of her apron pocket, reading, "YOU WILL OPEN YOUR DOOR TO A STRANGER BEARING GIFTS."

It was just as she had expected it would be—nonsense. It was simply one of the regular run-of-the-mill nonsensical fortunes that could mean almost anything you made it mean, just as she had known it would be. In fact she knew of several of the ladies in the tenement who had gotten the exact same fortune any number of times in the past twenty years, and she had heard many of them complain to the Greek that he ought to at least take the trouble to get some new fortunes printed once in a while, to which the Greek had supposedly answered (for like all Greeks, he was clever and knew that his answer was exactly the kind of thing which would satisfy anyone ignorant and superstitious enough to spend good money on his foolish fortunes in the first place), "There are only just so many kinds of fortune, you know. And my girl, she has them all in her drawers here—both the good and the bad. You might as well ask an old man to change life—eh?—as to ask him to change the fortunes." At least if she had been a number player like the widow, she might perhaps expect to open her door to a stranger bearing her winnings; smiling to herself at her disappointment and saying aloud as had become her habit during the past six months, "You are becoming as foolish as a schoolgirl in your old age, Martha."

And so, it is not as though she had really believed any of it, not the fortune or the widow's foolishness either; and yet, now, sitting here at the kitchen table under the raining skylight, thinking back over the past twenty-four hours in which the fabric of her life had seemed to be coming down around her like some kind of net against which it was useless to struggle, which somehow she had nevertheless managed to escape, not merely through her own quick thinking and practicality, but also through what seems to her now an incredible combination of circumstance and luck which could not possibly have happened to anyone (and especially not herself) unless she really and truly were living a charmed life (or at least a charmed day), and no matter how many times she tells herself how foolish it all is; she just cannot help listening for the knock on the door— the knock of the stranger bearing in his palm the gift, not of wealth or health and certainly not of happiness (it was much too late for that), but simply of peace, simply and only a plain impassive but permanent peace.

It was *that* she needed now more than anything. Enough had happened to her in the past twenty-four hours to last her a lifetime; and everything she had done, every secret she had hid, every lie she had told, had been offered as a sacrifice burned on the altar of the palm-bearing bird. She had not really thought very much about Marya at all last night. She was too busy worrying about her husband, the kitchen clock striking midnight and then one and two and three like a hammer nailing her mercilessly to the certainty that she had finally lost him not *despite* his having acted more like himself that evening, that entire day in fact, than he had in the past six months, so that he had even joked her before leaving for his evening walk, had joked about his playing the fool over Magda, promising that now that they were married and gone, it was all over and done with, and the rest would be all just growing old together . . . "and peace, Martha, only peace"; not *despite* that but because of it; thinking, " 'I will be home early tonight,' he said. 'I will not walk long. Just down Monroe Street. I will be home long before Marya returns from the dance' "; Marya's room still empty long after the clock had struck three and four and five; thinking, "As if I did not have enough. After all these months of telling her and telling her. Why did she have to pick tonight? And if I know her . . . It will be just like her to be with some no-good cigar-smoking bum with nothing in his pockets, who

if he ever does decide to marry her will do it only for my money
anyway, because why would any decent man even want to look
at her?" never dreaming that her daughter was in the tenement
all the while, because though she had got up out of bed barefoot in her nightgown and peeped out into the hall at every
sound, she somehow had missed them, and it was not until the
rain had begun, and she had got up to close the windows in the
parlor—the first light of dawn splashing in the streets about
Johnny's car parked there at the curb since a little after midnight—that she heard the knocking on the door and opened it
to find not her husband or her daughter or a stranger bearing
gifts, but Johnny crying, "Marya's bleeding to death."

After that, it all began to happen so fast that it was not until
she had already hung up the phone, standing there in her nightgown and slippers in the cold candy store, the big windows
beating under the huge dawn rain, the kitchen clock just striking
six far away across the hall, just as the key turned in the lock behind her and the bell rang matins over the jamb, and her husband
appeared out of the morning like a drowned man, the rain dripping off the brim of his cap and the ends of his mustache, ap-
pearing just in time to open the store; it was not until then
that she realized what a stroke of luck it had been for the widow
Nowicki to have stuck her head out of her door as she passed
on her mad rush up the six flights to Groszek's flat to find
Marya fully clothed lying there in a faint in Groszek's bed
bleeding under the blanket; the drunken widow Nowicki repeating her plea still standing there swaying in the doorway
calling after her as she hurried back down the final flight to the
candy store and the phone; the widow Nowicki yelling, "Please,
Pani, please call the doctor. The baby is all blue, and I am afraid
of the stairs," her unnatural voice rattling down the landing
and through the open door into the candy store as Martha stood
there looking up the number in the hall light that spread into
the store, thankful she had thought to ask Johnny who the

doctor was before he had got away (she could see through the dawn-lighted rain-washed windows that his car was no longer at the curb); thankful, as her husband appeared just as she hung up the phone, that she was able to say, "Dr. Paulus will be here in a few minutes. Send him up to Groszek's flat. I will take the baby up there where it is quiet. The widow's flat is like a pigsty; she has thrown up all over everything"; thankful too that her husband seemed only too happy not to prolong the conversation, not to have her question him about where he had been all night; thankful that he did not think to ask why it was necessary to make the doctor climb the six flights to Groszek's rooms when she could just as easily have brought the baby down one flight to their own flat; leaving him standing there wrapping the apron around his waist, saying nothing more to him about last night than, "Go change your clothes before you put on the apron. You will catch cold. If you did not have breakfast wherever you were with the ragpicker" (the old junk wagon pulling away from the flooded gutter behind the big store windows—the old junkman wrapped in a canvas tarpaulin under the beach umbrella behind the steaming horse) "there is coffee on the stove, just turn the gas on under it"; he not saying anything at all, simply nodding his head as she left the store and rushed back up the flight of stairs and into the widow's flat and removed the baby, blue and silent, out of its makeshift crib in an opened bureau drawer, recognizing immediately the gash in the dried-food-smeared cheek as she bundled the child into a blanket—the widow weeping something about the poor baby, and that her Lottie was a good-for-nothing tramp to run away and leave a poor helpless baby like that with a drunken old good-for-nothing like herself—and carried it up the remaining five flights to Groszek's flat, thankful that Lottie had not come home, had not been home now since Friday night; thankful that if it was the will of God that the innocent suffer, that at least the suffering of the poor little innocent she carried in her arms would

accomplish something, that at least she carried in her arms an
excuse for calling the doctor, an excuse to satisfy the terrible
curiosity of the ladies of the hall, who standing in their door-
ways in their slips and slippers or sticking pincurled or un-
combed heads around their doors, yawned, asking, "What is it,
Pani? What is all the commotion?" which questions she did not
even bother to answer, her breath heavy on the stairs, knowing
that the widow Nowicki—already calling up the stairs after her
—would explain it all just the way she, Martha, wanted her to,
would explain it not only to them but probably to her husband
too, from whom, even more than from the curious ladies of the
hall, she knew she must at all costs keep the truth.

She would bear the burden alone, the shame, the responsibility. She had to, there was no question about it. For it would
be bad enough for her husband to find out their daughter's
shame (because that was not the kind of thing a man would
ever be able to understand), but to find that it was Johnny,
his own son, who was responsible for that shame . . . it would
kill him. "And so I must keep it from him," she thought, "for
his own sake, if not for the sake of the children." She did not
know then, did not know until after her talk with Dr. Paulus,
that it was much more than that, did not realize until after he
had finished with the silent and practiced movements of over
thirty years in the profession which she watched sitting there
helpless at the kitchen table behind the locked door and under
the rain-beaten, shade-drawn skylight, watched as he administered to the baby whatever it was he had sent one of the ladies of
the hall to the drugstore to fetch for him, whatever it was which
brought the color back to its face, and which of course he did not
bring along with him in his bag since she had not even mentioned
the baby to him on the phone, having simply informed him
that she was John Groszek's aunt and that her daughter was in
bed bleeding and unconscious; watching him standing there at

the kitchen sink after he had come out of the bedroom, standing there drying his hands on the dishtowel hanging on the
sink rack just above the overflowing garbage pail, saying, "It
is no wonder you have rats," and she apologizing, saying she
could not help it if her tenants were too lazy to empty their
garbage regularly, realizing that she was wasting her breath because he was not even listening to her, that he was no more
concerned with rats at that point than she was, seeing as he
rolled down his sleeves that his hands were shaking, recalling
how just a few minutes before she had marveled at how calm
and sure he had seemed to be about everything, not only about
the baby but even about Marya.

Of course she did not know how he might have behaved in
the room behind the closed door, since he had not allowed her
into the bedroom with him, saying it would be better for Marya
if she did not have to face anyone just then, not even her
mother, not at least until after she woke out of the sedation
he would give her, which ought to be about three o'clock that
afternoon, at which time he would expect her to feed her daughter some broth and give her another sleeping powder which
would keep her until sometime that evening, at which time she
should be fed again and given another powder. Actually, as far
as he was concerned there was apparently nothing at all to worry
about, Marya would be as good as new after a few days of rest
and some good food to build up her strength and restore her
color, since after all she *had* lost a certain amount of blood
which was not unusual in such cases. And so really there was
nothing to worry about, he assured her; an assurance which
Martha found difficult to accept when she saw his hands begin
to shake the way they did as he stood there before the sink
rolling down his sleeves, saying, as he noticed her watching him,
"Of course I am frightened. This is not the kind of thing I
do every day. Thank God it was not any more serious than it is—
suppose she had *really* hemorrhaged?" she sitting there watch-

ing him, wondering *why* he had done it, why *he*, one of the most respected and prosperous doctors in Prescott, indeed in the entire county, would stoop to such a thing, would jeopardize everything; thinking, "It could be only one thing."

Why else would a good and respected man like Dr. Paulus stoop to such a thing if it were not to prevent the birth of a deformed child, a deaf mute perhaps or even worse, a monster born out of an impossible and sinful union between a brother and sister. Maybe it was even possible to do such a thing legally if it could be proved that it was a sister and brother involved, even a half brother and sister; but even if it were, how could it ever be proved that Johnny and Marya were blood relations when according to their birth certificates they were only cousins, and not even first cousins. Surely, he could not have done it for money; and so what else could it be? Two frightened children coming to him for help . . . And she felt like getting up from her chair and kneeling before him and kissing each of those hands which trembled so now, only now, after they had done what they had had to do with perfect and professional calm and precision. "The hands of a saint," she thought, though perhaps a damned one like herself. And perhaps she would actually have got down there on her knees and would actually have kissed those hands had he not gone on to ask, "Where is the boy?" she telling him that the blood had frightened him, that he had driven off somewhere in his car, but only God knew where; and he, getting into his coat, saying, "How many others know of this besides yourself?" and she, "No one but the four of us, not even my husband downstairs in the store, just you and me and Marya and the boy"; and he (her saint), saying, "Yes, just the four of us, and that sonofabitch, cigar-smoking greenhorn politician who got me into this."

She would not let him leave after that. Not until he told her all of it, she standing there against the door, whispering as though she were afraid one of the ladies of the hall had an ear to the door, whispering, "I do not understand. I do not understand"; and he, "The two of you make a good pair." And it was then, only then, that she learned not only why the doctor had performed the operation but why it was absolutely important that she keep the truth from her husband. Because actually the doctor had no idea Johnny and Marya were related in any way whatsoever, not until she herself had told him, not until after she had finally managed to get him to believe that she knew nothing of the situation at all previous to this morning when Johnny came crying to her that Marya was bleeding to death, that not only did she not know Groszek had been involved, she would never even have been able to imagine it. Only then did he sit down at the table across from her and tell her, sitting there, his hands flat atop the table beside his hat no longer shaking, just as calm as ever, a tall graying man with nothing at all in his face but age perhaps, not even fear any more, just nothing, answering her questions in that calm un-hurried voice which now had even less in it than the face, an-swering her questions just as simply and frankly as though she were asking him what he prescribed for a headache or a nose-bleed, the strong deep voice droning even in a whisper so that it seemed to her his voice was not really coming directly across the table at her, but as though he were speaking into a microphone there on the table between them, that grave becalmed voice coming to her out of a loudspeaker set up somewhere beyond the shade-drawn skylight way up there on the roof, as though he were broadcasting her shame to the entire neighborhood, to the entire world.

She kept bringing her finger up to her lips as though to shush him, as though to keep it from herself as well as from the neighbors and her husband, whom she imagined standing out there in the street in his apron and under an umbrella looking up at the loudspeaker on the roof, there amid the crowd, the entire neighborhood or at least all that had not been lucky enough to find standing room out there on the landing along with the others with their ears to the door or strung down the six flights of stairs waiting their turn at the keyhole; the doctor telling her how three nights ago Groszek had appeared at his home in the Third Ward wiping his feet on the welcome mat like a man who had just tramped through a manure pile, saying that his son had got some beautiful college girl from Hackensack in trouble and that she was already three months gone; the doctor telling it to her and smiling toward the bedroom door, saying, "College girl! As though anybody could mistake that poor little thing in there for anything but a little Polish schoolkid in her babushka and holey drawers"; telling her how Johnny and "the beautiful college girl" arrived at his place last night, just as he and Groszek had arranged it, and how Johnny had offered him three one-hundred-dollar bills for his services, which he did not accept, and which Martha could not understand because if he did not do it for money, and he could not have done it because they were brother and sister since he did not know that, then why? "Why, Doctor?" But all he would say was, "I am not sure myself, any more"; saying only, "This Groszek is a clever fellow. Too clever for his own good."

And so she sat there trying to explain to him why Groszek had done it, why Groszek had asked *him* to do it; explaining to him that Marya and Johnny were brother and sister, or at least half brother and sister; saying that she herself would have done the same thing if Marya had come to her the way Johnny had gone to Groszek, and that Groszek's telling him the lie about its being some college girl from Hackensack was just Groszek's way of trying to hide the family shame. And the more she tried to explain it away to the doctor the more she convinced herself that Groszek had not only been justified in doing what he had done, but had actually behaved nobly, had gone ahead and taken the entire thing on his own shoulders in order to keep her and her husband (yes, her husband too, who was after all, as she saw it, really himself responsible for the entire mess) from having to learn and face the shameful truth; thinking later, after the doctor had finally left saying he was sure he did not need to warn her of the importance of keeping the matter strictly between themselves, and that he hoped the boy would not be stupid enough to talk to anyone about it in his fright, warning her to see to it that Johnny stayed at home when he returned from wherever it was he had run off to; thinking as she sat there at the kitchen table under the raining skylight, "He is not a bad man. He never was. It is just that everybody always expects the worst of him, and you most of all, Martha. When anyone with any sense, anyone that knows the whole story, that can see the complete picture, can see that he has done what he has done not for himself (what does he have to gain by it?) but for the rest of us, for all of us, not only for Marya but for her father too, and for you too, Martha, for you too"; thinking, "But what would the rest of them say if they knew what he had done? They would say he was only thinking of himself. That he was only trying to keep his son from causing a scandal which would hurt him in the elections, that he would sacrifice even his own niece for his elections. Because what difference does it make if Johnny is not really his son, his name is still Groszek and that is what it would be in the newspapers. After all he is a smart politician and knows how to make the best of a bad thing. And nobody ever gave him credit for having a good thought in his entire life; because people are fools and so are you, Martha, always looking on the bad side of everything, as though only the worst can be the truth, and the good is always really only a lie and only seems good, and if you look long enough and deep enough you will always find the truth behind the lie, you will always find the snake in the grass and the worm in the apple, like fifteen cents for a good fortune, but twenty-five cents for the bad."

Indeed, the way Martha looks at it, the ladies out there in the hall were just as much to blame for what had happened as anybody—their voices there against the door after the doctor had left, like a chorus of witches, saying it just loud enough so that she would be sure to hear it, saying, "Why not? Paying for the doctor herself is the least she can do. He is not as expensive as the exterminator," and, "Why should she let us in? She has enough company talking to herself. Besides who else would tell her that when her husband stays out all night it is not because he is looking for a younger mattress to sleep on"— it was their suspecting her of sleeping with Janush even before Sadovi had died, their rumors which had painted her as something she would never in a million years have thought of being had they not put it into her head with their malicious talk, taking up with Groszek the way she had the very afternoon of her husband's funeral. She knew of course that she herself was not entirely blameless, that indeed she was completely responsible for her own actions and therefore completely guilty; but nevertheless she was convinced that in the eyes of God, the ladies of the hall were no less guilty, no less guilty than herself or Groszek or her husband even, and certainly infinitely more guilty than the children, who, as Martha sees it now, sitting here at the kitchen table almost twelve hours after the doctor had left, are hardly more guilty than the innocent asleep in her arms, whose mother or grandmother in the five months since he had been born had not yet found time to take him to the church and have him baptized and who might have died in Original Sin had the doctor not arrived in time or had Martha not thought to say as she stood there over the kitchen sink washing the gash in his cheek under the water tap before the doctor arrived, "I baptize thee in the name of the Father and of the Son and of the Holy Ghost. Amen."

For Martha, the children, like the baby in her arms, were less guilty of actual sin itself than of the effect of sin, of hers and Groszek's and her husband's and the ladies' of the hall. For how many times had she warned Groszek, saying, "The only reason he does not steal too, is because all he has to do is come to you and if it is a hundred or a thousand or three or four even, for gambling or for a new car or to buy some tramp a present, you will go straight to the City Hall and steal it for him"; Groszek simply biting off the end of a new cigar and smiling, saying, "Pah, you know better than that, Pani. You know my Johnny does not have to buy presents for girls; they buy them for him, just like you used to buy them for me once, eh? Do you remember, Pani? Like that old Packard, eh?" winking and playfully holding her hand over the twenty-five-cent cigars, saying, "And for the same reason too, eh, Pani? For the same reason"; she, simply smiling and turning away, wiping her hands on her apron, saying, "Two of a kind. Both of you have only one thing on your minds"; and he, "Can he help it if those rich college girls are always chasing after him? Could I help it when I was young if a rich widow . . ." And she, "Two of a kind, two good-for-nothings"; and he, laughing, "Good-for-nothing, eh! The future Mayor of Prescott? Yes, maybe it is true. Once maybe Groszek was a good-for-nothing, although you did not seem to mind it very much in those days, eh, Pani? Well, it is the same thing with the boy. Give him a little time to make up his mind what he is made for. Look at me, how long did it take me to find my place? So he drinks a little. So when I was his age I drank a little too, and long before I even had a beard. So he has quit school, so what? When even the law says it is all right to stop at sixteen. What can I do if he does not like school? Should I send him to the factory maybe with all the rest of the donkeys, to break his back for a few pennies to make somebody else rich? Never mind, Pani. Do not trouble yourself with my Johnny. He is all right. He helps me plenty. Last week he delivered over three thousand handbills all by himself. How could he do that without a car, eh? Tell me that. It is easy enough to say that a father is to see that a boy behaves himself, that he makes something of himself, instead of giving him everything he wants so he should become a bum. But I am not your husband, Pani, and Johnny is not your boy. So please save your advice for your husband, Pani, yes, and for our Roman."

And that would be the end of it, because she knew he was aware he could always count on mentioning *their* Roman to get her to stop nagging him about his Johnny, who was as far as she was concerned no more his than Roman was her husband's, though for almost nineteen years now she would no sooner admit to him that Johnny was her husband's than she would that Roman was any less her husband's than Marya was— Marya who lay asleep now in Groszek's bedroom behind the closed door, asleep since about three, at which hour she had awakened from the sedative, and, her eyes still full of sleep, had eaten the warm broth Martha fed her, not speaking, just opening her mouth and swallowing amid the constant dip dip dip of the spoon in the bowl in Martha's lap as she sat there on the chair beside Groszek's bed, not speaking either, just thinking, thinking of what her daughter must have gone through, how much worse it must have been than even what she herself had gone through that morning she discovered the cigar stump on the bedroom floor, what she might have had to go through if Janush had not been there to marry her; thinking, "What if she had died? What would I do then, with Roman away? How would I ever live with myself?" remembering the quarrels over the bath water, and all the rest of it, thinking, "But it will be different now. Everything is going to be all right, now, and

everything is going to be different." Because even though she
did not believe in fortunes, surely the way things had worked
themselves out in the past twenty-four hours was a sign.

Maybe there was no stranger come bearing gifts and glad
tidings but things had certainly turned out a lot better than
they might have, than they even *should* have or even *could*
have, considering the circumstances. For not only had her husband come back to her—her husband who had been gone not
only overnight but for an entire six months ever since the letter
had arrived—which was, she supposed, something of a gift in
itself; he had come back to her like a new man, having stopped
her in the hall that morning sometime after the doctor had left
and she had put the baby to sleep in a bureau drawer in Groszek's room and was busying herself in her own kitchen downstairs making the broth to take up to Marya, stopped her on
the stair, saying, "It is good of you to spend your day taking
care of the baby, Martha. I am sorry I have been so foolish the
past six months to even forget to call the exterminator"; she
simply nodding, holding the soup, saying, "Is there no one in
the store?" playing the part of the sullen wronged wife in hope
that he would be too concerned about his having stayed out all
night to even think to question her about why she was taking
the broth upstairs, and then going right on to explain it to him
even though he did not question, telling him that the doctor
had told her not to move the baby and that she was simply
taking herself some soup up there so that she could eat and
keep an eye on the child at the same time, since of course the
widow was in no condition even to take care of herself much
less a baby, and only God knew where Lottie was, her absence
being as far as Martha was concerned simply another sign that
her luck was holding, since it allowed her to use the baby as an
excuse for the entire day; her husband standing there at the banister, saying, "It is good of you to care for it like this, Martha,
and it is also good of you not to ask where I have been all night."

And as she walked up the stairs with the bowl of soup in her hands, saying, "I have left some for you on the stove. It would not hurt you to close for half an hour and eat a little. I will be too busy upstairs to relieve you," and looking back saw him standing there at the foot of the steps wiping his hands on his apron, his mustache smiling; she heard his voice like peace itself drifting up the stairs after her on the pipe smoke, saying, "Martha, everything is going to be all right now. From now on, Martha. Everything. You can count on it."

And she believed him. And a little after noon, when he climbed the six flights and knocked at the door and she let him into the kitchen and told him to be quiet so as not to wake the baby sleeping in Groszek's room behind the closed door, and she told him no there was nothing he could do and that she would be down later to make him something for supper, and then at five as she spooned his supper out of the pot into his dish and he asked her where Marya was because he had not seen her all day, she really felt like telling him. She was no longer afraid that he would not understand, that he would never be able to forgive Groszek and Johnny. But all she said was, "She has gone with Johnny for a ride to Asbury Park this morning," because she just could not bring herself to believe that he would ever be able to forgive *himself*, answering simply, when he questioned, "To Asbury Park in all this rain?" "It is not raining at the seashore. They will probably not be back till very late with all the Sunday traffic"; feeling safe in her lie, feeling sure that Johnny would not suddenly walk in the door and expose her, because the way things had gone so far she felt that anything she wished hard enough for would happen, and it was just not in the wind that he should do anything other than keep the family shame a secret or come home long after her husband and all the rest in the tenement were asleep so that they (she and Johnny) could help Marya (who by morning could not possibly be anything other than well enough), help her down the six flights before her father or the tenants awoke, and into her own bed, and she could explain to her husband when he awoke that Marya had to remain in bed all day because she had eaten too much on the boardwalk and was ill.

She did not even consider what she would do or what would happen if Johnny suddenly *did* turn up. She did not need to, not because she believed, really believed, in the fortune slip, but because God helps those who help themselves and He would not let her down now, neither her nor Groszek either, not after they had gone through so much to keep it from the others. She had used her head, she was a practical woman and had not allowed herself to break down under the strain. She knew how to make the best of a bad thing, to smooth things over, to maintain peace at any price just as well as Groszek did; for she was after all just completing the good work he had started by taking advantage of every possible opportunity, because opportunity only knocks once and God helps those who help themselves. And though she certainly was not the kind to sit around excusing herself for her own mistakes by blaming them on others, and was fully prepared to admit her own share in the blame for all that had happened, she knew that God at least would recognize ultimately, as she herself has suddenly come to recognize, that if not herself, at least Groszek, the one man the world would consider the guiltiest of all, was actually the most innocent of all—including herself. Because the way she sees it now, as far back as 1927 Groszek had been more sinned against than sinning, for it was her own fault that she had not recognized then that he had wanted to marry her not only for her money (though she was not so impractical even now not to recognize that her money was certainly a factor) but because he really and truly cared for her too, and it was only because everybody including herself expected him to want her *only* for her money that even *he* finally came to think that that was the only reason.

And it was not *his* fault, was it, that she had been so weak as to
allow him to sleep with her without marrying? Any other man
would have done the same, except Janush of course, who had
turned her away that night two weeks before the funeral, though
he apparently had not turned Eva away, had he?

Anyway, if she knew Eva, if Eva was anything like her mother
(which of course she must have been, because she not only
went to bed with Janush but even had a baby by him after she
was already married to Groszek), then it was Eva who was responsible for the cigar burn in the bedroom chair that night
and not Groszek. It was she who had done the seducing, and
after it was over what else could a decent man do but marry
her right away? And how was he to know that she, Martha,
had Roman in her belly at the time, since she had never mentioned it to him and indeed had just a few days before been
praying for strength to give him up completely and never even
see him again much less marry him? And nobody could say that
he had not tried to lead a decent life with Eva; but how could
any man live a decent life with a woman who was running
around with another man behind his back, even having another
man's baby? Surely, if anybody had been wronged it had been
Groszek. It all seems so simple and obvious now, she cannot
imagine why she had never looked at it in this light before—
all those years. Why, even his marrying "that woman" was just
another case of *his* being wronged, because surely he deserves
better, a woman like that, a tramp who would take up with an
eighteen-year-old boy, and not just any eighteen-year-old boy,
but his own son. It was just another case of Groszek's good
intentions turning on him (and how could anything be really
wrong if it was done in good faith?), his sponsoring this tramp
to save their son and being ensnared by her himself. Because that
was the story of Groszek's life, and just thank God "that
woman" had not succeeded in ensnaring Janush too, though
only God knows how close she may have come.

And for a second she even looks upon Groszek's marrying simply as a means of keeping the woman away from her own husband, as a favor to herself, to Martha—though she abandons that thought rather than follow it to its logical conclusion, which would mean assuming that marriage was any more guarantee than it had been with Eva. And only God knows what would have happened if Janush had let himself go, and thank God that now her husband has, or at least seems to have, complete control of himself once again, that he had come home this morning from wherever it was he had been last night, a new man, somehow purified of what she is sure had been a sinful desire for that woman. And as far as she is concerned now, she does not care where he had been last night or how he had rid himself of that desire, even if it had meant that he had had to go out to a tavern and take up with one of those women who like the widow Nowicki and her daughter prey on married men. She would not even blame him if he became one of those men who made a habit of that sort of thing (though of course she knew Janush was not that kind), just so long as everything else turned out the way she prayed it would; just so long as now that Groszek was married he would move out of the tenement and into the new home he had mortgaged in the Third Ward park section and that would be the end of that, and she and her husband would be allowed to grow old together in peace. She felt that now that Groszek was married she was as free of him at last as her husband was free of Groszek's new wife; just as she believed, without really needing to put it into words, that the thing between Marya and Johnny was somehow the last of it all, the final and terrible penance which freed them all from the bondage of their sins, that all that had happened ever since that day in the old country when Sadovi's letter had arrived—the very same letter in a way which had brought Eva to America fifteen years later and Magda twenty years after that—had gone up in smoke in Dr. Paulus' incinerator last night along with the fetal offering sacrificed by Groszek for all of them.

Groszek alone had had the courage to take matters into his own hands, saving them all (and especially her husband) from having to face what their sins (and especially her husband's sin with Eva, a sin which he had never even been man enough to admit) had resulted in. No matter what anybody else might think, including the Law and the Church, Groszek had done the only decent thing possible, the very thing she herself would have done if Marya had come to her as Johnny had gone to him. And so thank God, thank God he had had the courage and good sense to go ahead and do what had to be done, despite the Law and the Church and no matter how sinful it might look to anyone who does not know the whole story as she does, who does not see the complete picture; and thanks to Him, he had had the good sense to go about it in such a way that there was no one but the doctor outside of the children and herself who knew anything about it at all, much less the whole story, that even the doctor would never have known (what with the story of the college girl from Hackensack) if things had not begun to turn bad the way they had this morning, which, thank God, due to her own quick thinking and with the help of Lottie's baby she had at least managed to make the best of, so that now everything is as quiet and peaceful as the rain up there on the skylight, and the hopeful breathing of the baby in her arms; and so when she hears the feet on the stairs and then the pounding on the door and she gets up from the table, whispering, "Who is it?" and she hears his voice behind the door, saying, "Martha, it is me. Let me in"; and she opens it and sees him standing there, his Panama twisting in his hands and his voice rattling past the cold cigar stub amid the tears, she cannot believe it. Because he is a stranger all right, but a stranger

bringing not peace but a sword, the words there rattling like
scabbards under the skylight amid the infant's wailing in her
arms, "Martha, I did not know. Martha, I *swear* I did not know
it was Marya."

Chapters XI & XX

NIGHT

Ever since last Saturday night, or rather, early Sunday morning, Groszek had believed without question the story about the college girl from Hackensack. He had come home even later than usual that night, the clock striking three behind the door in the Novak flat as he started up the stairs, his corns absolutely killing him from all the dancing at the fund-raising picnic in the park, and his eyes heavy with lack of sleep, with three or four months of it, during which every night after leaving Magda off at her hotel and unless he could find a card game going under the lamps behind the wartime blackout curtains in the City Hall Council Chamber, since neither lack of sleep nor too much to drink nor anything else ever affected his card game any way but favorably, he would drive back to the tenement and climb the six flights up to his flat and into his bed feeling himself falling off to sleep almost immediately his head touched the pillow; thinking every night, "Ah, tonight is the night. Tonight I will have no trouble at all because now I am so tired after all these weeks of sleeplessness and it was just a question of getting myself tired enough and after all I have had to drink I am already asleep."

At that point, every single night just as regular as clockwork, he would find himself wide awake staring up at the ceiling and listening to the rats gnawing away in the walls or cavorting noisily amid the kitchen plumbing; thinking, "That was him again, I know it was him," or more often, "I did not see him tonight, that makes how many nights now I have not seen him?" because actually he had only seen him about three or four times in the entire six months, once or twice in the terminal bus stop, once standing outside the movie house, and that once in the hotel revolving door, each time having been early in the evening just before he and Magda would leave the hotel for dinner and a night out (he had made it a practice to take her out every single night of the week even though she begged him several times for a night to herself—*especially since* she begged him for a night to herself); thinking, "He could not be there now. How could he be? He is downstairs in bed with his wife. Everybody in the tenement knows he never stays out later than ten o'clock, and you never bring her home before midnight no matter how tired she says she is, or how tired she says *you* look." For though he never let on to Magda, the only real sleep he ever got was when he was out with her in a movie house or during those few minutes in the soft chair in her hotel room waiting for her to get ready, not to mention those few hours every morning at dawn after the rats had finally gone to sleep in the walls and he would suddenly find himself kneeling under the kitchen sink looking down into the hole in the floor which was sometimes a rat hole and sometimes a pipe hole made by a plumber in the wrong place and never patched up, knowing that he was not really there on his knees under the sink at all but flat on his back in bed dreaming it, knowing that if he was dreaming then he had to be sleeping too.

It was the same story every single night lying there waiting for dawn to brighten the window shade and those few hours of sleep to arrive, thinking, "You are making yourself sick over something that is not even possible. She is lying alone back there in that hotel room, just as alone as you are. Only she is asleep, and it is only in your mind that she is in bed with *him*." And even if he were to go and knock on Novak's door every night before coming up to bed (as he had actually done one night when he was exceptionally drunk, saying, "You will pardon me, Pan Novak, for waking you up. But I just wish to tell you that your friends and relations do not even bother to run away any more when I walk into my kitchen. They just look up at me with those beady little eyes and go right on eating the garbage under the sink. I know you have been a busy man these past few months what with standing every evening in the train station, but how much time does it take to call the exterminator, eh?"), even if Novak were to come and answer the door every night, what good would it do? "When you got up here to bed, you would still wonder if maybe he did not stay home just long enough to answer your knock and have you see him in his nightshirt and slippers, when all the while he had his pants rolled up to his knees under the nightshirt just waiting for you to get up the six flights and to hear your door close."

He thought these very same things last Saturday night as he climbed the six flights to his flat, his eyes heavy and his corns so sore after all the dancing at the picnic, that he had unlaced his shoes in the car on his way home from the hotel and stepped out of them just as soon as he entered the downstairs hall, walking up the six flights in his stocking feet and pausing on every landing to lean against the banister with his shoes under his arm and, like a stork standing on one leg, caress a foot in his hands, thinking, "Tonight I will fall asleep as soon as I finish my cigar. Tonight, I am already asleep"; removing his tie and his coat even before he got to the top of the stairs and not even bothering to go into the hall toilet to wash up, just turning the key in the latch—his shoes under his arm—the kitchen almost bright as day under the white night flooding down through the skylight across the kitchen floor and spilling into the bedroom where, as though frozen not only in the cold light of the moon but in the yellow glow of the hall bulb slanting across the kitchen into the bedroom, he saw, kneeling there on the piece of carpet between his bed and the bureau, himself.

At least that was the first thing that occurred to him. He imagined he was looking at himself kneeling there as he had not knelt for over nineteen years, not since the days Eva would not allow him to get into bed with her unless he first knelt down on his side of the bed as she did on hers, staring across at her in the dark as she mumbled her rosary while he supposedly concentrated on the mysteries when actually what he was concentrating on was how nice it would be after the baby came and she was all flat again and would at least allow him to take advantage of his husbandly privilege on Saturday nights again as she used to before she found herself pregnant; but almost immediately, even before he had got across the kitchen to pull the light string over the table, he had already made up his mind that it was Novak kneeling there; thinking, "But what for? What does he want? Am I dreaming? Surely, I am only dreaming this. I am finally asleep and dreaming. Maybe I am even still back at the picnic sitting at the dice cage with my shoes untied after all the dancing and am asleep between the turn of the cage and the time they call out the winner, and that noise in the walls I hear is not really the rats running away at my footsteps on the floor boards but only the sound of the dice rattling in the cages.

Because what would he be doing here kneeling by my bed? Unless . . ."

But that was just as preposterous, remembering—his back to the bedroom now, his hand reaching around for the light string which after the glare of the hall he just could not seem to locate even under the white night flooding down through the skylight, as though in one of those dreams in which you try and try and try and just cannot succeed; thinking, "If I cannot even see well enough to see the light string, how can I see well enough to know that it is him, or that it is anybody at all and not just my imagination?"—remembering the glint of light from the bed, which might very well have been the glint of metal, of the tin box. Why not? Whoever it was kneeling there could have knelt down not to pray, which was of course ridiculous, but to open the bureau drawer and remove the box, and then turn and place it on the bed to open it, still kneeling; thinking, "But that is just as crazy. What would he want in the box anyway? Not the money surely. He has more than enough of his own. So what else? Her wedding ring? Her rosary beads, the picture taken on the boardwalk in Atlantic City? Why would he want that? I am in it too. Besides, how could he even know it is there? Unless Marya told him. How stupid! I have imagined the whole thing. If I am not dreaming, then I have imagined the whole thing"; turning quickly as his hand found the light string, almost as though it were his eyes and not the kitchen bulb that had lighted up the empty bedroom floor, his eyes that had suddenly snapped on or open or whatever, as though the light and the emptiness had been there all the while and he had either been looking at it through his eyelids or had had his back to it like looking at shadow figures on the wall, imagining all sorts of things which when he opened his eyes, or turned around or whatever, did not really exist at all; the bedroom empty in the glare of the kitchen bulb slanting in on the floor between the bed and the bureau, except that the bottom drawer of the bureau was hanging wide open and the rug on the floor was crumpled a little and he could see distinctly the way the sheet crumpled along the edge of the bed as though someone had possibly just taken something off it, "like a box" he thought.

However, when he thought about it some more, he realized that it was more likely the aftermath of his dressing that evening, seeing one dirty sock crumpled on the carpet, the other one probably under the bed somewhere in one of his thirty-five-dollar extra-comfortable shoes bought especially for his corns and which he had made the mistake of taking off to put on "the patent-leather vises" he now carried under his arm, because a gentleman never wore brown shoes after six o'clock; smiling to himself, thinking, "I am so tired, it is no wonder I am seeing things," going over to the sink and taking down the bottle from the closet over it and pouring himself three fingers in a water glass, and tossing it off as he walked into the bedroom, glass and bottle in hand, and ankled the bureau drawer shut, seeing himself and the shadowy room behind him reversed in the dark mirror, the curtains blowing over the open window behind him and the fire escape behind it, the closet door open as usual just beside the window which, he told himself as he walked back into the kitchen, "could very easily have someone behind it, if there is someone in there, maybe waiting for me to go out into the hall toilet to wash up so he can slip back out the window and up the fire escape to the roof the way he came," pouring himself another three fingers, thinking, "I should have looked into the drawer before I closed it, just to see if the box is still there under the sheets"; smiling to himself, thinking, "Groszek, you are behaving like a frightened schoolboy. You know there is nobody there, that it is your imagination, and yet you are afraid to go back in there and look behind that closet door. You are afraid that nothing or maybe the darkness behind the door will hit you on the head, eh? Maybe even with the box, eh? Why not? The

box that is still there in the drawer for over seven years now ever
since the day your luck changed."

He downed another drink, and placing the bottle and the
glass down on the table and taking off his shirt and placing it
over the back of the chair and taking the towel off the rack by
the sink, he said out loud with his hand on the doorknob—giving himself the excuse that really he was very drunk and so was
entitled to behave like a schoolboy—"All right, now is your
chance. Groszek is going out to wash up now, as you have been
hoping, and you can leave through the window like you came.
But it will do you no good, because I have seen you, Jan"; and
as he turned the doorknob smiling to himself at his foolishness,
vowing that when he got back from the toilet he would not
even bother to look into the drawer to make sure, he heard the
footsteps on the floor boards behind him, and he felt his face
drain white and then almost immediately blush hot with embarrassment, and when he turned, already halfway out into the
hall, and saw him standing there in the bedroom doorway, blinking his eyes in the glare of the kitchen light, he could not help
laughing out loud. For it was *Jan* all right, come like a thief in
the night, the tin box held out before him like an offering. But
it was not Jan *Novak*.

When Groszek finally got control of himself long enough to
sit down at the table and pour himself a drink and consume it
and then pour another three fingers in the glass and push it
across the table, motioning to his son to sit down and have a
drink too—laughing out of sheer relief, out of the great and
overwhelming feeling of embarrassment he had felt in that less
than a minute between the time he heard the footsteps behind
him and turned to find not Novak but his son, that less than a
minute when he thought that he would actually have to confront Novak, the man he had caught on his knees in his own

bedroom groveling amid his dead wife's relics; shaking his head, still laughing, knowing that he would never be able to explain his laughing to Johnny (What could he say, "I thought you were Novak. These days everywhere I turn I think I see Novak"?), watching him sitting there across from him, the tin box there on the table between them beside the ashtray and whiskey bottle and the empty water glass; knowing he could not explain and so not even bothering to try, simply pouring himself another drink and asking the expected questions, the "What are you doing sneaking around like a thief in the dark? What do you want with your mother's money box anyway?" questions which he felt he must have already known the answers to even before Johnny finally spoke, saying, "I need a hundred dollars"; Groszek just shaking his head, saying, "Well, maybe Martha was right after all, eh? It has finally come to this, to stealing, eh?"

He supposed he must have really expected it to happen sooner or later, that he had really known Martha had been right about Johnny all along, that he had been much too easy with the boy from the very beginning. But what else could he have done? Every time he looked at Johnny, not only back there when he was still a baby at Martha's breast and his father was a worthless drunkard, but all throughout those years he was growing up, after his father's luck had changed and he had come to live up there in the flat with him, and even now, right now as he sat there across the table from him, tall and blond, and though like his mother almost too good-looking, nevertheless every bit a boy; every time he looked seriously at his son, whenever he managed quite unintentionally and purely by chance to salvage that little space of time during the day between all the rest of the meaningless things a man had to concern himself with every single day of his life, that little space of time when he could actually think of Johnny as "my son" and really just for a second actually feel all the mysterious and unfathomable implications of fatherhood, he could not prevent his eyes from beginning to water, could not prevent himself from being overwhelmed by a great feeling of pity for his boy, "my son."

Ever since the fall off the roof back in '27, he had never for a minute doubted that Johnny was any less his than Roman was. He knew Novak had not lied just as well as he knew that his wife, Eva, had not been the tramp everybody in the tenement seemed to have believed, as even he himself had allowed himself to believe in his drunken and self-pitying stupor the day of her death (something which even to this day he is not sure he ought to forgive himself for); knew that she would never have allowed any other man to touch her but her husband, that she was not that kind of girl no matter how much she might have despised him and desired Novak; knew without question that Johnny was indeed his own son, and that, precisely that, was the terrible and pitiful part of it. Because, if Johnny had been Novak's, it would have meant nothing at all to Groszek; it would simply have meant he had made a mistake and married a tramp (which would have been just what he had deserved) and that would have been that, and he could have hated Johnny just the way he would have hated Novak, and it would have all been very simple and understandable and not at all mysterious. And though it might very well have been terrible, it most surely would not have been in the least *pitiful*, and he would never have had to look at Johnny and think, "My boy, my son, what a pity, what a shame to be hated by his mother even before he was born, to have a mother who wished he never would be born, even though it could not possibly be *his* fault that such a worthless good-for-nothing had to be his father, a man whom his mother, probably even now, probably even up there in heaven, could never no matter how much she may have tried, even up there, even with all the past, present and future before her like a picture, could never bring herself to do any more than merely to forgive."

So what could anybody expect? So he was stealing, and from

his own father, which was perhaps even worse than stealing from a stranger even though they would not put him in jail for it, for it is always the crimes that they cannot put you in jail for that are always the worst. Still, at least it was certain he was not stealing simply to buy drink or women, since Groszek knew that, like himself when he was young, it was no problem for his son to find some nice girl to stand him a drink and whatever else he might need in the back seat of his car; knew that his son very seldom needed to spend the "few pennies" his father gave him for any of the pleasures of life other than gambling; and he was in a way proud of this. And though he was sorry to see that his son did not handle himself well enough in a card game to keep out of debt at least, was indeed foolish enough to play a hundred dollars over his head, he nevertheless smiled as he joked him about staying out of deep water until he learned how to swim. But when he saw that Johnny did not take to the kidding, that he just sat there across the table from him looking down at his hands fingering a hairpin, saying, "It's not for that. I never lose," Groszek was somewhat surprised; but not for long, not for more than a second, watching him fingering the hairpin, saying, "It is hers, eh?" and Johnny, looking up and pulling his hands off the table into his lap, "What?" and Groszek, "Did she give it to you to open your mother's money box, eh?" and Johnny, "Who?" and Groszek, "The one you have got into trouble. Who is she? The one from Hackensack, eh? The one who calls you every day on the telephone downstairs, the judge's daughter, eh?" saying, "All right, never mind, you do not have to tell me. I do not care. I knew it would happen sooner or later. So that is why you have not come to me, eh?—you were ashamed. That is why you come sneaking around your own house at night, coming in through the window like a thief. But if you really wanted me to think it was a burglar, why did you wait till so late at night? You know I am always home before this time. What, are you drunk?" and Johnny, "I'm not drunk";

and he, "Then why, then? You knew I would be home any minute. That is like waiting to steal the apple until you see the grocer coming. It does not make sense. It is just asking to be caught"; Johnny just sitting there unspeaking, shrugging his shoulders, and Groszek, "All right, then. If that is how it is. But if you wanted so bad to tell me, why did you not just come to me in the first place? All right, never mind. Tell me, how long has it been? Are you sure it is yours?" seeing the look the question brought to Johnny's face, saying, "Well, if you feel that way about her, why don't you marry her?" and Johnny, not saying anything, his face in his hands now, the rest of him beginning to go with sobbing; Groszek filling the glass full this time and pushing it across the table, saying, "So the judge's daughter will not have you, eh? You are good enough for her in the back seat of a car, but to marry is a different story, eh? Well then, if that is the way it is, my son, maybe this is one of those 'hands' it is smarter to let yourself lose."

That was what Groszek believed; believed it when he opened the box, opened it with the hairpin because the key had been lost long ago, long before that day seven years ago when his luck had changed and he had restored—with three crisp one-hundred-dollar bills out of his horse winnings—the money he had burned three days before; handing the bills to Johnny, saying, "Here, what kind of doctor can you get with only a hundred dollars? Take it, it is yours to begin with"; believed it, as Johnny explained how he would pay it all back, how he would pay him back for everything for all those years ever since he was a kid; Groszek saying, "Pay me back? For what? Since when does a son have to pay his own father back for what he has given him?" but Johnny going right on telling him how he didn't have to worry any more about his getting into trouble and ruining his chances for Mayor, that he wouldn't be in the way any more and he and his new wife wouldn't have to put up with him in their new house because he had joined the Army and would be leaving inside of a week just as soon as he got this business over with.

He believed it the next day when he drove to the Third Ward park section and wiped his feet on the welcome mat, apologizing to the doctor's wife for smelling up her house with his cigar, his hat in his hand, saying he had come to invite personally the doctor and Mrs. Paulus to honor himself and his bride with their presence at their wedding reception in the park the following night for since they had not RSVP'd apparently they had not received the invitations his future wife had sent out, admiring the books in the doctor's study as the doctor's wife left the room, fingering them, smiling, apologizing for getting a bit of cigar ash on the rug, saying, "It has always been my ambition to have such a library some day, though of course as Mayor I will probably be much too busy to read even the newspapers completely—except of course for the horse page, eh, Doctor? Just like you, eh? Because I do not suppose a doctor has any more time than a politician for reading—except the horse page, eh? Though perhaps you used to have more time to yourself for such things before you thought to do us the honor of sitting in on our little card games, these last few years. Ah yes, and since we are both such busy men, I will come to the point."

The point was that he would like the doctor to do him a little favor for all the little favors he had done the doctor—for instance his having offered on Election Day back in 1942 to take as security for the extension of some election and gambling debts to the amount of fifteen thousand dollars extending back several years plus another five thousand dollars' credit in that night's card game; to take as security a mortgage on the doctor's seventy-thousand-dollar home in the Third Ward park section payable some time in the remote future, "Oh, let us say, two or three years from now . . . or even better, how about four years? Let us say, just for the sake of the contract, next Election

Day, eh? That would be November four years from now—in
1946, right? How will that be, Doctor? Surely your luck will have
changed before then, eh? And with the way the war is going,
there is nothing to guarantee there will even be a house there
in 1946 or even a Groszek or a Dr. Paulus either, eh, my friend?"
And there were other favors too, favors done and favors still to
be done, especially after the election in November when as
Mayor he would exert even more influence over his "friends"
than he had previously—"friends" who held several of the good
doctor's notes and who would surely be willing to trade them
for certain "favors" Groszek would be in a position to offer
them, notes which were actually worthless to the holder since
it did not look as though the doctor would ever be able to pay
them, but which Groszek would be pleased to buy up for favors
and hold indefinitely until that day when the doctor's luck
would finally change, simply because he himself knew "what it
is like to have your luck go bad," and knew too that "if a man
will only have patience and sit it out and not do something
foolish to himself, his luck is bound to change, sooner or later,
because that is the way with luck." And anyway he liked and respected the doctor, and only wished he could do more for him
especially since it was not possible for him to extend the mortgage on the house, for "as everybody knows, I am already not
my own boss any more, and we are not even married yet. So you
can imagine what it will be like after tomorrow, eh?" saying,
"You know I am sorry to do it, my friend. But I cannot ask my
wife to live up there in the tenement, can I? And even as it is,
we will have to live in the hotel until November. Because believe me, my friend, if I could I would extend the mortgage another four years, because I know what it must be like to have
to leave all these books and all even if you do not have time
to read them any more. But what can I do? With the campaign
costing so much, I cannot afford to *buy* a house, and how would
it look to have the Mayor of Prescott living in a hotel room?"

and Paulus, "Come to the point"; and he, "My, my, such a busy man. Somebody would think I was keeping you from a card game or something. The point is this, I would like to be sure of the Jewish vote in the Third Ward."

"I told you it was all settled. How many times . . . ?"

"No, no. I know you will do all that is necessary in November —you do not have a choice, eh? But what about right now? Like tomorrow night for instance. How will it look if you are not at Groszek's wedding? Here I am, your friend, the man you are supporting for Mayor, and you do not even come to my wedding. Shame on you, Doctor. Maybe that shows good character, my friend, but it is bad politics, very bad politics.

"All right, I'll be there. But as for Mrs. Paulus . . ."

"Of course. Groszek can understand if Mrs. Paulus is not feeling well tomorrow evening. I even noticed tonight when she let me in she looked a little pale"; putting back a leather-bound volume he had been nosing, a volume by some fellow in gold letters named Gibbon, saying, "By golly, they even smell educated," and then standing there at the library door looking down into the crown of his Panama, his cigar going in his teeth, saying, "Oh yes, one more thing. My son Johnny has got some college girl from Hackensack in trouble. He has three hundred dollars but I am afraid he will take her to somebody with dirty hands. I will send him to you tomorrow morning to make arrangements. Take the money when he gives it to you—maybe it will change your luck."

And he believed it last night too in the wedding suite he had decided he would rent for the entire week, when after they had got back from the boardwalk bar he dug into his suitcase and handed Magda the mortgage papers, saying, "It is my wedding gift to you. I am sorry to be such a schoolboy sometimes, but I have not slept much lately and I have some things on my mind"; believed it when Magda sat him down in the soft chair after his bath and lighted a cigar for him and put new corn

plasters on his toes for him, saying, "What is it, Groszek? What
is worrying you?" and he just shook his head, saying, "Nothing,
just my boy. He is going to the Army next week. Nothing"; believed it when he lay in bed with her for the first time, marveling
after it was all over and just before falling into a sleep as sound
as a baby's, how very little different it was from the times with
Lottie (he was not even sure it was as good in a purely physical
sense); thinking, "That is all I have really needed all these
months, not only to make me sleep nights" (feeling the sleep
coming over him like pleasure) "but to keep me from acting
like a jealous crazy fool"; believed it this noon when the phone
rang beside the bed, and the day clerk's voice was there saying
something about a boy who said he was his son being on his
way up; believed it when he got into his robe knowing that
something had gone wrong, the rain rattling outside against
the windows, almost expecting to hear exactly what he heard
when he opened the door and found Johnny standing there
breathless, saying, "Pa, she's bleeding. Pa, she's bleeding to
death"; believed it was the college girl from Hackensack all the
time, saying, "Good God, what about the judge? Does the judge
know?" believing right up until the moment—and even beyond
it—when Johnny cried, "Pa, it's Marya. Don't you see, Pa? It's
Marya."

And so when they arrived at the tenement after the hundred-
and-twenty-mile trip through a downpour so heavy it was like
driving under water most of the way—a hundred and twenty
miles and four hours during which they must have stopped
along the highways at least a dozen times trying to put a call
through to the tenement, the operator saying each time that
the storm had disrupted service at that exchange, all along the
highways the wires down, snaking and sparking green in the
puddles, the car finally careening over the Market Street Bridge
into Prescott and screeching to a halt before the tenement—

he splashed across the pavement and up the three steps into the hall without even stopping to help Magda out of the car, and up the six flights, two stairs at a time, so that when he finally got to his door he was so winded he thought surely his heart would stop. And when he realized that it was a baby wailing away there in Martha's arms and that she was saying something about his being quiet or he would wake Marya, he did not know what to believe, falling into the chair at the kitchen table, unable to question, to speak even, after the stairs, puffing like a race horse and wiping the sweat pouring down his face, his Panama on the table beside him and his cigar gone cold in his teeth; thinking, "I am dying. I am having a heart attack," kicking off his shoes as though somehow they were responsible for his not being able to breathe; thinking, "And nobody even cares —least of all, me"; Martha standing there in the doorway saying something stupid about his not needing to lie to her, because she would have done the same thing if they had come to her, the baby still wailing away in her arms, and the feet there on the stairs, and he just sitting there too exhausted to move, sitting there with his hands dangling between his knees, his voice a kind of hoarse unnatural whisper, saying, "Are you crazy, woman? Can you believe it of me? If I had known it was Marya, do you think for a minute . . . ?"

He could not believe it. He could not understand any of it after that; not only Martha's talk after they had all collected in the kitchen behind the locked door—he still sitting there at the table, his cigar cold between his teeth now and his breath wheezing like the end of his life, Magda and Johnny sitting beside each other on the edge of the cot big-eyed and mute, their hands folded in their laps and their toes in-pointing like two blond-headed kids on the edge of their bed engrossed in a shadow play on the bedroom wall—Martha explaining that Marya was all right and insisting that he must not be blamed, that there was nothing else to be done, saying over and over

again that she would have done exactly as *he* had, that he had
done it for their sakes for the good of all, and especially for her
husband's sake because if it was anybody's fault it was Novak's;
not only that, but Novak's not blaming him either, Novak, who
just turned away from his wife and kind of revolved once around
the kitchen floor as though looking for some place to sit other
than directly across the table from himself, passing behind him
as he sat there still unable to catch his breath, his eyes closed
expecting to feel the hands close around his throat from behind,
to cut off completely the precious air he was trying so desperately to suck back into his lungs; thinking, "Go ahead, kill me!
I am going to die anyway"; Novak passing behind him and then
in front of him around the table and sitting down in the chair
directly opposite him, and burying his face in his hands, saying
only, "I know, Martha. I know."

None of it made any sense. Because, surely, it was not possible that anyone could believe that *he*, Groszek, would ever
have allowed such a thing to happen if he had known the girl
was Marya, even if she and Johnny really *were* brother and sister. That anybody could possibly *forgive* him for what he had
done, excuse him for any reason whatsoever, especially such
stupid ones, that Martha should actually make up reasons for
excusing him, seemed to Groszek unbelievable. It was as though
they were trying to cheat him, as though they had all banded
together to cheat him of his guilt, not only Martha, but her
husband too, who instead of taking him by the throat right
then and there, had instead simply moved around the table and
sat across from him like that, actually agreeing with his wife that
it was all his own fault. It seemed to Groszek to be not only
some kind of plot against himself, but one of the most detest-
able exhibitions of cowardice he had ever seen. It had to be
cowardice. What else could it be? It was one thing for Martha
to pretend she believed Johnny was her husband's son (Groszek
could even understand her *actually* believing it, for he would

not put anything past a woman; a woman was capable of believing anything, and the more fantastic a thing the easier for
a woman to believe it), but Novak? . . . for Novak to pretend
that he not only believed that his wife believed it, but that
Groszek believed it too, that Groszek had done what he had
done only for Novak's own good; when what Novak must really
have believed (because how could he possibly think otherwise,
especially since he knew nothing about the business of the college girl from Hackensack), was that Groszek had been willing
to sacrifice Novak's daughter as well as his grandchild, just to
. . . just to . . . what? For a second he could not think what
his motive might have been; thinking, "Of course. It is very
simple. I was afraid a scandal would hurt my chances in November. Of course. And to believe that, and to allow me to sit here
across the table from him like this and not take me by the
throat . . ."

Suddenly an overwhelming feeling of disappointment dropped
over him like a net. Perhaps it was merely a reaction after the
wonderful relief and joy and gratitude he had felt when he first
realized that Marya was not dead after all and was actually
peacefully asleep in his bedroom and would be good as new in a
few days—or at least almost. Perhaps it was just the sudden
discovery that he was not going to die himself, neither from an
imagined heart attack nor at the hands of the man he had
sneered and scoffed at for nearly twenty years now, whom he
had nevertheless also somehow always secretly admired—"Yes,
admired"; he might just as well admit it, since now there was
so plainly nothing, absolutely nothing at all, admirable about
him—the man Eva had cared for, admiring in him the very
things her own husband lacked; the man who in all the years
since her death had never once, as far as Groszek knew, behaved
in any way other than what a woman like Eva would have
admired—unless of course he had really lied that day on the
roof after all. But now he had shown his true self at last, had

behaved, finally, not like a man at all, and certainly not like the man Eva had cared for, the man Groszek could understand her caring for no matter how jealous he might have been. At least Eva had cared for something different from himself, and whatever had been denied him as her husband, had at least been denied for the sake of something he himself had lacked, something he could never find in himself, something he had actually respected her for admiring, because he could never have cared for a woman who admired somebody as worthless as himself— a vermin who deserved nothing better than to be taken by the throat. For Novak had not taken him by the throat as any real woman would have expected a man to do (Groszek had never considered Martha a real woman in the first place—"She is a ring of keys, not a woman, locking up everything inside of her just to keep the peace"); he had behaved instead like a coward and a liar, "and the worst kind too, the kind that will lie to himself even, like cheating in a game of solitaire, the kind you can never put anything past. Because you can never tell what a liar will do, especially a liar who also happens to be a coward. You never know whether maybe he is finally telling the truth now that you are making it a matter of life and death for him, or whether maybe he is just trying to win you over with one more lie, like the business on the roof."

And so now that Novak had proved himself unworthy of all that Eva had denied her own husband in order to give him, now that Novak had proved himself a vermin no better than himself, Groszek was left with one of those victories which come too late, one of those victories in which whatever is won is won at the expense of losing everything else, a victory which left him more victim than victor, sitting there at the table, a kind of subdued, unnatural laughter rising up out of him somewhere even though his face reflected back at him in Novak's spectacles was not even smiling; thinking, "What a shame. She should see him *now*. He is nothing. He is no better than me. Even *I* am better than this *janitor*. Because if I were Novak, and he were me, *I* would not be sitting here like this across the table from myself pretending I believed my wife's foolish excuses"; wondering whether perhaps he should not take pity on Novak, make it easier for him perhaps, give him even a better excuse for his cowardice than the one Martha had invented for him, "to tell him perhaps that I did not know it was Marya; to get Johnny to tell him that I did not really know. Then at least maybe he will be able to convince himself that there really *is* some reason to forgive me, instead of sitting there like that knowing better than anybody that everything his wife says is a lie, and that there is no excuse for what I have done at all. Unless of course . . ." And all of a sudden it occurred to him. Could it be? Could it be possible that Martha had been right after all? Could it be that Novak really had been lying that day on the roof? thinking, "But even if he *was* lying, what difference would it make? I would still kill me for what I have done."

He closed his eyes for a minute on the pain in his corns. He was breathing normally again and so he struck a kitchen match on the leg of the chair and relighted his cigar, thinking how "just" it would have been if he had actually been having a heart attack instead of only a bad case of indigestion and shortness of breath; and then, remembering that he had not eaten anything all day, thinking, "I could have been dying, and none of them even noticed it, not even Magda"; watching her sitting there on the cot behind Novak, there in the very kitchen in which Eva had once moved and breathed, watching her sitting there silent and becalmed, fingering the wedding ring, the cigarette burning between her knuckles as Martha, still shushing the baby, disappeared behind the bedroom door for several minutes, nobody speaking, as though waiting for her return, as though she had gone into the bedroom not only to deposit the dozing and bandaged baby amid the clean white sheets and rolled clean socks in the bottom bureau drawer, but to excavate from that drawer and bring out into the kitchen and place on the table between them like an offering, that little tin treasure chest in which the immaculate heart of Eva, still bleeding and bloody, lay amid the rosary beads and the boardwalk photograph and the unstamped and unpostmarked envelope addressed to Pan Roman Pawel Groszek, U.S.A., and the *absent* wedding ring.

All of it was silence, not only because no one spoke, but because the rain rattling above in the skylight had suddenly ceased almost as though Martha had closed the door on the heavens as well as on the bedroom, returning empty-handed, wringing her knuckles white and moving across the kitchen and pulling the shade cord and the chain to open the skylight—the cigar and cigarette smoke hanging like a cloud under the lamp, rising in the draft—and repeating the same old nonsense all over again, saying, "He did it for us, Janush, for you and for me. Because everybody knows the children are nothing to him." However, this time when he heard it, he actually laughed, actually stood up and leaned long across the table at Novak, his neck stretched out and his cigar pointing, saying, "You wonder why I am laughing, eh? Well, I will tell you. I am laughing at what a fool you are not to take me by the throat . . ."; Novak not even looking up, just sitting there with his head in his hand, saying, "Sit down, Groszek. I know you are not to blame. Johnny has told me on the stair. Now just sit down, Groszek, before I knock you down."

From then on, none of it made any sense at all. For Groszek did not sit down. He did not know what to say, but he did not sit down; saying, "Are you crazy?" because he just had to say something, saying, "Do not believe that bum. Of course I knew. You think I am a fool. Why should it make any difference to me. Even if I did not know it was Marya, what difference would it make when my political career is at stake? Why should I suffer because your daughter is a tramp?" He could not believe it when he heard it. He could not believe it was his own voice he was listening to rattling away there under the skylight. He knew he did not believe a word he was saying, and yet, he could not stop himself, saying, "And do not think I do not know why you are so anxious to say no hard feelings, to take all the blame on yourself like some kind of big-hearted saint or something. Maybe you think Groszek does not know what has been going on all these months—in the bus stop, eh? in the revolving door, and the other day with the flowers, eh? You think maybe if you forget this business today, I will overlook your playing around with Magda like you did with Eva, eh? You see, I know you, janitor. After all these years, I am the only one who really knows what you are—you, the ladies' man, the one they have all been so crazy for, and for what? You are no better than me. You are even worse, to allow me to go on living after what I have done, and to make believe it is all just some kind of Christian charity or something when really you are no better than a rat in a garbage pail—all eyes and appetite and nothing else. Because I know you, my friend. Because we have fed from the same pail, janitor. And so do not think you can forgive Groszek. Because you have no right to forgive Groszek, you nor anybody, no right to even talk of forgiveness. Because, by God! Groszek will not be forgiven!" And when he saw his hand hurl itself open against Novak's face, he was as surprised as anyone. And in the almost reverent hush that followed, like an acolyte's bell startling communicants to their knees, the infant wail rang out from behind the bedroom door and up against the skylight glass.

The night is clean and white under the moon. It is as though the rain had washed away the old clouds, grimy as grave clothes, and some insomniac old woman had wrung them damp and hung them out to dry in the damp breeze flapping the rain-soaked sheets and diapers on the clothesline. And standing there at the roof wall looking down into the fire escape, the bedroom curtains blowing gently on the down draft from the opened sky-

light in the kitchen seem to him to be drifting and blowing on
the Latin prayers of extreme unction being prayed over what
he keeps telling himself is the already grave-cold body of the
fifteen-year-old child he himself had as good as murdered. As
far as he is concerned, it was his yelling and screaming across
the table at Novak and all the terrible things he had said not
only about her father but about her too; his screaming and
yelling which had waked her and (hearing) had caused her to
do whatever it was she was trying to do during those few seconds
of silence following the slap across the kitchen table, the silence
in which the man across from him did not even have time to
turn the other cheek, almost as though it had not really been
the force of the blow which had turned him toward the bedroom door at all, as though he had not even been conscious of
having been struck, and had simply turned on the sound, as
though he had already been listening, had already heard something, was already moving toward the door though he had not
yet even fully risen from the chair, was already on his way to
the bedroom even before the baby's wail had reached through
the door and, seizing them all like a hand, dragged them into the
bedroom behind Novak, to find there, the bed empty and the
bureau drawer yawning open and the window open too and
the curtains blowing in the draft and (Groszek having raced
to the window past Novak and the others standing transfixed
over the empty bed) Marya lying out there on the fire escape,
barefooted in the bloody nightgown, with, lying beside her still
embraced in the crook of her arm, the blanketed baby howling
down the alley like a cat in heat.

Within fifteen minutes Paulus was there. Groszek had
phoned the City Hall from the candy store, saying "If you are
not here in ten minutes, Paulus . . . If anything happens to
her . . . If I do not kill you on the spot, I will see to it that the
only way you get out of jail is in a coffin." But it seemed hopeless; Paulus coming out of the room rolling down his sleeves, all

of them sitting just as they had sat before the scream, as though once the doctor had come in and chased them out of the bedroom and closed the door behind him, they had all gravitated back to their original positions as though that way they might somehow undo what had been done, somehow start all over again from the beginning, before the scream, before the slap, before the shouting and the insults, Paulus saying, "I will call an ambulance, but it is no use. I do not even think there will be time for a priest"; none of them even moving at first, not even speaking, Martha finally handing the baby to Magda and wringing her hands and circling the table once, looking up at the skylight as for an answer, saying finally, "Johnny, go and telephone the rectory"; and Groszek, "No, take the car . . . If you have to, drag them by the hair. Only make them hurry," fumbling in his pockets for the keys, saying, "I must have left them in the car"; the door closing behind Johnny and Paulus like a signal, Martha wailing, rushing into the bedroom and kneeling beside the bed kissing and weeping into the palm lying open atop the sheet; Groszek following her, kneeling across the bed from her with his hands folded on the bedclothes looking into the pale already seemingly lifeless face above the sheet, the long chestnut hair fanned dark upon the white pillows; kneeling there crossing himself "in the name of the Father and of the Son and of the Holy Ghost," his lips beginning to mumble the "I believe in God, the Father Almighty, creator of heaven and earth . . ."

He had not really thought to pray. At first he was not even conscious he was praying, his lips simply moving as they had moved before, had moved the last time he had ever knelt beside his bed like that, only then the bed was empty and across from him knelt not Martha but her niece. And when he finally realized what he was doing, that not only was he praying but the others were actually following him, that he was actually leading a rosary—Martha having begun first, repeating the Hail Mary after him, and then Magda, standing there at the foot of the bed hushing the baby in her arms amid the "Amens," and even Novak standing there beside her, his hands folded before him and his lips going—thinking, "What am I doing? Praying over her is as good as burying her," almost as though she might live longer if only he had just not begun the "goddamned" praying, as though praying over her were the final and ultimate recognition that they had given up hope, as though it were as good as telling her she was now free to give up the ghost since they had very conveniently succeeded in resigning themselves to their loss and that she was after all merely on her way to a "better world" or a "happier land" or whatever other nice name they could think of to call a hole six feet under; he rose and fled the room, yelling to Paulus, who was back from calling the ambulance and just sat there at the kitchen table with his hands before him, "Do something. Do not just sit there. Do something." But Paulus did not even look up at him; he simply reached for his hat, saying, "Can I drive you to the police station, Mr. Mayor?"

He did not answer. But what he probably should have said was, "No, not the police station, the hospital." For suddenly, almost immediately Paulus spoke, Groszek found he could not breathe, and in his chest (or was it his shoulder, or his arm?), not really a pain, more like the ache of a bad tooth; and only now, only up here on the roof looking over the wall into the fire escape—the Latin prayers blowing amid the lace curtains—only now can he breathe again, his breath wheezing as he leans heavily over the wall, his chest in his hands, wondering how Johnny could possibly have had time even to get to the rectory, much less be back already with a priest, wondering and wanting desperately to throw up over the wall the half-full bottle of whiskey he had snatched out of the closet over the sink and had consumed on his way up the single flight of stairs to the roof; thinking, "The police station will not be necessary. I am going to die," thinking, "That priest does not know it, but he is not only praying for *her*"; imagining the priest down there in the bedroom in his stole, anointing not Marya's forehead but his own, Groszek's—Magda and Novak standing there smiling down at him from the foot of the bed, smiling down at his death—thinking, "Well, that is just like me, thinking only of myself, with Marya down there dying," thinking how if he were any kind of a man at all he ought to welcome the coffin after what he had done, instead of worrying about leaving his wife for Novak; thinking, "It has got so bad now, that I not only imagine I see him every time I turn around, but now I hear him too."

For as he listens to the Latin prayers drifting up from the open window, he marvels at how much like Novak the priest sounds; thinking, "If I did not know better. If I did not know that I am nearly out of my mind with lack of sleep and worry, I would *swear* it is Novak." And then suddenly, almost as though the prayers to the Divine Physician for the healing of the body and the remission of sins were being answered ("at least the healing of the body business," he thinks, "though it is probably only a matter of just imagining I was dying in the first place, the lack of sleep during the past few months making every little thing seem like the end of the world or something, even just a little indigestion and shortness of breath"), the pain subsides in his chest and his breath returns, and even though the sweat still pours down his face like oil, he moves away from the wall and sits down on the crate beside the chimney, thinking in the glow of the skylight, "I am not as young as I used to be. I will have to take it easier or one of these days it will not just be a little heartburn and my imagination. And it would be a shame to have to go now after all the planning and the working and things looking so good for November, now with a new wife and a new house and all . . . to leave it all to him. Because you can bet your last dollar, Groszek, that if you were to go now, he would lose no time trying to step into your shoes," realizing for the first time that he had left his shoes down there under the kitchen table, that ever since he had slipped out of them he had been walking around the flat in his stocking feet and had not even been aware of it, his feet cold on the rain-soaked gravel and his corns beginning to ache again almost the second he thinks of them; thinking, "He would step right into them. They have been asking him to run for years now. Only he would rather be a janitor because he knows better than to run against Groszek in the primaries. But if Groszek were gone—ah!" seeing again those pictures in the Republican newspapers of the veiled woman in the incumbent Mayor's limousine and the caption underneath, "His Honor the Mayor and Mrs. Gold(?) Leave for a Weekend at Their Lake Hopatcong Hideaway"; thinking, "What are you doing, Groszek? You think I do not know what you are doing? You are making up excuses for not taking yourself by the throat and throwing yourself down the seven stories to the alley pavement."

The Latin prayers drift up out of the open skylight now, out of the bedroom and into the kitchen and up into the white night, almost as though it were Marya herself all clean and white and bodiless as the night rising up out of her bed on the prayers and up through the skylight glass and into the air past him as he sits here cowering like a criminal in the corner beside the chimney; thinking, "You will never see her again, Groszek, never. Not where she is going, anyway. And maybe it is for the best, because you would never be able to face her again anyway," thinking, "Because just suppose by some terrible mistake in the bookkeeping they sent *you* an invitation too, and you had to sit there at the speaker's table with all the saints and big-shot priests, maybe even right beside her. Just suppose . . ." imagining her sitting there next to him, not even looking at him, not paying any attention to him at all, and when he pulls her skirt and goes "pssst," just looking at him with that forgiving and pitying little smile on her face like it was bad enough to come so late in brown shoes and a Panama without making a racket right in the middle of His Honor's speech, and just turning right back to the rostrum, leaving him sitting there with his hands folded in his lap and his cigar gone cold in his mouth and his corns killing him after all the stairs, wondering why she could not even take a little time out to kiss and say hello to her uncle, because what could He be saying that was so important. "Because like those Latin prayers down there you would not be able to understand a word of it, Groszek. And so it is better just to tear up the invitation and pass right by the tuxedo store," thinking, "Because that must be what the priests mean," never quite able to understand before how anybody (even God) could possibly be both infinitely Just and infinitely Merciful at the same time, thinking, "Because there is no doubt where you would be better off, Groszek. With the fire burning under you and you and Novak gnawing at each other's brains like rats in the wall, it would be hell all right, but it would not be half so bad as heaven."

On the clothesline Lottie's sheets and diapers blow and flap under the moon like a family of ghosts dancing to a fiddle scraping away at a wedding reception somewhere down the block—the gravel roof bright as day under the white sky. He wishes he had another drink left in the bottle, telling himself it is useless because he has already had more than enough to do the job if the job were ever going to get done. But he knows he needs more than the kind of courage that comes out of a whiskey bottle if he is ever going to go so far as to throw himself off the roof. Frankly, he might just as well admit it, he had never really seriously considered it in the first place; it was all just talk. Since he had thought he was going to die anyway—why not? Suicide always got a bigger spread in the newspapers than a mere heart attack. But since it was only a little heartburn and shortness of breath resulting from lack of sleep and his not having eaten anything all day, and he would probably be around for some time yet, after all, it was a different story; thinking,

"Well, I will get there soon enough. There is no sense rushing things. No sense leaving all I have worked for to him." However, when he thinks about it, it looks as though Novak might get a chance to step into his shoes anyway. "Because where I will be for the next twenty years, or whatever the judge gives me . . . If I know Paulus he was not joking about the police station. He will do it just to spite me. And maybe no Jew will lend another one money just to gamble away, but let one of them get into real trouble and watch the way they stick together. He will get his Jew lawyers and his Jew judges and he will get off with a little fine and Groszek will end up in jail for twenty years. And Novak's name will be on the ballot come November, and Magda will be the woman behind the veil."

Why not? Everything was Novak's right from the beginning anyway, the tenement, the candy store, Eva, and who knows, maybe even the boys. "Pah!" He does not really believe it, any of it, either about the boys or about Magda either. He knows she is his, knows that no matter how much chasing Novak might do or had done, she neither had nor ever would have anything to do with him. "Because, a man just knows somehow. A man just knows when a woman is his and only his, knows that she would never lie to him. And yet . . ." And he wonders how it is possible, knowing this, that nevertheless every time he had seen truth and love written all over her face like an open book, he still could not help wondering whether maybe she was just a good actress after all and was really laughing at him behind her makeup all the while. Why, at times, like yesterday morning at Atlantic City, for instance, it was almost as though he had *wanted* to be deceived, had actually wanted to be laughed at, to be cast down on his knees there before the hole under the sink of his imagination and like a rat on his belly to squeeze down and down into that stinking hollow inside himself Magda naïvely called his "schoolboy jealousy."

And so even though everything else he has worked for all

these years has been lost, has died down there in the bed with Marya; there is still Magda, Magda whom he had fished out of a sewer like a lucky penny and, instead of spending her on himself that first afternoon, had saved away in his heart like a treasure in a chest. Because now Magda is his luck. And all the rest of it, all he has lost the past few hours, is nothing compared to what he has found; and Novak could have his tenement and his candy store and yes the boys too and even the election and the Mayor's limousine and the woman behind the veil. One thing was certain, the woman behind the veil would never be Magda, because Magda is his, and she would be waiting for him when he came back from wherever it is Paulus' judge would send him. Because Magda is his wife, and she is his luck. Because Magda is his angel. And so when he sees them, when he hears the praying cease and he looks down through the skylight into the bright kitchen and sees Novak appear out of the bedroom and sit down in his chair at the kitchen table, his head in his hands, and Magda following him, closing the bedroom door behind her and standing there before him with her cheeks in her hands and then kneeling and reaching and touching his face like a blind woman, the two of them down there alone together under the skylight, only the crowns of their heads visible from the roof, the two of them together in a kind of unspeaking communion, lasting, Groszek knows, not just two minutes or two hours or days or even months but decades, his tired old brown shoes staring up at him empty and mournful beside the chair; suddenly the sparrows fly up, flapping dark wings amid the clothesline; and overhead, the heavens, so fixed and firm just a moment before, come tumbling down around him; and the constellations, wheeling like whirlpools, all fire and fury, blow about the heavens as on a violent wind that *name*, the name which only after he plants his hands firmly around Novak's throat, does he realize he himself has been shouting, shouting it like a madman, stumbling drunkenly about the roof—the broken pieces of the whiskey bottle he had hurled against the roof wall a second before frightening the sparrows off the ledges, bleeding now under his stocking feet—shouting it up against the heavens which just will not stay still, as though the heavens themselves were shouting it, calling out the name of this impossibly lucky fellow who came running up the stairs to his grave as though to claim a prize at a picnic, this fellow who now gasps under his hands, his head and shoulders hanging over seven stories of nothing between roof and pavement below, this fellow who had pushed his luck just a little too far. Because even though it is probably just all in the game, really there is no other way, no other way to keep the sky in its place, to keep the stars from colliding in the heavens. "Because, truly, I do not wish to do this, my friend. Truly, I would give anything to let you go." Only, he knows that if he does, as soon as he does, the peace he feels now, feels even as Martha pulls and claws at him and Magda stands there helpless against the chimney with Lottie's baby wailing away in her arms—the street below glistening like fish scales under the lamps as he watches his Packard pull up to the curb behind the screaming ambulance, and Johnny and the priest get out—all of it would be blown away like a clothesline in a wind, and the stars would collide in the heavens and the stars come down; and so he smiles; he smiles and he says, "No hard feelings, my friend"; and as the air-spotter's beam sweeps long across the heavens like some huge windshield wiper, he flips themselves over the wall; flips themselves, like heads and tails of a gambler's coin, down against the spinning world and off into the eternal.

Chapters XII & XXI

CHRISTMAS MORNING, 1946

Because maybe Roman was right in the first place, maybe it *is* just because we never really get to see the whole picture, maybe there really *is* no such thing as chance or accident or coincidence or whatever, maybe, like he says, just so long as it was or is or ever will be you can be damn sure He's got a hand in it, because there's nothing, absolutely nothing, hasn't got the stink of the perspiring palm of providence about it somewhere.

Like maybe we're not the only ones sweating out the outcome, like maybe your hands weren't the only ones wet on that steering wheel last summer, like maybe she was right after all when she said, "Thank God!" sitting there like that in the back seat gobbing on the lipstick, saying, "Thank God for the makeup too," even though in the rear-view mirror, even without the makeup, she didn't look half bad at all for a doll who'd spent a night in jail and all the next day and night "trying to live it down, by living it up," like she said, and then sleeping it off in the back seat of your car; gobbing on the lipstick, saying, "Thank God you leave it unlocked, because when my boy friends left me off this morning, I knew I'd never make it up-stairs to my bed, and in all that rain . . ."

Yes, thank God! And thank Him too for the pint you kept in the glove compartment because she needed a pick-me-up. And thank God you'd stopped being so fickle "like your old man, get all you can from a girl and then all of a sudden act like you never knew her," because until three weeks ago you'd been go-ing at it hot and heavy together there in the back seat almost every night, until that afternoon Marya stopped you on the stairs and told you the world was coming to an end. And so thank God you'd stopped being so fickle even though you didn't actually look like you were overjoyed to see "your little Lottie," which of course you weren't, not to mention she'd nearly scared you half to death just a minute before, popping up out of the back seat like that all of a sudden and cupping her palms over your eyes right in the middle of Route 3, the road slick as glass in all the rain, saying, "Guess who?" and playing cute just long enough to give you near heart failure and to remind herself—plopping back in the seat like that and holding her head—that she wasn't exactly up to that kind of thing this morning, at least not until after she had her pick-me-up and got a chance to put on a little paint, for which, it being the Sabbath—the parish-ioners heading for six-thirty Mass under their umbrellas—she thanked God, because after all, it was the little things in life that really counted, like the booze and the paint and the fact that you'd finally smartened up enough to take her advice and kiss the old town good-bye once and for all and take off for

Florida with her and to hell with everybody and everything including her waitress job at the Owl's Tavern.

To hell even with bothering to turn around and pack a bag at least, because "you don't need clothes to do what we're going to be doing," and anyway with the three hundred bills you just happened by some miracle to have in your pocket (for which miracle she was humbly grateful and didn't even bother to ask where you got it because "you should never look a gift horse in the mouth") you could certainly afford to play Santa Claus, even if it *was* only July, and buy her some new stockings because she had a run and maybe a new pair of shoes because the rain had wrecked these and maybe even a new dress, because it was out of season in Florida and the room would be cheap and she'd be spending most of her time on the beach anyway and all she needed for that was "a couple of your hankies practically"; her face going suddenly sad and pouting for a minute in the mirror what with only her top lip painted, saying, "Anyway, we'll worry later about what to do when the money runs out. Maybe we can even wire your old man for more," saying, "Hell, I don't blame him. Not for anything. Not for tossing me in the cooler or anything. Because I wasn't even invited, and if they didn't stop me I would have torn up the whole dance pavilion. So I don't blame him for anything. In fact I wish them luck, both of them. Can't we stop somewhere for breakfast?" and you, just to change the subject, because you weren't stopping for anything except red lights and once in New Brunswick for gas, saying, "And what about the kid?" and her, "Okay, what about him?" and you, "Nothing, I guess your old lady'll make out"; and her, "I guess. There's a diner over there. I'm starved."

And she was starved all the way down into southern Jersey, and, "What are you, crazy, Johnny, expecting me to ride all the way to Florida without breakfast?" until you finally stopped like that right in the middle of the Delaware Bridge, the morning traffic blaring behind you and you wising-off to the trooper, saying, "Because I felt like it, that's why," and her leaning over the steering wheel to give him an eyeful and tell him not to mind you because you'd spent the war in a concentration camp and lost your head sometimes; and the dumb hick trooper shaking his head like if he had a medal he'd pin it on you, saying, "Okay, so you stalled. Now get moving, and good luck"; you cutting out like a bat out of hell, leaving him sitting there in his rain cape pumping on his cycle in the middle of your exhaust; the sign still there in your mind as you crossed over into Delaware and turned around and headed back over the bridge again and barreled down Route 40 and across the state to ATLANTIC CITY 75 miles and across the bay bridges and over to the board walk and the hotel, handing her the three hundred right there parked in the gutter, the motor still running, saying, "I don't want you to be here when I come down. Take a cab back if you have to. I don't care how you throw it away. Just promise me you'll spend at least a piece of it on the kid"; and not even waiting for an answer, just splashing up the hotel steps out of the rain.

So thank God then for the sign in the road too, and for your leaving the keys in the car so that when you got back down, there was not only no Lottie, but no brand new '46 baby-blue Buick either and there was nothing else to do but drive back with the old man, sitting there in the back seat smoking, trying not to think about anything, just not about anything at all, slumped down like that with your head up against the little window watching the huge rain running down it like silvering the back of a looking glass, her face mirrored there, or rather the side of it, the unrouged cheek, the naked ear lobe, the soft pale hair with just that little-girl pink ribbon knotted around it falling long over the back of the front seat, her hand coming up out of her lap every once in a while with the cigarette. You sat there trying not to think of anything, remembering how she looked back there in the hotel suite when you turned away from the window and found her standing behind you barefoot in one of those long old-lady white cotton nightgowns with the long drawstring sleeves and neck and the ribbons running clear up to the chin; standing there behind you kind of hugging herself like you had surprised her when you turned around, her hands criss-crossed over her breast like she was cold or maybe knew what you were thinking, the Polish words and the unpainted lips and the nightgown and all, somehow kind of out of place in the plush fifty-buck-a-day top-drawer hotel suite overlooking the ocean; the Polish words saying how sorry she was (because it wasn't till out in the car that the old man told her what it was all about), how the old man had told her you were like brother and sister and how she didn't even know Marya had been sick; and you not even listening hardly, thinking, "Nine'll get you ten her feet ain't all that's bare under that nightgown."

And so maybe you ought to thank Him for that too, that by the time the Packard pulled up in front of the tenement—the old man splashing up the steps even before the motor died—you almost had to think for a second before you remembered where the fire was, opening the door and holding the umbrella over her leaning like that on your arm to take off the heels because the stream flooding the gutter was too wide to jump; splashing across the pavement and up the steps and into the hall and up the six flights, watching the hall lights curving down the back of her, and actually congratulating yourself, sitting there on the cot beside her, congratulating yourself that Marya wasn't really a goner after all and that in a couple of days she'd be good as new like they said; sitting there beside her listening to the two of them eating themselves up over her, and only Marya's fumble on the fire escape postponing what you, as well as everybody else, must have known then was bound to happen sooner or later; and even in the car, when they sent you for the priest, you couldn't help looking up into the rear-view mirror and dreaming what it would be like if she wasn't married to your old man, what it would be like to feel those palms over your eyes and that voice coming up out of the back seat saying, "Guess who?" (only in Polish this time); what she would look like in a couple of those handkerchiefs Lottie joked about, and all the while Marya up there in that bed . . .

It wasn't till you got back with the priest just in time to pick up the pieces, just in time to watch them come spiraling down off the roof onto the pavement, the two of them lying there all bloody in the rain, all wrapped up in each other like a couple of star-crossed lovers up on a movie screen; only then did it come home to you; only then did you feel like throwing up not only your guts but your heart and head and hide too if you could right out there in the goddamned gutter and the old rain running like a herd of horses toward the sewers; throwing up just the way you feel like doing now, except now you've got enough drink in you to fool yourself into thinking it's only the booze; because those wheels might just as well be clacking along inside your head as out on those tracks out there for all the difference; and right now you'd just about be ready to trade your left testicle for just a handful of that morning snow all over everything out there, just to let it melt all cool and wet all over your lips and eyes and forehead because there's nothing in the world you need more right now unless maybe it's a sack back at camp— because trying to sleep sitting up like this . . . Or maybe a chance to take it all back.

Because maybe he was right in the first place. Maybe even after all you told him, all you wish to hell now you hadn't told him . . . Maybe even knowing all of it, if you really *do* know all of it, if anybody ever does . . . even knowing all anybody knows, or ever has known or will or ever can; maybe even so, even then there's no guarantee you got the whole picture. A chance to take it all back; to take back not only the cablegram, not only the wise-assed remarks at the wake about how it was

almost worth losing your old man and your old lady's widowed
husband like that just to have your "half brother" home from
overseas for a few days; not only that, but to be back there in
that rathskeller after Mass this morning, back there right now
listening to him playing schoolteacher again, running off at the
mouth about how stupid it was to think they were fighting over
her when all the while what they were really fighting over was
these three other girls, these Greek dolls from the carpet factory
and all the rest of that jazz about the loom of history and the
figure in the carpet and the perspiring palm of providence and
like that there; because, "Use your head, Johnny boy, you saw
as well as I did the way they acted like a couple of long-lost sisters all through the wake, and you don't think Mom'd offer a
partnership in the tenement and candy store to somebody'd
been making time with the old man, do you?" and "No," it was
true, "nobody, no, not her or Mom or Marya or you either"
bothered to tell him about the flowers or his standing in the
station under her window every night, or the junkman's story
about dragging him out of the river the night after the wedding;
no, nobody'd bothered to tell him much of anything at the
funeral, "but so what?" now that he knew "What difference does
it make?"

Wish you could be there again in that rathskeller, back there
in that rathskeller right now, saying, "You're right, Roman, it
doesn't make any difference at all. You've sold me. And that's
the only reason I came all this way, just so you could show me
it didn't make any difference, just so you could sell me. That's
why I signed up in the first place. That's why I put in for Europe. That's why on my first overnight pass overseas instead of
spending Christmas Eve in Paris seeing for myself whether Pari-
sian tail is all it's cracked up to be, I travel over a hundred miles
by train to Augsburg and . . ." saying *that* instead of what you
did say, sitting there like that across the table from him, half in
the bag and fishing in your khakis for your wallet, saying, "Okay,

Sarge, I take it back. How did it go? CONGRATULATIONS YOUR
OLDMAN AND MINE KILLED THEMSELVES FIGHTING OVER HER, exactly ten words, right? Okay, then I take it back. I sent it to the
wrong address. I should've sent it upstairs, right? It should've
said, CONGRATULATIONS GOD AND THANKS STOP THANKS FOR NOTH-
ING"; and him, "That's not even ten words"; and you, "Okay,
how about AND MERRY CHRISTMAS? Does that make it? I'll send
it when I get back to the train station—just in time for His
birthday"; and him, "You're drunk"; and you, "That's right,
cause I got a present for you, brother of mine. A holy picture,
in keeping with the spirit of the season. A picture of last season's lay, your old 'shack' and my old lady, my own little Mother
Superior taking the veil"; and him, "The veil?" and you, "Why
not?" handing him the newspaper clipping. "It was Thanks-
giving weekend. They're heading for the lake, like it says. That's
the new Mayor there. And there in the limousine window behind the veil . . . guess who?"

Overhead in the rathskeller window the snow drifted and
blew under the streetlamps, the Christmas carols squeezing out
of the accordion across the dance floor and drifting in the cigarette smoke over the heads of the dancers and over the GI's
caroling around the long table beside the Christmas tree, a
couple of them whistling at the German doll walking across the
dance floor to the ladies' room, and you wondering whether it
was worth it after all, whether maybe since you had to go around
playing Santa Claus handing out Christmas presents you might
not better have just given *yourself* one, like a night in a hotel
sack with something like that; Roman just sitting there, his
hands flat on the table over the picture and nothing at all in his
face, probably wondering, just like you were, what the hell kind
of bastard pleasure you got out of busting up the other kids'
sand castles, just like at Dachau yesterday afternoon when he
translated that bronze tablet over the "ovens" in that solemn

goddamned preacher tone of his, " 'Let not worms eat my body. Let it be consumed in fire and flame, for I have always loved the warmth of the light,' " saying, "There was only one way to get out of here, and that was in smoke up the neck of a chimney"; and you, just to get a rise out of him, because Jesus what a hell of a morbid way to spend Christmas Eve afternoon and only a "hell-raiser" like Roman would ever think of it, saying as you walked down the "Way to Heaven" to the cyanogen *Spritz Baden*, "They must have come out of there smelling like peach blossoms. And hell it's not as though it was a complete waste. Like it says under the glass, they at least used the hair to make industrial belts and socks for U-boat captains and sifted the gold teeth out of the ashes. Besides, what's a couple of million Polacks more or less, and you're not going to try to tell me anybody but another Jew would give a good goddamn what happened to . . ." saying, when you saw that "I ought to knock you on your ass" look on his face, "Well, for Chrissake what do you want from me? It wasn't my fault, was it? Anyway, where's your sense of humor?" knowing exactly what he'd say, all that crap about you know you don't mean that and how you're just trying to cover up how you really feel because "cynicism is only the refuge of the sentimentalist after all"; and when you finally admitted that it was enough to make you want to bawl and that it was too goddamned bad the Krauts surrendered before the atom bomb, his going off on that long-winded spiel about providence and The Big Picture and how nobody but the Man Himself ever knows the whole story and "there's a reason in His mind for everything even those ovens"; and you, "Crap. You trying to tell me it's nobody's fault but God's; you trying to say those sonofabitchin' Krauts . . ." and him, "No, I'm trying to say it's everybody's, including the victims'."

So you should have known this morning after you showed him the clipping in the rathskeller, that it wouldn't be the way you'd expected at all (or maybe only half expected, because if anybody knows him *you* do), sitting there across from him, watching him, his hands flat on the table beside the beer stein, because he hadn't yet switched to booze at that point—your bottle more than a quarter empty—not even nodding his head or shaking it or anything, just sitting there like that; and through all of it you expecting him to answer (knowing it wouldn't be Roman if he did, but expecting it anyway), expecting him to answer when you finally said, "Well now that you're filled in and got a look at The Big Picture, what do you say?" expecting him to answer, expecting him to shake his head and answer, "The bitch. The good-for-nothing bitch."

But of course you were wrong. He just didn't say anything at all for a while. He just sat there and didn't bother to answer you one way or the other at first, as though none of it really concerned him, as though maybe he didn't really believe you, didn't believe it was really *her* behind the veil in the first place, saying finally, as though snapped awake by the absence of music when the accordion finished the set, saying not to you really, not to anyone but himself, saying, "I don't blame her. After all she's been through . . ." And it did you no good at all to stand up like that, like a drunken soldier, and yell, "For Chrissake, Roman, are you nuts? You're still soft on her. You're as bad as the old man, both of them," yelling so loud that the barkeep came over wiping his hands in his apron, saying, "There should not be any trouble here, Private. Otherwise it is outside mit dir, mach schnell." And Roman, "It's okay, Karl. Send me over a clean glass, will you?" handing him the stein; and the Kraut, "Ein Schnapsglass, Sergeant?" and Roman nodding and smiling up at you, "Sit down, Private." And you, snapping him a quick thumb-to-nose salute, saying, "Up your backside, Sarge," and falling back into the chair; and Roman, smiling, "A little more respect, soldier. I had to do a lot of brown-nosing to get these stripes"; and you, "Too bad he shipped out. I would've liked to meet him. I would've liked to put my boot up there just to thank him for being such a sweet guy, making you sergeant and all, and helping my poor little old lady get her papers like that and all."

But you might as well have been talking to the wall, because you weren't even in the picture, not the one he was looking at anyway, sitting there looking down at it, saying, "I don't blame her at all"; you, practically downing a whole glass of the stuff straight, thinking, "This isn't going to be as easy as I thought. But if I don't pass out of the picture doing it, I'm going to fill it in for him if it kills me"; saying, "All right, so she had a rough time. So did a lot of other people during the war. She made her own goddamned bed and you ought to know it better than anybody seein' as how you slept in it"; and him, just smiling like that, looking somewhere beyond you, or rather before you, before either of you were even born, before you were even able to imagine there would come a day even before you reached your nineteenth birthday when the only thing you'd want for Christmas was not so much to fill your brother in as to have him fill *you* in, to convince you that the picture you carried around in your head only seemed as sordid and murky and meaningless as it did because you didn't see it in its "proper proportion" and that he would clear it all up for you. Only he didn't. Because when you asked him to explain it to you, to fill you in, to tell you how come it wasn't any more her fault than it was his or everybody else's including yours (though nobody had to tell you about its being yours), how anything that happened to her in the old country could possibly have anything to do with you, with any of them, how the hell it changed the picture at all; all he could say was—as though here it was and now the scales would fall from your eyes and you would see at last—"But what you didn't know was, when she was just a kid in Poland she was knocked up and damn near murdered by some crazy goddamned priest."

No, it was true you didn't know that. But after he told you,

you didn't see where it changed anything. If anything, it just made things worse, and it didn't even go one step toward explaining away those poor bastards lying there beside each other in those twin coffins six feet under St. Michael's; or her following behind that hearse with the coffins piled two high inside, probably already thinking, there under the black umbrella booming in the rain, about riding in the Mayor's limousine big and black and silent as any hearse. The whole thing only made you begin to feel a little more sick in the stomach, and by the time you got outside and climbed into the horsecab to head back to the railroad station—the citizens of Augsburg already heading toward the cathedral for six-o'clock Mass, their black umbrellas open against the snow gleaming under the street-lamps, the horse's hoofs silent as death on the snow-covered streets—you already felt like throwing up your guts, because you were sick, completely and thoroughly sick, but not only from the booze, though you had killed an entire fifth between you back there in the cellar, with you taking more than your share of the punishment; Roman just sitting there and sipping it like wine or something at first, sitting there smoking your cigarettes; and you looking across at him, thinking, "Like they say, get a whore your first time out, you're a whore lover ever after," listening to him telling it, all of it, three or four hours of it, because it was almost six in the morning by your watch before it was over (not even midnight on his; you might have known—overseas over a year and he's still on Eastern Standard Time), all that stuff about the war and that Kraut doc of hers they hoisted last January; and not only that, but all that impossible stuff in Poland, all that business about a crazy priest and sleeping powders and Christmas-morning operations; and all of it was "You don't say," and "That sure is a new twist," and "Even if it was true, what the hell does Christmas morning 1926 have to do with here and now, and Christmas morning '46?"

So instead of drinking the picture into any kind of focus, you were drinking it into a complete blur (which follows), more and more blurred with every sentence, with every drink, until the bottle was finally empty and when he asked you how about another and you felt your neck all kind of rubbery and your hair down in your eyes, you knew you'd had it; not to mention a three-stripe Sergeant of the Army Roman Novak, RA . . . whatever the hell his serial number is, who not only had a little bit of trouble getting into his overcoat but even though there was a taxi right there waiting at the curb, all of a sudden decided he felt like riding in a horsecab, whistling like a genuine sure-enough drunken soldier, like maybe there was some hope for him after all, because you'd never seen him even slightly high before, whistling with him, saying, "Listen to that echo, baby," the whistles bouncing off the cathedral steps and back across the square; and him, "That's no echo, soldier. That's God whistling back at us"; and you, "God, hell. We got better things to do than go to church, baby. Even if it *is* Christmas"; the cab horse stamping under the lamp, the snow drifting and blowing, the cab dark and warm and kind of insulating inside, and the cabby just a voice up top somewhere, "Geh, geh," and the single slap of the reins.

You had no idea at all you were going to hand it to him right there in the cab. You figured you'd at least wait till you got to the "house," after he was all spent and sick of himself just the way you'd been feeling for over seven months now; reaching the ten-spot up to the cabby and yelling, "Fräulein, Hause! Verstehen?" because after that whistle in the street you figured maybe he no more felt like hurrying back to his cot in the barracks than you wanted to get on that early train, though you knew he'd never have thought of it himself, because you knew him and even after *her* and over a year overseas you knew he still wasn't tuned in on that channel. And even though that was no doubt the most popular picture playing in the European theater this morning or any other morning, it hadn't even passed through *your* mind more than once or twice during the evening, because if anything you sure as hell weren't feeling anything *like* horny, even with three quarters of a fifth of booze in you; saying, "Don't worry, Roman, baby. Do not worry about A thing. Because Johnny'll take care of everything. Johnny'll get you something nice and big and blond with plenty up front to lose yourself in." With all the booze in you you weren't just his younger brother any more, you weren't just Private-1 Johnny Groszek; and you had a simple kid on your hands (smart with the books maybe, but pretty simple when it came to "life") and you were going to take care of him from there on in, for the rest of the morning at least, because the hell with it, you could catch a late train, and you didn't give a damn if they busted you all the way down to civilian. What the hell, if it wasn't one thing it would be another because, let's face it, you're just about the worst goddamned soldier in the whole damn European theater even though soldiering ought to be the one thing you ought to be able to do with your eyes closed because it sure as hell doesn't take a hell of a lot of brains or much of anything else to play soldier.

And he must have thought you were pretty damn funny, talking the way you were, because he just leaned over drunk as a skunk himself and put his arm around you, saying, "Forget the girls, soldier. What am I going to tell her when I get home next month and she asks me if her little boy's behaving himself?" And just like that, for no reason at all practically, except maybe you'd been just looking for an excuse to let him have it all along, it all fell away from you, saying, "Sure, and you can take a pair of my Army booties she can have bronzed." And so it must have been the booze, because it wasn't you, that was a cinch, you who never for a minute ever imagined you'd do anything so stupid as tell him the whole truth—the newspaper clipping, all right; but not all the rest, not after everybody including his old

lady had been so careful to keep it from him, never dreaming
until after it was all over that maybe that was really the reason
you were there in the first place, the real reason, and the newspaper clipping was just an excuse for coming without having to
admit the truth to yourself; the whiskey talking, saying, "Well,
if you're such a damn thoughtful sonofabitch and you're going
to run a messenger service between here and Prescott for me,
maybe I ought to return the favor"; and him, though he
couldn't have had any idea what was coming, "What for, I'll
be home in a month?" which was exactly what you wanted him
to say, because you weren't even sure you knew how or where to
begin; that's what *you* wanted, but the whiskey had other ideas,
still talking, saying, "You think I came all the way out here just
to show you that clipping, right? Well, to tell the truth that's
what *I* thought too. But we're both wrong. Because, baby, I got
a real Christmas present for you." Just like that, handing it to
him right there in the horsecab like that, not because you were
sore he didn't blame her, because that was really what you
wanted all along, that was really why you showed him the clipping in the first place, so he could maybe convince you it wasn't
what you knew it was, maybe even make *you* see it the way you
knew *he* would; only he hadn't done a goddamned thing about
making you see it his way at all, and so that was why you said
it, saying it as though it were *your* voice rattling down from upstairs all the while telling them all to take their places, you alone
that pulled the curtain, saying, "You think you know her, right?
You think you know your old lady too, right? and your old man
too, right? . . ." watching his face going away like that as you
talked and only that sad faraway smile there after a while like a
disappointed kid, like waking up on Christmas morning and running like hell into the parlor to find not a tree there, not a good
old-fashioned manger or any presents or even a stocking with
some coal and wood in it to start a little fire under yourself in
hell, nothing, just your old lady boozing it up in the armchair

watching your kid sister and brother hump away the holiday on
the horsehair sofa; the back of the horsecab dark as the inside of
a hearse, whirling round and round like the world as you told it,
like the whole goddamned world had gone berserk on its axis,
as you hung your head out the window finally throwing up your
guts all over the soft white snow, just like you feel like doing
now, wondering why the hell you had told him, because you
didn't have to do that, because what good did it do?

"You think you know her, right? You think you know your
old lady too, right? and your old man too, right? and your kid
sister?"

"Right."

"And now five months have gone by, and you've got a picture
there in your hand to prove you don't, and you still think so."

"Right."

"You know what your trouble is, Roman? You're just looking
for somebody else to blame. Because it was *you* sent her home
and nobody else. You know what you are, Roman? You're one
of these wise guys thinks he's got an answer for everything. Hell
of a lot of good reading all the books in the Third Street Library
did you. You got all kinds of big words to say about everything
and everybody, like that figure-in-the-carpet crap, but when it
comes down to one and one makes two like a guy and a girl . . .
I guess you still believe Marya was sick from an appendix operation when you were home."

"I know she was; she told me."

"That's what I mean. Suppose I told you she's a liar just like
any of the rest of us, that it was no appendix operation she had,
that she damn near died and the doc said it was only a miracle
she didn't. You wouldn't believe me, would you? You got a picture in your head of her and your old lady just like you have of
your old man that even all I told you about him can't change.
Well, you're in for a big fall, baby, when you get home next

month. Because things just don't happen to be the way you see them. Maybe that's the way they ought to be, but goddamn it they just ain't. Just like that clipping there."

"That doesn't mean anything and you know it."

"All right! I don't know why I'm even bothering with you. Anybody that can't tell the difference between a woman and a bitch in heat . . . You've been dreaming up all kinds of nice stories to explain things away ever since the funeral. Now I come and show you a clipping which only goes to prove what I been telling you all along, and you tell me to go jump in the river and sleep it off. So I don't know what the hell I'm wasting my time for."

"*I* do."

"Now what's that supposed to mean? *You* tell *me* then. What the hell am I doing here in the first place? You think I hold it against you for sending her home, right? Well, you're wrong. Forget the cablegram. I think you were stupid, but I know the kind of simple tool you are and it's exactly the kind of thing I'd expect from you, sending a whore home to the States. All I can say is, too bad that CO of yours didn't let you marry her. I still remember before you left and I told you you were going to lose it in the service for three dollars, just like all the rest, and you told me I was nuts because if you ever got to the point where you didn't give a damn about yourself there'd still be the girl to think about, because, 'What do you think those girls are selling you for three dollars? You think they're only selling you their bodies?' (or maybe a dose, eh?) 'Like hell, Johnny boy, you're trafficking in souls, you're one of the great consumer public, and the guy operating the cash register's the Great Consumer himself.' You see, baby, I can quote you just like you were up there on a shelf in the Third Street Library. And when I asked you how old the book was you got that crap out of, because nobody not even priests believed in the devil any more, you just asked me who the hell I thought was the 'goddamned *author* of disbelief'? It's been almost eighteen months now and I still remember that. Maybe I always gave you a hard time, Roman, but I used to listen to you. I used to think probably in the long run you were right too, but what the hell, we couldn't all be saints. You and your big talk and your high ideals, all nice words to impress a jerk like me so I almost start thinking maybe you got something, and then what do you do? . . . a two-bit tramp, twice your age . . ."

"If it was you instead of me it would've been okay, right?"

"You're goddamned right! I don't go sitting around in a corner all day pulling little plums out of books and yelling what a good boy am I, that's for damn sure. I don't go around making all kinds of fine distinctions about how paying a whore three dollars is bad bad bad but shacking with a bitch old enough to be my old lady's different somehow. No, don't interrupt, this time *I'm* going to do the talking for a change. All right, so maybe you never said it was all right to shack with her, but you did it, didn't you, and you see what happened. Because don't you see, if it had been me in the sack with her none of this would have happened. Because I'm not like you, Roman. I'm not the kind thinks once you put it to one of them you got to marry her or at least take care of her as though you owed her your whole damn life. And whether she happens to be the Virgin Mary or a two-bit whore makes no never mind. Don't you see what brought all this on? A guy like you just can't go out and shack and just take it for granted and let it go at that. No, it's got to be one of those things that goes on and on until something like what finally happened happens. Me, I would have paid her off and that would have been it—the roof over her head, the chow, a pair of stockings and some shoes and maybe a new dress now and then and that would have been it, and the world would have gone right on spinning around like always. Because that's what makes the world go round in the first place; I mean, knowing how much a thing is worth and paying for it, no more and no less. Because that's honesty, and it's only guys like you that put too high a price on everything and run around trying to overpay everybody for anything they give you that cause all the trouble in the world. You're just as bad as the guys that aren't willing to pay at all, the guys that just go around *taking* what they want. You know what you are, you're just like them, you're a thief. You go and steal from your own goddamned family so you can overpay a whore. And you know why? You know why you're always running around overpaying for everything? Not because you're such an idealist, but because you think anything that gives you pleasure has got to be wrong. And you're not really worrying about how much a whore's soul is really worth. You're just worrying about yourself, about doing enough penance to pay up your debt. Why, you would've even married her just so she could make you miserable. And when that didn't pan out, you sent her home to make your family miserable, which would make you miserable in turn like at the funeral. Maybe you didn't know it at the time, but you sent her home to do exactly what she did, and you're glad I showed you the picture because now you know for sure *what* you sent home and *what* they killed themselves over, because now you know damn well it wasn't the girls in the carpet factory, that it was *her*, and you sent her, and so it's all your fault and now you're miserable over it, and you're suffering, and after a while you'll figure you've paid up in full for your pleasure and you'll be all clean and good and holy again even though you had to go and kill off two pretty damn nice guys in the process. Because it all worked itself out for the best, just the way your Friend up there wanted it. Because like you said at the funeral, for one thing Lottie's baby, who never had a real mother before, has two now, because with Marya feeding it the bottle there in bed with her like her own and your old lady washing the diapers and all the rest and even paying out the rest of the installments on the car so they wouldn't have to go looking too hard for Lottie . . . The guiding hand of providence, you said, remember? Roman, baby, I know your kind . . ."

"You ought to."

"You bet I ought to."

"Because, you haven't only been talking about me, you know. Only difference between us is we don't see that clipping the same way, Johnny boy, and that means one of us has got to be wrong about what it proves, not only about her but about that Big Picture we been talking about. And all you came here for was to get me to convince you that the way you see it isn't really the way it is at all, because you really want to see it my way, don't you? Only there doesn't seem to be any kind of connection between this down here and whatever the hell is supposed to be going on in His mind up there. And so what you'd like is to have Him come round and visit maybe and maybe give you the word on things or at least to call down once in a while just to let a guy know there's somebody home upstairs. But Jesus, don't you see, He already did that once two thousand years ago and he's doing it again right now—back there in that cathedral."

"I don't see how that hocus-pocus satisfies an intelligent son-ofabitch like you're supposed to be. I thought the more books you read the smarter you were supposed to get, but I guess you're just a mama's boy after all, because your old man was as smart as they come and you never saw him in church. But maybe you're right. Maybe that was the trouble. Maybe that's why Whosit upstairs finished him off like that. Did you ever think of that? Maybe you're His instrument, baby. Like once I saw in a movie where this guy running around killing people said he was the instrument of the Lord. Maybe that's why He got you to send her over there, to knock them off, both of them, because Groszek wasn't exactly a priest lover either. Only I don't see how that would explain your old lady and Marya, because they both spent half their lives in church and you know what living angels they always were, and what the hell did Lottie's

baby do to deserve the old lady he got, he isn't even *old* enough
to go to church. What I mean is, things aren't exactly the way
they looked when you were home five months ago, baby. Because you know where Lottie's kid is now? St. Michael's Orphanage. Because Lottie's old lady not only drinks too much to take
care of a baby, but she got herself a new drinking partner and
they go through a couple of quarts a day together, and Marya's
too busy tending the store during the day, what with your old
lady tippling like she is, and since the operation she's filled out
quite a bit so that nobody'd ever take her for only sixteen and
I hear from the guys back home she's doing real well for herself
nights in the Owl's Tavern."

"My sister?"

"*Our* sister."

"You're drunk."

"Listen, I don't like being your brother any more than you do
—not even half."

"What the hell are you talking about? The hell with that
bull. You been listening to Lottie and her old lady too long.
What about Marya?"

"It was Marya told me."

"Told you what?"

"And it was your old lady told her."

"Mom? Why should she? Even if it was true. After all these
years of denying it, why believe her now? You said yourself she's
drinking."

"This was before she was drinking. Back last July."

"But why?"

"To stop her from marrying her brother."

"Marry? Why the hell would Marya want to marry *you?*"

"Because I knocked her up, that's why!"

"You what?"

"Ask the new Mayor. He's the doc that did the operation."

Under the lamps when the horsecab stopped, the snow was no longer swirling and blowing. It was falling straight down. There was a Christmas wreath on the door and a tree bright in the window and the cabby's voice came down out of the dark, saying, "Fräulein. Fräulein, drinnen." He just stood there in the street, Roman did, the snow sprinkling down on his cap like rice after a wedding. And he didn't say anything when you told him you'd changed your mind about the girls, that you weren't really in the mood after all. It was just before he closed the door on you that you found the buck in occupation scrip on the cab floor, Roman saying, "That's luck, buddy, like finding a penny"; and you, "Only better"; and him, "About a hundred *times* better," smiling, saying, "That and two more'll get you a real change of luck, inside. What do you say, John?" But even so, he probably really wasn't in the mood either, because out of the back window as the cab pulled away you could see him under the streetlamps walking back over the canal toward the cathedral square, watching him, his last words as he closed the door still there in the cab with you amid the horse's hoofs silent as dawn in the snow-covered streets.

"What'd you say the orphanage was?"

"St. Michael's. Why?"

"I was just wondering."

"You mean how the little bastard's makin' it."

"I guess."

"Well, let me know, will you? I mean anybody goes round picking money off the streets like I do, ought to be able to go a little handout for the homeless come payday."

"Okay, John D. See you."

"Take care yourself, Rome."

"About that cablegram . . ."

"What cablegram?"

"The one you're going to send upstairs."

"What about it?"

"I'd forget it if I were you."
"How come? What do you mean?"
"I mean it's a waste of time."
"You mean there's nobody home up there."
"I mean the cable's been cut."

ABOUT THE AUTHOR

RICHARD BANKOWSKY teaches English at Sacramento State College in California, where he, his wife and their two children now live. He was born in New Jersey in 1928, has degrees from Yale and Columbia Universities, and has studied at the State University of Iowa, where he taught prior to moving west. Mr. Bankowsky's third novel, *On a Dark Night*, is already under way.